JESSICA JUDE

King of Obsession

First edition

ISBN: 979-8-9906231-5-6

*This book was professionally typeset on Reedsy.
Find out more at reedsy.com*

*To anyone who's ever been left out or left behind—
not everyone who touches your heart deserves to hold it.*

Contents

Author's Note

Wesbourne is a fictional island country set in the middle of the Atlantic Ocean between North America and Europe. It is ruled by a queen, and you can read about her story in Queen of Wesbourne. While the country is a fantasy concocted in the playground of my mind, all of my books are contemporary and take place in the modern world.

This book is the third in a series, and while they can be read alone, I recommend starting with Book 1, Ace of Betrayal, for the full reading experience. Book 2, Queen of Vengeance, takes place before the majority of events in this book. However, there is a slight overlapping of timelines. The last scene in Queen is repeated through a different POV in Chapter 4, and all following events are subsequent.

The following book contains mature content and potential triggers, including: addiction, divorce, attempted assault, toxic marriage, recreational drug use, drug addiction, gambling addiction, verbal / emotional abuse, language, and explicit sexual content. It is not intended for readers under 18. If you prefer to keep the bedroom door closed, you may want to skip chapters 18, 20, 22, 26, and 40.

Each chapter is named after a song that fits its vibe. Listen if you'd like or chalk it up to me being extra. The choice is yours. Access the entire playlist by going to jessicajude.com/king-playlist.

And finally, I am not responsible for any damages inflicted on reading devices by the consumption of this book.

xoxo Jess

1

"Somebody That I Used to Know" - Gotye

Saylor

Do all men take this long to shit? Standing outside the bathroom, the only room in the whole flat with a door, I knock. "You're going to be late," I call through the thin wood.

Nate mutters something incomprehensible.

I move into the kitchen and pop open the ibuprofen bottle, then shake a few into my hand and toss them back. I'm washing them down with tap water when he finally emerges, forty-five minutes after retreating inside. I bite my tongue before a passive-aggressive "finally" can slip out.

He slings his deployment bag over his shoulder, eyes on the phone in his hand. "Guess this is it, then."

"I guess so." I edge around the kitchen counter.

He looks good in his uniform, almost exactly like he did when we first met a few years ago. Tall, close-cropped brown hair, blue eyes that promise the world. Over his shoulder I spot our wedding photo, taken on the steps of the courthouse. Just two fools who thought love could conquer all.

As if reminding me, a stab of pain shoots through my mouth. "Before you go—" I say.

He glances up from the screen, trying to mask his irritation, but I catch a glimpse of it behind that cool veneer.

"This toothache is getting worse. Is there enough in the bank to cover a dentist visit?"

He blinks twice, then lets out a mocking chuckle. "You have a job. Two, actually."

My lips part in surprise, an old instinct that hasn't fully worn off yet. I swallow the bile I feel rising in my throat. "I work for a nonprofit. It doesn't exactly pay well."

He slips his phone into his pocket and shifts his bag higher on his shoulder. "And whose choice is that?"

"Nate," I say as he heads for the front door.

He stops with his hand on the knob but doesn't turn around.

"It'll probably just be a few hundred," I add.

His fingers turn white as they clench the gaudy brass handle. "Yeah, well I don't have a few hundred."

I cross my arms over my chest, unable to help myself. "Don't tell me the last paycheck is already gone."

Finally, he turns, but only to glare at me. "That's my money, okay?" He points a finger at my chest. "I work hard for it. I don't just play around on social media all day." The corner of his mouth rises in a sneer. "If you want money to see the dentist, maybe you should get a real job."

I should be used to the pain of his words by now, but it still manages to catch me off guard as it slams into me. Squeezing my arms tighter around my midsection, I fill my voice with ice. "My work is important."

"Yeah, making a bunch of losers feel better about themselves."

"When did you become such an asshole?"

He narrows his eyes and pretends to think about this. "Maybe around the time I married you."

I clench my jaw tightly, stifling the tears that badly want to spring up. He's right, and we both know it. Neither of us was like this before. The last three years have been hellish, tolerable only when he's on tour. Which he has been most of the time, fortunately.

"I'm sorry, babe." Dropping his pack onto the floor, he strides toward me. His long legs eat up the space in two steps. He pulls me into his arms and, not caring that I'm still stiff as a board, just tucks my head beneath his chin. "That was shit of me to say."

Something melts inside me, draining away the animosity. For just a second, I allow myself to imagine the old Nate, the one I fell in love with at twenty-one. Back when I was a stupid girl who decided to get married because she thought she'd found someone who wanted the same things from life as her.

I sniff the rough fabric of his uniform where it's scratching my cheek. We met when he was on leave, started writing letters like we were in a Nicholas Sparks movie, and visited the courthouse the next time he was home, without having spent any real time together.

There's something intoxicating about young love. It convinces you that you're the only two people in the world to ever have experienced these emotions, that no one could possibly have felt the way you do before now, because if they had, how would they ever have gotten anything done?

I lean away from him, letting my hands run along his arms before dropping them at my sides. "Take care." My words are soft, but they are sincere. As much as I don't enjoy living with my husband, I don't want anything to happen to him.

"I will." He straightens his shoulders, his hand hesitating in the air as if he plans to tuck my hair behind my ear. At the last second, he brings it back down. "You too."

Pain bleeds through me. How did we end up here? I can still smell the bath salts he used to add to the bubble baths he drew for me. I can still feel his hands on my shoulders, rubbing out the tight knots after I'd worked a twelve-hour shift on the hotline.

He lifts his bag and slings it back over his shoulder. "Guess I'll see you when I see you."

"Yeah," I croak. "Be safe."

I can't remember the last time we said "I love you" to each other. The phrase fell out of our vocabulary the same way you fall out of a boat.

Nate opens the door and walks out, tossing me a quick glance before disappearing.

I pause in the doorway, listening to his footsteps on the stairs leading down to the car park. Should I have gone with him? Seen him off at the base? That's what a real military wife would do, isn't it? But it's been a long time since I felt like a wife and not a prisoner in a jail cell of my own making.

I move toward the 1950s dresser I thrifted soon after we moved in. The attached mirror is cracked right through the center, making my reflection look like something from a fun house.

I inherited my springy black curls from my Black dad and my turned-up nose from my Polish mum. My brown skin is a mix of both of them, along with my love of books—hence the teetering stacks throughout the room.

My jewelry box, a gift from my grandma, is sitting on top of the scratched surface. Twisting the ring on my left hand several times, I take a deep breath, tug it off, and tuck it into the box with the other trinkets. The old friendship bracelet I made at summer camp still lives there, tattered and faded after all these years, but I can't seem to toss it out. Nate accuses me of being sentimental as though it's a crime against humanity.

Opening the top drawer of the dresser, I pull out an oversized Pink

Floyd tee. Before I close it again, I lift up the stack of shirts. It's still there—the crisp manila envelope holding my freedom. I extract it and peek inside. "From the Desk of the Court of Family Affairs" parades across the top of the page. Nate's and my names are listed beneath it, along with the date of our impromptu wedding.

My phone blares from the kitchen counter, and I shove the documents back into the envelope before returning it to the bottom of the drawer. It's time to leave for work, and I'm not even dressed yet. Signing divorce papers will have to come later.

* * *

I dash up the stairs to the suite I've worked in for the past five years. You would think after all this time I would remember about the loose rubber strip at the top, but it trips me for the millionth time.

During my second year at university, in the evenings after my classes, I started volunteering at Restore Hope Initiative's crisis hotline. Nearly two years ago, they offered me an internship position, and I accepted, much to Nate's disapproval. I create content for our social media accounts that promotes mental health and addiction awareness, with the added purpose of trying to catch the eye of potential donors.

It's definitely not what I saw myself doing when I first started at uni. I was going to be a teacher like both of my parents. It was an easy way to make them happy, and I knew I would have no trouble getting a job at a local school. Teachers are harder to hold on to than wet fish. But after a few weeks working the hotline, I knew I had found my calling. I switched my major to communications and haven't looked back since.

I skid to a halt in front of the administrator's door and adjust my beanie. There's an unidentifiable smudge on my combat boots that I probably got on the train. I wipe it off with my palm, then straighten.

Sondra looks up from her desk when I rap on the doorjamb. "Hey, girl." She waves a hand. "Come on in."

I know I'm lucky when it comes to bosses. Sondra is the best.

"Sorry I'm late. Nate left this morning."

She tucks a loose strand of blond hair into a ponytail that's already messy, despite it only being eight in the morning. She blames her regularly disheveled state on her two kids running her ragged before they head for school. "For a second there, I thought you meant for good."

I exhale a tiny puff of air through my nose.

"I'm sorry," she says. "I just don't see why you're still married to that jerk."

Nausea swirls in my belly, churning the contents around until I can feel my breakfast rising. I tamp it down and force my lips into a smile. "It's complicated."

Sondra removes her reading glasses and holds them out to the side as if asking "And?"

"I loved him. Once."

Gnawing on the end of the earpiece, she lifts a single brow.

I sigh. "I need the housing stipend. And the health insurance." I hate admitting this out loud, especially to my boss, who is already fully aware of how little I make working here.

She closes her eyes. "I know your paycheck isn't large, but if that scumbag wouldn't gamble it all away—"

"I know," I rush to assure her. "I printed out the paperwork from the website you gave me."

She tosses her glasses onto the desk. "It's about time."

"I just haven't sent them in yet."

"Then get your ass in gear and get it done."

I take a deep breath and release it. "I will. Soon. I need to open a personal checking account first."

"Saylor." She blinks at me. "You haven't done that yet?"

"I didn't have enough until now." The bank requires a thousand dollars to open one. It's taken me four months of selling my old clothes and things around the flat to save it up. "I'm going over there on my lunch break."

I used to have my own account. But when we got married, Nate told me his credit score was shit. Bad enough that none of the local banks would let him open one. I agreed to add his name to mine, giving him access to both the money in it and my good standing with the bank. I lost control of it—and the money—soon after.

"That man will bring you down if you don't get out," Sondra says.

"You don't think it's cruel to file for divorce while he's on tour?"

She cocks her brow again.

"What if something happened to him because of it?" I add.

"Let me tell you something." She steeples her hands in front of her. "You are not responsible for that man. You're not responsible for anyone but yourself."

I fiddle with a string hanging from my distressed denim shorts. This feels a lot like a lecture from my parents.

"Just because he doesn't respect you, doesn't mean you shouldn't respect yourself," Sondra says.

Raising my head enough to meet her eyes, I nod. I know she's right. I also know she'll kick my ass if I don't do something about it. "I'll file the papers."

2

"Midnight Prayer" - Thirty Seconds to Mars

Rhett

Rehab was a bitch. But she was a predictable bitch, and I liked that. I strum a few chords and tweak my lyrics. "Rehab, you ol' bitch. A crazy-ass witch."

I give a frustrated downstroke and lean back in my chair. Why the fuck can't I compose anything since getting out? I wrote an entire album of songs in three months while I was in that place. A whole fucking *album*. Not that I had any intention of ever recording them while I was writing them.

My shrink wanted me to pick up a hobby. Painting, he suggested, or sculpting. I told him there's no way in hell I'm picking up a paintbrush. I tried the sculpting thing to make him happy, but when I showed him my penis masterpiece, he only raised one bushy brow and said, "Let's revisit this tomorrow."

Eventually, I asked if music counts as a hobby. He blinked at me a few times before saying, "Of course. I didn't realize you were musically inclined."

"I don't know about *inclined*," I said. "But I feel a lot better with a

8

guitar in my hands."

Two of my guitars arrived the next day via courier, courtesy of my mate Pierce. I was bummed he didn't bring them himself, but I felt a hell of a lot better holding the familiar instruments in my hands.

After that, rehab was only half the hellhole it had been. The uniforms were still sketch as fuck, but I got used to it. Some of the assistants were even kind of hot in them. I may or may not have divested a few of them of their starchy whites in a hall closet.

I sit up and adjust my guitar, strum a short melody. It's hanging there on the fringe of my memory, but I can't grab ahold of it. God, I used to be able to write a song in twenty-four hours. I've been trying to compose something new for days, and I'm as hollow as a TikTok trend after two weeks.

Maybe I need to go back for a visit, see if it fires up the old juices.

I set the guitar aside and walk to the kitchen to grab a grapefruit water from the fridge. Normally I'd reach for a beer, but they frown on that in rehab—no clue why—and I got hooked on these instead.

I pop the tab and riffle through the stack of mail on the counter. Most of it's a bunch of stupid invitations to galas and other shit. The worst part is, they can't just invite you and be done with it. Oh no, they want a response. "Please RSVP by May 2nd." Then if you don't fill out their bloody little card and send it back, they call you. "Hello, Mr. Cole. We haven't received your RSVP for our stupid charity auction, and I was wondering if you've decided to attend with the rest of our boring-as-fuck guest list."

When I was in rehab, I didn't have to mess with things like this. I hired someone to handle my mail, and they responded to each invitation with a simple, "Mr. Cole is out of the country until March 29th."

It was perfect. I could focus on my music, and as long as I showed up for my therapy sessions, they pretty much left me alone. My songs were good, too. I'm not sure what made the difference, but I think it had something to do with the lack of pressure. Before, I tried to release a new song every week on TikTok. That was fucking hard to do. I ended up regurgitating a bunch of hits.

I stayed off social media while I was inside—yet another suggestion from my therapist. The old guy actually knew a thing or two. Without the pressure of playing for my fans, I just wrote whatever I wanted.

Turns out, what I wanted and what they wanted were the same thing.

Since getting out, I've been shooting videos of myself playing the new stuff. It's all rough around the edges, but they are eating it up. I didn't intend to put out all of it, just a few of my favorites, but everyone has been begging for more.

My TikTok has climbed to three million followers in the three weeks since I've been out. That number alone is staggering, but it's especially shocking for my account, which has hovered in the hundred thousands for the past few years. I guess the new lyrics are striking the right chord for people.

I've been giving them what they want, but the well has dried up. Guess I need to check myself back into rehab to find my inspiration again.

My phone rings on the counter beside me. "Sam" flashes on the screen. I accept the call and tap the speaker button. "Samuel," I say, and take another sip of water. "How's the world's worst agent?"

"I'm about to become your favorite person in the world," he says. Sam has been shopping my songs around to record labels for over a year and a half. No takers so far.

"You know I'm my own favorite person."

He chuckles. "We have a meeting."

"A meeting." I drain the grapefruit water.

"With Lunar Echo."

I set the can down with a clatter. "You better not be fucking with me."

Sam laughs again. "I swear, I'm not fucking with you. They want to meet tomorrow morning. I think they're going to offer you a contract, mate."

* * *

Tomorrow morning takes forever to arrive. I am so jittery I start to question if I somehow managed to sleepwalk myself to my dealer's house for a hit.

A fucking record deal.

I've been prepping for this ever since my dad put a guitar in my hands at age four. God, just wait until he hears about this. He didn't sign his contract until he was twenty-seven, so I beat him by a whole year.

Sam picks me up in his ten-year-old Audi. My red Maserati would have made a bigger splash pulling into the car park at the record label, but I'm too fucked up to drive anywhere right now.

Sam is in his midthirties, but for an old guy, he knows how to dress. It's the main reason I hired him. Image is everything, baby. Today, he's wearing tight jeans, a white shirt, and a black blazer. "Chill out, mate," he reminds me when we get out of the car. "You've got the upper hand here."

I try to remember that as we walk into the sleek office building. A bright wall mural of Bob Marley greets us before the receptionist sitting in front of it does. Shiny leather and chrome sofas and chairs dot the reception area.

"Hello," the woman says as Sam and I approach the curved desk. "Rhett Cole. I'm a big fan."

She grins and sticks out her hand for me to shake. Her black hair is streaked with blue and pulled back into two buns that stick out at least three inches on each side of her head. Not my usual type, but a pair of long legs peek out from under her short skirt. I can definitely work with that.

"Sounds like you have good taste," I say with a wink. Beside me, I can feel Sam roll his eyes. If we sign a contract, he can fucking wait for me in the car while I see what else is under that skirt.

"Please have a seat. I think they're almost ready for you." The woman motions toward a black leather sofa against the wall.

Sam and I sit down, and my leg immediately starts bouncing. Even the thought of getting it on behind that desk isn't enough to chase away my nerves.

"Relax," he says from the side of his mouth.

Several minutes later, the door to a large conference room opens. A man in a gray suit waves us in. I'm guessing he's got two kids and a dog at home. "You must be Rhett," he says, offering his hand. "I'm Eddie. A and R. I'm in charge of artist-label relationships."

I shake his hand, then do the same with the other suits in the room. There are six of them altogether, and I'm starting to wish I'd never gone to rehab. I could really use something to calm me down.

We all take a seat around the big-ass wooden table. My gaze flits to the pictures lining the wall. Artists they've signed in the past—many of whom became huge national sensations—gold albums, and even pictures with Queen Celia.

Lunar Echo Records is no small fish.

The people around the table have introduced themselves, but I've forgotten everyone's name already. I'm terrible with names, and they all look alike in their suits and button-downs. I'm wearing a white T-shirt with a Coca-Cola logo and black jeans, for god's sake, and probably look like a dipshit. I push my hair out of my eyes, wishing I'd gotten it cut before this meeting.

Eddie sits across the table from me and touches his impeccably styled dark hair. "It's so good to have you here, Rhett. We are really liking what we're hearing." He messes with his phone for a few seconds, then my voice comes through the speakers.

It's one of my new songs and one of my biggest hits on TikTok. The audio needs a lot of help—I recorded the bloody thing on my phone—but I gotta admit, the song is good. They were right to snatch me up. I glance around at the rest of the execs. Some of them are looking down at their notes, but a few are nodding their heads to the beat.

Eddie kills the music, then looks me in the eye. "I'm going to cut straight to the chase here, Rhett. You've got talent. Considering who your dad is, that doesn't come as a surprise."

There are a few chuckles around the room. Is he bullshitting me right now? "My success has nothing to do with my dad—"

Eddie holds up his hand, stopping me midsentence. "Of course not. The Cole Brothers are legendary, but that's not why we want to sign you."

I relax into my seat.

"Your talent is raw and needs developing." He nods at one of the guys at the end of the table. "That's what Jason is for. But I see the potential in you. Potential to take the world by storm."

My heart is ricocheting around my chest. I am sitting on the brink of the best thing that's ever happened to me. I just need him to say the words.

"We want to offer you a contract," he continues, "for three years."

Beside me, Sam sits up a little straighter in his chair.

"And a concert tour," Eddie says, "in the US."

I lean into the table. "Are you fucking serious?"

Eddie grins. "Dead serious. We don't typically move this quickly, but I convinced everyone that we need to capitalize on your success before it's too late."

My brain trips over this, but I don't stop to consider what it means. "Yeah, absolutely. We'll take it."

Sam nudges me with his knee. "Let's hear the terms first."

Eddie's smile slips a tad, but he quickly recovers it. "Of course. Your contract will include an album release, which we'd like to fast-track. You already have the songs, and while they need some development, they're quite good as is."

I push aside the offense that creeps in at his words. Obviously my songs need work. I grab a ballpoint pen from the table and click it on and off.

"Because of the sensation your songs are becoming on TikTok, we really think time is of the essence here. We all know how quickly these trends die, so we want to strike while the iron is hot. We'd like to produce your album within three months."

I can't keep my eyes from bugging out of my head. Three fucking months? Holy shit. Most albums take close to a year to produce. They're going to have to throw all of their resources toward this thing to get it done in time.

"Normally, we don't offer a concert tour until we see how well the album does on the charts. But again, considering your social media success, we're willing to throw in a tour deal." Eddie sits back in his chair, waiting for my response.

I glance sideways at Sam. He's technically supposed to speak for me at these meetings, but he seems a little speechless at the moment.

"That sounds great," I say. "When do we start?"

This knocks Sam out of his daze. "Just a minute. What's the catch?"

"Catch?" Eddie blinks at him. "What catch?"

"Come on, mate," Sam says. "Read us the fine print."

They stare each other down for a few seconds. Finally, Eddie drops his eyes to the paper in front of him. "I wouldn't consider this a catch, per se, but there is one contingency we have." He looks up at me. "You'll need to keep your nose clean."

I shift in my seat and hope he plans to elaborate, because I really don't want to have to ask what he means by this.

"The plan is to present you as a clean Justin Bieber. Tori will go over all of that with you later." He nods to a woman with fiery red hair. "All you need to know right now is that we have the right to terminate your contract at any time if there's even a hint of scandal."

"And what constitutes a scandal?" Sam presses.

I continue clicking the pen in my hand as I wait for Eddie's answer. The room feels hot and stuffy. I'm glad now that I just wore a T-shirt.

"Drugs, affairs, making a scene in public, pregnancies, lewd displays, drunken orgies." Eddie gives us both a tight smile. "Anything you'd find in a Netflix drama."

Sam snorts. "Those things go hand in hand with the music scene."

"Not anymore, they don't." Eddie folds his hands on the table. "Times are changing in the industry. People want to see celebrities they can look up to. Everyone is shifting toward health, personal growth, mental health, and charity work. Like I said, a clean Justin Bieber." He glances between Sam and me. "Will that be a problem?"

I meet Eddie's gaze head-on. "No, sir. It won't."

His blindingly white smile lights up his face. "Glad to hear it. Now we can move on to signing the paperwork."

As the lawyer distributes copies of the contract, it hits me—they don't have a clue that I was in rehab. I did my best to keep it under wraps, but you can never be too sure about things like that. But if their goal is to present me as a clean and wholesome pop star, there's no way they know about the drugs.

They have no clue that every song they want to put on my album was written while I was in treatment. They have no clue that each song is about my journey to overcome my addiction.

My job is to make sure they never find out.

16

3

"invisible string" - Taylor Swift

Saylor

God, it's good to be on my own again. Nobody else's dishes molding in the sink. No more waiting for a bathroom that always seems to be occupied. No more waking up cold because all of the blankets were pulled off in the middle of the night.

Nate shipped out two weeks ago, and it's been like a dream. The only part that hasn't improved is the money, or rather, the lack thereof.

It's hard enough to live in the city on a full-time income, but part-time? Nearly impossible. Hence, me sitting in Sondra's office right now, my foot twitching in time with the second hand on the clock above her desk. I've been waiting for a few minutes already, and it's nearly five.

She ends her call with a sigh and sets the phone back down. "Sorry about that. Another donor."

I frown. "Pulling their support?"

She gives me a weak smile. "We'll be fine."

A month ago, a local newspaper ran a story on Restore Hope, which would normally be a good thing, but this particular story featured an interview with a previous addict we'd tried to help but who wasn't interested. We've lost nearly 25 percent of our support since then.

"I guess now isn't a good time for me to ask about a full-time position?" I say.

Sondra's shoulders sag, and the corners of her eyes mimic the motion. "Saylor . . ."

"It's fine." I hold up my hand before she can apologize. "I totally understand."

"You deserve it," she says. "We just don't have the money right now."

"Yeah, I get it."

Restore Hope relies fully on donations. Losing a quarter of our annual support probably means some of us will be losing our jobs. I was hoping I'd finally be able to schedule a dentist appointment, but it looks like I'll need to restock the ibuprofen instead.

"You've been here for two years. I want nothing more than to offer you a full-time position."

My tooth throbs in response.

"The only way I can afford to promote you is if someone else quits."

"Sondra, it's fine. I'll just pick up more shifts at the thrift shop." I sound more optimistic than I feel. I'm pretty sure I've taken all the available shifts already, but I'm certainly not going to ask Sondra to fire someone so I can take their job. I stand up and cinch the flannel around my waist tighter.

"I feel terrible about this," she says.

I offer her a bright smile. I'm disappointed, but it's not like I'm going to leave Restore Hope just because of this. "You're not losing me. I love my work." I head for the door, which is open six inches thanks to a latch that has been broken for as long as I can remember.

"Saylor."

I turn back to Sondra, whose face wears a pinched expression.

"I have to let you go." Her voice wobbles on the last word.

My mouth falls open. "What?"

"We can no longer afford your salary, small as it may be."

I sink back into the chair I just vacated, not sure I'm hearing her correctly. "I've been here for two and a half years. I just thought—" I break off, not sure how to put it into words that I thought others would lose their positions before I did.

"Unfortunately, your responsibilities are more easily turned over to someone else than some of the other positions."

I stare at her, half expecting her to laugh and say the whole thing is just a joke.

"Besides, I think this will be the best for you anyway."

I find my voice again. "What's that supposed to mean?"

"Have you had your tooth looked at yet?"

Instinctively, I raise a hand to my jaw. "I was going to, until I lost my job." I can't resist a tiny glare in her direction.

Sondra shakes her head and gets to her feet. "You're wasting your life here."

"I'm *helping* people. How can you call that a waste?"

"Oh, love." She tries to smile, but it looks more like a grimace. "You're twenty-five years old. You have your whole life ahead of you. Now isn't the time to scrape together pennies to be able to buy ramen for dinner."

I open my mouth to protest, but I've had ramen for the past five nights.

"You know I don't want to do this—"

"Then don't," I say.

"You need to be able to support yourself. And Restore Hope just isn't able to do that for you right now."

"I'll survive." I lift my chin to prove my point. "I've made it this far, haven't I?" Never mind the fact that my rent is due at the end of the month and I don't have a fucking clue where I'll find the money to pay it.

"I'm sorry. You deserve so much better than what I'm able to give you here." Sondra shakes her head, blond wisps falling from her low bun and framing her face. "There are some boxes in the storage closet for your things."

* * *

I cannot believe that the sum of the five years I've spent at Restore Hope Initiative—two and a half volunteering and two and half as a paid intern—can be packed into two cardboard cartons and hauled away. I have poured my heart into this organization. My friends work here. I care about our mission.

And yet somehow, I find myself walking the dingy hall of the Hamilton Building where Restore Hope rents a suite, carrying my heavy boxes and dragging an even heavier heart.

Sondra said she'd pay me through the end of the month, in lieu of advance notice, to give me time to find something else before my rent is due. She also admonished me to get to the dentist, but at this moment, the throbbing in my chest is much worse than that in my mouth.

This building used to be a school, but now it houses a bunch of different businesses and organizations. It still bears mementos of its past life—broken water fountains in the corridors, heavy wooden doors with narrow windows, metal placards that used to mark classrooms.

It's in bad need of updates, but like many buildings in this part of the city, it's not high on the list of anyone's priorities. The boxes in my arms prevent me from seeing where I'm going, but I've walked this hallway so many times, my feet know each and every inch.

Unfortunately, they have forgotten about the loose rubber strip at the top of the stairs, which again trips me up, causing me to pitch forward and my cartons to fly out of my arms. My arms windmill, trying to find purchase. They collide with something solid and warm. Strong hands prop me up, keeping me from tumbling down the stairs and joining the mess of my things at the bottom.

"Easy." The low, rumbling voice is masculine, with a slight rasp. The man straightens me, then joins me at the top of the stairs. I catch a whiff of his scent—leather, cedar, and a hint of peppermint. The bowler hat on my head shifts as he readjusts it.

My heart is racing a thousand miles an hour, and even though I can see past my hat again, I'm too embarrassed to look up at my rescuer. God, what kind of idiot tries to traverse stairs without being able to see where they're going?

"You okay?" he asks.

I take a deep breath. The least I can do is thank him. I tilt my face upward to meet his eyes, and the words on my tongue dry up.

You've got to be kidding me.

I look around the hallway for the camera crew. There's no way this is real. There's no one filming, which means I must have fallen down the stairs, suffered a concussion, and am daydreaming this part. I shake my head and try the stairs again, careful to hold on to the railing this time.

"Wait," he calls out, because of course he does. This is a dream.

I move down the steps gingerly—I don't want to further injure my head, even if this is a dream—and begin collecting my things, now scattered across the tile floor.

Footsteps squeak behind me, but I don't turn around. By now, he's probably turned into a fantasy man with flawless skin, a million-dollar smile, and bottomless brown eyes. The dream versions are always crazy and completely untrustworthy.

"Let me help." My hero squats down beside me and begins to gather the random office supplies and trinkets strewn everywhere. His right hand has a tattoo of a pair of dice. It brushes against mine as we both reach for the same pen. His skin feels surprisingly warm for a dream.

That warm hand stretches out toward me, offering to help me to my feet. I accept, because this is a concussion-induced vision, after all. Why wouldn't I take advantage of it? His grip is firm and solid, and the sensation of a thousand scurrying ants travels up my arm.

When we're both upright again, he graces me with a panty-dropping smile. Twin dimples pop out on both his cheeks. Did I actually remember that detail, or is my brain tripping and adding fantasy elements now? I have likely spent too much time thinking about—

"Rhett Cole." He keeps hold of my hand and gently squeezes it, his smile only increasing in wattage as I stare at him. Does he think I don't know who he is?

Fourteen-year-old Saylor is screaming right now. She does not believe this is a dream. This is her fantasy come to life. Rhett Cole, in the flesh, right in front of her. She would throw her arms around his neck and say something stupid like, "I knew we'd find each other again."

The acidic taste of bile hits the back of my throat. Stupid, stupid girl.

I yank my hand away and shake my head, knocking my hat askew once more. I clamp it down before it can fall off. If this were a fantasy, he would remember me, not reintroduce himself like we're strangers. Which means—

"Oh my god," I say. "Is this— Are we—" I squint at him. If you try to look at something too closely in a dream, it disappears. He stays where he is, cocky grin growing wider the longer I stare. Dark brown waves have fallen into his face, but he makes no move to brush them aside.

"Are you a fan?" he asks, that stupid smile somehow managing to grow even cockier.

Am I a *fan*? As in, have I followed him on TikTok, watched his videos on repeat, and occasionally imagined seeing him on the street? Do I have his brand-new album on my Spotify?

Of course not. I am a modern woman. I don't *moon* over men. I've lived an entire life since the last time I saw Rhett Cole in the flesh.

And so, it seems, has he.

"I'm sorry." I raise a hand to my forehead and frown. "Who are you?"

"Rhett Cole," he says again. "I thought maybe—"

"Oh." I snap my fingers. "You're on the billboard over on Twenty-Fifth."

It's his turn to frown. "No. I—"

"Oh, I know! You did an interview with that one guy on TV."

He shakes his head. "Not me."

"Are you sure? I swear, you look just like him."

A wry chuckle slips out of his mouth, but he's not smiling. "I'm sure."

I shrug. "Sorry. Guess I don't recognize you after all. Thanks for the help, though."

God. As though I'm going to humiliate myself any further by explaining to Rhett fucking Cole that of course I know who he is and he should remember who I am, too.

Lifting my boxes once more, I pretend he no longer exists and move toward the exit. Fortunately, it has one of those old metal push bars, allowing me to leave without needing to fiddle with a knob, because it seems Mr. Cole has completed his gentlemanly duty for the day.

The door has just slammed shut behind me when I hear him yell. I keep walking.

"Wait," he calls again, following me outside.

I shift the cartons in my arms a little higher and continue heading for the train station two blocks down.

He comes up beside me and matches me step for step. "Wait. Please."

I don't slow my pace. "Why?"

"I want to talk to you."

"I have things to do." Like look for a new job. And, if there's time, remind myself of what an idiot I am.

"Pine Acres Summer Camp."

My steps falter, and my eyes dart to his instinctively. "What?"

"I remember you."

I halt, and he does the same. I've got to get rid of this guy. "Congratulations. Would you like a star?"

He winks—fucking *winks* at me—then says, "Already am a star, but thanks." He reaches for the boxes in my arms. "Let me take these for you."

"I've got them." I tighten my grip on the cardboard.

He relents and rocks back on his heels. "I recognized you right away, but I'm bloody terrible with names."

The fact that he feels the need to explain himself tells me everything I need to know. Rhett Cole may have been *my* first kiss eleven years ago, but I highly doubt I was his.

"I need to go." If he expects me to help him out with my name, he's about to be sorely disappointed.

"Please." He stops me with a hand on my arm, singeing my bare skin. "I'd love to catch up."

Catch up? With *Rhett Cole*? What would I even say? I married the wrong guy, picked the wrong career, and am currently considering whoring myself out to pay my rent?

"I don't think so," I say.

"We could grab a coffee." His dark eyes twinkle as he directs that imploring gaze my way. God, is this how he lands women? They must throw themselves at him.

"I come with a lot of baggage." I heft the boxes higher.

"Let me at least help you to your car with this stuff."

"I'm taking the train," I say, and nod in the direction of the station.

"With all of this shit?"

I narrow my eyes. "I don't have much choice, seeing as I don't have a car." It's not like I can afford an Uber, but I'm definitely not telling him that. I take off down the street again.

He bolts ahead of me and stops, blocking my way. His fingers dive into his thick hair, shoving it off his forehead. "Give me that stuff. I'll take you home."

A short laugh bursts from my throat. "I don't think so."

"It's the least I can do."

"I don't know anything about you. For all I know, you're a psychopath, and I'm about to become your next victim."

"*First* victim, actually," he says, a smile playing at the corners of his mouth.

"Not a risk I'm willing to take."

"Come on," he says. "I owe you for not calling you back."

I blink at him. We had a cliché summer camp romance—thrown together for six weeks, "fell in love," then went back to our separate lives. We texted a few times, but it soon became apparent that whatever *I* thought we had started that summer stayed at camp for him.

"Say yes, Saylor." His voice has grown quiet, barely louder than a whisper.

Images flood my memory—cuddling next to him at a bonfire, holding hands; the wink he'd throw my way across the mess hall; him tucking a strand of hair behind my ear right before kissing me.

It's the fact that he remembers my name after all that does it.

"Okay." I whisper it back, not trusting my vocal cords.

A grin splits Rhett's face. He takes the boxes from my hands and gestures over his shoulder with his chin. "I'm parked over here."

I follow him to a cherry-red sports car that looks more like a toy than an operational vehicle. So this is why he wanted to take me home. Impress the girl, score the goal.

I can't wait to disappoint him.

He sets the boxes on the roof to open my door—I guess he found another reservoir of chivalry—and after I'm settled, he deposits my things in the boot. Who the fuck would have believed I'd end a very shitty day in Rhett Cole's Maserati? Timie would insist on getting every last detail if talking was still something we did with any regularity.

The car emits an air of luxury I should not be inhaling. People like me don't ride in vehicles like this. I check the soles of my boots, but they're not too dirty, considering how many miles of city streets they've traversed. In a moment of defiance, I fill my lungs with the spicy leather and expensive cologne scent.

Rhett slides into the driver's seat and starts the car, Prince's voice bleeding through the speakers. But instead of pulling out of the parking spot, he turns to look at me, that stupid smile still stretched across his very nice mouth. I remember that mouth well.

"Tell me what you've been up to."

What I've been up to? He says it like I just popped over to the shops for the day and we're catching up over dinner.

I blink at him. "For the past eleven years?" I return my gaze to the windshield and tick off my fingers. "Well, let's see. Last night I binged *Suits* on Netflix. Have you seen it? Highly recommend."

He shakes his head, his smile somehow even wider, and pulls the car into traffic. We'll probably cause an accident in this ostentatious thing, people blowing red lights as they crane their necks for a better look.

"How about the big stuff," he says, glancing at the hand in my lap with its bare ring finger. "Husband? Kids?"

"God, I'm only twenty-five." I am *not* talking about my failure of a marriage with Rhett Cole.

"I forgot. Still a baby." He clucks his tongue.

I snort loudly and sink further back into the seat. This leather is exquisite. I feel like I'm being cocooned in butter. "You're, like, a year older than me."

He cackles at this. "Touché. Where are we going?"

I give him directions to my flat, trying not to notice the way his hands grip the steering wheel—casually, like he's used to handling this much power. His hands are large and have several tattoos each. A subtle sideways glance reveals they're sprinkled up his arms too. I wonder how many are on his chest before murdering that thought.

He's wearing a rust-orange knit polo that looks like it's straight from the '70s, along with cream-colored jeans. It's like looking at my fantasy version of Billy Dunne from *Daisy Jones and the Six*. Sam Claflin is hot, but Rhett Cole is . . . mesmerizing.

"What were you doing at the Hamilton Building?" I blurt out before I can stop myself. I can't think of a single reason someone who drives a fucking Maserati would have for being on this side of town. Everything we have, they have in overpriced droves where he comes from.

The shrug he gives me is so casual, so practiced. "Running errands."

As if Rhett Cole doesn't have people to run his errands for him. It's a bald-faced lie, but I let it go. "How's Princess Beatrice?"

I haven't overplayed my hand with this question, because anyone who hasn't lived under a rock for the past five years knows about his on-again-off-again relationship with the Princess Royal.

"Good, I assume." His eyes dart toward me. "I haven't seen her in a long time."

I shove my tongue into the side of my cheek and stare at the passing shops.

"Do you have any animals?" he asks.

"Nope," I say to the window.

"No dog?"

An image of Charlie flashes through my mind, followed by that now-familiar dull ache. "They're animals the last time I checked."

He laughs. "Closer to people if you ask me." Several beats of tense silence pass, then he says, "Not even a goldfish?"

I hold up a finger, but keep my eyes averted. "Not an animal. And no. Why do you keep asking?"

I feel, rather than see, his shrug. "Just remembered how much you liked animals is all," he mumbles.

Fortunately, the world's awkwardest car ride comes to a stop a few minutes later as he pulls up in front of my building.

"Thanks for the ride." I climb out of the car before he can get any ideas about opening my door again.

He's already lifting my boxes out of the boot.

"I can take those." I reach for them.

Twisting his body away from me, he says, "Lead the way."

I roll my eyes and head for the metal staircase. If he wants to play Cary Grant, he can play fucking Cary Grant. But he's not setting foot inside my door.

He waits patiently while I dig the key from my bag. It's buried at the bottom, as usual.

My neighbor sticks her head out into the hallway, bright pink curlers buried in her bottle-red hair. "Saylor," she hisses. "Must you make so much noise? Luca is sleeping."

"Hi, Paula." I twist the key in the lock. "We'll try to be quieter."

"Who's Luca?" Rhett asks after Paula retreats into her flat.

"Her reborn doll."

His left brow quirks upward. "Do I want to know?"

"Probably not." The door swings inward, and I grasp it before it opens further and accidentally invites my unwelcome visitor inside. "But if you're feeling adventurous, Google it."

He looks reluctant to hand over the cartons, but I weasel them from his hands anyway. "Hold it right there," he says, and rummages through his pocket.

I hear the scratch of a marker on cardboard. "Please don't tell me you carry a Sharpie with you."

He emerges from the other side of the stack of boxes with that shit-eating grin. "Actually, it's a Dango." He wiggles the silver pen back and forth.

I close my eyes. "My god."

"What are you doing tonight?" he says, shoving his hands back into his pockets.

"Anything but you. Sorry." I edge backward into my flat. "Thanks again for the ride."

"My pleasure." His eyes flick downward. "Nice shoes."

Under his attention, my feet grow hot inside my special edition Doc Martens X Keith Haring 1460 black combat boots. I shift awkwardly, unsure what to do with his gaze. It feels like live coals. "Thanks," I say.

He winks—*again*—then adds, "If you ever want to redo those really bad kisses, just let me know."

4

"All My Friends" - A Day to Remember

Rhett

My tour schedule is waiting in my inbox when I park in the underground garage of the Atlantis for poker night. I open it before getting out of the car. New York City, Boston, Cincinnati, Chicago, Seattle. My heart pounds faster just scanning the list. *Nashville.*

Will he show up? Come listen to his kid play? Or will he be too busy doing his own shows to pay any attention to me? It's hard to believe I'll be in the same city as my dad in a few weeks. I haven't seen him in five years.

I slide my phone into my pocket and head upstairs to Pierce's flat. The label has a lot riding on this tour, and I can't afford to let them down by thinking about Randy Cole. The album is doing well, and several of my songs are climbing the charts. I didn't get to choose my band members, but I met them a few weeks ago, and they seem great. My manager, Marcus, is cool too.

There's nothing to worry about. So then why do I feel so apprehensive about the whole thing?

I punch the lift button for Pierce's floor and force myself to think about something else. Images of Saylor in her little bowler hat pop

30

into my mind. She had no idea how damn cute she looked in that thing.

I recognized her the second I saw her face, which was only after I kept her from face-planting down a flight of stairs. I lied about forgetting her name, because I wasn't sure she remembered me, and there is nothing worse than being the one forgotten.

Our kisses were terrible, that much was true. What else can you expect from a couple of first-timers who don't have a fucking clue what they're doing? If she'd give me a chance, I could show her exactly how much I've learned in the past decade.

I wasn't sure I'd hear from her after I scrawled my digits on her box of shit, so I was surprised when a random number popped up on my screen with a link to a TikTok video. At first I thought it was a scam text, and I was about to delete it when another message appeared—a single clown emoji.

I clicked through to watch the video, which was about the creepiest dolls I've ever seen. They weren't the horror movie variety, and that somehow made them even worse. They looked *real*. It was disturbing. Laughing, I texted her back.

I'm gonna have nightmares for a month. Thanks for that.

She responded with the victory sign emoji. That only made me smile harder. What is it about this girl that makes me feel lighter?

I snap a goofy-ass selfie in the elevator and send it to her, without a fucking reason except that I want to hear from her again.

Tonight's poker game proceeds the way they usually do. Maeve is uptight when I tell everyone I'm going on tour for six weeks. Heath and Walker can barely keep their hands to themselves. Pierce looks like he has a stick shoved so far up his ass he can taste the bark. And Lux brought her boyfriend—a first for our group. Fortunately, Slate and I have become good friends since he got me into rehab.

When the game is over, I head to the kitchen to refill my glass. I need something to help me relax, and since weed is no longer in the picture for me, Pierce's top-shelf whiskey will have to do. I'm trying not to stress about the tour, but so far I've been largely unsuccessful. I knock a shot back and am pouring another when Lux walks in.

She leans against the sleek counter, watching me. "Hey. Everything okay?"

I toss back the second shot and wipe my mouth. "Why wouldn't it be?"

"You didn't seem as thrilled about the tour as I would have expected."

"I'm excited."

"Rhett." She touches my arm. "Isn't this everything you've ever wanted?"

"Of course it is." I spin my glass on the wooden countertop. "It's just—" I rake fingers through my hair, searching for the right words. Lux is the only person here I can be honest with.

"Just what?"

I glance at her and shrug. "I'm scared."

"You're scared," she parrots back. She looks like she isn't sure she heard me correctly.

"I've been clean for four months." *And my entire career is riding on me staying that way.*

"And you think the tour will mess with that?"

"Do you know what it's like out there?"

"Not exactly. But that doesn't mean you have to be a part of it, does it?"

I shake my head. "The pressure—it's intense."

"What if you took someone with you? To help?"

"Help with what?" There's something crusted on the countertop that Pierce's maid must have missed. I scratch at it with my thumbnail.

"To, like, help you say no?" Lux says.

"What, like a handler?"

"Sort of." Her delicate shoulders rise and fall. "Someone to remind you of why you're clean in the first place."

I shoot her a look. "I don't need a babysitter."

"My god, Rhett. That's not what I was suggesting. Just a mate to stand beside you."

"I don't know. People will get suspicious. The record label can't find out about the rehab."

"What if your handler was a girl?"

"You mean so I could bang her instead of shooting up?"

She looks nonplussed. "Of course not. But what if you let people think you were dating? As a way to explain her presence."

What she's suggesting works its way into my brain. "A fake relationship."

"Exactly."

I let myself picture it for just a second. "That could be . . . fun." I'm sure the grin on my face looks malicious, but I can't help it. It *does* sound like fun.

"If you can find someone for the job."

I fight the urge to chuckle. "I already have the perfect person in mind."

Now I just need her to agree.

* * *

I walk back to the poker room with buoyed spirits. If Lux's plan really works, and I can get Saylor to agree to it . . . The thought of having her on tour with me has adrenaline pumping through my veins.

Pierce has finally loosened his tie and is staring glumly at the stack of chips in front of him. He looks up when I sit down, and I can tell he's about to start interrogating me about the tour. I need to redirect, and fast.

"You'll never believe who I saw together at the Carlton," I say, more loudly than necessary, but everyone stops talking and looks at me. I keep my gaze focused on Maeve. She narrows her eyes. "Maeve and Preston Ansley."

Pierce snorts loudly. I expect Maeve to sock his arm, but she only intensifies her glare at me, a death threat now lurking in those dark depths.

"I didn't realize it was a crime," she says. Her face has taken on a scarlet tint, but that might just be the reflection of her red dress or the glowing lights all over the room.

"It is if he's married," Lux singsongs under her breath.

"Or if he's a tool like Ansley," I add, unwrapping a toothpick and sticking it between my teeth.

Maeve's cheeks darken even further. Definitely not the dress, then. "You don't even know him."

"Uh . . ." I chuckle, wondering what can of worms I've unintentionally opened. "I know enough."

I expected her to fly off the handle at my insinuation that something happened between them, making us listen to five minutes of her raging about what a wanker he is and how they were only meeting up so she could pump him for information. I did not expect my insinuation to be . . . correct.

"You okay, Maeve?" Walker asks.

Maeve ignores her. "Preston is not who you think."

"So he's *not* married?" Lux asks.

Maeve turns her glare on Lux. "Not for much longer."

Heath groans and leans back in his chair. "Don't fall for that line, Maeve."

She looks ready to snap. "It's not a line. His wife is atrocious. If you'd ever spent five minutes with the woman, you'd know the only topic of conversation in her wheelhouse is her distant connection to the queen." Her eyes scan each of us in turn, begging us to understand. "Preston can't take it anymore. He's going to file for divorce."

I glance across the table at Pierce, who is studiously avoiding eye contact with everyone and twisting a poker chip in his hands. Lux shares a look with Slate, who has one very large tattooed hand clamped on her thigh. Walker catches my eye, and I can read the question there. *What do we do?*

I shrug. Trying to talk Maeve into or out of anything is as easy as getting a table at Rao's when you're not a regular.

"You really should break it off," Walker finally tells her when it becomes obvious no one else is going to say anything.

Maeve's eyebrows are nearly touching in the center of her forehead. "That's not happening."

"For fuck's sake, Maeve," I say. "The bloke's married."

"And I told you, he's in the middle of a divorce," she shoots back.

"Actually, you said he was going to *file* for divorce," Lux says. "Which literally means nothing coming from a married man."

"I guess you would know." Maeve's voice is brimming with hostility.

Lux colors and drops her gaze to the table. Beside her, Slate growls at Maeve.

"She's right," Walker says. "Married men are notorious for telling their mistresses they're getting divorced. How do you not know this?"

"Preston is different."

Mother of god. I never thought I'd see the day Maeve Wilson would fall for a load of crap.

"Did you look at the new budget yet?" Pierce's voice surprises all of us. He's been so quiet throughout this whole conversation, I almost forgot he was in the room.

"Oh, god," Lux says under her breath. "Here we go."

Maeve turns to him. "I glanced at it. It's still three million over what we agreed."

Pierce shifts in his chair. "There's no way to do it for less."

"Then maybe you should kiss the deal goodbye."

Heath shoots me a droll look. One thing I will not miss on tour is Maeve and Pierce's bickering over shit between their companies.

"Since we just established that your judgment is rubbish, I don't think that's a good idea," Pierce says.

Maeve stands up so fast her chair knocks over. Her face is so red, I'm not sure there's blood left anywhere else in her body. "You bastard." She grabs her purse from beneath the table and stalks out. Seconds later, the crash of the door slamming reverberates through the game room.

"Fuck," Pierce mutters.

"Nice job, mate," I tell him.

Walker stands up. "I'll go see if she's alright."

Pierce motions for her to sit. "It was my fault. I'll go."

I sure hope he can get her to calm down, because if not, we might just have had our last poker night.

5

"Check Yes Juliet" - We The Kings

Saylor

How is this my life? I wedge the cold compress between my shoulder and cheek the way one might a phone while I fiddle with the ibuprofen bottle. At this rate, I'm going to give myself an ulcer, and then I'll have to deal with that in addition to the toothache, which is starting to feel debilitating.

I think about my credit card longingly. Once upon a time, I kept a minimal balance on it, paying it off every month. My credit score was fantastic. But thanks to my wonderful husband and his gambling addiction, the card has since been maxed out—with steep payments I'm still responsible for—and my score has tanked so low that I get laughed off if I even attempt to apply for another card.

Everything is fucking terrific.

I've got the thousand I deposited in the bank when I opened my new account, but they fine you if the balance falls below the initial deposit. And try as I might, I've been unable to scrape together enough to cover my rent *and* a dental visit.

I'm prioritizing the roof over my head, which means I'm officially screwed and will just have to ride out the toothache until I find a new job. God, I love my life.

The compress has warmed and is now more nuisance than help, so I toss it on the counter and peek into the fridge. I don't want to take the painkiller on an empty stomach, but given the lack of food, that might be my only option.

There's a half-full bottle of ketchup, a jar of Nate's jalapeño olives—no idea why those are still in there—and a jar of blackberry jam my mum gave me for Christmas last year that tastes like a Fruit Roll-Up that gave up on life. I haven't had the heart to throw it out, in case she asks about it the next time she's here. Unless I'm willing to eat condiment soup, I'll just have to risk the ulcer thing.

It looks like my last paycheck from Restore Hope will go toward restocking my sad fridge. Which means it's time to start job hunting. I've been putting it off since Sondra let me go on Friday, but I can't ignore the inevitable any longer. I will starve to death if I don't find another source of income.

I carry my laptop over to the sofa and plop down. I would rather get my tooth extracted without numbing medication than look for another job. How will I ever find anything that compares to Restore Hope? My work there mattered, and I already know I'll hold everything else up in comparison.

As I wait for my computer to boot up, my phone rings. I blink in surprise at the name on the screen. He's never called me before.

"Hello?" I answer tentatively.

"Saylor Jones." I can hear the smile in his voice already.

"Rhett Cole," I say back.

"I have a proposition for you."

"No, I'm not giving you sex tips."

"You slay me." I picture him clutching his heart in mock pain. "My offer has nothing to do with sex, you pervert. Also, I don't need tips, thank you very much."

"I assumed you were as useless in bed as you are at chess." We tried playing several games at summer camp, and when I say the guy doesn't know his pawn from his king, I'm not exaggerating.

"God, you are mean." His laugh has a light, airy quality to it. "I'm beginning to reconsider my offer."

He has my curiosity piqued, but I'm not about to tell him that. "That's probably better anyway. I'm a very busy person."

"Oh, yeah?" Something that sounds like a guitar strum comes through the phone. "What are you doing right now?"

I glance down at the lock screen on my computer. I shift it off my lap and tuck my feet underneath the thrifted oversized Metallica T-shirt I'm wearing as a dress. "That's classified information."

A pause. "And what do I need to do to gain access?"

"I'm afraid I'm out of your league. Sorry."

He groans. "I'm fully aware of that. But it won't stop me from trying anyway."

I bite my lip through a grin. Flirting with Rhett is . . . fun. And I haven't done anything resembling fun in a very long time. Still, there's no point to it, and I'm just procrastinating, avoiding doing something that will actually keep me alive. "How about I save us both the time? It was nice running into you again, but I don't think this is going to work."

"You haven't even heard me out yet."

No, but I heard my heart pick up speed when your name flashed on my screen. This is a dangerous game I have no business playing. "Like I said, I'm very—"

"This will only take a second."

"Fine." I say it with a sigh, but a small part of me—a very small part—is excited by his insistence.

I hear a faint "yes" on the other end. I imagine him pumping his fist into the air like he's actually achieved something. I hope he knows he's only setting himself up for disappointment, because whatever he's offering, I'm turning it down.

I pick up the mug of lukewarm tea from the coffee table and wait for him to go on.

"I need you to pose as my girlfriend."

I choke on my drink. When I'm done coughing, I hold the phone back to my ear. "Sorry, I didn't catch what you said."

"I want you to pretend to be my girlfriend on tour."

I laugh. Loudly. "That is . . . wow. Do you try that line on all women you want to sleep with?"

"Who said I want to sleep with you?"

"I thought guys like you considered another notch in their bedpost to be the greatest possible achievement."

"Guys like me," he repeats.

"Guys like you."

There's silence for a few seconds, and I'm beginning to think I've offended him.

"Are you calling me a slut?" he says. The question is absurd, given how many times he's appeared in the tabloids, his arms slung around women so beautiful it hurts to look at them.

I laugh awkwardly and stroke the blanket tossed over the back of the sofa. "I didn't say that."

"I can own that I have . . . slutty *behaviors*—"

"Behaviors?" It comes out on another laugh.

"But I was actually serious, Saylor."

Something catches in my chest at his tone. Probably just left over from my choking fit. I clear my throat. "I can't do it."

"Why?"

"I'm not sure I'm required to give you that information."

More strumming. "What can I say to convince you?" he asks.

I bite my lip and push my toes into the orange velvet of the sofa.

"My answer isn't going to change, but you can tell me why you're asking." No one said I can't be curious.

A soft melody floats across the line. I wonder if he's perched on the edge of a chair to play or slumped back against a couch, guitar on his chest.

"I'm an addict."

The words are so unexpected, I blink and set my tea down before I spill it all over myself.

"I got out of rehab earlier this year," he continues. "In March."

"You're clean?" I say.

"Five months."

"Congratulations."

"Thanks." He sighs, and there's a rustle of movement. "The record label doesn't know. If they did, they probably wouldn't have signed me."

"I thought drugs were par for the course in the music world."

"They want a polished image. 'A clean Justin Bieber.'" Mockery coats his words.

I snort. Rhett is nothing like the Biebs. "How do I play into all of this?"

"I was hoping you'd be my handler. You work with addicts, right?"

"Not exactly." I create social media content about addiction—well, I did—and volunteer on the hotline, but that's not the same thing. Not even close. "I've never been anyone's sponsor."

"I already have a sponsor. But he's old and fat, and no one would believe he was my boyfriend."

I cackle. "Why do you need to date your sponsor?"

"To hide the real reason for their presence?" His voice rises at the end, the question hanging there, as though he's still trying to convince himself this fucked-up plan could actually work.

It makes sense in a way. If he's hiding his addiction from the record label, he can't exactly broadcast that he's bringing a handler along. "I wish I could help you."

"You can."

I let out a wry chuckle. "No, Rhett, I can't." Not only is it a bad idea on so many levels, but I already know how it would end. Not pretty.

"Why not? Didn't you just get fired?"

My jaw tightens at the reminder. "I was let go."

"Potato, po-tah-to."

I tug the '70s afghan I thrifted a few weeks ago onto my lap. Why am I suddenly cold? "My answer is still no."

"Have you found a new job?" he says.

"Not yet, but I—"

"Now you don't have to look."

My sigh is loud. I push my fingers through the crocheted holes in the blanket. "It's not that easy."

"What's so hard about it? You need a job, and I'm offering you one. The pay will be better than anything else you'll find."

"You think I can't find a high-paying job?"

"Not this high." He quotes the figure.

My mouth falls open, and I have to remind myself to shut it. "That's insane. You're going to pay someone that much to pretend to be your girlfriend?"

"Not *someone*. You. And technically, it's payment for being my handler."

"I can't do it." I force the words out before my brain can trick me into mentally spending every cent he just offered me.

"Can't you even think about it before saying no?" His voice is soft, wiggling its way into my core, invoking more sympathy than I should be feeling right now.

"There must be a thousand girls who would say yes."

"I don't want them. I want you."

I do my best not to let his words flatter me, not to read into what is a very convincing charm. "You don't even know me."

"Come on tour with me, and I'll change that."

I shake my head, a smile tugging at my lips. God, he's relentless. An even better reason to stay far away. "I don't think so."

"Please."

I laugh at his pleading tone. "You must have been awful as a child."

"I go after what I want."

"I noticed."

"What I want is you, Saylor Jones."

My heart beats a staccato. *He's a player*, I remind myself. He thinks what he wants is me, but I know better. "You'll just have to find someone else."

"Come on. Think about it. Traveling the United States, all expenses paid, for six weeks. With the hottest artist on the planet."

I ignore the flash of excitement that lights up my brain. "You're going to the US?"

"I'd go to the moon if it meant you'd say yes."

Part of me wants to reward him for his persistence. Another part of me really wants that money. With that much cash, I could fix my tooth, stock my fridge, and go back to working at Restore Hope, for no pay this time. Hell, with that much money I could make a down payment on a house. A little cottage with pipes that don't creak every time you turn on the hot water and a little flower garden out front and— *Shit, Saylor. What are you doing?*

"I could be your social media manager instead," I say before I can reconsider. Maybe there's a way for both of us to win. "And your handler." It's still a bad idea, but if it's just for six weeks, it might not be a complete disaster.

"I don't need someone for social media."

"Uh, yeah, you do," I say. "Your TikToks suck."

"You follow me." The smugness in his tone is blatant.

"I looked you up." Rhett Cole on screen is addictive. I can only imagine the kind of magic he will bring to the stage.

His songs have always been good, if maybe a little generic. Recently, his lyrics have become more raw and vulnerable, the music edgier, grittier. His voice is throaty and makes something deep inside me pulse when he sings.

"I wouldn't take my photographer to an after-party," he says.

"Why not?"

"Because that'd be weird?"

"But you could," I point out. "The fans would love the behind-the-scenes stuff."

"Fine," he says. "You do the social media shit *and* play my girlfriend, and I'll double the price."

My eyes nearly bug out of my head. "Can you repeat that?" I stammer.

"I'm serious."

Goddamnit, why does he have to make this so hard? "I can't. I'm sorry." I feel physical pain saying the words. The things I could do with that much money. But it's not worth it. If I say yes, it'll only destroy me.

Several seconds pass before he says, "I can offer more."

"God, Rhett. It's not about the money."

"Then what is it?" A brief pause, then he adds quietly, "Is it me?"

Images of him flood my mind, and the memory of his scent clogs my senses until he's all I can smell. "No, it's not you." I mean, it *is* him, just not in the way he thinks.

"Tell me what I need to fix, and I'll fix it."

"There's nothing to be fixed." Some things just aren't meant to be. "I can't do it."

"And you won't tell me why?" he says.

I squeeze my eyes shut, my fingers clenching the afghan. "I just think it's a bad idea. The kind that blows up in your face."

"Aren't those the best ideas?" His smile bleeds through the phone, but it sounds sad.

"My answer is still no."

"I'm not giving up."

"You're wasting your time."

A pause, then: "I don't think I am."

6

"Lonely" - Justin Bieber + benny blanco

Rhett

How can you listen to this shit?

My kid sister can write better songs than this.

Wonder how much he paid for his followers.

The comments roll in faster than I can delete and block. I toss my phone aside, and it hits the sofa with a soft plop. I shove my fingers through my hair and lean forward on my knees.

Maybe I should take it as a compliment that they feel the need to attack me so relentlessly, but it feels like shit. As soon as I block their accounts, they just make new ones and come after me again. It's getting old.

The price you pay for fame, I guess. At least in the twenty-first century. Pretty sure my dad never had to deal with social media trolls in the early 2000s.

I sigh and reach for my phone again. Better to deal with this than pretend it's not happening.

This guy's a joke. His music sucks as bad as his hair.

Hey wanker. Leave the hair alone, I reply.

Not that it'll do any good. There will just be five more replies agreeing with him that my hair sucks. Does my hair suck? I run my hand through it again. Considering the hundreds I pay for each haircut, I'm going to assume it does not suck.

The most recent comment flashes on my screen. *Only reason this guy's famous is because of his dad.*

That one hits in the center of my chest with a hard thwack. Mainly because I'm scared it's actually true. I can defend my haircut until I'm dead, but I have no way of knowing how much of my success can be attributed to him. Randy Cole is a household name. What record label wouldn't want the chance to make the son as famous as the father?

My phone rings as I'm pressing the delete button on the comment.

"Hey, Eddie," I answer. "How's it going?"

The A and R rep clears his throat on the other end. "Well, to be honest, not great."

My heart sinks. What the fuck is going on now? "Oh?" I force my voice to remain cool and detached.

"We've been monitoring your social media accounts. You've seen some of your latest comments, I presume?"

I close my eyes and squeeze the bridge of my nose. "Yeah."

"Is this going to be a problem?"

"No, sir. You know how people are."

"I do," he hedges, "but these ones seem particularly malicious."

I want to welcome him to the TikTok era, but I don't. "I'm handling it," I say, not sure exactly how I'll continue doing so while I'm touring. Ten-hour days, producing new music, trying to get enough sleep so I don't look like a washed-up star.

"This is important, Rhett." Eddie's voice grows more stern. "Your contract—"

"Yeah, I know," I snap. Fuck the bloody contract. That thing's going to come back to bite me in the ass. "Sorry, sir. I will do my best to keep it under control."

He sighs through the phone, and I wonder if he already regrets signing me. If so, I'll just have to prove him wrong.

"See to it that you do," he says. "Otherwise—"

"Will do, sir," I cut in before he can threaten to terminate our agreement. "You won't be disappointed."

His answering grunt does not seem to agree, but I will take the fact that he doesn't press it further as a good sign. I can handle this. I just need a game plan.

"All right, Rhett. We'll give it another shot. I recommend not screwing it up."

"Yes, sir," I say, ending the call. "Fuck!" I hurl my phone across the room. Fortunately, it hits the other sofa and doesn't break.

I push to my feet and pace the floor, kicking a moving box out of the way. I've lived here for two years, and I still haven't fully unpacked. Maybe the trolls are right, and I am just a dipshit.

What I wouldn't give for a hit of insidion right now. One of those little white vials could make this whole thing disappear, fade into the background and allow me a little breathing room.

But those vials are the reason I'm here in the first place. Starting up again would be the absolute worst thing I could do for my career. It would make the social media trolls look like adoring fans.

My phone pings again, and I walk toward it out of instinct, even though I'm slightly terrified it's Eddie telling me the rest of the team voted to cut me. I let out an audible sigh of relief when I see Lux's name on the screen.

Lux: *Did you give my idea any more thought? xx*

Me: *Skinny dipping tonight?*

Lux: *No, you idiot. About a GIRLLLL*

After Maeve stormed out the other night and Pierce went after her, things got awkward. I guess it's to be expected that we'll fight occasionally, but I've never seen Maeve that mad. Maybe whatever she has going on with that wanker, Preston, is more serious than we all thought. But fuck it if it is. She shouldn't be messing around with a married bloke.

Pierce returned fifteen minutes later, sans Maeve. He said she had finally cooled down but didn't feel like coming back upstairs. Thankfully, she hasn't been ignoring our group chat, so it looks like our poker games will continue for the time being.

I bring my attention back to my conversation with Lux and type out a reply.

Me: *She said no*

Lux: *I wasn't aware it needed to be someone in particular??*

Me: *It doesn't. I just really wanted this one*

Lux: *So ask her again. xx*

I sigh and shake my head. I hate admitting how much Saylor's rejection stung. Until she told me no, I didn't realize how much I was already visualizing the two of us on tour together, getting to know her again, maybe falling back into the place where we were as kids.

Me: *She's going to hate me*

Lux: *She must already if she told you no.*

Me: *Ouch*

Lux: *Just kidding!!!!! xxxxxx*

Me: *Well she's definitely not a fan*

Lux: *Who is she? I'll cut her. How can she not be a fan? You're Rhett Cole!*

Me: *Please don't. And you don't know her*

Lux: *Just ask someone else!*

Me: *Will you be my fake girlfriend on tour while simultaneously keeping me from doing drugs and washing my career down the drain?*

Lux: *Cute.*

Lux: *And I'm deleting that text so Slate doesn't kill you.*

I could ask someone else. If I were smart, that's what I would do.

But now that I've imagined Saylor doing it, I don't want anyone else pretending to be my girlfriend.

I really want to see her again. I want to see her so badly, I've actually dreamed about her a few times. Nothing *too* inappropriate.

The day I drove her home felt like destiny. What are the odds the two of us would run into each other like that? Literally, if I had stopped at Restore Hope to drop off the check later that day, she would've been gone, and I would never have known how much I'd missed out on. If fate wants us together, she can't stand in the way.

I pull up our text thread. We've hardly talked since the day I called her and she turned me down. I've texted her a few times, but she rarely responds. She's either very busy—which I doubt, given the loss of her job—or she doesn't want anything to do with me—more likely, but harder to swallow.

Her not answering makes me think about her even more. Most girls won't stop texting me, asking what I'm doing or when they can see me again, until I'm ready to become a monk just so I don't have to put up with the clinginess. But at the end of the day, sex always wins out, and I end up giving my number to yet another girl who won't take the hint that I'm not interested in anything more.

But with Saylor, it's different. We've never slept together, but I'm not even thinking about sex, to be honest. I just find myself wondering what she's up to when I'm driving, or picturing her face while I'm working on a new song.

I read through our messages once more, automatically smiling at the exchange. She's funny, and goddamn, funny girls are hard to find. Funny girls who don't send a million texts a day? A goddamn rarity.

The tour is only a few weeks away, and I need a handler before then. If Saylor refuses to do it, I'll have to suck it up and look for someone else. But that doesn't mean I'm giving up on her just yet. I've been known to charm pricklier things than my summer camp crush.

Me: *Hey*

I regret the text as soon as I send it. What better way to sound like a twelve-year-old wanker than to start a conversation with "hey." I try again.

Me: *Sorry that was my dog hitting on you*

Several minutes pass, and I can't help checking for a response every thirty seconds. When the speech bubble finally pops up next to her name, my pulse picks up speed. I knew the dog comment would get her.

Saylor: *You have a dog?*

Me: *It was a hypothetical dog*

Saylor: *...*

Me: *What would you say if I asked you to please reconsider my offer?*

Saylor: *I'd tell you to kindly fuck off.*

Me: *Wince. Are you always this sweet?*

Saylor: *Only with dogs trying to get with me.*

Okay, I deserved that.

Me: *What if I told you I wasn't interested in you like that?*

There's a long pause before she finally replies.

Saylor: *I'd ask if that's supposed to be a compliment.*

Me: *No. Also not the truth*

Saylor: *I can appreciate the honesty.*

Me: *But I'm willing to make it the truth if you'll reconsider*

Saylor: *I already gave you my answer.*

Me: *Hence the reconsideration*

Saylor: *You can point in any direction and find a hundred women willing to take you up on it.*

Me: *And if I don't want them?*

Her response takes an agonizingly long time to arrive.

Saylor: *I thought it was supposed to be fake.*

I bite my lip as I consider my response. She is taking no bullshit from me, and I'm loving it. I'm so used to girls throwing themselves at me that this kind of verbal firing is actually refreshing.

Me: *I'll double my offer*

Saylor: *You already did.*

Me: *I'll double the double*

Saylor: *Put your money to better use.*

Me: *Is there anything I can say that would change your mind?*

Saylor: *Nope.*

My chest deflates like a balloon slowly releasing air. I take back everything I just said about this being refreshing. It feels like I've been sucker punched and am reeling for breath.

I am royally fucked.

7

"Hard Times" - Paramore

Saylor

I cringe as the clerk scans the last item on the belt—a box of generic crackers—and my total appears on the screen. My reusable shopping tote isn't even bulging, and the total still manages to take a nice chunk out of my last paycheck.

I swing the bag over my shoulder and head home. Food would probably be cheaper at one of the bigger supermarkets, but then I'd have to take public transit, which is undesirable for several reasons. For starters, it costs a lot more than walking, and I'm a big sucker for free. Second, I know myself, and myself would try to make the trip worth it by buying enough for several weeks, which I can't afford to do.

So for now, the neighborhood market, which carries only two brands of toothpaste—both with fluoride—will have to suffice. And of course, it starts raining on my way home, making me regret my dedication to walking.

My tooth throbs as I jog up the stairs to my flat, as though it wants to remind me that it, too, has needs. It's become like a pet after all this time, waking me up in the middle of the night, costing more than my dinner, preventing me from getting anything done with its incessant nagging.

The thrift store won't pay me until this weekend, and even when they do, it will only be enough to cover a small portion of my rent. I took the job for the sweet discount, not for the pay.

Thank God I still have the housing allotment—the only reason I still haven't filed the divorce paperwork—but I have to find the money for the rest of the rent, which is due in less than two weeks. No one is going to hire and pay me in that amount of time, even if I do manage to find a job, which means I'll have to dip into the minimum balance in my account. It kills me, because the fine isn't cheap, and it took me months to save up that money. But I'll be damned if I lose this flat.

I put the groceries away, then reach for the bottle of painkillers. There's a single pill left. "Crap," I mutter, and put the cap back on. Saving it for tonight when the pain won't let me sleep is the wise thing to do.

Naturally, I forgot to grab more at the shop, which means either another trip—in the rain—or some alternate method for pain relief. Thunder cracks loudly, as though helping make my decision. Guess I'll try my hand at home remedies.

A quick online search gives me a few different options, and I call the thrift shop while I set the tea kettle on to boil.

"Justine's Attic."

"Hey, Justine. It's Saylor."

"You calling in sick?" Justine is no-nonsense and as predictable as tax season.

I fill a cup with water and add a spoonful of salt. My gag reflex activates, and I haven't even held it to my lips yet. "Actually, I was wondering about picking up some extra shifts."

She *tsks* into the phone, a bad sign. "Oh, girl. I wish I had some to give you."

"I'm free any time of day. I'll even work Saturday nights." *No one wants to work Saturday nights.*

"Don't you already work Saturdays?"

I blink at my reflection in the window above the sink. The sky has grown dark, rain slashing against the windows. "Maybe I could clone myself?"

Her chuckle sounds more tired than amused. "I'm afraid I don't have anything available."

"Darn. You sure? Damian calls in sick so often—"

"I'm sorry, hun, but I've got too many people in the same boat as you."

I sigh and stir the saltwater with a spoon. "It's fine. If anything opens up, keep me in mind?"

She assures me she will and ends the call.

I slump against the counter, already feeling defeated, and I haven't even started looking for jobs yet. Before I can talk myself out of it, I take a large mouthful of saltwater and swish it around my tooth.

It's disgusting. I spit it into the sink, then get a fresh glass from the tap while my laptop reboots. Time to stop delaying the inevitable. If I want to stay alive, I'm going to need to find a new job.

Rhett's proposal taps me on the shoulder, reminding me I've already received a better job offer than I'm likely to get again in my lifetime, if you're only considering the pay. But since I'm not, I shove it away. While I'm drawn to the idea of helping him avoid falling back into addiction, I'm more worried about how drawn I feel toward *him.*

Better not to play with fire.

I soak a cotton ball in clove oil—as per the instructions I find online—and sit down to see what kind of jobs are out there. I've never done an official job hunt before. Restore Hope and Justine's Attic both fell into my lap at an opportune time, and I'm not one to look a gift horse in the mouth.

I stick the cotton ball onto my tooth and bite down while I scan the postings. The first one is for a "Social Media Sorcerer," whatever the heck that is. I click to read more, but the description doesn't shed much light.

"Seeking a Social Media Sorcerer to conjure up compelling content that charms followers and boosts engagement. Ideal candidates are wizards in crafting viral posts, have experience in brewing up magic marketing strategies, and can spellbind audiences on Instagram, TikTok, and Threads."

Okay, then. I click back to the rest of the results. They are just as bleak, but with fewer wizards and more CEO talk. I have the skill set for most of them, but I can't imagine wasting it on promoting their mindless products. How am I supposed to face myself after posting about a supplement that promises to make your hair grow an inch a day?

I have a BA in communications, but I feel like a high school dropout looking at these jobs. There isn't a single charity listed. I was actually helping people at Restore Hope. Now I'm supposed to sit in a cubicle all day, tweeting about Miley Cyrus?

I shut my laptop in frustration and go to grab my kettle, which has been whistling at me for the past minute. There's one bag of peppermint tea left, and I add it to the hot water rather than my cup to make it stretch further.

My phone rings on the coffee table, and my first thought is that it might be Rhett. My second is that if it is, I will take him up on his offer, threat of hellfire be damned.

It's not Rhett. It's a FaceTime call from my parents, who are currently traveling in southern Asia. I sit on the couch and accept the call. Their faces press together to fit on the screen. Behind them, I can make out what appears to be a lush green rainforest.

"Hi, love!" my mum says, louder than necessary. "How are you?"

"I'm good!" I insert an extra dose of enthusiasm into my voice. My tooth pulses with pain at my lie, and I quickly turn my head away from the screen to remove the cotton ball from my mouth. "How's Indonesia?"

"Beautiful," my dad answers at the same time my mum says, "Stunning." They give each other goofy smiles, then my dad waits for her to continue.

"We just got back from a monkey sanctuary," she says. "It was incredible. You would have loved it."

"I'm sure I would have," I say.

"We wanted to hike up Mount Bromo, but with your dad's heart condition, they didn't recommend it. We're not in the same shape we were twenty years ago." She giggles at this and shares another look with Dad.

My gut pinches. I'm happy that they're able to finally do this, but the truth is, they would have gone much sooner if it hadn't been for me. I was an "accident," although they've never worded it like that. "A happy accident," my mum would say if she could read my thoughts.

Thankfully, she can't. She prattles on about the things they've experienced so far. It's been a culture shock for them.

Neither of them has ever left the country before, but it's been their dream my entire life. Our home was always full of travel guides, atlases, and globes. They watched foreign films every night they weren't grading papers or planning lessons for the next day. I knew how badly they wanted to travel, but living in the city on two teacher salaries isn't easy. It definitely doesn't leave money for luxuries like travel, especially not once you add in a child.

I ignore my tooth, which badly wants attention right now. If I asked them for the money, I'd have it by the end of the day. I could schedule an appointment with a dentist tomorrow.

But I know how long they've saved and planned for this trip. I refuse to do anything to jeopardize it. They deserve this. They cared for me for eighteen years. It's time to be a big girl and take care of myself.

58

8

"Counting Stars" - OneRepublic

Rhett

The text comes during my last set of bench presses. I hook the weights back into place and grab a towel from the rack. Rubbing it over my face, I head for the showers. When I've set all of my shit down on the bench, I drape the towel around my neck and pull my phone from my gym bag.

Saylor: *OK.*

My thumb hovers over the question mark key. What the fuck does she mean?

Instead of replying right away, I jump into the shower and mull it over. It isn't until I'm lathering up that it hits me.

OK.

She's accepting my proposal. She's actually agreeing.

At least that's what I hope it means, and not just that she accidentally texted the wrong person. I rush through the rest of the shower and jog out to my car, tossing my bag into the back seat.

There's only one way to find out.

I still have her address in my GPS history, thank fuck, so I find the flat with no problem. Was the building this dingy the day I dropped

59

her off? I don't remember the cement being stained or her neighbor's junk piled outside their door.

My palms start to sweat as I walk up the stairs. What if she's not home? Or worse, what if she's home but not alone? Shit. I definitely should've texted her back, but it's too late for that now.

I rap on the door with my fist. She doesn't even have a doorbell. The same woman as before sticks her head out of the flat next to Saylor's. She gives me a pinched once-over before retreating inside to her reborn dolls. I shudder. I'm about to knock again when the door swings open, and there she is.

Saylor couldn't convey her surprise at seeing me any more blatantly if she tattooed it across her forehead. Her mouth drops open into this adorable little O shape, and her eyes widen just enough for the light to hit them.

It's a little embarrassing how often I've thought about her in the past few weeks. Something about those eyes haunts me every time I slow down long enough for them to appear in my memory.

Her black hair is pulled back into a ponytail that accentuates her cheekbones. She's wearing long fuzzy socks and a tiny pair of floral-printed shorts, leaving her brown legs gloriously exposed. Her matching camisole shows she's not just a pretty face. She also has an impressive rack that has definitely filled out since summer camp.

We process this information at the same time. I react by letting a slow grin spread across my face. She reacts by reaching for something behind the door. At first, I'm afraid it's a can of pepper spray—wouldn't put it past her—but when she slips her arms into a big sweater that hangs past her thighs, I increase the wattage of my smile.

"Hi," I say, leaning against the door frame as she tugs the cardigan closed in front of her.

Her eyes narrow. "What are you doing here?"

"I got your text."

She blinks a few times, expression blank. "My text inviting you over? Sorry, wrong flat. Try Paula next door." The door starts to swing shut.

I block it with my hand. "Saylor, you have to talk to me sometime."

She halts the door, but her jaw has the definitive set of someone who is not pleased.

"I'm sorry for coming over unannounced," I say. "I wasn't thinking."

"I accept your apology." She sniffs. "I'll call you tonight."

This time it's my mouth that drops open. Is she seriously sending me away? She's agreeing to my proposal, but she won't talk to me in person?

Damn. Why am I turned on by her rejection? I shove a hand through my hair and turn toward the stairs, unable to keep a smile from my face as I do. God, the next six weeks are going to be fun. And probably miserable as fuck.

My feet are on the first step when her voice sounds behind me. "Rhett, wait."

I turn back slowly.

She's still in the doorway, clutching that cardigan shut like it will save her from a predator. Is that what I'm supposed to be? "You're here, so . . ." Her voice trails off, but I'm not about to make any further assumptions. They haven't gotten me anywhere yet.

"So what?" I make her say it.

"We'll talk." Her words come out in a rush, and then she's gone, disappearing into the flat but leaving the door standing open.

I'm not going to wait for a second invitation. I follow her inside, shutting the door behind me.

The place is small. Actually, my living room is small. This is *tiny*. I could stretch my arms out and nearly touch both walls. It's not cluttered, but there is a lot of stuff. The most jarring bit is all of the colors. Orange sofa, green chair, humongous rug that covers nearly the entire floor and looks like rainbow vomit. Plants line the long windowsill along the far wall.

It's chaotic and way more color than I'm used to, but somehow it suits her. All the same, I can't help teasing her. "Couldn't decide on a color, so you used them all?"

She looks at me, unamused, arms crossed over her chest. "It must hurt your eyes to venture out of your sleek bachelor pad." Her finger taps against her lip. It's the most distracting thing I've seen all day. "Let me guess. Sofas too uncomfortable to sit on, edges sharp enough to cut you, and enough chrome to replace the mirrors?"

Ouch. Has she stalked me or something?

She moves over to her own sofa, which looks like something from the set of *Mad Men*, and folds herself gracefully onto one side of it. She takes up so little room that I could sprawl out and still not touch her. Which is the point, I think.

I sit down on the other end, making sure she's aware that I have no nefarious intentions. Not today, anyway. I don't say anything, just watch her. The ball is fully in her court, and we both know it.

I've tried reaching out to other girls with my proposition. By tried, I mean I thought of a few contenders. But every time I brought up one of their numbers on my phone, I couldn't send the text. Saylor's face kept coming to mind, taunting me with what I can't have.

I've never been more grateful for anything in my life.

She shifts on the sofa, tucking her feet even more thoroughly under her legs. How long is she going to make herself uncomfortable to stay as far from me as possible? "We should probably discuss things."

She bites her lip, and my eyes zero in on it, suddenly unable to remember why I'm here. It's to fuck her, right? That's why I'm here.

She releases the lip, leaving it cherry colored and slightly swollen. God, what it would be like to kiss it, bite it with my own teeth, watch it double in size.

She clears her throat, and my gaze moves back to her eyes, which don't look impressed.

Shit. I lean forward with my elbows on my knees. "Yes, there's a lot we should discuss." I force my eyes to stay on hers, rather than traverse her entire body the way they very much want to.

"If I do this, there will be boundaries."

I nod as if that isn't my least favorite word in the English language. "Boundaries. Good idea."

"I'll pose as your girlfriend, but only when necessary."

My forehead pinches as I process this. "What does that mean?"

She picks at a thread on her sweater. "Nothing in public."

"No publicity. Got it." I'm nodding so much now, there's a good chance my head will roll right off my shoulders. Outwardly, I'm in agreement. Inwardly, my brain is already skipping ten steps ahead. "When you say not in public, what does that mean exactly?"

"Well, when are you needing me to . . . help?"

I haven't thought through the logistics of it yet, mostly because I didn't think this was actually going to happen. "Mostly at the after-parties," I say. "That's when things get a little crazy."

She nods. "Okay. At the after-parties then. Nothing else."

My brow furrows. "No one's going to believe you're my girlfriend if we're not together other times."

"What, then?" Her sigh is heavy, and it punches me in the gut that she's this repulsed by me.

"At least around the band. Backstage. On the bus. Everyone in the industry, really. They're the ones I need to sell the idea to."

Saylor blinks as she considers this. "Will there be publicity in those places?"

"Not usually."

"What about phones at the after-parties? I don't want any photos taken."

Damn, she really doesn't want to be seen with me. "Okay."

"Okay?"

"I'll ban phones from the parties. Anything else?"

"My name and face won't be leaked?"

"I can't promise anything, but I'll do my best."

"Thank you. Okay." The muscles in her shoulders loosen, and she reaches for the crocheted blanket on the back of the sofa. "Okay," she says again, tucking the colorful afghan around her legs. She's taking up more space now.

"Is that what you're worried about? Being in the spotlight?"

She tilts her chin forward. "That's one thing, yes."

"What else?" I have the sudden urge to vanquish all of her doubts and fears.

"Physical boundaries."

My heart rate kicks up a notch, both in dread of the boundaries she wants to set and in anticipation of physical contact between us. "Yeah, absolutely," I say, as though I was thinking the same thing and not about how much I would like to lay her beneath me on this sofa.

"No kissing."

The floor of my stomach drops out. "None? I'm not sure anyone will be convinced if we don't kiss occasionally."

Her eyes flicker down to my mouth for the briefest of seconds. Is she thinking about our first kiss, too? "Fine, but no tongue."

The side of my mouth quirks upward. "Deal." I'm going to have a hell of a time planning a kiss spectacular enough that she changes her mind. "Is holding your hand okay?"

"Touching is permitted, but no boobs or ass."

I notice she doesn't mention her legs or the area between them, but I'm not about to bring this to her attention. "Stay away from the best parts. Got it."

Her glare heats up, making my grin widen. "And absolutely no shenanigans," she says.

A laugh slips out before I can stop it. "You want that in writing?"

"I do."

God, she is hardballing me so bad, and my balls are here for it. "What constitutes a shenanigan?" I ask.

"I think you already know."

"Enlighten me."

"Something tells me you are the king of shenanigans."

"What in the world gave you that idea?"

Amusement lights her eyes as the atmosphere in the flat shifts. She's warming up to me again, and I can't say it doesn't make me feel like I could fly a fucking plane. "I see the headlines."

"Fuck," I mutter under my breath. "What if I said you can't believe everything you read?"

An actual smile blooms on her face, and it's the most beautiful thing I've ever seen, like watching a flower open for the sun. "I'd say that I guess I'll find out."

"I guess so." I shift back in my seat, my hands aching to pull her into my lap and show her why shenanigans should definitely be on the table.

"What about our breakup?" she says.

"Our what?" I blink at her.

"After the tour? Won't you need to tell people we're no longer together?"

"Yeah, of course." How is it that she's thinking of everything, and the only thing I can think is that I'm not sure I want there to be a breakup, and is that bad?

"Mutual and friendly, right? No hard feelings afterwards?"

I mumble something in agreement. Meanwhile, my head is so full of shit, I can barely think straight. She's like a drug. Once in your blood, impossible to stop. She's already planning the end of this thing, and I'm trying to figure out how to hold on to every single moment.

"All right, then." She pushes to her feet, blanket discarded on the sofa, damn sweater still covering everything. It's enough to shake me out of my stupor.

I stand up as well. "Thank you for agreeing to do this," I say. Do I hug her? Shake her hand?

She keeps her arms wrapped around herself, so I do neither. "It's kind of hard to resist that much money."

"And here I thought it was my charm that won you over."

"I agreed in spite of you."

"Ouch."

She shakes her head, a smile lingering on her lips. "When do we leave?"

"Saturday morning. I hope your passport is up to date."

"It is."

I take a step backward, in the direction of the door. "Should we kiss, just for practice?" I shrug like it's no big deal.

She holds her finger up. "Shenanigan."

"Shenanigans are the spice of life."

"No spice allowed."

"You drive a mean bargain."

She tilts her head to the side, completely unapologetic. "You're the one who wanted this."

"Don't make me regret it."

"Mr. Cole, what did you think my mission was going to be?"

I breathe out a laugh and dig my hand into my hair. It's hitting me that I lost the upper hand the minute we met. "By the way, my agent will email you an NDA to sign."

Her smile melts away. "Do you actually think I'll tell anyone about this?"

I think she'd rather cut off her own arm than leak that she's pretending to be with me. "It's not for me. The record label requires it of everyone."

She nods. "Okay."

I expected more pushback, to be honest. I open the door, then turn back to her and frown. "You don't have a boyfriend who's going to beat me up, right?"

She smirks and leans her shoulder against the wall. "No promises."

I leave her in her colorful flat, already counting the hours until Saturday morning.

9

"Hello Brooklyn" - All Time Low

Rhett

I cannot believe this day has actually arrived. I've been dreaming of going on tour my whole life, but now that I'm standing here in the airport with my band—waiting to board a plane to the United States, of all fucking places—it's impossible to make it feel real.

The guys are sprawled out across the seats in the VIP lounge, messing around on their phones or napping. I don't know how any of them can be relaxed enough to sleep, but maybe they haven't been fantasizing about this ever since discovering their dad is a famous rock star.

A tinny voice announces flights on the intercom, but it's become background noise by now. Noah, our tour manager, is in charge of travel. He's currently flirting with the stewardess at the desk, so as long as they don't sneak off to the restroom for a quickie, he won't let us miss the flight.

I head to the bar. The three martinis I threw back earlier haven't done shit for my nerves. I order another, then glance behind me as the bartender mixes it. Saylor's still not here. I've been telling myself not to worry, that she said she'd come, but it hasn't kept me from pacing the lounge and glancing at the clock every five minutes.

The bartender slides my drink across the smooth countertop, and I down it in three gulps. I toss him a large bill as a tip, and he nods his thanks. The alcohol hits my empty stomach, but it's not enough to shake my anxiety. I know it's ten in the morning, and my therapist would have my head if he knew how much I was drinking, but at least I'm not taking anything harder. Instead, I pull a peppermint-flavored toothpick from my wallet and unwrap it. I scoffed at the idea initially, but they're actually pretty dang effective when the cravings come.

I make my way back to the band. Jentry, our bass guitarist, glances up from his phone with a smirk. "Mate, you need to chill. There's still forty minutes until our flight."

I want to tell him to fuck off, but he's right. I'm stewing for no reason. Saylor has plenty of time to get here. If she wasn't coming, she would have called me.

When I announced that I'd be bringing my girlfriend on tour, my manager, Marcus, nearly shit his pants. Noah also thought it was a terrible idea, until I assured both of them that Saylor was my muse, and that my music would only improve if she came along.

They're both lies, of course. But since having Saylor there will prevent the label's investment—me—from making stupid decisions, which is their only concern, I'd say it's more of a fib than an outright lie.

"Can't wait to meet this girl," Diego says without opening his eyes. He's slumped in his chair, arms crossed, ball cap pulled low over his face. "She must be *fine* if she has you this bothered."

My jaw clenches. "I'm not bothered, you asshole. I'm just afraid she's going to make us late."

"Even Rhett Cole doesn't have the power to delay the plane," Jentry says. "Don't worry, mate. If she's late, she'll catch the next flight."

If she's late, I'm afraid she'll never come. I won't relax until she's strapped into the seat next to me.

Jamal whistles from the chair to my right. "Yo, mates. This one's mine."

One of the personal protection officers nearest him moves, and I turn to see what they're looking at.

And there she is, strolling across the lounge in a vintage David Bowie T-shirt and leather pants. Her tight black curls are covered by a knit beanie. She looks fucking adorable. A tiny smile brightens her eyes when they land on me.

I flick the toothpick into the nearest rubbish bin without looking. Bolting across the room, I swing Saylor around in my arms the way they do in those historical military movies Maeve is always forcing the rest of us to watch.

Surprise jolts through her. "Put me down this fucking instant," she hisses.

I chuckle into her hair, but obey, burying my face in her neck—she smells really fucking good—and say softly, "I thought you weren't coming."

She has her arms wrapped around my neck, but she manages to find a piece of loose skin on my shoulder and pinch it. "I don't break my word."

I can feel the eyes of the band on us, so I slowly release her, less willing to do so than I'd like to admit. I should've gotten laid before leaving, something I'm starting to regret as I think about platonically sharing a suite with Saylor for the next six weeks.

I link our fingers and lead her back to the rest of the group, who are all awake now and staring at my girl with obvious interest. "Boys, this is Saylor," I say, looking at her the way I imagine an adoring boyfriend would. "My girl."

She doesn't meet my eyes, just gives the guys a wave. "Nice to meet you all. Thanks for letting me tag along."

There's a muffled chorus of hellos as they shift in their seats.

Jamal sticks out his hand and introduces himself. "Rhythm guitar," he says, throwing her a wink as she shakes his hand. I'm going to have to keep an eye on the bastard.

I introduce the rest of the guys—Jentry, bass guitar; Diego, drums; Chase, keys—and when I've finished, I place a hand over my chest. "Rhett, front man and love of your life."

She rolls her eyes in that way girls do, saying "Oh my god, isn't he adorable" without words.

"You want something to eat or drink?" I ask, pulling her away. I'm already greedy for her full attention. Her hand is still wrapped in mine, and I intend to relish every second of it.

She shakes her head. "I just had breakfast."

"You got your luggage checked in?"

"Yep." She shifts the tote bag on her shoulder. "Everything except this."

I take it from her. "Let me carry that."

I tug on her hand, leading her to an empty section of seats. We sit down, and it's amazing how much calmer I feel now that she's here. Maybe she'll end up being my muse after all.

She still hasn't untangled her fingers from mine, and I'm desperate to know if she's just trying to keep up the ruse, or if this feels as natural for her as it does for me. I wasn't worried about touching her—plenty of experience with that—but it's easier with some girls than others.

With Saylor, it's like breathing. Like being underwater for way too fucking long and suddenly breaking the surface, gulping in huge lungfuls of air.

Is it possible that our bodies remember each other? We didn't do anything at that stupid camp besides kissing and some heavy petting, but maybe it has a bigger impact when you're young.

I gesture toward her Bowie shirt. "Will you wear my face?"

She smirks at me, and a tiny thrill of pleasure races up my spine at the thought. "Maybe."

"Who's taking care of your plants?" I ask as she lets go of my hand to pull a sweater from her bag.

"Paula." She sticks her arms into the sleeves, and I mourn the loss of the small amount of skin she was showing.

"The reborn doll lady?"

"The one and only."

"You trust her inside your flat?" I leave my hand palm up on the armrest on the off chance she'll take it again.

She doesn't, just wraps her arms around herself as if she's still cold. "She's not that bad. If you can overlook the dolls."

I'm already shrugging out of my navy hoodie. "Overlooking the dolls seems dangerous to anyone's mental health."

My T-shirt rides up as I pull the sweatshirt over my head, and I catch her eyeing my bare stomach. She looks away immediately, but her gaze lingered just long enough for my cock to wonder what else she might find attractive.

I drop the hoodie onto her lap. "Here."

"I have a sweater," she says.

"Yeah, but you're still cold."

She makes no move to pick it up, so I tug it over her head. She obediently pushes her arms through the sleeves, giving me an exasperated look as I pull her hair through the opening. "Is this what I can expect for the next six weeks?"

"What? Chivalry?"

She shakes her head, but a tiny smile lurks in the shadows of her face. "You look normal for once. How does it feel?"

I glance down at my solid gray T-shirt and jeans. "I dress like this. Sometimes."

Her only response is a cocked brow.

"Do you always wear those boots?" I lean forward to take another look at the worn Doc Martens on her feet. They're the same ones she had on that day outside Restore Hope.

"Do you have a problem with it if I do?" she asks.

"Not in the least," I assure her. They fit her vibe. "I like them."

"Your dad lives in the US, doesn't he?"

The question takes me by surprise. I don't know if she remembers that from camp or if she's been visiting my Wikipedia page. The verdict is still out on which would make me happier. "Last I heard."

"Are you planning to see him?"

I shake my head. "I haven't talked to him in three years."

"But he knows you're going on tour, doesn't he?"

"Unless he's been living under a rock." It's not a subject I like to dwell on. I learned a long time ago not to expect shit from my dad, but somehow he still always manages to disappoint me.

"I bet he'll come to a concert." She reaches into her bag and pulls out her passport. My eyes flick downward as she opens it, taking in the name printed at the top: Saylor Seegmiller.

What the actual fuck?

I wipe my palms on my jeans and look away. My pulse is going crazy again, and I reach for another toothpick. This cannot be happening.

She was Saylor Jones at summer camp. I remember, because it's the perfect girl-next-door name. If that's not her name anymore, it can only mean one thing.

"You're *married*?" I say.

I can't have a married woman pretending to be my girlfriend, for obvious reasons. If the record label caught wind of it—hell, if my fans caught wind of it—my career would be over before it even began.

She glances at me, that deer-in-the-headlights look on her face, but it vanishes in a millisecond. "Relax." She snaps the passport shut. "I just haven't changed my name back yet."

Relief floods my veins as fast as a hit of insidion, and it feels nearly as good. "Why didn't you tell me?"

"You mean about my terrible decision to get married at twenty-one to a guy I didn't know well enough and who turned out to be an asshole? Gee, I don't know, Rhett."

I close my eyes for a second and sink back into my chair. I hate the thought of her having been married, but thinking about someone mistreating her is even worse. "Did he—"

"Hurt me?" she asks, eyes on her bag as she rummages through it for something else. "Not in the way you're thinking."

"You don't know what I'm thinking," I grumble, and grab her wrist. Not if she thinks I only care about physical abuse.

She stops rifling through the bag and looks at me long and hard, unblinking. I see a million things in her eyes, a million moments she's lived, a million times she's been hurt, a million instances no one was there for her. Every single one of them kills me a little, until I'm nothing but a shell of a man, walking around with a million stab wounds and a million reasons to hate myself.

Her eyes flutter shut, and she tugs her hand out of my grip to pull her phone out.

"I'm sorry," I say quietly.

"For what?" She doesn't meet my eyes.

"Whatever he did."

She opens WhatsApp and starts typing a message. "It's not your problem, Rhett."

"For the next six weeks, it is."

This gets her attention. She swings her gaze toward me, a hard edge in it. "I don't need you to fix me. This"—she motions between us—"is fake. I don't need you swooping in with your savior complex and upending my life, okay?"

I let out a humorless laugh and hold my hands up. "Fuck, woman.

I got it." I shift in my seat. "And for the record, I don't have a savior complex."

Her attention is already back on her device, thumbs furiously tapping on the screen. "No savior complex. Noted." She finishes the message with alarming speed and tosses the phone into her bag. "What else do I need to know about you?"

* * *

We board the plane a few minutes later, leaving the sharp metallic scent of luggage and diesel fuel behind and heading for the first-class suites.

"What are we doing?" Saylor hisses, yanking on my hand.

I turn to her with a frown. "Boarding the plane?"

"Aren't we supposed to be back there?" Her attempt at a whisper is hilarious. She motions to the coach cabin behind us.

I give it a cursory glance before looking down at her again. "You're with me now."

"Oh," she says. It's full of wonder, that "oh."

We stop in front of our suite. It's an unnecessary upgrade, since it's not an overnight flight, but the look on Saylor's face is worth every cent. Inside are two ergonomic chairs, a flat-screen TV, and two beds that have been combined into one double bed, rose petals scattered across its stark white linens. Her eyes nearly bulge out of her head when she sees it.

I glance down the corridor to make sure none of the guys are watching. The label paid for business-class tickets, but I upgraded Saylor and myself personally. "Don't worry. It's only a seven-hour flight," I say, nudging her into the suite.

We may not be sharing a bed on the plane, but judging from her reaction, she isn't expecting to share a bed with me at all. Probably a

75

conversation we should have had before crossing the Atlantic together.

"So." I drop her tote bag onto one of the chairs. "We should probably discuss sleeping arrangements."

She spins around to face me. "What about them?"

I shove a hand into my hair. "You get that we'll be sharing a hotel room, right?"

A tiny crease forms on her forehead. "Of course. I just assumed there would be two beds."

"There will. I'll make sure of it."

She nods as though that solves everything and bends down to see out the plane window. We haven't lifted off yet, and the baggage handlers are still loading the cargo hold.

"The tour bus, though—" I stop, unsure of how to phrase this in a way that won't send her running back down the corridor and off the plane. "There's only one bed."

Her spine straightens as she slowly stands, but she doesn't turn back around. "I assumed there'd be bunks."

"They rented one with a bedroom when they found out you were coming along."

She whirls on me. "You agreed to no shenanigans."

"It wasn't me, I swear." I'm once again holding up my palms, defending myself to this girl. It's not a lie. I didn't request the bedroom, but I sure as hell didn't object when they told me.

10

"Welcome to New York" - Taylor Swift

I am in New. York. City. It's the first thought I have when I open my eyes. None of that disorientation of waking in a new place, wondering where you are. I'm fully aware that I'm in the Big Apple, a place I never dreamed I'd ever go, not because I didn't want to, but because I'm practical. I have no intention of ever taking a corporate job that might send me to the United States on business, and unlike my parents, I haven't carried the dream of traveling my whole life. After Nate wiped me out, it became obvious that practicality was the way to go.

I swing my legs out of bed with a mixture of excitement and regret. These sheets are the softest thing I've ever touched, and I feel stupid for leaving them. On the other hand, how can I possibly waste a single moment in New York?

We're staying in a fancy hotel that I never caught the name of, and which is posh enough not to have it splayed all over the room. Our suite is high up enough that when I look out the window, the people scurrying across the pavement below look as tiny as ants. Iconic yellow taxi cabs still dot the streets, but I've heard they're becoming fewer and fewer as ridesharing takes over.

My decision to take Rhett up on his offer came suddenly, which meant I had to scramble to get ready. I almost forgot to drop the divorce paperwork in the mail before leaving, but fortunately I saw the file when I was packing. God, what a nightmare that would've been if anyone found out I was still legally married while "dating" Rhett. Thankfully, Wesbourne divorce law grants immediate separation once the papers are filed, which means I am a free woman for the first time in four years.

We arrived at JFK yesterday evening. Due to the time change, it was still afternoon in the city, and we hit the ground running. The label had scheduled a dinner for Rhett and the band with some minor celebrities in the city—hoping for their endorsement, no doubt. Since he wasn't going to need his hair and makeup team, he lent them to me so I could get ready.

I didn't have anything appropriate for dinner at a four-star restaurant, but Rhett sent someone to Bloomingdale's, and they came back with a gorgeous black cocktail dress that I will definitely never have the opportunity to wear again. It's currently hanging in the closet of our suite, awaiting pickup for the dry cleaner's, arranged by someone who is not me.

I took my first limo ride last night. I had my first glass of real champagne. The bottle probably cost as much as my rent, but I didn't waste a drop. I rubbed shoulders with famous people and didn't combust. I wore a pair of ankle-breaking heels and *didn't* break an ankle, although I'm sticking to my Docs from now on.

Is this a dream? Because it sure as hell feels like one.

I look around the room. I think of it as a room, because that's what you say when referring to a booking at a hotel. "Room for one, please" or "My hotel room had a great view." But in reality, there are four rooms. A bathroom, sitting room, and not one, but two bedrooms.

After Rhett's announcement on the plane about sharing sleeping quarters, I was beginning to regret ever agreeing to the world's stupidest arrangement. These things never work out, romcoms be damned. I have no desire for this to turn into a happily-ever-after, thank you very much.

To be completely honest, I didn't believe him when he said he'd get two rooms. It sounded just like him to manage to end up in the same bed as me, although I will admit that most of my opinion of him comes from the tabloids and not from spending any real amount of time with the guy. Not since summer camp anyway, and who doesn't change in eleven years?

Which is part of the problem. We don't know each other, so pretending to be in love is difficult. I forgot to mention the tiny fact that I'm a vegetarian to him, and he offered me a bite of his mahi-mahi at the restaurant. Fortunately, no one was looking at us, so I quickly whispered the truth in his ear, but it's definitely the kind of thing a boyfriend would know.

So was I expecting a king-sized bed strewn with rose petals and fancy chocolates when I stepped into the suite last night? One hundred percent. If Rhett saw the surprise on my face when he told me to choose a bedroom, he didn't acknowledge it, just further unbuttoned his shirt and flopped onto one of the chairs in the sitting room.

He's been a perfect gentleman so far. Maybe this won't become quite the disaster I envisioned. Of course, I should probably wait to make a final assessment until we share a bed on the tour bus, something I am dreading with every cell of my being.

My tooth throbs as I open the door into the rest of the suite, and it's the first twinge of pain I've experienced since setting foot in the US. Apparently, luxury is as effective a painkiller as aspirin.

Rhett isn't in the sitting room, but there's a note propped up on the small entryway table, along with the room service menu. Beside it is a black Amex.

Had to leave for sound check but your day is on me xx R

Is he suggesting I take his Black Card and waltz around NYC in my Doc Martens? The thought is laughable. That card is for places I would never set foot inside. The vintage boutiques and record shops probably don't even accept American Express.

I have no intention of swiping it anywhere, but I pick it up anyway, weighing it in my hand—when will I ever get this opportunity again?—and holy shit, that baby is heavy. I drop it back onto the table with a clatter.

It's just after eight in the morning, which is probably the best time I'll have all day to call my parents. I texted them after we landed and promised I'd call when I woke up.

We exchange travel stories—they're in Cambodia right now—and I give them a virtual tour of the hotel suite. My mum nearly swoons when she sees the city skyline through the huge windows in the sitting room.

"Oh my god, Gerald." She grabs my dad's arm. "Can we change our flight to New York instead?"

He gives her an amused look. "I thought you were dying to see Laos?"

Her face twists. "But it's been weeks since we've seen our girl."

"I'm fine. Really." I give her a genuine smile. "Both of our trips will pass quickly. We should enjoy them while we can."

She pulls her lips into a pout. "I worry about you."

"Why?" I think I've done a good job hiding the things that would cause her the most concern, but her intuition can be eerily accurate.

"For one thing, you're traipsing around a foreign country with that boy—"

"He's twenty-six, Mum."

"—and Nate is—"

"Nate's fine." I can't confirm this, since we haven't spoken in ages, but I think it's safe to say that he can take care of himself. My mum, on the other hand, has always had a soft spot for her soon-to-be ex-son-in-law and will worry about anyone who will allow it.

She lets out a long sigh. "Are you sure you know what you're doing, Saylor?"

I fight the urge to laugh out loud. I don't have a fucking clue what I'm doing, but that is not what she needs to hear. "Of course I do. You've always called me an old soul."

"That's because you like older music than she does," my dad chimes in.

She socks him in the stomach with her elbow. "You *are* an old soul, and wise beyond your years."

Oh boy, here we go. "Not the *wise* lecture, Mum."

"But sometimes you prioritize others' needs before your own," she continues as though I haven't spoken.

I take a deep breath, letting my eyelids lower. "Are you done?"

"Always put on your own oxygen mask first."

"Not yet? Okay," I mumble under my breath.

She's given this speech so often, even my dad has it memorized. I catch his eye roll and hide my answering grin behind a fake yawn.

"I know you two think I'm just a crazy old woman," Mum says, which we both emphatically protest. "But you are my only child, and I am entitled to worry about you if I want to." She punctuates this by lifting her nose in the air.

"I think Saylor can handle herself," my dad says, placing his large black hand on her shoulder. "We raised her right."

"We didn't raise her to follow some wannabe singer around the globe."

So that's what this is about. "I'm just doing his social media for him," I say. "It pays really well."

"And what if he develops feelings for you?" she insists.

I tuck my lips into my mouth as I consider the best answer to give her. If I deny the possibility, she'll sniff out the lie like a bloodhound. Best to make her think I have a plan in place. "He'll be busy doing music stuff, so we'll hardly be spending any time together. I'm just taking pictures during the concerts." The thought comes in a streak of brilliance. "Besides, his girlfriend came along."

Relief washes across Mum's face. I try not to be offended that she doesn't trust me, her own daughter, but she trusts a man she's never met to stay faithful to his fake girlfriend. Does she know how many people get cheated on every day?

We end the call soon after, with her reassured that I will stay out of trouble. I place an order for breakfast, then jump into the shower. The water pressure is so strong, it makes my own back home seem like little more than a dripping faucet. The towels are as soft as rose petals, and I wonder if they'll notice if I stick a few in my bag. I would never, but the thought is tempting.

Room service arrives while I'm still wrapped in a fluffy bathrobe. It would probably be inappropriate to wear to the concert tonight, but I'm considering it anyway. The rolling cart is covered in white linen and holds a vase of fresh flowers and several shiny cloches. I lift one to reveal a beautifully golden vegetable frittata. The other covers ricotta pancakes as delicate as clouds. A sparkling crystal flute of orange juice sits next to a steaming cup of Earl Grey, and there's a small bowl of fruit topped with a sprig of fresh basil.

How is this my life right now?

I instinctively pull out my phone to send a picture to Timie before remembering that that's not something we do anymore.

I need to remember that this all ends in six weeks. My mum was right to worry—not about Rhett, but about me becoming too used to this level of pampering. Before I know it, I'll be back home with my uneven hardwood floor and neighbors with an affinity for 2 a.m.

karaoke. This trip will be nothing more than a hazy memory.

11

"A Sky Full of Stars" - Coldplay

Saylor

It's stupid, I know. I'm in New York City for a full day, with an *Amex Black Card*, for god's sake, and a personal protection officer who has assured me he's willing to escort me anywhere I wish to go. I'm guessing the hotel swimming pool and spa were not what he had in mind.

But here I am. I shift on the massage table, the hot stones on my back now cold.

I didn't know where else to go. I've never been here before, and I don't have a NYC bucket list as long as my arm. If Timie were here, we'd have the time of our lives exploring. But she's not, nor does she have any desire to be.

I haven't seen Rhett all day. I debated texting him a few times but decided if he wanted to check up on me, he would. Maybe I'm supposed to stay tucked out of sight until he needs me. If that's what he wants, I can't complain about the arrangement.

We never discussed the concerts. I have no idea what he expects. Does he want me to attend? Do girlfriends usually attend? Do *I* want to attend? I ponder that last question as the massage therapist works the knots out of my shoulders.

I've been to my fair share of concerts, but always firmly in the back, where the view is sketchy and the tickets are cheapest. Special front row privileges might be kind of nice, at least for one show.

After leaving the spa, I ask my newly-assigned personal protection officer, Leo, what I'm meant to do during tonight's concert. He assures me he'd be happy to escort me to the venue whenever I'd like. He's a big guy with fists the size of my neck and a buzzcut that reminds me of Nate. I squash that thought as quickly as it appears.

As I'm choosing my outfit, I realize this is yet another thing Rhett and I haven't discussed. A quick "what do rock stars' girlfriends wear" Google search yields no helpful results. Maybe he expected me to shop for a new wardrobe today, hence the credit card. But if that's what he wanted, he should have said so. As it is, he's stuck with the clothes I packed, all of which suddenly seem woefully inadequate for the level of fame I think Rhett is on the cusp of.

I settle on a pair of light wash jeans and a cropped black T-shirt—classic and put together without drawing unwanted attention. I give last night's heels a disdainful look as I pull on my Docs. I still have a blister on my ankle from the thin straps.

Leo has arranged for a private car to take us to the venue. We both sit in the back seat, and I make small talk at first, but when he seems less than eager to chat, I shut up and take in the sights of the city through the window.

The concert hall is massive, and a huge billboard with Rhett's grinning face is posted out front. There's already a line of people forming at the door, and the show doesn't start for another two hours.

I wipe my sweaty palms on my thighs as the car slows. Leo leans across the front seat and says something to the driver, who continues past the venue, then circles the block and pulls up in an alley at what I assume is the back entrance.

My heart is thudding behind my ribs. Everything so far has had a dreamlike quality to it. Meeting the band, the plane ride in our ridiculous suite, the glamorous dinner, the exquisite hotel. I've been living in a bubble up until now, but it's all about to become very real. Rhett and I will have to put on the show of our lives if we're to convince anyone that we're so in love we can't bear to be apart for six weeks.

Leo escorts me inside, one hand on my elbow at all times. I'm not sure if he's afraid I'll trip or run away, but the tiny gesture is comforting all the same. The back of the venue is dark and slightly claustrophobic, with tight corridors and flickering lights. Even with the haunted house vibe, there's an energy buzzing through the place. I can feel my blood start to hum the minute we enter.

We walk down one hallway and up another, winding our way through the belly of this place until there's no way in hell I could find the exit again. Finally, we stop outside a door labeled "Practice Room."

I almost tell Leo I've changed my mind. "Thank you," I say instead, and take a deep breath. It's been nearly twenty-four hours since I've seen Rhett, and that thought alone is responsible for at least half the butterflies in my stomach.

I turn the doorknob, praying to anyone listening that I won't be interrupting. I expect one of those sound rooms like in the movies, where you can watch the musicians through a two-way mirror without them seeing you. I definitely don't expect to waltz directly into the band's practice session.

As the realization hits me, I freeze. The band keeps playing, even though their eyes all flick to where I'm standing just inside the door. I wince and give a little wave. The guy on rhythm guitar—Jamal, I think—grins and nods.

Rhett is on the far side of the room, intently playing his guitar. If he's noticed me, he isn't showing it. I watch him, completely mesmerized. His videos have always entranced me, but seeing him in person is something different altogether. He moves as though he's one with his guitar, and the sounds pouring out of it are raw and vulnerable. My throat tightens the longer I stare.

He leans toward the mic in front of him and lifts his eyes. They connect with mine, and time stands still for one brief instant. Then he swings the instrument behind his back and walks over to me like it's the most natural thing in the world.

His guitar cord trails behind him, the music trails off, and my thoughts trail away, but he doesn't slow down. When he reaches me, he brings both hands up to cup my face. I'm terrified he's going to kiss me—I am not prepared for this—but he just leans in close and whispers, "Trust me?"

I give a barely perceptible nod, and then his lips are on mine.

Have I imagined this moment? Maybe a few times. Was it ever this good? Definitely not. It should be noted that Rhett Cole has gotten *much* better at kissing. I don't even know what to do with my mouth, but it doesn't matter, because he is doing enough for both of us. I had insisted on no tongue during our negotiations, but my mouth doesn't care, just opens for him as though he holds a members-only pass.

He does not wait for further invitation, just invades my mouth with the skill of a guy who has done this *a lot*. His hands claim my face with the same intensity with which his lips claim my mouth, like I belong to him. Which I kind of do for the next six weeks.

I don't know what to do with my hands either, so I rest them on his elbows, holding him as he holds me, and somehow it feels like whatever happens next, I don't need to worry about anything, because he's got me. He's not going to let anything bad happen to me.

It's a comforting thought that I desperately want to hold on to, but the snarky voice in my head doesn't care what I want. *But what if he's the bad thing?*

It's the antidote I need for whatever fever Rhett's lips have inspired in me. I break off the kiss, and the instant I do, reality snaps back into focus.

The band is watching us but pretending not to. Rhett is staring down at me with a kind of wonder that I need to rectify immediately, because no one else can see it, which means it's not for show.

"God, I missed you," he says, just quiet enough that I can't tell if it's meant for the band to overhear.

I give him a weak smile. "Me too."

He pulls back then, maybe sensing my unease. "Did you have fun?"

"Not the kind you imagined, I'm sure." I pull his credit card from my pocket and hand it to him.

He looks from it back to me with an amused look before sliding it into his wallet. "Come on. Let's grab some pizza." He slings an arm around my neck and pulls me into his side.

I go willingly, show or not, because something about him changes something about me. It should scare me, because I can't identify it, but I'll worry about that later. Right now, I'm pretending to date a rock star.

Rhett smells like leather and sweat, and as repulsive as that sounds, the last thing it does is repulse me. It feels raw and gritty, a little like him, and something bubbles deep inside me, something that will become dangerous if I pay it any heed.

So I don't, just let him tuck me against his side as he slips the guitar over his head and hands it to someone. Then we're walking toward the greenroom, where he assures me several large pizzas are waiting.

"One of them is just cheese," he says.

I glance up at him from my position under his arm.

"I remembered," he says with a wink.

The bubbling intensifies, but this cannot happen. He will break my heart if I give in.

As soon as we're inside the greenroom—which is not green, but decorated like a swanky living room—I slip out from beneath Rhett's arm, pretending to be completely parched as I guzzle one of the water bottles that have been set out.

Cardboard boxes of pizza are stacked on the coffee table in the center of the room. Rhett opens one of them, pulling out a slice covered in melted cheese and holding it out for me. I'm about to take it from him when I realize he wants me to take a bite. I hesitate, then lean forward when I hear the guys outside the door. They walk in just as I'm biting through the crust, and Rhett and I share a look.

He hands me the slice along with a napkin, and we settle next to each other on one of the sofas as we munch our pizza. He's wearing a white shirt unbuttoned halfway down his muscled chest and tight black jeans. I look away before the bubbling returns.

"Are you nervous?" I ask after he returns with another piece of pizza for me.

He shrugs with what I'm beginning to recognize as faux nonchalance. "Not really."

I nudge him with my elbow. "Really."

He looks at me, then back down at his own slice. "Maybe a little."

"You'll be great."

His eyebrows waggle. "Are you going to be watching?"

"I wanted to ask you about that." I pick at a string of gooey mozzarella. "I don't know what girlfriends usually do."

He shrugs again, his shoulder rubbing against mine as he does. "I don't either. Which means you can do whatever you want." When I don't reply right away, he glances at me. "So? What do you want?"

"I don't want to be in the way." I don't know what goes on backstage during a concert, but I imagine lots of bustling around and activity that I would only trip up.

He rolls his eyes like I've just said something ridiculous. "You could never be in the way, Saylor."

Bubble, bubble. I sit up straighter. "Maybe I can watch from the side stage?"

"Sure." He nods. "Leo can stay with you."

"You won't do something embarrassing, will you? Like point me out during the show?"

The side of his mouth quirks upward at a rate that does not bring me comfort. "Of course not."

When the pizza's nearly gone, someone wearing a headset sticks their head into the room. "Opening act is up in five."

"That's our cue, mates," Rhett says. He stands, then reaches a hand down to help me up.

We walk to the backstage area, where the din from the crowd is becoming audible. The opening band, Velvet Inferno, plays through their set, and the energy from the audience increases with every song. I'm not even going to be visible, and I'm feeling nervous.

There's a jitteriness flowing through the band, and they practice various ways of relaxing. Diego takes a puff of vape, Jentry moves his shoulders in circles, and Chase leans against the wall and closes his eyes.

Jamal doesn't appear to be nervous at all, and when I smile at him, he throws me another wink. I glance at Rhett, but he's facing the stage.

I wrap my hands around his arm and squeeze gently. "You're going to be amazing."

He turns to me with a grim smile. "Sure hope so."

The radio DJ hosting the show takes over the stage, throwing out tidbits about Rhett, which makes the crowd go wild.

"Do people still say 'break a leg'?" I ask.

"I'd rather have another kiss."

I stand on tiptoes and press my lips to his cheek, where his stubble is just starting to break the surface.

"Not the kind I meant," he growls.

I give him a syrupy smile. "But the only kind you're getting tonight."

"We'll see." With that, he turns and follows the band onstage.

12

"Bad Habits" - Nerv

Rhett

I don't think I've ever been this high in my life. They should recommend performing in rehab, not that stupid journaling shit, although those songs are technically what landed me here in the first place.

The crowd is wild, abso-fucking-lutely *wild*. And it's only the first night. My very first show of the tour, and it's insane. Fans are needing to be hauled back by security, girls are throwing their tops toward the stage, and the energy level is about to lift the roof off the stadium.

No wonder my dad couldn't get enough of this. It's fifty times better than any drug I've ever taken. I would do this every single night for the rest of my life if I could.

Unfortunately, I've already played my two encore songs. I swing my guitar behind my back and wave at the crowd. They go even wilder.

Grinning, I lean into the microphone. "You lot have been fantastic."

Ear-splitting cheers.

"It's been a great night." I pause to let the noise die down. "I'll see you at my next show. Goodbye, New York."

The stage goes dark, and I use the time before the house lights come on to slip into the shadows. A big group of people is waiting backstage with congratulations and bottles of water. I drink one greedily as my eyes scan the crowd around me. Where the fuck did they all come from? There must be at least a dozen roadies waiting to tear down the equipment, the production crew wrapping up the show, and a fuck-load of people I don't recognize.

Noah, the tour manager, approaches. "Terrific show, mate. They loved you."

I flash him a smile. "God, it was amazing."

"You've got five minutes before the meet and greet," he says, staring down at his phone, where tonight's itinerary is pulled up.

Shit. I completely forgot that my job isn't over after I leave the stage. Glancing around for Saylor, I start to pull the shirt over my head.

Noah glances at me. "What are you doing?"

I look at him, my shirt halfway off. "Changing?"

He shakes his head. "Don't bother. These fans want just-walked-off-stage Rhett."

"Dude, I'm drenched in sweat."

He scans me and shrugs. "They eat that stuff up."

I blink as he walks away to talk to the rest of the band, then tug my shirt back down. As disgusting as it sounds, if that's what my fans want, I'm obliged to give it to them. I rummage through my bag for cologne to at least help mask some of the smell.

Saylor still hasn't appeared by the time Noah and several PPOs lead me down the corridors to where the meet and greet is happening. "Do you know where my girlfriend is?" I ask when we stop in front of an unmarked door.

"Haven't seen her, mate," Noah says, then swings the door open.

The room is full of fans, 99 percent female, 100 percent rabid. They descend on me like wolves. My security team keeps them from getting too close, creating order out of the chaos.

I smile to lessen the sting of it and start greeting my number one fans.

* * *

The event lasts an hour. By the end, I'm so fucking ready for a shower, but Noah tosses me a clean T-shirt and says I'll have to make do until the after-party is over. No one knows where Saylor is, but if she's not at the venue, she must have gone back to the hotel. She doesn't answer when I call, so I send her a text.

See you at the after party?

I change into a fresh set of clothes in the back of the limo. By the time we pull into the parking garage of the hotel, she still hasn't texted back, and I'm starting to get nervous. I call her again, but it just rings through.

Fuck. Where is she? I rub my palms across my thighs, trying to still the twitch in my legs, but it doesn't help. I move on to cracking my knuckles, until Noah shoots me an annoyed look from the other seat.

We make our way to one of the top floors of the hotel, where a suite has been reserved for the after-party. I glance at my phone every couple of seconds, but there's still nothing from Saylor. My heart races as we exit the elevator, PPOs on both sides of me. I note with relief that neither of them is Leo, Saylor's personal protection officer. At least she's safe, wherever she is. But she should be here, damn it. That's what I'm paying her for, isn't it?

When we reach the double doors to the party suite, a ripped Black guy is standing outside collecting phones. It occurs to me that she might already be waiting for me inside. That would explain why she's not texting me back. I completely forgot that I had Eddie add it to my rider—no phones at the after-parties—and I check mine in along with everyone else's.

The party feels tame after the concert, but a hypnotic energy still buzzes throughout the room. People are drinking all around the suite, which has an incredible view of the New York skyline. My album is playing over the sound system, but the din of voices mostly drowns it out.

My entrance seems to disrupt the balance. People flock over for autographs and slaps on the back. Someone must have invited groupies, because I recognize a few faces from the meet and greet. How the hell did they beat me here?

I dutifully sign merch, albums, and bare skin, but all I can think is *Where's my girl? Where the fuck is my girl?* And then I have to remind myself that she's not my girl. She's only playing a role.

The drugs make me nervous. I know they'll start circulating soon—if they haven't already—and that's the part I'm worried about the most. That's the whole reason Saylor is here. I'm twitching so bad, I'm afraid even a joint will lower my defenses enough that I'll spiral. I search my pockets for a toothpick, but they're empty.

I scan the crowd, but the girls hanging on to my arms make it difficult to get a good look. One of them pulls my head down to whisper something in my ear. The noise in the room drowns it out, but it doesn't take much to imagine what her offer is. She must have been one of the ones who chose to throw their shirts at the stage, because she's topless except for a hot-pink lace bra.

I'm about to tell her I have a girlfriend when I see the silver tray coming. My pulse speeds up even further, and my palms are drenched. I wipe them on my pants, but they immediately start sweating again.

Someone shoves the platter against my chest. "The guest of honor should have first pick."

I give a tight smile in the direction of the voice, but my gaze is focused on the offering in front of me. The noise in the room is so thick that drowning it out actually becomes easy.

All of the usual players are here—ecstasy, cocaine, GHB, special K, speed, and those familiar white vials—insidion. I can feel sweat beading along my hairline and desperately hope my hair covers it from sight.

I could take something harmless—speed, maybe—to take the edge off and get everyone off my back. I can feel them watching me, and god, I want it. I want it in my system, flooding out the stress from the show, the weight of everyone's expectations. I want to feel like I'm in paradise, like I'm the fucking king of the world.

My hand reaches up of its own accord and sorts through the options. The insidion calls to me the loudest, but I'm not stupid. My fingers close around the bag of coke. One small line won't hurt.

I glance up—looking for what, I don't know. My therapist? My sponsor?

And there she is, striding across the room like a vengeful goddess. She doesn't slow when she reaches me, just knocks people and the tray out of her way, throws her arms around my neck, and plants her mouth on mine.

I drop any hold I had on the drugs and grab her. My fingers plunge into her glorious mane like they already have well-worn grooves mapped out. Her lips are pressed together like she's hanging on to the last remnants of her chastity, but at the flick of my tongue, she parts them and allows me access.

The taste of her has a shadowy richness to it, like the dark chocolate lava cake at Jolie's. I want to drown, spin, spiral into it, into her, into this feeling that she is the only thing I need. Somehow it manages to be even better than the high from the show and the high from insidion, while also leaving me wanting more than I've ever wanted before. It satisfies and depletes in equal portions, and I'm both richer and poorer for having known her, because now that I've tasted her, how am I ever supposed to stop?

She breaks it off, and it's like popping a balloon. I'm suddenly aware of the people around us, cheering and whooping as they watch us make out.

Saylor's cheeks turn a gorgeous shade of pink, and I'm pretty sure her breathing is more labored than usual. I reach for her hand, entwining our fingers and tugging her back against me. I drop another kiss on her lips, then lean down to whisper into her ear. "Wanna get out of here?"

She freezes in my arms, and I can practically hear the gears in her head turning as she tries to figure out exactly what I mean by that and what her response should be.

I torture her for a few more seconds before saying, "I can't stay here."

Her eyes flicker up to meet mine, and she nods.

I can't stop the grin that takes over my face as I lead her from the room amid catcalls and more cheers. Let them think what they want. There's nothing wrong with fucking my girlfriend, and if that's the only thing that gets back to the label, Saylor's presence will have been a success.

We walk to our suite in silence. I keep expecting her to mention the show, but she doesn't say anything, just waits patiently while I unlock the door.

Once we're inside, I head to the minibar to pour a few drinks. I haven't had anything since the concert, and although I'm not doing substances, I'm sure as fuck not going to be completely sober. Especially not if I can't fuck the girl who's in my room.

I hand her a vodka cranberry. "Thank you for that," I say, and pour a second splash of vodka into my own glass.

She takes a small sip and shrugs. "It's what I'm paid to do, right?" She moves to the window overlooking the city, and I see her reflection in the glass.

There's something about how flippantly she says it that disturbs me. It's almost word for word what I thought earlier when I couldn't get ahold of her. So why does it bother me?

"Yeah," I mutter, and throw back my drink. The alcohol burns, but it does nothing for the confusing ache that's growing in my chest. I pour another, then join her at the window.

"Were you actually going to do it?" She turns to look at me, her eyes wide with concern. "Take that line, I mean."

I blow out a breath and keep my eyes fixed on the glass. "I don't know. Maybe." I take another sip. "Probably."

Neither of us says anything for a long time, and the alcohol begins to dull my reasoning just enough for me to wonder what she'd do if I asked her to have sex with me tonight.

Just when I'm imagining laying her down on those Egyptian cotton sheets, she says, "You should tell them."

My mind spins as I try to remember if we were having some conversation I'm unaware of. "What?" I finally say, unable to piece it together.

"Your fans. You should tell them about your addiction and recovery."

A choking laugh rips from my throat. "You're joking, right?"

"No."

I look at her for the first time since joining her. Her hair is wisping around her face in a way that makes her look fucking adorable, which she would hate me mentioning. Her jaw and eyes carry a steely determination that is actually a little scary.

"I can't," I say.

"Why not?" she challenges, tilting her chin a fraction of an inch.

"Because I'd lose my credibility. And my record deal."

"You think they'll respect you less for struggling?"

I shrug with my shoulders and mouth.

"They'll respect you more for fighting your way back," she says, her eyes bright.

"I'm pretty sure they just want good music."

"The only thing more powerful than your music is the story behind it."

Frowning, I say, "No one cares about that."

"You really think they don't want to know what inspired the songs they're listening to?"

I shake my head and drain my glass. "I know they don't."

It's not technically true, since I don't have a fucking clue what my fans want—besides sweaty selfies with me, apparently—but it doesn't matter, because I'd die before I confessed to the world the circumstances my songs were written under.

"We need a secret signal," I say, partly because it's true, partly in an effort to change the subject.

"A what?" Saylor looks at me like I've lost my mind.

"A secret signal. You know, to communicate across the room?"

Her mouth drops open into an incredulous smile. "You're joking, right? What are we, seven?"

I set my glass down on the table. "Come on. If we're across the room from each other, how am I supposed to let you know I need you to rescue me if I can't text you?"

She blinks once, twice, three times. "I'm sorry. Did you just say that *I'm* to rescue *you*?"

I grin, sensing where this is heading. "I did."

Her smile matches mine, and she shakes her head. "Okay, James Bond. What did you have in mind?"

We run through a couple of options before finally settling on a classic chin tilt—first to my chest, then back up again.

"Where were you tonight?" I ask, wishing my glass wasn't empty.

"When?"

"After the show. I looked for you, called you. I was starting to freak out." Fresh goosebumps break out over my skin as I remember the way it felt to have lost all connection with her for those few minutes. Even during the show I could see her from the stage, and god, she looked hot standing there.

"I headed to the hotel right after. I was already at the party when you got there, but you didn't see me." Tiny frown lines appear between her brows. "Why were you freaking out?"

It's a good question. A great question.

Why the hell *was* I freaking out?

13

"Electric Touch" - Taylor Swift + Fall Out Boy

Saylor

I'm exhausted, and it's only the fourth night of the tour. We're in Boston, and Rhett is playing another sold-out show. I don't know how he's still so full of that boundless energy—just watching him makes me more tired.

He gives me a lazy smile from where he's waiting with the band near the stage entrance, and my heart trips over itself.

Careful, Saylor, I warn myself. *Not a path you can afford to travel.*

I smile back at him, then lift my phone and snap a photo. It's a great shot, but then it's pretty much impossible to take a bad photo of Rhett Cole. He comes alive for the camera, just like he does onstage.

I post it to his stories before letting Leo escort me to the door. I'm watching from the VIP section tonight. I've spent the previous concerts on the side stage, but the front has better angles for pictures.

While Rhett spends his time practicing with the band and playing around with new compositions, I've been shooting footage and uploading it to social media in my downtime. Of which there is a lot. Thanks to all of the time I've been able to dedicate to his accounts, they're growing like wildfires. Several of his songs are trending audios right now, which is only increasing his ticket sales as we start to cross the country.

Leo drops me at the side entrance and hands me a VIP badge. Rhett and I decided earlier that a bodyguard in the pit would only draw attention, and since I'm more worried about public scrutiny than being personally harmed, it seems safer to pretend I'm just another groupie. The crew has been strict with their no-phone policy at the after-parties, and not a single picture of me has been leaked.

Tonight, my aim is to blend in, so I'm wearing a Rhett Cole band T-shirt, loose fit jeans with big holes in the knees and fishnet tights underneath, my combat boots, and a crossbody fanny pack. I slip into the crowd in the pit, which is already getting pumped by the second half of the opening act. As their energy levels increase, their volume is going to follow suit. Maybe I should've brought ear plugs.

Then Rhett comes onstage, and I forget all of it.

I've been to enough concerts in my life to know that Rhett has something special. Every front man needs a certain charisma to make a show a success, but it positively drips from him. Calling his a panty-dropping smile is not an exaggeration—one girl actually slips off her underwear and tosses it toward the stage.

I have to stand at the very back of the pit to avoid my camera getting jostled by the crazed fans surrounding me, but once I've recorded clips of several songs, I tuck my phone away and edge closer to the front.

The experience here is so different from on the side stage. You can smell the sweat of the people around you, feel the crowd pulsing behind you, and while the excitement is always intoxicating no matter where you're standing, being in the pit is like the difference between watching a football game and actually being on the field.

The beat of the music thrums through my body, like Rhett is

plucking at my veins rather than his guitar strings. All of his songs carry an intoxicating rhythm that is impossible not to dance to, probably the reason he launched onto the charts so quickly. My lips mouth the lyrics I have memorized by now, but my attention is focused on Rhett, not the music.

He's wearing a black sleeveless shirt that shows off the tattoos on his arms and how much time he spends in the gym. I happen to know the muscles beneath that shirt are just as sculpted, because he has no qualms about stripping it off in front of anyone.

His hands wrap around the microphone as he sings into it, and my brain immediately flashes to the way his hands feel on my face when he kisses me. I know those kisses don't mean anything, but my stupid heart wonders what it would be like if they did.

The hair on his forehead is already damp with sweat, and he shoves it out of his eyes. It immediately flops back into place, which lends him that boyish charm everyone is fanatical about. He leans back to play a mean guitar solo, and the crowd goes wild.

I can't decide which I like the best—his ability to shred a guitar, his raw lyrics, or his sultry voice crooning in my ear. The man is talented; that much is obvious.

My eyes ping between his hands on the strings and his devastatingly gorgeous face. I know I should be giving the entire band equal attention, but it's impossible to tear my gaze from Rhett. He knows how to work a crowd, and he apparently also knows how to work me.

Someone knocks into me—not unusual down here—but it's hard enough to jar me out of the haze I've been in for the past hour. There's a feeling in my stomach, light and fluttery, almost nauseating in its sweetness. I haven't had it since the summer I met Nate. It's tinged with sadness, which only makes it that much more addictive.

A *crush*. I have a fucking *crush* on Rhett Cole.

God, I am the worst kind of person. I have a crush on the guy

I'm faking a relationship with. I'm supposed to be helping him, and instead I'm mooning over him like a fourteen-year-old. The same fourteen-year-old who never got over her infatuation with the guy who gave her her first kiss and told her she was beautiful.

I knew this was a risk from the moment I ran into him again—literally—but I didn't realize it had reached this point already. If I don't stop it, this crush will turn into something else, something much worse.

The beat of the music shifts, and I recognize the opening chords of "Electric Heartbeat," Rhett's current number one hit. The crowd does too, and they go bonkers, waving their signs and screaming about how much they love him and want to have his babies.

Okay. I may have chosen the wrong place to hang out.

I try to retreat to the back of the pit, ready to escape to the hotel, but the groupies are crowding as close to the stage as they can get. There is literally no way to get out without shoving people out of my way. I generally consider myself a nice person, so it seems I'm stuck here until the end of the concert.

"There's a spark in the air when you're next to me," Rhett sings, the cheering almost loud enough to drown out his voice. "A current that runs, baby, naturally." He grins at the audience, then his focus shifts to the pit, giving the groupies the attention they paid for with their overpriced tickets.

"Every glance, every move, it's pulling me in / You're the light in the dark / where my world begins."

The song continues, but I'm no longer paying attention to the lyrics. My eyes are hungrily taking in Rhett's every move, the way he's bending over to brush his hands across the ones reaching for him like he's a god. He's still singing into the microphone in his hand and doesn't miss a single beat as he brings girls to the brink of passing out. No longer is he the guy I'm touring with, the one who's had his lips pressed to mine more times than is healthy to think about. Right now he's a musical genius whom I would very much like to be noticed by.

He's on the left side of the stage, but I don't think he's seen me. Actually, I *know* he hasn't seen me, because it becomes obvious the second he does. His eyes are scanning the sea of faces without registering them, but when they pass over me, he does a double take and stops singing. Somehow, his grin becomes even wider, and his eyes soften like butter in the sun. It's over in a matter of seconds, but it's long enough for him to have missed an entire line of the song.

He bounces back onto his feet and belts out the lyrics like nothing happened. "You're the pulse that keeps me breathing." But then, before retreating back to the center of the stage, he lifts his arm, points at me, and winks.

The bottom of my stomach drops out.

He could have thrown a lit firework into the pit, and it would have caused less disturbance than that wink. The groupies around me lose their shit, screaming and launching themselves toward the stage. He doesn't even notice, just slips back into his performance like he hasn't just rocked the ground beneath my feet.

* * *

I leave before the concert is over. It takes me five minutes to fight my way out of the pit, but I can't stay and allow myself to fantasize over what that wink meant. I need to get some fresh air. This groupie nonsense is turning my head to mush.

Leo is waiting to escort me back to the hotel. I use the short car ride to upload a video I shot during the concert. While I'm still logged in, I scroll through the hashtags Rhett's fans use. There's the usual stuff—crowds lined up for the concert, footage of the show itself, proclamations of undying love for Rhett. But a video that was uploaded just minutes ago catches my attention.

It was taken at tonight's show from directly behind the pit. The on-screen text says, "Rhett Cole winking at a fan." Sure enough, the camera caught him pointing and winking at me, but fortunately, they were too far away to be able to identify who he was looking at. The video hasn't gone viral yet, but it's only a matter of time.

Fuck. Even if no one knew who I was—or am currently pretending to be—it's flirting with danger. All it takes is one TikTok sleuth to put the pieces together, and my life will blow up in my face. Looks like I'll be watching the show from anywhere but the pit from now on.

I keep to the edges during the after-party, which is being thrown on the top floor of a swanky downtown bar, not wanting to risk being recognized by any of the fans here. It's unlikely—they were all too enamored with Rhett to pay attention to the people around them—but it's still a chance I'm not willing to take.

The room is dark and hazy, a drunken stupor seeming to permeate the atmosphere. Couples are making out on sofas or against the walls, people are snorting lines of coke from the coffee tables, and two bartenders are running to keep a drink in everyone's hand. No wonder Rhett was worried about the tour. It's like a scene from a bad '70s movie.

In spite of the fact that it's too dim to see properly in here, I know exactly where Rhett is, as if his body contains a homing beacon, drawing me to him. Several girls are currently draped over him, plying him with their long fingernails and fake boobs, begging for autographs—and probably a lot more.

I shoot a glare in that direction and take another sip of my rum and Coke. My miserable attempt to distract myself by watching the other partygoers doesn't last long. Fuck Rhett Cole and that stupid bloody wink.

My eyes travel over to where he is now somehow buried in even more women. Maybe he really does have a homing beacon, because the second I look at him, his gaze meets mine—just cuts through the cluster of desperate women around him and centers on me. He could have touched my face, and it wouldn't have felt any more sensual than that look.

Then, while I'm still watching, he slowly lowers his chin to his chest and back up. I'm too stunned to move, let alone think about what it means. My brain is still trying to remind my heart that falling for Rhett Cole would be the worst possible thing I could do.

He repeats the movement, and I snap back to reality. "Shit," I mutter, and hand my drink to a dumbfounded waiter. I make my way through the drunken party guests to the other side of the room, where Rhett is knee-deep in groupies. I never saw drugs over here, but maybe he's still feeling tempted.

Right before I reach the outer ring of his circle of fans, he shakes off the last of them and meets me. "Hi," he says, and smiles down at me with that blowtorch smile, melting me into a gooey, molten mess.

"Hi." I swallow the swirl of emotions in my throat. "Ready to get out of here?"

"In a sec." Then those strong sexy hands I just watched tear the most beautiful music from a guitar reach up and cradle my face. His lips capture mine in a kiss that, although short and sweet, does nothing to ease the storm of desire raging in my gut.

He releases my mouth, then rests his forehead against mine, sending a message loud and clear to the groupies I can feel watching us. *I'm taken.*

Unfortunately, it also sends a message to my heart.

I am so fucked.

14

"Lovely" - Fly by Midnight

Saylor

Escaping the party is a relief. My muscles are sore from traveling in the bus all day and dancing in the pit all night. I'm tired from the exhausting schedule we've been keeping. My body longs for the comfort of home and my familiar mattress, even if it's lumpier than a bag of potatoes. Still, I can't wait to fall into a bed and sleep like the dead.

That thought quickly evaporates when Rhett leads me to the tour bus instead of a hired car. My feet catch on the pavement, and he reaches for my arm to steady me. In the haze of the concert, I managed to forget that tonight is our first night sleeping on the bus. In a shared bedroom.

In a shared bed.

Dear god, I'd rather go back to the pit than set foot inside that forty-five-foot torture chamber.

Rhett has no such hesitations. He stands back to let me climb the steps first, and I do so with a racing heart. Was that what the wink was about? Him letting me know he was looking forward to tonight?

If so, he's about to be majorly disappointed.

He warned me this was coming, but I'm still not prepared to sleep beside him. Not with this crazy sexual tension between us. Not when nothing—and I mean *nothing*—is going to happen between us.

We pass through the bunk room, and I glance at the single beds with longing before Rhett opens the door to the back bedroom. It's not very big, which only makes the situation worse. Lights glow in strips near the ceiling, and a large bed covered in white linens takes up most of the room. It's at least a queen-size, but it swallows up the entire space, leaving no doubt in anyone's mind about the two things expected to take place here—sleeping and fucking.

I feel the need to emphasize that only the first will be happening on this tour. "I can just sleep in one of the bunks," I say, and jerk my thumb over my shoulder. "That way you can have the bed to yourself."

"Don't be ridiculous. There's plenty of room for both of us." Rhett reaches behind him and pulls his black T-shirt over his head. I avert my eyes. "Besides, the bunks are full."

I force my eyes away from the ridges of muscle that make up his torso. They want nothing more than to study every inch of that blessed physique, but doing so would be one of the worst decisions I could possibly make. I know my own weakness for a chiseled man. It's best to stay far, far away.

Unfortunately, it looks like I won't be going very far tonight.

"Do you want to use the bathroom first?" he asks, nodding toward a small door.

I grab my things from one of the tiny closets tucked into the walls—Rhett arguably has about three times as many clothes as I do—and duck inside the cupboard-sized en suite. I'm eager for the opportunity to escape the temptation of those abs and that smile he could pull out at any minute, sending me melting onto the floor.

When I come back out, Rhett is sitting on the bed with his guitar, still shirtless. He glances up, gives me a sloppy half smile, and I nearly drop the bag in my hand. I scurry to the other side of the room, where he's no longer facing me. He sets the guitar down and retreats into the restroom.

I breathe a sigh of relief and crawl into bed. My plan is to be asleep before he comes back, but as luck would have it, I can't sleep. My eyes refuse to so much as shut. Before I know it, I'm reaching for my phone. Staring at a screen always makes me tired.

I'm still logged into Rhett's account when I open TikTok, and I have instant regrets. As predicted, Rhett's wink at tonight's show has gone viral. There is a social media *storm*, with everyone trying to figure out who it was directed at. Multiple girls have posted videos saying they've been in a relationship with Rhett for months and that the wink was for them.

I don't know whether to be amused, irritated, or scared. As long as these wannabes are distracting people with their wild stories, it keeps the focus off me. But part of me is still annoyed that the world seems to think they own part of Rhett, as if he's nothing more than a book in the public domain.

The bathroom door opens, and I immediately lock my phone. Either he was very fast in there, or I've been scrolling much longer than I realized.

The bed shifts as he crawls into it, and every single hair on my arms stands straight up. I clutch the blanket in my hands, not sure how it's going to protect me, but unwilling to let it go. The scent of men's body wash drifts over, and I inhale deeply before thinking better of it. God, why does he have to smell so good?

"Do you have enough room?" His voice is low and gravely, as though he just woke up, but I've discovered by now that it's actually from belting his heart out during the show.

"Plenty," I say, even though I'm hugging the edge of the bed.

"I'm not going to do anything, you know," he says after a minute.

"You don't have to fall out of bed to stay away from me."

"I'm not." Then, to prove my point, I roll over so I'm facing him. "It's not like you'd get anywhere if you tried, so . . ." I want to swallow the words as soon as they leave my mouth. They sound way too flirty.

I can feel his grin, even though it's too dark to see it. It works its way across the bed, tangled with the heat from his body. How am I supposed to endure another five and a half weeks of this?

"Noted," he says, every letter of the word wrapped in that damn smile.

I search my brain for a way to change the subject. I cannot go to sleep with these being our last words of the night. "Your wink caused quite a stir."

Silence. Then finally, "Did it?" Another pause. "For who?"

"Everyone. They want to know who you were winking at."

"And you?"

"Me what?"

"Did it cause a stir for you?"

"I—" I clench my jaw. How am I supposed to answer that? Not truthfully, obviously. I force a laugh. "Why would it cause a stir for me? I'm pretending to be your girlfriend. These things are expected."

He huffs out a soft laugh. "Okay."

I prop myself up on one elbow and stare at his shape in the dark. "What does that mean? 'Okay'?"

"It means okay."

* * *

Midmorning, the bus stops at a hole-in-the-wall diner for breakfast. The eight hours of sleep I got did nothing to improve my mood—if you can call lying in a bed "sleeping." I'm pretty sure I only got around four hours of actual REM. On top of that, my tooth still feels like the devil is shoving his pitchfork into it.

Then there was the godawful restroom shuffle. The bus braked hard at the exact moment Rhett and I were passing each other in the en suite doorway. The lurch made my braless chest rub against his shirtless one, while his morning wood brushed against my waist. My cheeks flamed, and we both darted in opposite directions like we'd been shocked.

I slipped off the bus the minute it came to a stop in the car park, eager for both fresh air and distance from Rhett. Unfortunately, we still have an act to keep up in front of the crew, so when Rhett slides into the vinyl-covered booth I claimed for myself, I can't be surprised or irritated, except that I'm both.

"How'd you sleep?" he asks, dousing his platter of pancakes in syrup.

I tear off a hunk of my toast with my teeth. "Fantastic." Then, just to be polite, I say, "You?"

He nods, his mouth full. "Terrific."

It's as much a lie as mine was. I heard him tossing and turning all night, and the dark circles under his eyes aren't covered with makeup the way mine are.

I take another bite, and my sensitive tooth shouts its discomfort. Grabbing my cheek, I grimace with pain that is too severe to conceal.

Rhett's fork clatters onto his plate as he reaches across the table for me. "What's wrong?"

I shake my head, but the agony is still too strong to hide. "Just a bloody toothache."

The concern doesn't leave his eyes for the rest of the meal, but neither of us says much.

We hop back on the bus for another long day of traveling. I stick a clove-soaked cotton ball onto my tooth and try to get more sleep while Rhett and the band hang out in the lounge. I can't have slept more than twenty minutes when he knocks softly and opens the bedroom door.

"Are you up for a surprise?" he says when I blink at him.

Kill me now. "Depends on the surprise," I mumble.

The bus has stopped moving, so I sit up. How are we in Chicago already?

Rhett reaches out to me. "Come on."

Ignoring his outstretched hand, I swing my legs over the side of the bed. I follow him out the door, smoothing down the curls that rebelled during my nap.

The band is sprawled across the bus lounge when we pass through, and Jamal gives me a wicked smile. Rhett doesn't stop though, just heads for the door of the bus.

We step into the bright sunshine. We're in a random deserted car park. There's nothing here except a boarded-up building and a bright yellow sports car. The car door opens, and Leo steps out.

I cock a brow at Rhett. "What is this?"

"This"—he runs a hand fondly over the bonnet of the car—"is a Lamborghini Huracán."

"I have no idea what you just said."

He grins. "Just get in."

I do, and it occurs to me I could probably buy one of these myself with the amount of money he's paying me.

The leather feels like butter, and I make a note to capture this moment, because something like this will likely never happen again in my lifetime. There's no way I would actually waste Rhett's money on something so ridiculous. The interior has a distinct new car smell—not like Rhett's Maserati, which smelled like him, dark and mysterious.

We peel out of the car park, kicking up dust behind us. Within seconds, the tour bus is nothing but a speck in the rearview mirrors.

I glance over at Rhett. The hoodie he's wearing is gray, which may be my favorite color on him. Jeans, a baseball cap, and sunglasses complete his small-town look. He casually drapes his wrist on the steering wheel, even though the speedometer shows we are going a breezy one hundred miles per hour.

I clear my throat and turn my attention to the windshield. "Where are we going?"

"To have fun. But first"—he slows the car gracefully as we enter city limits—"we're going to the dentist."

I swivel to look at him. "What?"

He keeps his eyes on the road and the GPS. "You have a toothache, right?"

I can only nod dumbly.

"So we're taking care of it."

"Just like that?"

"Just like that."

Soon, we're pulling into the car park of a dental practice. I don't know how Rhett thinks we'll get an appointment right away, but when he tells them my name, they lead me right to the back.

Thirty minutes later, my toothache is greatly reduced, thanks to my new filling. My strength to resist Rhett is also greatly reduced.

"How did you do that?" I ask once we're back in the car.

"I had Noah get you an appointment." He shrugs like it's no big deal.

A thick lump clogs my throat. "Thank you," I say softly.

I'm more aware than ever of his presence beside me. We're closer than we were in bed last night. He's ditched the sweatshirt now, and the lower half of one of his tattoos peeks out below the sleeve of his dark green relaxed polo. I want to lift the fabric so I can see the whole thing.

I try to imagine Nate doing for me what Rhett just did, and I can't. He wouldn't even give me the money for the dentist, let alone set up the appointment and take me himself.

God help me. If I'm not careful, I will fall for this man, and it will be like plummeting from Mount Everest.

"I'm sorry, by the way."

Rhett's voice startles me out of my daydream spiral, and I glance at him in surprise. "What?"

He flicks his eyes toward me before returning them to the road. "For not calling you. After camp."

I blink—one, two, three times—trying to process his words. He's sorry?

"I never apologized for that dick move."

My mouth feels as dry as cotton, but I manage to say, "It's okay."

From my peripheral vision, I see him shake his head, but I keep my gaze firmly fixed out the windshield. "No, it's not. I really did like you back then, but—"

There's always a but. I tap my fingers on the door's armrest, wishing we could skip the part where he makes me feel like summer camp leftovers, the kind of thing you look back at with a fond smile, giving yourself a pat on the back for having grown up since then.

"I got shipped off to boarding school that fall," he says. I feel his eyes on me, but I still don't turn. "Things got really crazy after that, and . . ."

He doesn't need to finish that sentence. We both know how it ends. *I forgot about you.*

"It's fine." I shrug as if I didn't spend the six months after that scrolling through the pictures of us on my phone before finally deleting them and deciding never to fall for someone out of my league again.

Guess that lesson is still in the works.

Clearing my throat, I ask, "Have you heard from your dad?"

I regret my choice of topic the second I see Rhett's face tighten. "Nope." He flips on his blinker and waits for the light to turn green.

"I'm sure he'll call," I say, fighting the urge to place my hand on his arm. Not because I think it would give him the wrong impression, but because I know it would give my heart more firepower than it can handle right now.

"Well, that makes one of us," he says, his jaw set.

While he may be trying to hide it, it's obvious to me that Rhett Cole still very much craves his dad's approval. And Randy Cole is a fucking asshole if he's not planning to see his son while he's touring in the United States.

"It's his loss," I say quietly. But maybe this is one thing I can fix.

15

"Honey" - Taylor Swift

Saylor

The Chicago concert is incredible—helped, no doubt, by the fact that my tooth is no longer trying to murder me. Also helped by the fact that, after what he did, my crush on Rhett has only grown bigger.

I know it's stupid and risky as fuck. But the heart wants what the heart wants, and all that shit. So I'm going to play a little game with myself. I'm allowed to fantasize about Rhett all I want when I'm not actually *with* him. But as soon as we're together, the shields go up. It's been working so far, but only because we haven't been together since I invented the rules of the game.

Rhett exits the stage and, after exchanging a few words with Noah, he walks over to me with a huge grin on his face. *Calm the fuck down,* I remind my enthusiastic heart. He takes my face in his hands the way he did the other day, and I'm prepared for what's coming, I swear I am, but fireworks of pleasure still shoot through me the second our lips meet.

There is no hesitation in this man when he goes after what he wants. And for the ten seconds the kiss lasts, I become convinced that what he wants is me. It's a dangerous game I'm playing, one that will have devastating consequences if I don't maintain control of my heart.

I end the kiss and toss him a smile that I hope looks nonchalant. "You're an excellent actor," I whisper, just centimeters from his mouth.

His smile grows a little wider. "Who said I was acting?"

I roll my eyes and pull back so that his hands are forced to fall from my face. "You have fans to greet," I say, pointing to Noah, who is watching us with his arms crossed.

Rhett throws me one more smile before heading for his meet and greet. I follow Leo outside to the car. Taking a deep breath of the chilly night air, I let the cold cool my heated skin. That whole encounter violated the rules of my game. It's a good thing we're staying at a hotel tonight, because I'm not sure how well my rules would hold up if I had to sleep next to Rhett all night.

Since I know he won't be at the after-party for a while, I use the time to take a shower and freshen up. Doing so before the concert always feels pointless, since I inevitably end up gross and sweaty from the crowd anyway.

When I finally arrive at the party and turn my phone in at the door, the hotel suite is full of people, but I find Rhett immediately. He's in the center of a group as usual, talking animatedly with the fans around him. As if he can feel my presence, he turns from the guy he's talking to and fixes his eyes on me.

He laughs at something, his gaze still locked with mine. Then he excuses himself and walks toward me. His mouth slips into that lazy smile I've come to love, one side hitching higher than the other. I remind myself that the game ends as soon as he's beside me.

"Hi," he says, and slips a hand around my waist to tug me close. His nose nuzzles the hair at the nape of my neck. "Mmm, you smell good."

Behind him, people are watching us and murmuring to each other. My cheeks heat with their attention, his utter disregard for it, and the feelings his touch evokes. His lips play over the skin on my collarbone, and it's so nice that I'm tempted to let my imagination have free rein.

Rhett pulls back but keeps his hand on my waist. In fact, he keeps a hand on me all night. At the small of my back when we're talking to someone, on my thigh when we're sitting on a sofa, on my waist when we're alone, letting the world know that I'm his with his quiet possession.

I know it's just an act. I *know*. I keep reminding my heart over and over that this is fake, this doesn't mean anything, but it refuses to listen. It's melting and molding itself into a Rhett-shaped form, as if he is becoming necessary for survival.

And he can't. He cannot be a necessary part of my life, because the moment he is, everything changes, everything falls to pieces.

Rhett and I leave the party together, and I focus on killing the butterflies in my stomach one by one as his thumb strokes the skin of my wrist while he holds my hand. There isn't anyone here to see us besides our PPOs, so why is he still pretending?

I slip into the bathroom as soon as we're back in the suite. I need space, I need time, I need a fucking miracle, but it doesn't look like I'll get any of them. Try as I might, Rhett is becoming harder and harder to resist. The way he looks at me makes me feel as if I could fly a fucking plane if I wanted. It's dangerous. Lethal, even. But that doesn't stop me from craving it.

* * *

My phone rings the next afternoon while the band is practicing and I'm working on editing videos of last night's concert. The name on the screen makes me freeze, my thumb hovering over the accept call button, my brain quickly trying to decide if I should or shouldn't.

Timie.

It's been months since we've talked. We haven't even texted in weeks, and whenever we do, it only lasts a few minutes. Things are just too different now. The friendship we once shared got dumped into the rubbish bin the day she packed her bags and left for some little village no one had ever heard of.

I have no clue why she's calling me now. Unless it's an emergency? I tap the button and regret my decision the second I hear her voice. It sends a sharp stab of pain through my abdomen. She sounds so . . . *happy*.

"Saylor! Oh my god, it rang so many times, I thought you weren't going to answer."

I give a weak laugh. "Sorry about that. I didn't hear it at first." The lie slips out easily, because that's what she's reduced us to. There was a time when I would rather have chopped off my own thumb than lied to my best friend.

"How have you been? It's been so long. I feel like I don't know anything that's going on with you."

Ice coats my internal organs. Does she know I'm on tour with Rhett? Is she calling to get the inside scoop? Maybe she's running out of gossip for the other playground mums.

"I'm good," I say. Another lie, because the last word I would use to truthfully describe myself right now is *good*. "Busy." Maybe she'll take the hint and let me go. And if she knows about the tour, this will give her the perfect segway to bring it up.

But she doesn't do either. "How is Nate?"

It's a testament to how far we've drifted that she would bring him up. Before Timie moved, she and Javiar were close with Nate and me. The four of us hung out at least once a week when Nate was home. When things went south in our marriage, Timie was already gone, off to start her fairy-tale life far away from me.

"Well, he's deployed, so . . ." I'm not about to delve into the topic of our divorce.

"That's right. I forgot. Silly me." There's a clatter in the background, and she murmurs something to her son. "Between the piles of laundry and the towers of dishes, the details sometimes slip my mind." She giggles, as though Nate shipping out is a "detail." "And how are you holding up?"

"I'm good. Really." And I'm more than ready to quit this interrogation before she asks something I can't lie my way through. I shut my laptop and set it beside me on the bus's sofa. "Tell me what's been going on with you."

It's the perfect thing to say. Timie has never struggled for words in any situation, but since moving to Timbuktu, she has more to say than ever. Probably because she has fewer people to talk to. I can't imagine conversations with a toddler are very stimulating.

As she chatters on, I walk to the kitchenette and browse the contents of the fridge, phone pressed to my ear. I fix myself a plate of veggies, pita chips, and hummus before she runs out of breath.

"If you ever decide to leave the city, you should totally come to Ferncombe," she says. "It's so lovely here."

I don't know if she means to live or just for a visit, but both are out of the question. Sitting back down on the sofa, I say, "I'll keep it in mind. How is Javiar?"

"He's wonderful," she says, and I envy the joy in her voice. "The best husband in the world. The other day he came home with roses, a bottle of wine, and a box of chocolates. When I asked what the occasion was, he said he was celebrating having the most beautiful wife in the world."

I know I'm supposed to melt at this, so I give a weak "aww," but in reality, I want to hurl.

She continues regaling me with details about their house renovation project, little Remi's potty training escapades, the puppy they just got, and their travel plans for next year. The overarching theme of everything? *My life improved a thousand times after I left the city and you.*

When we finally end the call, I've lost my appetite. I carry my untouched plate back to the kitchenette and set it in the sink before retreating to the bedroom. I'll deal with it later. Slipping into the restroom, I slide to the cool tile floor, rest my face in my hands, and let myself grieve what Timie and I lost.

We were best friends. There was a time in my life when I couldn't have imagined not talking to her every day. Now, sometimes entire months go by without a single text exchange. What does it say about me that I'm replaceable in her life, but three years later, my own heart still bears the gaping hole that she used to fill?

I don't know how much time passes, but when there's a knock on the door, my face is damp with tears.

"Saylor? Are you okay?" Rhett asks from the other side.

"I'm fine," I call, but my voice sounds thick and cloudy.

The knob turns, and he steps inside. He takes one look at me and sits down on the floor beside me. "What's wrong?"

I sniff out a laugh. "What if I had been puking my guts out?"

"Then I would've held your hair."

"Right." He probably would have, which is a problem.

He lays a tentative hand on my back. "You wanna talk about it?"

I shake my head, wiping my face on my sleeve.

He hands me a roll of bathroom tissue. "You sure? I'm a great listener."

I'm tempted to test that theory. Guys hate when girls cry, and this is the perfect opportunity to send him away. "You're not scared off by crying?"

He tucks my hair behind my ear. "It makes me feel useful for once in my life," he says, crossing his long legs in front of him, as though he's planning to stay awhile.

That only makes more tears spring to my eyes. He rips off a piece of tissue and hands it to me.

"I ruin everything I love." I blow my nose loudly. If my tears don't scare him away, maybe my emotional outpour will.

"Not true." His hand continues lazily stroking my back, warm through my shirt.

"You wouldn't know."

"Then tell me."

So I do. "Nate changed after our wedding. We weren't together very long before getting married, but afterwards . . . He was different."

I feel Rhett stiffen beside me. "That's on him, not you."

"There's more." A lot more. "You asked if I have animals? I did." I nod vigorously. "I rescued a dog once—Charlie—and he was the best dog ever. I had him for two weeks, then he got sick and died. There was nothing the vet could do."

"God, Saylor," he says quietly. "That wasn't your fault."

"My best friend moved away. We did everything together before that—and I mean *everything*. I thought we wanted the same things from life, but one day she announced she was moving away to some godforsaken town to live the life of her dreams. Now we hardly speak, and she's happier than I've ever seen her before."

"But what does that have to do with you?" Rhett quietly presses.

I risk a glance at him, turning my tear-streaked face toward him. "I was holding her back."

He tugs me against him—just tucks me into his shoulder like I belong there. And for a second, I let myself believe that I do. "Of course you weren't."

"My parents . . ." I stop, because complaining about my parents to Rhett feels especially cruel. My parents are amazing, and they devoted their entire lives to me. He hasn't spoken to his dad in years.

His fingers rub circles over my arm. "What about them?" he says.

"They've always dreamed of traveling. Even when I was little, it was all they talked about. They loved me, of course, but we never had enough money, so they lived the dream by talking about it." I swallow the lump in my throat and force myself to go on. "Now they're finally able to travel, but they're too old to do the things they dreamed of doing all those years."

He tilts my chin up so I'm looking at him again. "Again, what does that have to do with you?"

I shrug, but it gets lost in his embrace. "They could've gone sooner if they hadn't had me."

Rhett sighs and grabs the back of my head, pulling me into his chest. "Your theory is ridiculous."

It isn't, but his scent is too intoxicating to form coherent thoughts. He smells of leather and those peppermint toothpicks he's always chewing. I want to spend the rest of my life here, just curled up in Rhett Cole's arms, breathing him in and letting him scare away the monsters in my closet.

The moment is sweet, him comforting me, but we both sense the second it changes. Electricity crackles through the air, and I'm suddenly aware of how close we are. His mouth is mere inches from mine, and, as if he's just come to the same realization, he draws back slightly, his eyes flicking down to my lips, then back up to my eyes.

My body doesn't care about the game, and neither does my heart. They gang up on my brain, which is desperately trying to keep us from imploding. My lips part in invitation, and Rhett doesn't hesitate. His mouth is on mine immediately.

Kissing Rhett is like listening to the greatest hits of all time. He's both soft and hard, his hands both soothing and searching, his mouth giving and taking. He still has a hand wrapped around my waist, and he uses it to pull me closer, until I'm practically in his lap. With the other, he cradles my face in that way I've started to dream about.

His fingers press into my skin as though he can't get enough of me. The hand on my cheek slides lower until it's wrapped around my throat, not tightly, but in a way that makes moisture dampen my thighs. My own fists are clenched in the soft fabric of his T-shirt, with no intention of letting go in this millennium.

He breaks the kiss long enough to whisper, "God, you're fucking beautiful" and move his mouth to my neck. The hand on my waist skims over my thigh, then finds the source of my heat. His fingers drag back and forth over the denim of my jeans, making desire flash hot down there.

I groan as he reaches for the zipper of my pants, and that tiny movement is enough to break the trance.

What are we doing?

I scramble away from him, wiping my mouth with the back of my hand.

Rhett looks resigned, as though he should have expected this. "I'm sorry," he says.

I shake my head. "We can't," I whisper. Even after three years, one conversation with Timie still makes me cry. If I fall for Rhett, our inevitable breakup will be a million times worse.

16

"All the Small Things" - Blink182

Rhett

Tonight was another knock-out success, another sold-out show, and we're in the fucking *music capital of the world.* Some days I still can't believe I made it this far.

I jog down the steps to the backstage area, where our routine has been smoothed to a high shine. Noah tosses me a towel to wipe the sweat from my face and neck, a protein bar, and a peppermint toothpick, then my PPO, Bear, walks me to the meet and greet room.

The Lunar Echo execs are very happy right now, as they should be. "Electric Heartbeat" is number one on the charts in the United States, which is huge in and of itself, but "Chasing Shadows" and "One More Night" are also in the top ten.

My dad had four hits on the charts at once, so I've still got some work to do, but this is my first year as a signed artist. Pretty sure I'm not only going to match his record—I'm going to annihilate it.

Saylor thinks my success is because the songs I wrote in rehab are authentic and shit, talking about my addiction, but I don't know if I believe it. Several of my top hits weren't even written by me. The execs thought I needed some "different vibes" on the album, too. Whatever.

Sometimes you just need a stroke of luck to get your break.

After the meet and greet, Bear escorts me toward the greenroom, where a huge buffet of food better be waiting for me, because I am starving. That protein bar earlier did little to fill the gaping hole that is my stomach.

When we enter, there are more people than usual in the room, but the snack bar still looks pretty stocked, thank god. I'm heading that way when Saylor comes up to me. My heart rate kicks up a notch. She looks fucking hot as always in that tight black dress Leo picked up in New York. Over it, she's wearing a red-and-white Bruno Mars T-shirt I'm pretty sure she stole from my closet.

"Hey," I say. "What are you doing here?" Then, because we're in a group of people, I pull her in for a kiss. Ever since we almost did something more in the bathroom, she's been skittish. I haven't dared kiss her when we've been alone, even if it's practically all I think about.

"Waiting for you."

Fuck. Blood surges to my cock. I would love nothing more than to properly thank her for waiting, maybe on the sofa in the corner or against the wall, but I highly doubt she'd be down for any of it. "You didn't have to do that," I say, and reach for a bag of crisps on the table. Normally, she heads back to the hotel or the bus as soon as the concert is over, and I don't blame her. Touring life takes its toll on everyone.

"I know," she says, and tucks some hair behind her ear, something she does when she's nervous. "But I have a surprise for you."

My lips curve into a half smile as I open the bag. "A surprise. Please tell me it's new lingerie under that shirt you stole from me." I can say these things in public without her freaking out, and the blush that stains her cheeks only makes her that much more gorgeous.

"Stop it," she hisses, but there's a flash of pleasure in her eyes; I'm sure of it. She likes flirting with me, even if she pretends otherwise.

"Then what is it?" I pop a crisp into my mouth, then slip my hand around her waist and pull her close, desperate for another whiff of her smoky scent. It's mingled with a hint of my cologne, and fuck me seven ways to Sunday if that isn't the hottest thing ever. Her wearing my clothes, my scent imprinted on her? Is she trying to kill me?

She comes to me willingly, which gives me hope that this will turn into something more than a show for an audience before the tour's over. This whole thing would be much more fun if we were having sex.

My nose is still buried in her hair, so I notice the cowboy boots first. I release Saylor so I can greet the person approaching us. But when I look up, I realize it's not a person. Well, it is, but it's also . . . my dad.

"Surprise," Saylor says softly beside me.

Randy Cole—legendary musician and leader of the rock band Cole Brothers—is standing in front of me. He's at least six three, topping me by two whole inches, something that aggravates me more than it should. He also looks ten years younger than he is, thanks to the tight black T-shirt and white jeans he's wearing. Even though it's streaked with gray, his hair is still thick, and he has it styled in a trendy fade.

A blindingly white smile splits across his face as he looks at me. Then he throws one beefy arm around my shoulders and slaps me on the back. "Congratulations, son."

My throat is too tight for me to say more than a mumbled "thanks." All of the people stuffed into this room suddenly make sense.

I haven't seen my dad in five years, not since my twenty-first birthday party, when he popped in for a few minutes to give me a new guitar, then disappeared to god only knows where. We've talked on the phone several times since then, but he's always been too busy for a conversation lasting more than a couple of minutes.

Saylor says something beside me, but I don't even hear what it is. I'm too stunned. My dad is *here*. He knows about my success. I have dreamed of this moment more than all of the tour stuff combined.

"You were at the show?" I finally manage to ask.

He nods and takes another bite out of the apple he's holding, the crunch loud in spite of the noise level in the room. "I was. It was pretty good." He turns his grin on Saylor. "Your pretty girlfriend here invited me."

I don't miss the patronizing way he talks to Saylor, but I'm still reeling at the revelation that Randy Cole was in the audience tonight and I didn't even know it. "I played the Martin," I say, realizing as soon as the words are out of my mouth how ridiculous they sound.

"I know. I saw it." Randy tosses the apple core into the rubbish bin. "The old girl sounds good."

He gave me the Martin D-45 when I turned eight. Birthday guitars became a tradition after that, at least on the ones he showed up for.

"So, what'd you think?" I sound like a little kid who needs his parent's approval. I don't; I'm strictly interested in his opinion as a professional.

Randy shrugs and wipes his mouth with the back of his hand. "There were spots that could use a little help, but you sounded pretty good for a first-timer."

A *first-timer.* Leave it to Dad to bring even crazy success down a peg or two.

"Do you want to come to the after-party?" I ask.

I already know he'll say no, that he has somewhere he needs to be—it's his favorite excuse—so when he says, "Attend my son's after-party? Of course I do," I couldn't be more surprised.

Fortunately, Saylor doesn't seem to be struggling to maintain her composure, even in the presence of one of the most famous rock stars of all time. She lets the security team know we're ready to leave, and as we head out the door, I'm still holding the bag of crisps, my raging appetite vanished in the wake of my dad's appearance.

The party is a blur of bodies and drinks and music. Not my songs this time, but original Cole Brothers hits that are at least fifteen years old. Who the fuck picked the playlist?

I pictured sitting on a sofa with my dad, discussing different chord progressions or the latest guitars he's added to his collection, or even just life. I have no idea what he's been up to recently. His Instagram page isn't any help. It's just a bunch of staged photos that make it look like he's having the time of his life. Maybe he is.

I'm certainly not. I've barely said ten words to the guy since we got here. He's more interested in talking to people he's never met before than his own son.

"I'm going to get a drink," Saylor says beside me. We're standing at one of the bar-top tables scattered around the room. "Do you want one?"

"Whatever," I say, eyes still on my dad, who's chatting up Diego. Watch him try to steal my own band out from under my nose.

Saylor returns several minutes later and hands me a cup. I don't even stop to see what it is before chugging it.

"Steady on," she murmurs.

I ignore her. A stunning redhead walks past us, and I reach out a hand before she can join the cluster of people around my dad. "Hey," I say as she turns. "Didn't I see you at the show tonight?"

It has the intended effect. Her face brightens like a light bulb, and she begins fawning over me and the show and my skills with a guitar. For a few minutes, I'm able to forget what a jackass my dad is.

When the girl wanders off, I realize I'm alone. Saylor must have disappeared during our conversation, and now I don't see her anywhere. Go figure. I walk over to one of the empty sofas and sink into it, nursing a second drink that I don't even remember getting.

My dad has a group around him, all laughing uproariously at whatever he's saying. The guy's not even that funny. I'm about to get the piss out of here when I spot Saylor in his clusterfuck of admirers.

Apparently, even my own girlfriend thinks he hung the moon and stars. What a load of shit.

"Why do you keep wandering off?" I ask her when she takes the seat beside me several minutes later.

"Because you're sulking, and it's boring."

"I'm not sulking." I take another swig from my drink.

"This"—she wags her finger in the air around where I'm slumped on the sofa—"is sulking."

I roll my eyes, then immediately scan the crowd for Randy. He's surrounded by groupies—*my* groupies—who are younger than I am. There should be a law against that.

"I think you're with the wrong Cole," I mutter.

"What's that supposed to mean?"

"Come on. You invited him here."

She jerks her head around to look at me. "Yeah, for you."

"You expect me to believe not even a little bit of it was for you?"

"Honestly? I think the guy's a jerk."

Furrows form between my brows. "That's my dad you're talking about."

She levels me with a hard stare. "Maybe that's where you get it from." Then she turns and walks out of the room.

17

"She Knows It" - Steven Rodriguez

Saylor

Rhett's gone when I return from the restroom. I check the entire party suite, but he's not in any of the small groups clustered around the edges of the space, and he sure as hell isn't in the crowd of groupies mooning over Randy Cole.

Do they have any idea how desperate they look, clawing at him, laughing at his stupid jokes, tossing their hair over their shoulders? I wonder which one of them—or rather, how many of them—will be "lucky" enough to go back to Randy's room with him.

It's disgusting, but it's also par for the course in this world.

Maybe that's where Rhett is right now, banging some eager groupie in a hotel room while I search for him. The thought fills me with dread, but I can't be mad, can I? We're not a real couple—definitely not in that way—so if he wants to sleep with someone else, he has every right.

The only way to lessen the chances of that would be to sleep with him myself. He's got to be missing sex by now. God knows I am, but when your spouse is in the military, you learn to get really good at using a vibrator.

Moral of the story? I'm not sleeping with Rhett, no matter how badly either of us may want it. And the queasy feeling in the pit of my stomach at the thought of him fucking some other girl against a hotel room door needs to get the hell out of town. Because Rhett and I are nothing more than platonic friends.

It's more probable that he's fallen into trouble, snuck off to do a line of coke—or god forbid, insidion—in a room where I won't see him.

As soon as the thought registers, the likelihood of it slams into me. His father's a jackass, there's no denying that. And as much as Rhett might want to defend him to me, I know that he knows it's the truth.

What do you do when you've waited five years to see your dad again, only for him to ignore you in favor of a bunch of girls who barely look old enough to drink?

If you're Rhett Cole, you probably try to drown out the noise.

Leo is standing outside in the corridor, doing something on his phone. He snaps to attention when I approach. His brows furrow at what must be a stricken look on my face. "What's wrong?" he says.

"I can't find Rhett. I'm afraid—" I stop. I'm the only one here who knows about his addiction. "I just need to know where he is."

If he ends up being strung out in a back alley somewhere, he can claw his own way out of the shitstorm that will bring. Finding him before he does something even more stupid is more important than keeping his security team from discovering the truth.

Leo touches his earpiece and murmurs something quietly. Then he looks at me. "He's on the bus."

Relief courses through me before I realize he could be defiling the bus with his debauchery just as easily as anywhere else. Maybe more easily. There's only one way to find out.

"Take me there?" I say. We're leaving tonight anyway, and I've had enough of the Randy Cole after-party.

Bear is standing outside the luxury tour bus, and he opens the door so I can climb on. The lounge lights are dim, and the sound of soft music floats in the air. *Shit.* What if he does have a girl here? Do I play the part of betrayed woman or flippant girlfriend who's only here for the perks?

I'm still trying to decide as I quietly walk through the lounge. A startled scream gets caught in my throat when I spy Rhett sitting on one of the sofas, guitar propped on his legs.

"Fuck, you scared me," I say, clutching my heart.

He doesn't look up, just keeps strumming. "Where'd you think I was?"

"Uh, the bedroom?"

Strum, strum, strum. "Doing what?"

"I don't know." I sink onto the sofa opposite him. "Maybe not what, but *whom?*"

His eyes flick up, catching me in his gaze. "You thought I was fucking someone? In our bed?"

I frown. "It's not *our* bed. It's . . ." I trail off because I don't know what it is. Technically, we both sleep there, but that's a far cry from labeling it "our bed."

His fingers halt on the strings. "Until this arrangement is over, it's our bed."

I swallow the lump in my throat, which is now the size of my fist. "Okay. Our bed." I nod, even though my heart is racing a million miles an hour around a racetrack I have no idea how to get off of or if I even want to, because this is what he does to me.

He drops his gaze back to his guitar. "And for the record, I will never fuck someone else while we're together."

My throat and mouth go dry. I try swallowing again, but it doesn't do much good. "But we're not really together," I squeak out.

"Let me tell you something, Saylor." His eyes flash like lightning. "I don't cheat. Not on my real girlfriends, and not on my fake ones."

This settles into my heart like a dog searching for the perfect spot to curl up for a nap. My guilt buzzes, a fly preventing full relaxation.

"I'm sorry," I say. "I shouldn't have assumed. To be honest, I was more worried I'd find you passed out in an alley somewhere."

Rhett snorts but starts playing again. "I don't need a babysitter."

"Then why did you hire one?"

He gives one final downstroke, then moves the guitar off his lap with such speed, I sit back in my chair and blink at him. "What do you want, Saylor?"

What are words again? "I just want to make sure you're okay."

"I'm fine," he bites out.

"You don't sound fine."

He stands up abruptly and stalks to the small fridge, yanking it open. He grabs a can of grapefruit water and pops the tab before taking a long drink. Then he wipes his mouth with his wrist. "I was fine. I was fucking great until you invited *him* here."

I'm speechless. It doesn't happen often, and the feeling is crippling.

Ever since Rhett took me to the dentist to get my toothache taken care of, I've wanted to do something for him. It took me a dozen tries and multiple gatekeepers to finally get ahold of Randy Cole. Convincing him to attend his son's concert was easier. I had no idea what a prick he was, but even if I'd known, I probably would've invited him anyway, knowing how much it would mean to Rhett.

"Excuse me," I say, getting to my feet as I discover language again. "You're the one who wouldn't shut up about wanting to see your dad. I was trying to do something nice."

I heard something once, probably in a TikTok video. "When a woman does something for a man, he doesn't think she's great. He thinks *he* is." Rhett will always have that perspective of me. I uprooted my entire life to help him out, and what do I get out of it? Several hundred thousand and the heartbreak of the century.

My words seem to suck the energy out of him. He sets his drink down and sags against the counter. "I know. I'm sorry." He rubs a hand over his haggard face. "God, I shouldn't have blamed you. None of this is your fault."

I take a step closer, fighting the urge to comfort him. "I honestly thought you would appreciate it." I wrap my arms around my middle, since I can't wrap them around him.

"I did. I do," he says. "It's not your fault my dad's a world-class jackass."

"Has he always been like that?"

Rhett nods and sips his soda. "For as long as I can remember. He'd come around sometimes, but only when he stood to gain something from it. Publicity, a stroke to his ego, a quick fuck with my mum." He shakes his head in disgust. "He only wanted us for what we could do for him."

I roll his words around in my head, trying to decide if I should say what I'm thinking or stay quiet. Finally, I can't hold it back any longer. "Sometimes that's how I feel," I say softly.

His brow pinches. "What do you mean?"

I close my eyes, already regretting mentioning anything. "Nothing."

"Saylor." Rhett's voice holds a warning tone that makes my thighs clench together. The rest is unspoken, but it hangs in the air all the same. *Tell me, or I'll flip you over the sofa and fuck you senseless.*

When did the tension in the room change? With every pulse of blood through my veins, my body becomes increasingly aware of his, mere feet away. I pinch the bridge of my nose. "That you only want me around for what I can do for you?" I say to the beige carpet.

His hands on my arms surprise me, but they feel right, like they belong there, like they're the missing puzzle piece I've been searching for for days. He doesn't move them, just holds on until I finally lift my gaze from the floor.

"I'm sorry. That's not at all how I feel." His face is earnest, his eyes wider than usual. "Forgive me?"

"Of course." I nod quickly, ready to get this weird confrontation over with. I thought he'd get mad and we'd keep arguing. I definitely didn't expect an apology and his touch searing my skin.

"You have my full attention the rest of the night. What do you want to do?"

I blink at him, my mouth hanging open. What do I want to do? What a loaded question. I glance around the room, searching for something to put distance between us, something to keep me from voicing what we both want.

My eyes land on the guitar propped against the sofa. "Teach me to play?"

His hands slide further down my arms, coming to rest at my elbows as he turns to look at it. "You really want to learn?"

It's never crossed my mind before, not in any serious way, but suddenly the idea holds a strange appeal. "Yeah," I say, "but I doubt I'll be any good."

He *tsks* and moves to sit back down. "Come here," he says, and pats his legs.

I bite my lip and take a step closer. Before I can protest, he grabs my arm and pulls me into his lap. Technically, I'm sitting between his legs, his chest pressing into my back, his breath warm in my ear, his strong arms wrapped around mine, but the idea is the same.

He settles the guitar on my lap, then lifts my hands into the right position. "You're going to put this finger here"—he presses it down on a string—"and this one here, and this one here." After my left hand is in place, he hands me the pick. "Now strum."

I do, and it sounds terrible. "You make it look so easy."

His chuckle rumbles, sending tremors through my back. "I've been playing since I was four."

He teaches me a few more chords, and by the time we're done, I've made something that sounds halfway like music come out of the instrument.

"See?" he says, his mouth only inches away from my skin. "A natural talent." He sets the guitar aside but doesn't move me from between his legs.

"I'm not sure I'd call that natural," I say, my voice sounding breathless.

"Oh yeah?" His fingers trail up my arm, causing goosebumps to break out. He seems to enjoy that, because he keeps doing it until I'm on the verge of shivering.

"Yeah," I breathe out. I'm not even sure what we're talking about anymore.

He brushes his warm lips against my shoulder, and I nearly combust. It feels a million times more intimate than any of the kisses we've shared, and those have been hot enough to earn a spot of their own in the galaxy.

"You're wearing my shirt," he murmurs, his mouth still pressed against my skin, branding me with his warmth, his scent, his intoxicating presence. "That's so fucking hot."

He lifts my hair and nuzzles the nape of my neck, sending a thousand sensations through my body that I most definitely should not be feeling for this man, who is nothing more than one bad idea away from breaking me forever.

18

"Dress" - Taylor Swift

Saylor

I force myself to focus. Rhett's mouth is still hovering over my skin, his hot breath blazing a trail of desire down the entire length of my body.

Leaning forward, I break the contact while my heart begs him to never stop touching me, never stop kissing me, never stop giving me hope that there's more for me than the future I've created for myself.

My feet move me away from the sofa, while my heart is still very much curled in Rhett's arms. I glance back at him. "I'm going to get ready for bed." It isn't until I'm walking to the bedroom that I realize that it sounded like an invitation.

Once I'm ensconced in the tiny bathroom, where I'm safe from my own devious intentions, I look at myself in the mirror for a pep talk. "Nothing is going to happen," I say under my breath to my reflection. "You are going to go out there, crawl into bed as usual, and keep your hands to yourself."

The devil on my shoulder pipes up. *What would it hurt to get it out of our systems?*

I shoot him a nasty glare. "I've seen the movies. There's no such thing."

So don't read anything into it. Just sex, nothing more.

I shake my head as I squeeze toothpaste onto my toothbrush. "That might work for some people, but it won't work for me."

I've had sex with exactly three men in my lifetime, and one of those was a one-night stand that was mediocre at best. For years, it's bugged me that I can't remember if his name was Mike or Mark.

Can I have sex again that doesn't mean anything? Yeah, probably. Can I have sex with Rhett Cole without it meaning anything?

The odds are not in my favor.

I slip Rhett's T-shirt over my head, inhaling his scent one last time before tugging at the zipper of my dress. It's the black designer one he bought for me our first night in New York. I wore it tonight in honor of his dad being there, but I have major regrets as soon as the zipper gets stuck partway down.

I've always scoffed at girls whose zippers "get stuck." I mean, come on. We all know that's just an excuse to get a guy to unzip you. But after struggling for several minutes with the bloody thing, which managed to snag in the *worst* possible place—right between my shoulder blades, where I can't reach it properly—I have to admit defeat. I can only hope that Rhett doesn't feel the same way about stuck zippers as I do and take this as further invitation for something to happen.

Opening the door quietly, I see him sitting on his side of the bed, ankles crossed, phone in his hand. He glances up, and I grimace, then walk in, clutching my dress against me as though it might decide to flee my body of its own volition.

I turn my back to him. "Do you mind?" I say, holding my hair out of the way.

He swings his legs over the side of the bed to take a look. "God, woman. What were you doing to this thing?"

"This is why I never wear dresses," I mutter.

His fingers brush against my bare back as he fiddles with the zipper. The touch feels electric, and I imagine what it would feel like to have those hands on every inch of my skin. Would he move slow or fast? Be rough or gentle?

Finally, the telltale whir of the zipper sounds, and cool air floats through the open back of my dress. Before I can thank Rhett, I feel his thumb moving over a scar on my lower back. "What's this?" he says, his voice little more than a breath.

My nerves stand at full attention as he strokes the three-inch mark. "Just an old scar," I say. "Thanks for your help." I try to move away, but he puts a hand on my stomach to hold me in place.

"What happened?"

I dart a glance at him over my shoulder. I can't be hurt that he doesn't remember. It was eleven years ago. Why would he? "A stack of canoes fell over—"

"—right on top of you," he finishes. "I forgot about that."

I slip out of his hands before they can make me lose all common sense. "At least you were a gentleman and saved me."

He snorts. "After snogging you behind the canoes, I think it was only proper that I pulled you out from beneath them when they toppled."

"Pretty sure we did more than kiss back there." A blush climbs my neck and settles in my cheeks. It only takes a hop, skip, and a jump to remember exactly how I felt every time Rhett pulled me aside to kiss me—among other things—as if he couldn't possibly get enough of me in the short time we had together. If I had known then how much he would only improve in both looks and skills . . .

"Thanks for the zipper," I say, and slip back into the bathroom. The more distance between us, the better. Maybe I can think of an excuse to sleep on the sofa tonight.

When I emerge ten minutes later, Rhett is on the bed again, but he's changed into a long-sleeve gray T-shirt and loose black sweatpants. He looks casual and cozy. He looks like home. Before I've fully processed the idea, I snap a photo with my phone.

He looks up. "What was that?"

I open my editing app. "A picture."

He's out of bed in a flash. I don't realize his intentions until his fingers are already on my phone. "Let me see."

I show him the photo.

"That's terrible. Delete it."

I tighten my grip. "No way. People need to see that you own sweatpants. Besides, it's not terrible." It's actually quite good, but it does paint him in a different light than usual, more boyfriend material than gorgeous fuckboy. I have yet to decide which I prefer.

"Saylor." There's that warning tone again, which sets off a clanging alarm bell inside me. I have the sudden urge to see what he'll do if I press him.

Pulling my hand from his, I hold the phone away. "I'm going to post it."

"No, you're not," he says, and casually reaches over my head for my arm. Damn him for being so tall. His fingers snake around my wrist and tug it down with hardly any effort.

I let out a laugh-scream as I spin away from him, turning my body so he can't steal the phone. His hands clamp around my middle, holding me in place as I try to squirm away. Then he does the absolute worst thing possible. His fingers work their way into my sides, and I do my damndest not to let it affect me, but it only lasts half a second before I am convulsing with giggles and desperation.

"I seem to remember something," he whispers heavily into my ear as he holds me against himself, showing no mercy. "You're ticklish as fuck."

"No," I squeal, fighting him now. "I'm not."

His laughter is deep and a little dirty as his hands move closer to my armpits. "Is that right?"

I make one last concentrated effort to move away from him and actually manage to put a little distance between us. However, he's blocking the rest of the room, so the only place to go is the bed. I take the leap and land in the middle of it.

He growls and crawls onto it after me. I shriek and launch myself to the other side, but I get tangled up in the blankets. By the time I've freed myself, he's caught up to me, and now we're both stuck in the two feet of space beside the bed.

Rhett props his arm on the wall above our heads, but he doesn't touch me. My mouth goes dry as he stares at me with his lids at half-mast, the desire in his eyes so blatant that my panties grow damp just looking at him.

He plucks the phone from my hand and tosses it behind him on the bed. I make no effort to retrieve it, no longer giving two fucks if he deletes the picture or not. He moves closer, but there's still a sliver of space between our bodies, big enough that I have to fight to keep my hands from reaching out to pull him closer.

Our breathing is ragged, and I'd pay a million dollars to know what he's thinking right now. His eyes travel every inch of my face, as though he's memorizing it to savor later. I can't do anything but lose myself in those dark eyes, which have the power to wreck me so thoroughly.

He touches my face with the back of his hand, and my eyes flutter shut at the butterfly softness of it. I feel his warm breath on my neck as he leans in. "Is this okay?" he asks.

I nod, eyes still closed, because what else is there to do when your first crush, your first kiss—your first love, probably—is touching you and asking if it's okay? Because how could it ever be okay for him to *not* be touching you, and how will you be okay when this is over, when he goes back to his life and forgets about you and you're left with the memory of his skin against yours and the leathery scent of him and the taste of peppermint that prevents you from ever chewing gum again without thinking of him? How is that okay?

My body trembles as his fingers stroke my cheek with the utmost gentleness. I want to ask him to do something—anything—other than this slow, torturous dance around what we both want, but I'm terrified what it will all mean. And isn't that the point anyway? For this whole thing not to mean anything?

"Relax," he whispers. "I won't do anything you don't want me to."

"I know," I say. He's been nothing but a gentleman so far, in spite of the fact that I've been sleeping only inches away from him for the past two weeks.

His hand grows heavier on my cheek. "Then what are you scared of?"

I swallow the thick lump in my throat. "I'm scared of what I want you to do."

That's all it takes. He pushes me up against the wall, hands firmly clamped around my face, and says, "Tell me when to stop, baby."

My mouth opens with a gasp as his descends upon it. There's something about Rhett's lips. They're pillowy and soft, but they have a strength behind them that you'd never know unless he kissed you. They pluck at my lips like a pick on guitar strings.

His thumbs rest on my cheeks, gently stroking back and forth as he tilts my face up toward him, then holds it in place with those incredibly flexible hands. I feel like I could melt into the floor at his touch. It carries enough power to start earthquakes and hurricanes—if not in the world, then at least inside me.

He moves his mouth to my jaw, tracing the entire line of it with kisses before moving to the column of my neck. My head tilts back of its own accord, and I'm no longer able to focus on anything but the feeling of Rhett's lips against my skin.

He arrives at my collarbone, tugging my shirt away to be able to reach it. It's a crewneck, so not the easiest thing to do, but I specifically chose this old Van Halen shirt to wear to bed because it covered the most amount of skin.

He tugs on the hem. "Take this off," he murmurs, his words muffled by my body.

I slip it over my head, causing him to take a step back. I'm left in nothing but a pair of tattered sweatpants—possibly the least sexy thing I own—and he sucks in a shuddering breath as his gaze sweeps over me.

He rests his hands on my hips. "Have these been underneath this whole time?" he asks, eyes on my 32D chest, then on my waist, then back on my boobs.

I bite my lip. Warmth spreads through me at his admiration, but it still makes me slightly uncomfortable. "I think so?" It comes out as a question.

He slides his hands around the small of my waist, dwarfing me with the width of their spread. It has the same effect as swirling a hot knife through butter—instant liquefaction. He yanks me against him, and my nipples rub up against the softness of his T-shirt—something I was admiring before, but now want to disintegrate.

His fingers make their way up the curve of my spine, and he groans before dropping his mouth onto mine again. After another scorching kiss, he shifts and kneels in front of me. The sight of Rhett Cole kneeling before me will never be erased from my memory as long as I live.

He moves his attention to my breasts, pulling them into his mouth one by one and sucking until my knees buckle. I feel his grin, and it prompts me to open my eyes and watch him. He looks up at me, his eyes alight with something I can't put into words. Elation maybe, if I had to settle on something.

His mouth moves downward, following the faint line between my abs to my navel. I let out a shuddering breath as he sprinkles a circle of kisses around my belly button.

The waist of my sweatpants prevents him from going any further, but he slowly eases them down, immediately chasing the newly exposed skin with his kisses. Carefully lifting each leg, he helps me step out of the pants.

I'm now wearing nothing but a pair of lavender lace underwear, and Rhett Cole's face is less than two inches away from them. He's looking at me like he's never seen a naked woman before, which the entire world knows is a lie.

He lets out a ragged exhale, then rubs his palm over my panties. "You're shaking," he says.

He's right. Tiny tremors rack my entire body, and there's nothing I can do to stop them.

"Are you scared?" His eyes pull mine to them like a magnet.

I shake my head, not trusting words right now. It's not a lie. I'm not scared, exactly. More like aware that I'm standing at the edge of a cliff, and the second I choose to take the plunge, there's no going back.

Rhett studies me for another beat before leaning back on his heels and pulling his phone out of his pocket. Several seconds later, the sultry notes of a piano float through the bedroom speakers. "Better?" he asks.

I nod as the music sinks into my bones, calming me in a way I didn't know was possible.

"We don't have to do this," he says quietly.

"I want to." It nearly comes out as a whimper. The depths of that want might be what scares me the most. I'm not sure I've ever wanted anything as badly as I want him.

He reaches around to my ass, tugging me toward him. The heat of his mouth is so intense, I glance down to see if he's melted my panties right off my body. They're still there, but are doing little to shield me.

A cry escapes my lips as he nips at me through the fabric. This turns him ravenous, and he moves the crotch of my underwear aside with greedy speed.

The first flick of his tongue nearly does me in. It's hot and wet, and it hits every single nerve of my clit. My hands fly to his hair, pulling him closer as I thrust my hips into his face. He growls into my pussy and, with his hands still on my ass, drags me even nearer.

His tongue travels further back, then dives into me with so much force I cry out again. After several pulses, he moves his hand so he can use his fingers to drive in even further. A sudden sharp thrust brings a scream to my lips.

"God, how many fingers is that?" I gasp.

"Three," he grunts, ramming them in with perfectly timed precision.

I sag against the wall as he continues ministering to me, making me feel so many things at once that thoughts become a distant memory. When he leans in to use his tongue again, my climax unleashes. I cling to his head like it will save me from the storm.

He fucks me with his tongue and hand until my orgasm ends and I collapse against him, completely spent. A chuckle rumbles through him as he tugs my soaked underwear down my legs, then lifts me and gently lays me on the bed.

He climbs on after me and positions himself between my thighs, which he spreads wide with those hot, heavy hands. My brain has enough battery life left to notice that he's still fully clothed, while I'm sprawled naked under the strip lights of the bus bedroom.

Lifting both of my legs, he throws them over his shoulders, leaving me even more open and exposed. I'm about to protest when his mouth finds me again, eradicating vocabulary entirely. With long sweeps of his tongue, he somehow brings me to another climax.

When I've come down from it, he lowers my legs back down and pulls his shirt over his head. No matter how long I live, I will never tire of watching guys do that, especially when they look like Rhett. Hard, sculpted muscles make up his torso, and there doesn't appear to be an ounce of fat on him. A handful of tattoos are scattered across his shoulders and down his arms. A faint trail of hair disappears into his sweatpants. I reach up and trace it, soaking up the way it makes him shudder.

His eyes have gone black, and he's watching me with more seriousness than I've ever seen him wear before. Gone is charming, teasing Rhett. In his place is a man who is on the brink of losing control.

The power of it is intoxicating.

I slip my hand beneath his waistband, finding what I'm looking for immediately, thanks to his lack of underwear. His eyes flutter shut as I wrap my hand around his hot cock, squeezing and pulling it.

"Fuck, Saylor," he whispers as I rub my thumb over his tip.

"You should," I whisper back, making his eyes fly open.

He yanks his pants down with lightning speed, leaving me holding his cock in the light. It's a beautiful masterpiece, all veins and tight, pink flesh. I drag my eyes back up his body, meeting his gaze.

Without a word, he reaches for the drawer beside the bed, returning with a condom. I glance at it, then back at him, my confidence returning now that I've brought him to his knees. "Was that meant for me or someone else?"

The corners of his mouth lift in a smile as he rolls it on. "Let's call it wishful thinking," he says. His eyes are still black, but lit by a spark that is quickly becoming my favorite thing in the world.

"That doesn't really answer my question."

His smile vanishes as he lines himself up at my entrance. "Does this?" He thrusts inside me in a single fluid motion, entering and filling me with such force that my vision goes black for a heartbeat.

I wrap my legs around him as he buries himself deeper. He leans forward on his elbows, nuzzling my chest as he fucks me. His lips close around my nipple, and then I feel the telltale sting of teeth. I gasp as it makes me clench tighter around him. He groans and thrusts extra hard.

We must be rocking the entire bus, advertising our activities to anyone watching. The surprising thing is that I don't care. Everyone thinks we're together anyway. This is less alarming than if we weren't having sex.

My third climax is building, and Rhett looks like he's barely holding it together. He reaches for me, shifting my body for a slightly different angle. I thought he was already as deep as he could go, but it turns out I was wrong. He's buried so far that I can feel his balls slapping against me with every thrust.

I let out a shaky gasp as I feel it coming again. He chases it with his own moaning growl, and for the first time in my life, I orgasm at the same time as someone else.

19

"Chills" - James Barker Band

Rhett

I can't believe I once thought an insidion high was the optimal mountain peak. Since then, I've discovered the euphoria that comes from performing for a stadium full of adoring fans screaming and flashing their boobs at me, my name scrawled across them in block letters. Even seeing my dad in the greenroom, knowing he watched my show, flew me higher than any drug ever has. Until he revealed that he's as much of a jackass as ever, of course.

But even better than all of that is Saylor Elizabeth Jones.

Last night may have been the best night of my life. She slept in my arms naked after I gave her three orgasms (still patting myself on the back for that one), and when I woke up during the night, hard as a motherfucker, we had another go.

But god, it's not even the sex. It's *her*. I look at her, and the rest of the world goes black—just fades into nothing like a background vocal trailing off.

Now she walks out of the bathroom, pajamas clutched under one arm, wearing denim shorts and tights with a flannel tied around her waist. I shoot her a grin, and it only stretches wider when a faint blush rises in her brown cheeks. I waggle my eyebrows, hoping she'll agree to another round.

She rolls her eyes, but a tiny smile plays on her lips. "Don't you have rehearsal?" she says, stuffing her clothes into her closet.

"It can wait." I grab her hand and tug her closer to the bed, which isn't difficult given how little space there is in here. Tonight we'll have an entire hotel suite.

She comes willingly, but only to drop a kiss on my lips. Then she spins away and opens the door. "I'm hungry," she says before slipping out.

I growl, but the door's already closing. "I'll show her hungry," I mutter, and swing my legs over the side of the bed.

By the time I'm done showering and have grabbed one of the breakfast sandwiches Noah had delivered, the roadies have our equipment set up in the practice room we'll be using all day. I'm surprised to find Saylor talking to Jamal when I walk in.

"Hey, babe." I wrap an arm around her waist and plant a kiss on the side of her face.

She turns to smile at me. "Jamal was just telling me about the party last night. Apparently, we missed Diego dancing on a table?"

"Thank god for small mercies," I say, not letting go of her. Definitely not around Jamal, who looks at Saylor like he'd very much like to have his tongue down her throat, the bastard.

He goes to get his guitar, and Saylor pulls away from me. "I should go. Let you guys practice," she says.

I tighten my grip on her waist. "You could stay."

"And do what?" She bites her full bottom lip, and I want to pull it into my mouth.

"Watch," I say, staring at it.

She blushes beneath my gaze, and I'm starting to realize how much I like the sight. "I don't want to be in the way."

I scoff. "That's the last thing you'd be. I want you here." I'm going to be throwing around some new lyrics this morning, seeing what the guys think and possibly adding music to some of them. I suddenly want her here more than anything. "Please stay?"

She blinks several times, her eyes wide and luminous. Her face has a glow to it that wasn't there before. *I put that there.*

"Okay," she whispers.

I add a new entry to my list of highs.

20

"Sex on Fire" - Kings of Leon

Saylor

Thanks to me, there are no phones allowed into the after-parties, and since the hotel is right next to tonight's venue, I didn't have the drive over to upload the concert footage to social media the way I usually do. So I take a few minutes in the corridor outside the party to get everything posted.

I'm beginning to regret offering to handle Rhett's socials. It gave me something to do during the first few weeks of the tour, but as his fame grows, the number of troll comments is increasing as well. And to be honest, he's been keeping me so . . . busy . . . that I've spent less time than ever on his accounts.

We're staying in the hotel tonight, which will be a nice relief from the bus, which we've slept on for most of the past week. Not that Rhett and I have done much sleeping. My gut tightens just thinking about his arms around me, holding me close as he makes my entire body sing.

It's becoming hard to remember that none of this is real. When we're with the rest of the band, he puts his hands on me, leans in close when I talk, gives me a quick kiss before heading onstage. He did all of those things before, too. The only thing that's changed is that we have sex now.

It's stupid, I know. Possibly the stupidest thing I've ever done, with the exception of marrying Nate. But god, the sex is good. But is it good enough that I'm willing to throw my life away for it? Because that's what will happen if things continue down this path.

Like I said, stupid.

I upload the last batch of photos to Rhett's story, then hand my phone to the security officer at the door and enter the party. The hotel's Wi-Fi is slow, and it took me longer than usual to post everything. I feel bad for leaving Rhett alone for so long. What if he got into trouble while I was outside?

It takes all of two seconds to determine that I needn't have worried. He's not sitting in the corner shooting up or even smoking a doobie. There's no tray of drugs in front of him like there was that first night. Tonight's buffet is of a different sort.

Surrounding Rhett is a ring of groupies so blond there's no way a single strand of hair among them is its natural color. He doesn't notice me entering the room, and why would he? He has both arms slung around members of his fan club, and judging by the smile on his face, I'm pretty sure the only way he could be happier is if he were an octopus with eight arms instead of just two.

They're pawing at him—hands on his chest, in his hair, on his arms. He's not exactly pawing them in return—nothing that could get him in legal trouble, anyway—but between the massive grin and his relaxed posture, it's obvious there isn't a place on earth he'd rather be.

I head to the bar along the wall and order a cocktail. I can't even remember what I asked for until the bartender slides the glass across the counter and I take a sip. Why the fuck did I get a Manhattan? I don't even like them.

Forcing myself to turn around, I sip my disgusting drink and scan the room, trying to look everywhere—anywhere—but at Rhett and his posse. We agreed this wouldn't mean anything. I'm here to act a part. And while it sucks to play the humiliated girlfriend, at least it's not real. No one even glances my way. Apparently, they don't care any more about my feelings than Rhett does.

I finally allow my eyes to rest on him again, but he's still entangled in the bronze limbs of those American girls, with their flawless skin, short dresses revealing way too much ass, and nasal drawls. How am I supposed to respect a guy who thinks that kind of attention is the ultimate achievement?

I down the rest of my drink in two swallows and turn to go, since I'm evidently not needed here. There's no way Rhett is trading that kind of attention for a drug of any sort.

Back in our hotel room, I change into my bathing suit. Nothing like a late-night swim to clear my head and help me form a plan.

The water does just that. There's no one else here, so I swim my laps in peace. Swimming lessons were the one extracurricular my parents could afford, and I've never been more grateful.

I'm about to wrap it up for the night and head back to the suite when the door to the pool room opens. I open my mouth to say hello, but snap it shut again when I realize who's just entered.

Rhett's black floral-print shirt hangs loosely from his shoulders, his hands shoved into the pockets of his white jeans. He walks to the edge of the pool and gazes down at me. "I looked everywhere for you."

I fight the urge to snort. We both know "looking everywhere" means asking Leo for my location. "Here I am."

He crouches down so we're closer to eye level, but I stay in the middle of the pool. "You didn't come to the after-party."

This time I can't hold back a biting laugh. "Or maybe you just didn't notice me there."

"I thought your job was to stick with me."

I narrow my eyes. "You looked taken care of."

He doesn't say anything, just stares at me without an expression. The light reflecting off the water dances on the ceiling and across his face.

I move into a backstroke, swimming away from him along the length of the pool on the other side. When I reach the end, I glance in his direction. He's no longer crouching, but he's still looking at me in a way I can't read.

As I watch, his fingers move to the buttons on his shirt. He undoes all of them—only half of which were done up in the first place—while I doggy-paddle at the far end of the pool. *Fuck.*

"You gonna tell me what's wrong?" he calls. He tosses the shirt aside, leaving those mouth-watering abs on full display. Even from here, I can make out all the dips and ridges I've enjoyed exploring the past seven days.

I swallow thickly, my mouth as dry as chalk. "Nothing." My voice carries across the water.

Rhett reaches for the buckle of his belt. "Saylor."

My heart pounds at that familiar warning in his tone. I paddle in place faster, wishing now that I'd gotten out earlier so he wouldn't have me at a disadvantage. Although, as he yanks the belt from his pants, then works to unfasten those as well, it hardly seems like a disadvantage.

"Were you jealous?" he asks, eyes on me as his jeans fall to the deck.

"Don't be ridiculous."

He stands there, wearing nothing but a pair of black boxer briefs. It's a glorious sight, and my heart starts racing as he moves in the direction of the pool stairs. "Do you know who those girls were?" His foot touches the first step.

I shake my head, moving backward while keeping him in my line of sight.

"They were big shot influencers, all of whom were instrumental in me going viral." He's fully in the water now, and it swirls around his torso as if it too can't get enough of him. "I owed them some attention. The label execs called this afternoon to let me know they would be there and that I was expected to schmooze with them."

It makes sense. I know how much pressure the label's been putting on him. But it doesn't completely erase the sting of him ignoring me or the ugly feeling rising in my chest as I watched him lap up their attention.

He's only a few feet away from me now. I tried paddling backward, but it was nearly impossible to do while also watching him.

"You didn't look like you minded too much." The words squeak out of my mouth.

His gaze darkens as he closes the remaining distance between us. "They're beautiful," he says, "but you're a fucking goddess." He reaches a hand toward my face, and my eyes close unwittingly at his touch.

He tugs me closer, until there's no longer a gap separating our bodies, and my nipples press against his hard chest. He slips his thumb into the bottom of my boring-as-fuck one piece, stroking those sensitive folds several times before dragging it back out. I gasp as he lifts me out of the pool and sets me on the ledge.

He grins up at me wickedly. "I think it's time for me to pay homage."

He spreads my legs on the cool tile, and I catch myself by propping my hands behind me. Slowly, he eases the crotch of my swimsuit to the side, then stares down at me for several long seconds. Nothing has ever felt as intimate as him gently peeling back the fabric covering my pussy and gazing at it like he's never seen anything more beautiful.

At the first stroke of his warm tongue, a strangled cry rips from my throat. He takes another long drag before pulling back to give me a smug smile. The bastard is way too pleased with himself.

With his hands under my ass and his mouth properly occupied

again, he drags me to the brim of the pool, tilting me back so he can reach me better. I have to lean on my elbows to keep from collapsing.

My feet are dangling in the water, and I thrash when he slips a finger inside while tormenting my clit with his tongue. Nothing in the world should feel this good. My climax is building fast. As though he can sense it, he shoves another finger in to join the first, urging me closer and closer to the edge of both my orgasm and the tile.

When it finally breaks, I splash us both with a spray of water. He keeps his mouth and hands on me, making the wave last forever and ever. The sensation is too much.

I pant and look up at the ceiling of the pool room. At some point, my arms gave out, and I collapsed onto the deck. It occurs to me now that I should maybe be worried about someone finding us here, hotel staff especially, but the idea carries no weight.

Let them find us. Let them arrest us.

I just had the best orgasm of my life, and after the last week, that's saying something.

Rhett lowers me back into the water. "That was the hottest thing ever," he murmurs into my ear. "When your pussy squeezed my tongue, I nearly came."

My brows shoot up. "You nearly came from going down on me?"

"Oh, baby." He chuckles. "If you're surprised by that, you have no idea how fine your pussy is."

Heat creeps up my neck, while my insides turn to Jell-O. For this moment only, I'm going to let myself pretend he means it.

He's holding me close, but his fingers are already finding their way back between my legs. I'm still so osensitive, but the ache is growing rapidly. He slips my swimsuit to the side and pushes two fingers inside again.

I moan and let my head drop onto his shoulder. His arm is fastened tightly around my waist, holding us both up in the water as he pumps his hand in and out of me. Then he moves us toward the shallow end so we can both stand. I realize why as soon as he lowers his briefs.

"We don't have a condom," I say as his hard length presses into my stomach.

"I got tested before the tour." He rubs his cock against me with one hand, the other still busily working me over.

"Me too," I pant. "And I'm on birth control." A gulping breath. "But I was thinking more about contaminating the pool."

His grin widens as he removes his fingers and drags his cock through my folds. "They have filters."

I whimper as he rubs circles over my bud. Using his palm, he pushes my bathing suit out of the way, then plunges himself fully into me. I let out a gasping breath. The water only heightens the experience of feeling impaled on him.

Hands on my waist, he pumps me up and down over his cock. I struggle to stay upright, wanting nothing more than to sink into this feeling and never come back up.

It's not real, I tell myself.

It's not real.

But as we simultaneously climax again and I feel his warm cum filling me, that truth becomes hazier than ever.

21

"Jealous" - Nick Jonas

Rhett

There's a bite in the air that makes its way into my lungs as I jog. It's the perfect antidote for the raging libido I've had since this trip started. I'm lucky Saylor is as eager to fuck as I am, or I'd be even better acquainted with my right hand than I already am.

Things have been . . . good between us. After she got over what she perceived as me flirting the other night (okay, it may have been *slight* flirting, but only because the label demanded it), we've hardly been apart except during my shows. I'm working on some new stuff, and she always manages to thread her way through the lyrics.

We're in Seattle for one more night, then hitting the road tomorrow. It will give us the perfect chance to get out of the hotel room and spend some time together.

I nod at the doorman as I walk into the lobby, already planning what I'm going to do to Saylor after my shower. Maybe I can convince her to join me. She was still sleeping when I left, but she should be awake by now.

She's not in the living room when I get inside, so maybe she's still in bed after all. I'm heading for the bathroom when I hear someone talking on the other side of the suite. I turn and follow the sound to the second bedroom, the one I originally booked for Saylor but which we haven't used because she's been spending every night in my bed.

I recognize her voice as I approach. Who the fuck is she talking to at eight in the morning? My first instinct is to barge into the room like a caveman, ready to protect his woman's honor. Then I remember that she's not my "woman," and she has a right to her privacy.

But that doesn't mean I'm above a little eavesdropping.

The door is slightly ajar, so I gently push it open far enough to be able to see into the room. Saylor is sitting on the bed, her back to me. In front of her, a silver laptop is open on the duvet. A man's face is on the screen.

I can't make out what he's saying, but I can see his features well enough. The bloke is average looking, although he has that kind of face girls seem to think is hot. Personally, I don't see the appeal. Sandy-brown hair cropped close to his head, a jawline you could use to cut a line, and light-colored eyes, either blue or gray.

Saylor responds in her soft, sultry voice. My anger surges as I listen to her, although I can't make out what she's saying either.

Who the hell is this guy, and what's he doing talking to my girl?

I pull the door shut again and stalk down the hall toward our bedroom. Is this her idea of payback for the other night? Who gives a fuck if I was flirting? It didn't mean anything. It's not like I was going to sleep with any of those girls, so who cares if I macked on them?

Grabbing a clean set of clothes, I can't decide if I'm glad I caught her or not. At least now I know that to her this relationship is as fake as a Kardashian. Better to be aware than act like a bloody fool who thinks it might be something more.

On the other hand, now I'm pissed. At her, at myself—I don't even fucking know, but it's ruined what was supposed to be a good day. Instead, I have to live with the knowledge that she's talking to other guys behind my back. Am I supposed to just be okay with it?

Fuck that.

Fuck this bullshit mess I've gotten us both into.

When I get out of the shower, I have several new messages. Some of the anger dissipates when I see who they're from. God, I miss my friends.

Pierce: *How's the tour going, mate?*

Walker: *You and your girlfriend have been blowing up the news lately. When do we get to meet her?? xx*

Maeve: *God, yes. I need fresh meat to sink my teeth into.*

I wince at that one.

Lux: *We'll make her behave, Rhett!!! xx*

Me: *Tour's fucking unbelievable. Most days I still can't believe I get to do this. That would be a no to the gf*

Lux: *Whyyyyyy?*

She should know better. It was her idea, after all.

I pull on a pair of jeans, and the image of Saylor sitting on that bed, talking to some guy whose name I don't even know, fills my head. Apparently, the shower did less than I thought to cool me off. I type out a reply.

Me: *Because it's fake*

I may have just shot myself in the foot revealing that, but I don't give a fuck right now. Besides, none of my friends are going to blab, and it feels good to finally tell someone the truth.

Me: *She's talking to her lover as we speak*

I'm not interested in their opinions on the subject, so I send a third text.

Me: *So Maeve, still with Preston?*

Heath: *Snort*

Pierce: *Yeah, Maeve. Do tell us how the pinprick penis is treating you these days.*

Lux: *Is it actually that small??*
Maeve: *FUCK. OFF.*

* * *

I forget about the date I arranged with Saylor until it's six o'clock and too late to cancel. Our dinner reservation is at seven thirty.

She steps out of the bedroom wearing the tight black dress I bought for her. It hugs her in all the right places, and for two seconds, I forget that I'm mad at her.

My eyes sweep her from head to toe. "I thought you swore off dresses."

She glances down at it and approaches the armchair I'm sitting in. "It's too nice to waste." Her hand skirts across the silky fabric. "Besides, it was this or ripped jeans." A flicker of a smile crosses her mouth as she looks down at me.

I blink to clear my head before returning my attention to my phone. "Good choice."

If she's hurt by my less-than-stellar reaction to her outfit, she doesn't say anything, just starts setting up an area for the hair and makeup team to come in and give her a hand, since I'm not performing tonight anyway.

Our reservation is at a quiet restaurant, one of those places that advertise "intimacy." When I booked it, I thought it would be the perfect place to take Saylor. Give us a chance to drink good wine and get to know each other. Real date stuff. Not being stuck in the back bedroom on a tour bus, banging each other on every possible surface. (There are nine. We counted.)

Not that there's anything wrong with that, but this feels different than most of my flings. Like there's something of substance here. I'm not usually first in line to take a girl on a date, but for some reason it's different with Saylor. I *want* to take her out.

When we arrive promptly at seven thirty, the maître d' escorts us to a private alcove in the shape of a half circle. Thick red curtains hang across the opening and line the inside of the room. He shows us how to unfasten them if we want more privacy.

Beside me, Saylor turns pink. I let her slide into the velvet-covered booth first, then move in beside her. It's arranged in such a way that we're both next to and across from each other. Several small candles flicker on the table. The rest of the alcove is dark.

"This is nice," she says quietly.

I murmur my agreement, then place an order for a bottle of wine.

"Are you glad for a night off?" she asks after the maître d' leaves.

"Yep."

A stilted awkwardness hangs in the air between us, but she pushes ahead as if she's not talking to other guys behind my back, pretending to be into me while she's making plans to fuck them later. "I heard that 'Take a Chance on Me' is moving up the charts."

I nod and taste the sample the sommelier pours from the bottle. I give him a thumbs up, and he retreats after serving each of us a glass.

"How's the new song coming along?" Saylor asks, taking a sip of hers.

"It's fine." I swirl my wine, the dark red liquid sloshing up the sides.

A tense minute passes, then finally, she says, "Are you going to tell me what's wrong, or are you going to keep acting like a child for the rest of the evening?"

I meet her eyes for the first time all night. "I don't want to talk about music."

She gives me a peevish look. "That would be a first."

I stick my tongue in my cheek and stare at her. She really is so fucking beautiful. That thick black hair, her smooth brown skin, those bottomless dark eyes . . . Too bad she has commitment issues.

"First time for everything."

"Rhett, I don't understand what's going on. Did I do something?"

My laugh is sharp enough that a lady at a table near us turns to look. I give her a tight smile and turn back to Saylor. "Yeah, you did something. Or maybe I should say *someone*."

To her credit, she actually manages to look confused. Maybe she should take up acting. "I don't know what you're talking about."

I pick up my glass. "Really? Bloke with the hair"—I move my hand in a vague circle in front of me—"and the face?"

"Are you on drugs?" she says.

"Don't joke about that." I take a long swig of wine.

"I'm not."

I set the goblet back down with a little extra force. "I saw you on the video call this morning. Ring any bells?"

Her eyes widen. "Nate? You're talking about *Nate*?"

"I don't know how many there are."

A tiny scoff blows from her nose as she lifts her glass to her lips and takes a sip. "Wow."

"Glad I amuse you."

"I'm sorry, were you *jealous*?" She says it like that in itself borders on hilarity.

I clench my jaw so hard something pops. "No."

She bites the side of her lip, and I know it's to hold back a smile. "You don't need to be jealous."

"I'm not." I cross my arms and lean against the back of the booth.

She bends across the table as though she's making up for the space I've added between us. "Nate's my husband."

I don't school my features in time to hide my surprise, both at the revelation and her use of the present tense. "*Ex*-husband, you mean."

She deflates at this, dropping her gaze and picking at her nails. "He's on tour, and they lost several squad members today."

"Oh, shit." I reach across the table for her hand. "That's fucked up."

She doesn't look up, not even when the server brings our plates.

"Why did he call you, though?" I ask gently. It's hard to tell how upset she is, since she won't look at me. I scoot her plate toward her.

Taking it, she spreads her napkin over her lap. "Both of his parents are gone, and he's an only child." Her eyes finally rise to meet mine. "As difficult as our marriage was, I'm all he has."

22

"Treat You Better" - Shawn Mendes

Saylor

As I listen to what sounds a lot like jealousy in Rhett's voice, a bad feeling crawls over me. His hand is still lying on top of mine on the table, but after I tell him that I'm all Nate has left, he slowly removes it and picks up his steak knife. He doesn't say anything for a few moments, just chews his food in silence, a surprising feat for Rhett Cole.

I want to say something to break this awkward tension that's been between us all day, which I now realize came from him thinking that Nate was—what? Somehow a threat to him? As if.

But what is there to say? I'm as scared and fucked up as Rhett is. I don't *want* to care what he thinks, because the practical side of me knows this will all be over in a few weeks. We've been down this road before, Rhett and I, eleven years ago. He made me think I was his whole world back then, too, and we didn't even have sex that time.

I'm not upset about it. I get it. Our worlds don't fit together, no matter how hard we might try to force the pieces. He forgets that when we're together, but as soon as he has his normal life back, with his friends and cars and luxury bachelor pad, the shine of these weeks will wear off, and he'll see that I wasn't any different from the dozens of other girls he's slept with and forgotten.

Because of this, it's imperative that I protect my heart. I know the danger I pose to myself, the ease with which I read so much more into things than I should. My heart wants to translate Rhett's irritation over Nate into the good kind of jealousy, the kind alpha heroes in romance novels have. But my brain—ever practical and looking out for me—reminds me that this is a childish jealousy. To Rhett, I'm his plaything for six weeks, here for *him*, to help him keep his nose clean. And apparently to bang whenever he feels like it as well.

Where is my backbone? Have I really reached the point where he can just look at me with those eyes and shift his mouth into that pouty smile and I'm done for? Anyone viewing us from the outside would say so.

I should be happy with this arrangement. As a modern woman, I should take what I want from the relationship—and I mean, the sex is incredible—and be prepared to walk away as soon as we're back on Wesbourne soil.

My experience with Nate should have taught me this, at least. Men are never who they appear to be at first. I've already seen firsthand what happens when Rhett steps outside the bubble of a relationship. There is no reason to think this time will be any different.

"What happened between you?" Rhett's voice is quiet, measured, but it still surprises me.

"What?" I glance up at him.

He's focused on his plate, cutting his steak, which is not tough enough to deserve the kind of vengeance it's currently receiving. "You and . . . him."

I blink, trying to put together what he's asking. "Between me and Nate?"

His eyes flash with irritation as he finally looks at me. "Fuck, Saylor.

Yes."

I've never heard so much anger in his tone before. I shift backward in my seat before even realizing I'm doing it.

Things with Nate started out good, too, even though in hindsight, I can see that the signs were all there. The biggest issue was that I married him too quickly to notice them.

"We fell in love fast." I dab my mouth with the cloth napkin, my appetite gone. Our relationship was a romantic whirlwind. Nate was—is—handsome and charming. He completely swept me off my feet.

"Did he treat you well?" Rhett's eyes are dull as he says this.

"Yes. At first, at least."

Rhett looks away. Maybe he'd prefer to hear that I was mistreated?

"So what happened?"

"We had a courthouse wedding because he was leaving to finish his military tour." I shrug and take another sip of wine. "The gambling started soon after. Or maybe before, I don't know."

I never knew if he was gambling before we met and just hid it really well, or if it started as a way to escape the realities of married life, but I suspected the latter. I don't want to think about those days, about standing at the grocery store till and being told that my debit card was declined. About his anger when I questioned him about it. The way he implied I was the reason he gambled, that he was trying to make back the money I spent on "thrift store junk." Junk, I might add, that he definitely didn't have a problem sitting on or eating from.

Rhett frowns. "He has a gambling addiction?"

"He still did the last time I saw him."

He appears to be mulling something over in his mind. Finally, he says, "Do addictions scare you?"

I fumble the napkin ring I've been toying with, and it rolls across the table. "What?"

"You said he's addicted to gambling. I imagine it caused a lot of problems." He raises his brows, waiting for my agreement. After I nod, he continues. "I'm an addict too."

Realization sets in, and I reach for his hand. "I worked with addicts for years. It's different with those who can admit they have a problem and ask for help. Nate never did that."

"I would never hurt you, Saylor," Rhett says, eyes earnest and full of emotion that I'm too scared to unpack.

You would never intentionally *hurt me*, I mentally correct him.

* * *

The air has turned brisk by the time we leave the restaurant, and I've never been so thankful to have a car and driver waiting for us. Rhett texts furiously beside me in the back seat, so I keep my eyes on the window as the streets of Seattle pass by.

When we pull up in front of the hotel, he leans forward and says something to the driver that I can't hear. Bear is waiting outside and passes Rhett a big bag of stuff.

I glance at Rhett in confusion as we drive away from the hotel entrance. "What's going on?"

He grins at me, pulling out all the stops with that mouth of his, and tucks me under his arm. "Don't worry."

I try to peek into the bag, but he just tightens his grip around my shoulders. "Are you planning to murder me?"

He pretends to consider this. "It *would* cement 'Electric Heartbeat' at number one for the rest of the year."

I pinch what little loose skin I can find on his side—not much. He squirms away from me but doesn't loosen his hold on me. That grin somehow stretches even further across his face.

Reaching into the bag at his feet, he pulls out a pair of socks and sneakers. "Here. Put these on."

I take them gratefully. They look stupid with the designer dress I'm wearing, but these heels are killing my feet.

The car stops, and I look up to see the lights of the city reflected on the water ahead of us. Rhett and I climb out, and he tells me we're at Pocket Beach. I immediately see where it got its name. It's a rough semicircle tucked in along the coastline. Rocks and driftwood are scattered across the sand.

"Come on." Rhett grabs my hand and leads me to several logs a short distance from the water. In his other hand, he carries the bag from Bear. Once we're seated, he pulls out a blanket and tucks it around our legs.

"Ah," I say. "I thought this was to hide the body in."

He sniffs a laugh and wraps his arm around me again, then hands me a Thermos.

I take a sip. "Hot chocolate?"

He nods. "Spiked with vodka."

I murmur in appreciation and take another drink before handing it back to him. "So what's the occasion?"

Rhett nestles the Thermos between our legs. "Occasion for what?"

I gesture to the beach. "This. Us. Here."

I feel his shrug against my shoulder. "No occasion."

"I'm serious."

He looks down at me, and I can't make out more than a fleck of light in his eyes. "So am I."

My mouth goes dry at the intensity in his gaze, a gaze I can feel more than see. I swallow loudly.

"I mean it, Saylor. I'm serious." His tone has shifted, and I don't think he's referring to this moment anymore.

I pull my eyes away from the face that is already making its way into my dreams night and day. I know how this ends. I'll fall—hard—and when he leaves, there will be no one there to pick up the pieces of what's left of my heart, the pieces he threw out the window as he drove off, the leftover fragments still clutched in his hand, embedded so deeply into his skin that it's now a part of him as much as it is of me.

The breeze that blows off the water is cold, and I wrap my arms more tightly around my middle as protection from both the wind and the man sitting next to me, easing his fingers around my beating heart, ready to grab it and run at a moment's notice.

Rhett pulls me closer into his side, using his body to shield me from the brunt of the cold. I wish he wouldn't do things like that. They only give him a stronger grip on this heart of mine.

He rubs his arm against the sleeve of my leather jacket. "I'm not him, you know."

I press my hand against the thump of his heart inside his coat. "I know."

And then, somehow, we're kissing. I'm not even sure how it happens. One second I'm curled in his arms, the next my face is wrapped in his hands like a present.

His lips, warm against mine, heat me up faster than the hot chocolate, blanket, and my jacket could as a team effort. I whimper as his hand slides down my neck and rests at the base of it. He gives it a gentle squeeze.

I never thought I was one of those girls with a kink for dominance, but when his fingers tighten around my neck—not enough to affect my air flow, but enough to show his strength—motherfucker, I am done for.

My hands are fisted in his shirt. How they got there, I don't remember. I scoot closer to him on the log until I'm practically in his lap. Then I *am* in his lap, because he picks me up and deposits me there. He moves his hips upward, grinding against where I need him most. He's already thick and hard, as ready as I am.

I shift my weight back and forth so that I drag across his tip again and again. He groans into my mouth. His hand fumbles beneath my dress, which is probably destined for the rubbish bin after tonight. When he reaches my panties, I feel his shuddering exhale.

The positioning is all bad, and when I move to accommodate him, the wind whips around us and right up my dress. Breaking off the kiss, I suck in a loud breath. "Damn, that's cold."

"You're right," he says, and moves me off his lap. "We should get back to the car."

I walk beside him, hiding my disappointment—it's for the best, really—and he reaches for my hand. We've held hands before, but always when others were around. It's not even a form of foreplay, this entwining of our fingers. It feels . . . intimate.

Rhett lets me into the black car first, then slides in after me. I've barely buckled my seatbelt when his hand is up my dress again.

I whirl around on him with wide eyes. "What are you doing?" I hiss, quietly enough that I'm pretty sure the driver can't hear.

Rhett bares his white teeth in a shit-eating grin. "Do I need to explain it to you?" he says in a normal voice.

My eyes flick to the front seat, where our driver appears to be oblivious, although I'm pretty sure he can hear every word. Rhett looks confused, so I do it again, more obviously this time. His thumb is stroking circles over the satin of my underwear, and it is taking 99 percent of my willpower to ignore it. I use the other 1 percent to give him an exasperated look.

Finally, it dawns on him what I mean. He presses a button with his free hand, and the divider between the front and back seats goes up. As soon as it clicks into place, he lunges at me.

His mouth claims mine in a kiss so possessive, there's no way in hell to resist it. Not that I'm inclined to, but as soon as I get the chance, I sputter, "We can't do this here. He'll hear us." My voice is barely loud enough for Rhett to hear me, but I'm not taking any chances.

He pulls back from where he was planting kisses along my collarbone. "Relax. It's soundproof."

"He still knows what we're doing," I mutter as his mouth clamps onto my skin again. But it feels so good that I soon forget about the driver entirely.

Rhett's fingers find their way inside my panties to where I'm a wet mess for him. "Fuck, I'm ready for dessert." His voice is the strum of a bass guitar. He reaches for the buckle of my seat belt and undoes it. Grabbing my underwear with both hands, he pulls it down my legs and discards it on the floor.

I start shivering, even though the car is toasty and warm.

"Scoot back against the car door," he directs me in a murmur. After I comply, he hoists my dress up around my hips. "One leg on the floor. The other"—he tosses it over his shoulder—"right here."

He leans down between my legs—not an easy feat in the small space—to where I'm splayed open for him. I buck against his tongue, but he holds me in place until he's had his fill.

"Look at that pink pussy," he says, stroking it with his finger. "Like a rosebud just for me." Then he takes me with his mouth again, not letting up until I climax around his tongue and fingers.

When he finally sits up again, he's done nothing to satiate my hunger. I want him more now than I did on the beach. I reach for his belt frantically, like a woman possessed.

He gives me a lazy smile and lifts his shirt, as though my need for him is amusing. After I divest him of his clothes, I grab his cock. It throbs, hot in my hand, and I slide my palm up and down the length of it while he throws his head back and groans.

I shift backward on the seat and usher him to my entrance. His eyes meet mine, dark and stormy, before he grunts his way inside me. We stay like that the whole time, eyes locked, staring into each other's souls.

The angles in the car are all wrong for this, and there are probably a million positions that would work better for getting us both off, but neither of us makes any attempt to move. His grunts grow more ragged as the speed of his thrusting increases. I recognize by now the signs that he's close to his own climax.

As happens almost every time we have sex, him building and then releasing is enough to bring about my own orgasm. I clutch his shoulders and bury my mouth against his skin as we both come undone.

When it's over, I don't let go of him, just keep him clutched against me, and he makes no effort to move, in spite of the fact that we're both as uncomfortable as fuck.

We're lying there in the dark of the back seat when it occurs to me.

I'm falling in love with a very bad idea.

23

"Monster" - Shawn Mendes + Justin Bieber

Rhett

This practice session is shit. Chase keeps screwing up on the keys, and I swear if Jamal waggles his eyebrows at me one more time, I'm going to punch him in the throat. Sure, I've forgotten a few lines here and there, but we've done this show nearly every night for the past month. It's time to get our shit together.

My phone rings from the pocket of my jacket on the other side of the room. I walk over in the middle of the song to answer it. It's not like we were getting anywhere anyway.

When I see the name on the screen, I move to take the call outside.

"Eddie, my man," I say once I've left the practice room. "What's up?"

"Rhett." The tone of his voice does not match the enthusiasm in mine. Shit. What now? "We need to discuss a few things."

God, I hate the word *discuss*. It sounds like something white men in stodgy suits do around a big-ass table laden with donuts. "Shoot," I say.

Eddie doesn't beat around the bush. "Your record sales are down."

My brows knit together, and I kick at a wadded napkin in the corridor. "Nah, mate. My shows are mostly sold out."

He clears his throat. "Ticket sales are down as well. You've received some bad press recently. The label is afraid people are moving on."

Bad press? What the fuck? I force a laugh. "I don't know what you're talking about. My fans love me."

"Your fans do, yes. But what's concerning the label is the rate at which you're making fans. Or in this case, not making them."

My blood runs cold. This can't be happening. "What are you saying?"

"I'm saying that unless things change, and soon, the label is thinking about cutting your contract short."

"They can't do that." That's the whole point of signing a contract.

"They can, and they will, if they feel you are in breach."

"What am I supposed to do?"

"I'm sure you'll think of something." He ends the call.

I slap my palm against the cold block wall. The smack echoes down the hallway. First the fucked-up practice session, and now this. Today might be the worst fucking day of my life.

I slide down the wall until I'm sitting on the floor. Propping my arms on my bent knees, I start searching for this "bad press." I won't know how to fix it if I don't know what people are saying.

I log into social media, and holy fuck, Saylor was right. My socials have blown up since she took over. I make a mental note to show my appreciation later.

It doesn't take long to find what Eddie was talking about. There are a handful of videos of my concerts, with people claiming it was the most boring show they've ever attended. Someone even claims to have fallen asleep during it, which is bollocks. The hardest punch is the one labeling me as just another washed-up pop star who thinks he's someone.

That is, until I find my dad's interview.

It's a clip from a longer video, only about thirty seconds long. The interviewer asks him to confirm that Rhett Cole is his son and that he recently attended one of his shows.

"That's right," Randy says, with a short nod. No change in his expression.

"And what was it like? Seeing your son onstage?" the interviewer asks.

My dad ponders this for a second, then says, "It was great. I gave him his first guitar, you know. I don't know if he has what it takes to make it to the top, but for a new artist, he's decent."

The phone falls from my hands, the interview already replaying on the screen. Cold from the wall seeps through my thin T-shirt, chilling my skin until it's the same temperature as my heart.

I know I shouldn't have watched those bloody videos, especially the one of my dad, but fuck me. I wasn't expecting *that*.

I'm *decent*? God, would it have killed him to share a single fleck of the spotlight?

I head back to the hotel. If the guys are wondering what happened to our session, they can go fuck off. Maybe they can use this time to figure their shit out.

The bartender at the hotel bar is young and hot, with a nice set of tits under her tight T-shirt. Unfortunately, the only thing I'm interested in right now is getting smashed. Fortunately, with one flash of my smile, she's more than happy to serve me as many drinks as I want.

* * *

If the shot glasses lined up in front of me on the bar are any indication, I've accomplished my goal. I grin at Macy, the bartender, and she leans down to whisper conspiratorially, "I think you've had enough."

"Macy," I say, using my sexiest drawl, "I'm just getting started."

I know the effect my Wesbournian accent has on women. Macy is not immune. It, combined with my good looks and the knowledge of who I am, has her wrapped around my little finger.

She bites her bottom lip and glances to the side before picking up the bottle of Don Julio. "Okay, maybe just one more. And then you really should stop."

I grin and knock the shot back as soon as she pours it. "You're the best, Macy."

She's about to say something in reply when her eyes dart to the door behind me. Straightening, she backs away a few steps.

"There you are."

I turn to see Saylor marching toward me, face tight with anger. I offer her the same smile I did Macy, but it does not have the same effect. "Hey, babe," I say, reaching out a hand.

She slaps it away and stares at me. "What are you doing?"

I lift an empty shot glass. "What does it look like?"

"You have a show in three hours."

"You're sexy when you're mad." I hold up the glass toward Macy for another refill, but she shakes her head and turns away from us.

"God, you're absolutely plastered." Saylor turns toward the door, and I think she's going to leave me alone. Instead, Bear and Leo join us, each grabbing one of my arms.

"What the fuck, fellows?" I protest when they lift me out of my barstool. "Leave a man some dignity."

When they release me, however, I nearly crash into a table, so I permit them to help me to my room, ignoring the stares from the other hotel guests. If they know who I am, fuck them. Maybe this will give them something to talk about that isn't what a suckfest my shows are.

Once we're inside the suite, Saylor starts barking orders at the PPOs. I cover my ears to block out her voice. "And you"—she yanks my hands down—"are getting in the shower."

I'm too scared to not do what she says. The water's way too fucking cold, and I yelp when it hits my body. Saylor glares at me, so I stay under the spray of icicles.

Once I'm out and dried off, Bear shoves a bottle of electrolytes at me. I dutifully drink the whole thing. When I'm done, I take the plate of food Leo's holding.

"You can stop hovering," I tell them as I tuck into the sandwich.

"We all have a vested interest in you making it onstage tonight," Saylor says, hands on her hips. God, she's hot. She turns to Bear and Leo. "You guys can go. I'll keep an eye on him."

After they're gone, I turn to her with a grin. "My thoughts exactly."

Her face doesn't hold a single emotion. "You're getting nothing from me, except maybe a slap in the face."

"Come on, baby. Don't be like that." I wipe my hands on the napkin and reach for her.

She skirts away from me and over to my suitcase. "Put these on." She tosses a silk orange shirt and black leather pants onto the bed.

"I'm not going," I call as she walks out of the room.

Her raised middle finger is the only indication she heard me.

I put the clothes on because I'm still wearing only a towel, and I'm pretty sure Saylor was right about that slap. If I thought it might lead somewhere fun, I'd risk it, but that woman means business. I'm not about to get in her way.

We soon arrive at the venue, and the drive there feels like a blur, maybe because I slept the whole way. Bear and Leo hustle me inside. I'm perfectly capable of walking on my own, but I guess they're not about to take any chances. I'm not sure how they think I'm getting onstage to perform.

There's a strange energy buzzing backstage. The band members are all here, and they give me wary looks as I walk in. I ignore them and look for Saylor. She's in what appears to be a serious conversation with Noah. They're both frowning, and when she spots me, they both turn an appraising look in my direction. I grin and flip them both off.

Saylor stalks over. "What is wrong with you?"

I don't drop the smile. "Fuck this."

"What?" she hisses.

"All of it."

Her eyes narrow. "What are you talking about?"

"I'm not going up there." I nod in the direction of the stage, where Velvet Inferno's playing their third song, and cross my arms.

"Yes you are, even if I have to push you myself."

"That could be fun."

"Would you stop it? God, drinking makes you obnoxious."

"Obnoxious, washed-up, fucking *decent*. I'm just raking in the compliments today." I roll my shoulders to work out the tension that's gathered there.

Saylor's face softens. "You weren't supposed to see those."

"Well, I did. And nobody wants to watch a wasted fuckup, so let's head back to the hotel and do something fun."

"You're not a fuckup."

I drop the mask and meet her eyes. "You ready to die on that hill alone?"

"Yes." Her chin lifts. "But I'm not alone. Do you hear all of those fans?"

I let my attention shift to our surroundings. We're still backstage, but the band and the production crew have disappeared. Velvet Inferno is done with their set and packing up their equipment.

Then I hear what Saylor means. The noise level is insane. With the rest of the band already onstage, the audience is going nuts. But then I remember the videos and the comments. I shake my head. "I can't do it."

Saylor grabs my face in her hands. "They're cheering for you. Some of them drove hours to be here tonight. Some paid *hundreds* to get a ticket in the pit. Are you really going to do that to them?"

"They'll find someone else to follow," I say thickly.

Her palm hits my cheek with a resounding smack. "How dare you do that to me."

Lifting my hand to my face, I blink at her. I'm not sure what surprised me more, the slap or her words. "Do what to you?"

"I came on this tour to support you, to help you show the world that you have what it takes. And you're just going to throw all of that out the window and give up?"

Who is this woman, and where has she been my whole life?

My sigh carries the weight of the world on its back. "Do you have any idea how hard it is to get up there on a night when I'm feeling good? I don't have what it takes, baby." The term of endearment slips out before I can stop it.

"Of course you have what it takes," she says. "You have a number one hit and three others on the charts. You got an expedited album *and* a six-week tour deal from one of the top record labels in the country. You have twelve million followers on TikTok, and that number climbs every day." She pauses for a breath before continuing. "You somehow, against all odds and my better judgment, convinced me to follow you around the United States for a month and a half and play your girlfriend." Her tongue flicks out to lick those luscious lips. "Do you think I would do that for anyone but you?"

Something happens while she is talking. My heart gets noticeably lighter, like someone has tied it to a hot-air balloon and fired it up. Instead of a black cloud of despair hanging over my head, I can make out the colors of a rainbow.

"You are Rhett fucking Cole, so get out there and show people what that means," she says quietly.

I don't think. This isn't a moment for thinking; it's a moment for doing. So I grab her and kiss her soundly, taking her mouth with mine like it belongs there—because it fucking does, and it feels so good, she feels so good. But Noah is at my side, barking something in my ear about needing to get out there.

I drop another peck on Saylor's lips, give her the biggest grin in my arsenal, and follow my tour manager to the stage entrance. At the top of the steps, I turn back and give her a wink. I'm pleased to see that she's still flushed and those pink lips are still swollen from our kiss.

The crowd goes wild as I walk out to center stage and grab the microphone. "Hello, Dallas," I say into it, and they lose their shit.

Maybe Saylor's right and Eddie's wrong. Maybe I'm not done yet.

I don't have a plan for how to bring my image back and keep the label happy. Right now, I'm just focusing on getting to the end of tonight's show without any major catastrophes. So when the thought pops into my head, I go with it.

I wait for the applause and cheers to die down, then grin into the mic, letting the cool metal of the grille brush against my lips. "I've got a surprise for you all tonight."

24

"Rolling in the Deep" - Adele

Saylor

I feel like I just ran a marathon. Sagging against the wall backstage, I hear Rhett getting the crowd excited, but I'm not listening to his words. I'm calculating whether I have enough time to head back to the hotel for a quick nap before the party.

No one ever tells you running after a rock star is so hard.

For a few minutes there, I didn't think I'd convince him to get onstage. The look in his eyes—it will haunt me forever.

They tore him to shreds online. That may happen to a lot of celebrities and public figures, but Rhett's more sensitive than people think. There's a lot to unpack with that, and it's not something I'm prepared to do. Leave that one to his therapist.

My mission is accomplished, and I'd prefer to get out of here. I'm missing home and my plants and the peace inside my flat. Hell, I'm even missing Paula barking at me through the walls to turn my music down.

Only a few more weeks of this tour, then I'll be back to my normal life. Only it won't be normal at all, not after spending the best weeks of my life with—

Noah, Rhett's tour manager, is looking at me funny.

"What?" I say, and reach a hand up to my mouth, wiping the corners in case of any stray chocolate smears. Do I have spinach in my teeth? I didn't even eat a salad today.

I scan the space for Leo so I can ask him to drive me back to the hotel, but Noah approaches before I can locate him. He looks a little like Glen Powell but shorter. "Are you going up there?"

I blink a few times. "What are you talking about? Going where?" Am I so tired that I can't even follow simple conversations?

He nods toward the stage entrance. "He's calling for you."

I turn my horrified eyes toward the stage. My ears snap into action for the first time since pushing Rhett out there. And then I understand what Noah is talking about.

"Saylor." Rhett's voice is magnified by the speakers, my name bleeding out of every pore of the building. "Where are you, baby?"

I close my eyes and sag into the wall. What the fuck is he doing?

When I reopen them, Noah is still standing in front of me, a questioning look on his face. "You need to get up there."

"What—" I try to make the words come, but my mouth is simply a gaping hole.

"You need to give the audience what they want," he says.

The cheers from the crowd register. They've taken up chanting my name until even my heart is beating in time to "Saylor, Saylor, Saylor."

I shake my head, tongue still thick and numb. "I can't."

We agreed there'd be no cameras. Rhett promised to keep my name out of the press. If I go out there, the entire world will know who his mystery girlfriend is by the end of the night. My quiet life as Saylor Jones will be over.

"You don't have much choice." Noah grabs my arm—not hard, but firmly—and leads me to the stage steps. "Just go out there, smile and wave, and you can come back down."

The roar from Rhett's fans is insane. My ears are on the verge of popping.

"Saylor," Rhett calls through the mic. "Get out here."

I pause with my foot on the first step and turn back to Noah. "I really don't want to do this."

He shrugs with indifference. "It'll be fine. They'll love you." He gives me a nudge with his hand. "Now go."

I ascend the stairs like a zombie, dread filling my stomach so quickly I can already taste the bile. The lights blind me as I leave the shadows of backstage. When I step into view, the crowd completely loses it. They're screaming louder for me than they usually do for Rhett himself. I'm not sure if that should make me feel good or even more terrified.

Rhett looks like he's just won the lottery. If his grin grows any wider, I'm scared that beautiful face will break in two. He either can't read the terror on my face or just doesn't care, because he grabs my hand and drags me to the front of the stage.

I shoot Jamal a *help me* look, but he just shrugs and smiles down at his guitar. My feet follow Rhett to his microphone because they're out of other options. I'm here now; I can't very well slink backstage without causing an uproar. The lights make my eyes squint until they're nearly shut. How does Rhett stand this every night?

Hand still firmly clamped around mine, he leans into the mic. "I am madly in love with this girl."

He's looking at the audience as he says it, and that crazy-ass grin is cemented on his face, but my heart still skips a beat. There's no way he meant that, right? It's just part of the act.

I'm still trying to convince myself of that when Rhett places both hands on my jaw, cupping me between them like he always does, and leans in to claim my lips with his own.

We've kissed hundreds of times by now, but this one feels different somehow. Like I've become untethered from the buoy keeping me afloat. Like someone snipped the strings of my hot air balloon heart and I'm drifting toward heaven.

He tastes like the peppermint toothpick he spit out right before taking the stage. He tastes like adrenaline and energy and nerves. He tastes like an expensive mistake, the kind you never tell your mum about because you don't want to hear her lecture on life choices.

He tastes like finding that hidden treasure at the thrift shop, the one you squeal when you spot and bury in your cart before anyone else can see it. He tastes like a rainy day curled up with a tattered copy of *Pride and Prejudice* on the sofa. He tastes like the soaring joy you feel when you help someone weaker than yourself, when you watch their eyes brighten for a moment as they say thank you.

He tastes like the best moments of your life preserved in a scrapbook, ready to be flipped through again and again.

He tastes like . . . *home*.

Rhett ends the kiss slowly, drawing back, eyes fixed on me. His smile has disappeared. In its place is something I can't identify, because I've never seen him wearing this expression before, and it makes me nervous to not know what he's thinking right now.

We stand that way for five, ten, twenty seconds. I'm not keeping track, because I don't have the ability to move, let alone do anything as complicated as counting.

As slow as molasses, he lets his hands fall from my face, his gaze still muddled together with mine. Then, like the crack of a gunshot, the moment is broken.

Immediately, the noise of the crowd breaks through the fog in my head. If they were excited to see me enter the stage, they're going *ballistic* now. Out of the corner of my eye, I can see security keeping crazed fans from approaching us.

As the sounds around me start registering, so does what just happened.

Rhett just dragged me onstage during a show, kissed me soundly, and introduced me *by name* to the crowd. The whole thing will be splattered across the internet in a matter of minutes if it hasn't been already.

He's back at the mic now, although he's angling his body toward me, prompting every eye in the place to focus on me as well. "That was the best kiss of my life," he says, and the audience roars. "I'm not sure how I'm going to play the set."

The dizzying high I was experiencing up until this moment fades away, and I'm left with a growing realization of what this all means. I narrow my eyes and stare at Rhett coolly, but subtly enough that no one who isn't within a few feet of us would be able to make it out.

There's no going back now. The damage is done. Turning to the crowd, I wave as Noah instructed, then blow a few kisses for good measure. This delights the fuck out of them, so I wave for a few more seconds before retreating.

As I'm leaving, Rhett's voice rings out once more. "Isn't she amazing? Ladies and gentlemen, my girl!"

The din of cheering chases me all the way backstage. I don't even pause at the bottom of the steps. Leo is standing near the exit, and I head directly for him. "Let's go," I say.

He ushers me out of the building and toward the car. I'm a lady, so I'll wait until Rhett has completed his show, but then I'm going to murder that bastard.

25

"Stay" - The Kid LAROI + Justin Bieber

Rhett

Tonight's show was by far my best one yet. I can feel it in the air, buzzing around like a downed wire. The fans loved it, they loved me, but they went ballistic over Saylor. Bringing her up to join me was the most inspired idea I've had since writing during rehab.

I don't see Saylor backstage as I'm being escorted to the meet and greet, but she's probably already headed to the club for the after-party. All of the groupies waiting for me are clamoring for more details about our relationship, and I put them off as best I can. It's better for business to make them guess, keep them on the hook longer.

But there's no denying that things shifted tonight. The excitement coursing through the crowd as I played felt different, more electric. I can't wait to see how social media responds to this. They're going to eat it up, and then Eddie will have to eat shit.

The meet and greet can't end quickly enough for me. I'm desperate to get back to my girl, to find a dark corner somewhere and recreate that incredible kiss. Out of the dozens of women I've kissed in my lifetime, none of them have come close to being that incredible. There's something about Saylor that drives me to the edge. And apparently I'm not the only one who feels that way.

When Bear ushers me inside the VIP room of the club the label rented for the party, my eyes immediately scan the space for her. It's dark, lit only by colored glow lights near the floor. I make my way around the room, shaking hands, accepting congratulations, and signing autographs, all the while keeping my eyes peeled for her.

By the time I've circled the space, I'm confident she's not here. Besides, if she were, she would have come up to me by now. You don't kiss someone like that and *not* want to spend every second with them afterward.

Right?

The image of her on the bed talking to her fucking ex-husband, who had to go and have an honorable career like being in the bloody military, haunts me. What if she's talking to him right now? What if the kiss wasn't real for her the way it was for me?

I set my lowball glass down hard on the table next to me, and the girl who's been chattering at me for the past five minutes jumps. She glances down at my hand, then back up at my face, worry now lurking in her eyes.

"Sorry," I mutter, before draining the contents of the glass. I need to get out of here. Without excusing myself, I head over to Bear. "Where's Saylor?"

He must have been prepared for this question, because he doesn't even radio Leo. "They're at the hotel."

I snap my fingers, already halfway to the door. "Let's go."

* * *

The drive to the hotel is only a few minutes, thank fuck, because my mind is working against me full-time. Is Saylor sick? Is she exhausted? Is she sick and exhausted of me? Is she talking to him?

Is she planning to get back together with him? My brain generates every single disaster and fires it at me.

Every single fucked-up scenario but one.

I walk into our hotel suite and stop short. Saylor is a mad whirlwind, flying around the bedroom and throwing things into the open suitcase on the bed. My brain, which was overactive just seconds ago, decides that now is a great time to take a vacation.

"What the fuck is going on?"

I don't realize I've said it out loud until she whirls around, her eyes full of a crazed energy. No, not energy—*anger*. I've never seen that look on her face before, and it scares me. Not for myself, but for her. Even when she accused me of flirting, she just looked pissed. This is something different entirely.

She doesn't say anything, just stares at me with those wide eyes, frozen with something akin to fear.

"Hey," I say, and reach out a tentative hand, as though she's an injured kitten. "What's going on?"

"What's going on?" she repeats in a hysterical voice, tossing the shirt she's holding into the bag. "Are you really asking me that?"

I wait several beats for a better answer to present itself, but when none comes, I say, "Yes?"

Her eyebrows drop lower, and she turns away. She picks the shirt back up and refolds it. "Unbelievable," she says under her breath.

"Babe, tell me what's going on." *I really want to be kissing you right now.* I take a step closer, then stop, not wanting to frighten her off.

Her chest rises and falls with her breathing, which I note carries a hint of panic. Did something happen between the concert and now? Did someone try to hurt her? My imagination runs wild again. Did—

"Not all of us are obsessed with the spotlight." She punctuates this sentence by slamming the lid on her bag and zipping it shut.

"Okay," I say slowly. She's told me this a million times. "But why are you packing?"

The look she throws my way could cut a vein. "If you really have to ask me that, you're more stupid than I thought."

I've never felt more like a Neanderthal than I do at this moment. "We don't leave for Houston until tomorrow morning," I offer. I feel her eye roll in my gut.

"I'm sleeping on the bus." She yanks the suitcase off the bed and heads for the door.

Panic washes over me like a tidal flood. I'm still clueless as fuck, but I'll be damned if I'm going to spend the night away from this woman. "Saylor," I say to her retreating back. "Wait."

She doesn't, just keeps walking. When I realize she has no intention of talking to me further, I move instinctively, running to reach the door before she can and blocking it with my body. Her eyes narrow as she takes me in, arms spread to prevent her from getting out.

"Talk to me," I say, my voice an octave higher thanks to the desperation coating each syllable. "Please."

Fire dances in those dark eyes, and I want nothing more than to reach out and grab her, to kiss away everything between us until she forgets why she's mad and that this was all supposed to be fake.

"You promised." Her words are watery, and a crack splinters through the center of my heart.

I slump against the door. "Promised what, baby?"

Her chin trembles, but at least she's meeting my eyes. "You promised to keep me out of the limelight."

"I said I'd *try*."

The sadness evaporates from her face, chased away by anger. "Was that you trying tonight, then?"

Is that what this is about? I let out a sigh of relief and move away from the door. "Babe, it was bound to happen at some point."

"Yeah, from a rogue camera that made it into an after-party or a crazed fan who happened to snap a picture as we were leaving. Not because you *dragged me onstage.*"

The venom in her words slaps me across the cheek. I blink away the sting of it. Is she . . . embarrassed to be with me?

"I'm sorry," I say quietly. "I just got caught up in the moment."

She sniffs loudly, and I realize the anger is just a front to cover up the pain she's actually feeling. Using the sleeve of her sweatshirt, she swipes at her nose.

Extending my hand, I take another step toward her, but she backs away just as quickly. My heart plummets off a cliff. "I'm sorry," I say again.

She wipes away the trail of tears on her cheek, then tilts her chin upward, the picture of stoicism. "You don't need to pretend to be in love with me to sell records, Rhett."

Is that what she thinks? That this whole thing was a ploy to increase sales? "Oh, baby." I move close enough to grab her waist and tug her against me. With my other hand, I tuck her hair behind her ear. "I haven't been pretending for a long time."

26

"we fell in love in october" - girl in red

Saylor

I pretend to be asleep when Rhett leans down to press a kiss to my hairline. I'm not ready to face the music yet, but since we're heading to Houston today, I don't have much choice. After I hear the door to the suite shut, I swing my legs over the side of the bed and make my way to the bathroom. I've got at least half an hour before he returns from his run.

I allow myself the space of one shower to dwell on the events of last night. As the hot stream hits my back—the water pressure in this hotel really is something—I remember the way Rhett's mouth moved over my body, the way his hands seemed to cradle me, chasing away whatever lurked in the shadowy recesses of my soul.

I try not to think about what he said. *I haven't been pretending for a long time.*

We didn't talk about it then, and I have no intention of doing so now. What is there to talk about? I don't think he's lying. I think he truly believes he loves me. But Rhett Cole falls in love with a new girl every two weeks. I'm just another pretty face and hot body in his bed, but I refuse to be yet another broken heart he tucks away in his jacket

194

pocket as a souvenir.

I force myself to turn off the spray and the fantasies still playing on a loop in my head. Now is not the time to imagine a future with Rhett. It will never happen, and picturing it will only lead to further disappointment. The best thing to do right now is pretend that nothing happened last night. Or at least nothing besides sex.

I was even planning to forget about what happened at the concert, but once I'm settled in the armchair in the sitting room with a cup of black tea and my phone, I realize the rest of the world has no intention of doing the same.

It's *everywhere*.

My feed is filled with videos of our onstage kiss and users trying to uncover my identity. It's like the wink multiplied by ten. They can't stop talking about the way he grabbed my face, the look in his eyes, the look in mine. Apparently, it was the best kiss in the history of kisses. I'm not sure how they've verified this, but after watching some of the footage, I will admit it does look pretty hot. It *was* hot, even if I was too terrified and angry to fully enjoy it.

A quick Google search confirms that even some of the celebrity gossip sites are picking up the story. My only saving grace is that Rhett didn't use my last name, but it's only a matter of time before they discover it.

I set my mug aside, my stomach suddenly queasy. This was never meant to happen. It's exactly why I made Rhett promise to keep my identity a secret. I have no desire to be a feeding source for those vultures. They'll pick at my bones for years to come.

A premonition of this exact thing happening has been playing at the edges of my mind this entire trip. It's why I hesitated in the first place. Sure, I wasn't thrilled at the thought of being Rhett's plaything for six weeks, especially knowing my weakness for him, but *this* was the real reason I didn't want to do it.

Rhett's relationships have been in the tabloids for years now, ever since the first time he dated Princess Beatrice. It seems the public has as much of a thing for a bad boy rock star as I do.

When he inevitably drops me at the end of the tour, I was hoping to be able to return to my life as it was before, not continually haunted by photos and videos of our time together.

But after last night, that is nothing but a pipe dream.

* * *

The tour bus is loud. Six men, little more than overgrown children hyped up after playing shows night after night, are splayed out on the furniture of the lounge. I step out of the bunk room with my laptop. I thought I'd be able to work on the bed, but I need better back support than that.

Jamal watches me settle in at the small table in the corner, a wicked gleam in his eyes. "Saylor," he calls. "You can come sit with me."

I toss him an amused smile and fire up my computer. I know he does it just to get a rise out of Rhett.

Like a dog needing to mark his territory, Rhett gets up from his position on the sofa and walks over to me. I've managed to avoid him all morning, but now that we're with the band, I have to keep up the act of being the adoring girlfriend who just had the hottest kiss of her life in front of a stadium packed with people.

He looks so good—dark green joggers, a black short-sleeve mesh top, and a pair of scuffed Vans. His hands are shoved into his pockets as he approaches, and I know that means he's nervous. Rhett Cole doesn't *get* nervous, so I'm not sure what this is about. Is he afraid I'll bring up what he said last night? I smile to let him know I have no intention of doing so.

He still looks tentative as he bends down to give me a kiss, a chaste one on my cheek. "Hi," he whispers, breath tickling my ear.

"Hi," I whisper back. Now *I'm* nervous.

"Can I join you?" he asks.

I give the small booth I'm sitting in a pointed look. "I'm working on the content calendar for next week . . ." I let my voice trail off, hoping the insinuation is clear enough and that I don't have to spell it out for him. I don't want to hurt him, but I don't want to sit next to him in agony for the next three hours either.

"So I'll watch you." He slips a hand over my jaw and into my hair.

I can sense Jamal's eyes on us, so I smile sweetly back at Rhett. "You'll distract me."

A grin spreads across his face. "I certainly hope so."

After dropping a kiss on my lips—less chaste this time—he slides into the seat next to me. I stifle the irritation I feel and scoot over to make room. Of course the guy couldn't take a hint and leave me alone. Fucking fantastic.

I try to focus on my screen and ignore him, but within thirty seconds, it becomes obvious this will be impossible. He places his hand on my thigh, innocently at first, but then it creeps higher, squeezing tighter, wandering inward. I squirm in my seat and elbow him in the ribs.

"Ow," he says, even though there's no way I hurt him.

"I'm trying to work," I say quietly as his hand reaches the seam between my hip and thigh.

"Me too," he says, keeping his eyes focused on the front of the bus.

"Really?" I mutter. "How's that, exactly?"

"You're my inspiration. I'm getting inspired."

I snort and open my calendar. There are less than ten days left of this tour. I can't decide if I'm excited or disappointed by that. On one hand, I know I'll be thrilled to be home again, but— I refuse to think about Rhett or the hole that will be left in my heart when we say goodbye.

I knock his hand off my leg. "You're keeping me from doing the exact thing you're paying me for."

He moves it right back. "I'm paying you for other things, and if you want to head to the bedroom, I can remind you of what those are."

I whip my head to the side to look at him. "I sincerely hope you're joking."

He blinks at me. "About which part?"

"You are not paying me for sex," I hiss.

"Of course not." His face is the perfect mask of innocence. "That's simply a perk."

I roll my eyes and turn to face my computer again. When he starts rubbing his hand over my knee, I finally snap. "Rhett, please. Just—" I force myself to look at him so he'll take me seriously. "Just leave me alone. I can't get anything done like this."

Several beats pass as he stares at me, then he gets up and walks back to the sofa. A strange uneasiness washes over me as I watch him go, as though I've just sent a stray dog from the back porch without a meal.

Now that he's gone, I should be able to work, to actually accomplish something instead of mooning over a man who will most definitely break my heart if I let him. Still, it feels like a small hairline fracture has already spread across the surface.

Rhett picks up his guitar and starts playing. The other guys are talking too loudly for me to pick out the notes, but the melancholy way he's sitting, the way he avoids looking at me—I don't need to be able to hear it to know what it sounds like.

He's sad, and I made him that way.

Great. Even when he's not with me, he's still making it impossible to get anything done. My eyes keep drifting to the way his fingers are moving along the neck of the guitar. I can almost feel them on my own neck. My brain is only too happy to supply memories of the way those hands feel on my body, the way they drag over my skin as if trying to memorize it.

After a few minutes, he looks up and meets my gaze. Instinctively, I drop my eyes back to my screen, but I can already feel the flush climbing. When I glance back a little later, a tiny smile is playing at the corners of his mouth.

I give myself a mental slap. *Focus, Saylor.* I pull up recent job postings for back home. I've been scanning nonprofits for openings, but nothing has popped up yet that feels like a good fit. Fortunately, Rhett's generous payment for me joining him on this tour will last me for a little while. I plan to save most of it to maybe buy my own flat someday. It's a good thing I opened that separate account when I did. I shudder to think what might happen if—

Rhett stands abruptly and walks toward me, a man on a mission. I bite my lip as he approaches.

When he reaches me, he tugs it out from between my teeth. "Don't bite your lip unless you want me to fuck your mouth."

On impulse, I release it. My heartbeat drums through my chest. Slowly and deliberately, I sink my teeth back into my bottom lip.

Fire dances in his eyes. "I see," he murmurs. Then before I have a chance to react, he yanks me from the booth. "Let's go."

My pulse drums so loudly it could replace Diego in the band. Speaking of the band, I glance back over my shoulder to where they are all watching us with amused looks. "Rhett," I whisper as he tugs me toward the bedroom. "Everyone will know what we're doing."

He shuts the bunk room door behind us, then presses me up against it. "Why do you assume I give a shit?"

"Um." I search my mind for a reasonable answer, but none is forthcoming.

He leans in close, his words feathering over my ear. "Now get on your knees and suck my cock the way you know you want to."

As if he's spoken directly to them, my knees buckle beneath me, and

I find myself on the carpeted floor of the bunk room. I don't think the door behind us even locks. If someone finds us in here, I will die of mortification on the spot. But the thought of putting Rhett in my mouth? It surpasses all thoughts of embarrassment.

He moves so that he's the one leaning against the door, then unzips his joggers. The sound of that zipper alone is enough to spike my libido. Saliva fills my mouth as he tugs his pants down and frees himself from his black Calvin Kleins. He fists his cock and rubs his tip over my lips. My tongue darts out to taste him. As I make contact, he rolls his head back and groans.

I lean forward and pull him into my mouth. He groans even louder, loud enough that I wonder if the guys can hear us. They're just on the other side of this door, and somehow that makes the whole thing even hotter.

Sucking Rhett deep, I cover my teeth with my lips and move over the length of him. I'm not sure he's even aware of what he's doing, but his hands reach up to cradle my head and guide me up and down. All of a sudden, his eyes fly open, and he looks down at me. The pressure on my head increases as he thrusts into my mouth harder and harder. I blink back tears and try not to gag.

A grunt accompanies each thrust of his hips, and I know he's close. I suck harder, deeper, faster, and suddenly he comes, releasing into the back of my throat like a fire hose. I swallow every drop of him, then lick my lips after he pulls out.

His eyes turn devious as he watches me lick his cum off my mouth. He swipes at a spot I missed and sticks his thumb past my lips. I dutifully suck on it, and he gets this wrecked look on his face, as though that act is sexier than the blow job I just gave him.

Suddenly and without warning, he pulls me to my feet, grin stretching wide as he pushes me toward the bedroom. "Your turn," he whispers.

27

"Seven Devils" - Florence and the Machine

Saylor

There's an awkward tension in the bus, no doubt thanks to Rhett's and my rather loud hookup in the bunk room and the fact that he hasn't been able to keep his hands off me ever since. I can't say I've forgiven him for what went down onstage last night, but here's me hoping it'll all blow over soon.

Rhett and I are sitting together on the sofa as he works on a new song. The bus slows, and through the tinted windows I can see the streets of Houston surrounding us. We've only been on the road a little over three hours, but I'm already sick of the stale recycled air in the bus. I can't wait to breathe in the sultry Texas heat.

The driver parks outside the music venue, and we all gather our things. I think the band is probably even more eager to leave the bus than I am.

I'm packing up my laptop when I notice a shift in the atmosphere. I glance up to see that Noah is on the phone, his face tight. The rest of the guys are also staring at him, as though they're waiting on a verdict.

Noah ends the call. "That was security. We're to stay inside the bus for now."

"What?" Jamal does not mask his irritation very well. "What the fuck for?"

Before Noah can answer, Rhett hops onto the sofa and peers through the blinds. "Holy shit," he says under his breath.

The others clamber over him to see what's going on. The window in the kitchenette is closer to me and unoccupied, so I move over there to see what they're looking at, and holy shit is right.

A sea of fans is being held back by no less than six security officers on the other side of the bus. Some of them look like they've been here for a while. The guards are doing what they can to keep them at bay, but the order to stay on the bus suddenly makes sense.

One of the guys whoops, but I don't turn to see who. My gaze is focused on the signs being held up by the crowd. Most are some variation of "I love you, Rhett," but a few are directed at me. "Sailor, who R U?" and "We want Saylor." I release the blinds and take a step back.

Rhett appears at my side almost instantly. "You okay?" he asks, running his hand up and down my back.

I nod and swallow the lump growing in my throat. Am I okay? Definitely not. Am I going to tell him that right before what might be the biggest show of his life? Definitely not. I direct a blinding smile his way. "Great."

He answers with a smile of his own, then drops his mouth to mine. "Since we're stuck here anyway . . ." he murmurs.

I sniff out a laugh. "I think the band might stage a mutiny."

He shrugs and leans in for another kiss. "Then they'd be out of a job."

"Still, better not to risk it," I say, unsure if I'm referring to the band or the state of my heart.

He groans and straightens. "You're a vixen."

Before I can respond, his phone rings. I can't hear the voice on the other end, but given the way Rhett's shoulders stiffen, I assume it's someone from the record label.

"Uh, thank you, sir." His eyes flash to mine before quickly darting away. "That wasn't really my intention—"

There's a pause as the other person interrupts.

Rhett's face colors. "I'd rather not."

They apparently don't care whether he would or wouldn't, because the color in his face deepens more the longer they talk.

Finally, he says, "That's not happening," and ends the call.

I raise a brow. "What was that?"

He shoves the phone into his back pocket. "They thought bringing you onstage was a ploy to increase ticket sales."

"Wasn't it?" I cross my arms over my chest.

His face goes the way a person's might when they're being accused of a terrible crime. "Of course not."

I'm not sure if I believe him or not. Is he actually delusional enough to think he's in love with me, and *that's* why he did it?

* * *

Thirty minutes later, the security team finally lets us off the bus. They called in local law enforcement to help, and we won't be allowed to leave the venue until after the show tonight.

We're ushered into the greenroom, where I'll be spending the rest of the day while the band practices and runs through sound check. At least I'll have plenty of distraction-free time to focus on searching for jobs.

I'm too scared to open social media. After the shitstorm outside, I'm terrified to see what's going on online. Rhett needs to get a new social media manager, and he needs to do it soon. We're heading home in a matter of days, and I have no intention of sticking around to run his accounts after we get back. My heart couldn't handle it.

Maybe I should spend some time looking for someone to take my place, because there's no way Rhett can go back to doing it himself after this.

My phone rings just when my eyes are ready to bleed from staring at the screen. It's my mum, and I've never been happier to hear from her in my life. I shift my laptop off my lap and stand as I accept the call. The makeup crew is setting up next to me, so I head out to find a quieter spot.

"Hi, Mum," I say, closing the door behind me. I'm backstage now, where the band gathers before the show. It looks different than it will tonight, all lit up and bustling with people at the moment.

"Hi, baby." Mum says something else too, but with the roadies setting up for the show, it's too loud to hear.

I cover my other ear with my hand and move down the corridor. "What was that?"

At the end of the hallway, a neon-red exit sign glows, and after a quick glance around, I decide to risk it. The fans will all have disappeared by now. Besides, this is a rarely used side entrance. No one will even see me.

The door leads into a back alley holding several rubbish bins and surrounded by a chain-link fence. Not a place I'd want to visit at night, but it seems harmless enough in the middle of the day.

After Mum gives me the latest details about her and Dad's travels, there's a significant pause, then she says, "Anything you want to tell me?"

I realize now why she's calling me. It's not to catch up.

I pretend to search for an answer. "Nope, can't think of anything."

"Saylor, I've watched the videos."

Oh, fuck. This is even worse than I thought. If she'd just read an article, I could have played it off as stupid celeb gossip. "What videos?"

I say, because I'm stalling, not because I want to hear her say it.

"You kissed him. In front of cameras." The tone in her voice says a whole lot more than her words do. *What were you thinking?*

"It was just an act, Mum."

"And what kind of act is that?"

I sigh heavily into the phone. I don't have the time or mental bandwidth to explain the whole thing to her now. Besides, she wouldn't understand, even if I had all day. "It was his idea. He was just trying to please the crowd."

"What about Nate, baby?" Her voice is quiet—too quiet.

I really don't want to get into the dirty details of the divorce with her over the phone, certainly not when we're separated by oceans, but she deserves to believe she raised me right. "I filed for divorce."

There's a beat of silence as she processes this, and I picture her covering her open mouth with her hand. "Why didn't you tell us?"

"It all happened kind of quickly." Well, not *that* quickly, but I don't want her to feel guilty about traveling. "I'll explain more when you get home."

"I'm worried about you, Saylor. We can come home if you need us to."

I consider saying, "Yes please, I miss you," but discard the thought just as quickly as it came. They are on the trip of a lifetime, and I'm not about to ask them to cancel it because of a stupid boy—or rather two stupid boys—who broke my heart. "I'm fine, really. I promise. You don't need to worry."

"But honey, you know that's what I do best."

A chuckle slips past my lips. "Yep, I'm aware of that. Try to relax, though."

She murmurs something, but a flash of movement on my right grabs my attention, and I miss her words. A guy has just rounded the corner of the alley and is headed my way. I ignore him and ask my mum to repeat herself.

She does, and we chat a bit more, until I realize the man is slowing his pace. I glance over at him, and when our eyes meet, the sides of his mouth pull upward into a creepy-ass smile. I frown and tell Mum I need to go.

"Okay, I love you. Make good choices," she says. The line goes dead, and I'm left with the gravity of the mistake I've just made. This man does not appear trustworthy, and I just severed my only connection to another person. What kind of idiot am I?

The door into the building is between us, but I'm closer to it than he is. I bolt toward it and yank on the handle, but nothing happens. It's locked. I curse myself for not propping it open. This is taking idiocy to a whole new level.

The man is still approaching. He leers at me, not even attempting to hide his glee. "Looks like it's locked, honey." His voice sends chills down my spine.

I unlock my phone and search for Leo's number in my contacts.

"You don't need to do that," the guy says, moving close enough that I can smell the body odor emanating from him.

I stifle a gag and take a step backward. He moves faster, though, and swipes the phone from my hand. A small cry of protest leaves my lips.

"I'll just hold on to this for a second," he says, and slips it into the pocket of his jeans. "Now." He takes another step closer, and I retreat until I'm pressed against the brick of the building with nowhere to go. "What's a guy gotta do to get a kiss like the one you gave onstage last night?"

"I don't know what you're talking about." I look down the alley to my right, but the street is a long ways off, and I have no doubt this man could outrun me. He's got at least twelve inches on me.

He laughs, and the sound makes nausea churn in my gut. "Don't mess with me, baby. I know who you are."

Why didn't I take those self-defense classes I kept meaning to sign up for? Because I couldn't afford them, obviously. But I would rather have gone without food for a week than be in this position.

"I'm just on the makeup crew," I say, jerking a thumb over my shoulder. "Came out here for a smoke break."

His smile falters for just a second before he glances down. "I don't see any cigarettes."

"I'm feeling uncomfortable," I say. "Please leave me alone."

He chuckles as though I've just requested he bring me a Happy Meal. "Why don't you stop talking now and do what we both know you're so good at?"

I open my mouth to reply as he comes closer. I have to breathe through my mouth in order to avoid gagging from the stench. My mouth is as dry as the Sahara, but I try swallowing anyway. "And what's that exactly?" It's nothing more than a croak. I don't have a hope of hiding my fear anymore.

"Why don't I open my pants, and we'll see." The man leans that disgusting face closer, and I clench my hand into a fist, but I can't remember if you're supposed to tuck your thumb inside or not.

He runs one beefy finger down the side of my face, and I do my best not to let my shudder be visible. Fear will only egg him on, and repulsion will only make him rougher.

"Please," I say. "Just leave me alone." I settle for leaving my thumb outside. It seems like the safer option.

"You'll be saying please when—"

The rest of his sentence is cut off by the door opening so hard and fast it slams against the brick on the other side. Rhett barrels through, followed by Bear and Leo. Before the PPOs can stop him, Rhett sends the man reeling backward with a single fist to the jaw. He doesn't even wait to see what kind of damage he's inflicted, just grabs me and leads me back in, letting Bear and Leo handle the trash outside.

Rhett and I stop right inside the corridor, a single shaking mass. I'm not sure which of us is trembling harder. I clutch the front of his shirt and bury my face in his chest. His hands don't stop rubbing my back, alternating between long strokes and gentle circles.

"I can't decide if I'm angrier at you or Leo," he says quietly.

I lift my head, unable to keep the sarcasm from my voice in spite of what almost happened. "Or maybe the perv outside?"

He glances down at me. "Oh, he's going to die."

28

"In the End" - Linkin Park

Rhett

I climb the steps to the stage more shakily than I ever have before. Even before my first show of the tour—in fucking New York City—my hands weren't trembling like this. I can barely hold on to my guitar pick. I have no idea how I'm going to pull this off.

Swinging my guitar behind my back, I walk up to the microphone. The crowd goes wild as the lights come on and they see me for the first time. I grin out at them, and some of the tremors in my hands ease. I can't for the life of me remember which city we're in, so I glance down at the ink scrawled across my palm.

"Hello, Houston!" I yell.

The returning roar is deafening, and it works wonders at dispelling the image of Saylor pinned against the building, that creep's hands—

"How are y'all doing tonight?" I do my best to put on a Texan accent, but it muddles with my Wesbournian one into a ridiculous mashup that sounds more like a cartoon character than John Wayne. Fortunately, my fans find it amusing. "Are you ready for some music?"

As they shout their enthusiasm, I toss a look over my shoulder at the band, even though the guys are familiar with the routine by now.

We break into the intro of "Chasing Shadows," and the crowd goes even wilder, if that's possible.

I can play the set in my sleep, and sometimes I do. Being onstage loses some of its luster when you play thirty shows back-to-back, but I don't think the high from playing for a crowd this size will ever get old.

Finding my girlfriend being attacked, on the other hand . . . That's the kind of shit that will haunt me all night long.

I can't think about what might have happened if I hadn't gone outside when I did, if I hadn't demanded to see her before the show, if we'd given up on finding her after searching the entire building with no luck. If I can't keep those thoughts away, this show will end up a disaster, and my contract and reputation will land in the gutter.

Get your head in the game, Rhett.

Leo has promised to never leave her side, even if she needs to use the restroom. An agreement I thought we'd already made, but apparently I was the only one who thought so. I nearly ripped his head from his shoulders when I discovered he wasn't keeping an eye on her. And that was *before* we found her. He'll be lucky to have a job after this.

The ending notes of the song bleed into the next one, "Take a Chance on Me," which is currently sitting at number three on the charts, and which no one but Saylor knows is about my stint in rehab. I wrote it after four weeks of sitting in that place, when not a single one of my friends had come to see me, with the exception of Slate.

I guess you could psychoanalyze the lyrics and probably find something that points back to my relationship with my dad, blah blah blah. But none of that shit matters, because my fans love it. It can apply to anyone in any situation, and that's what makes a hit song. Write something people can relate to, put a good beat to it, and watch it soar to the top of the charts.

The crowd seems wilder tonight, thanks to the media attention after that bloody kiss. I'm almost beginning to regret it. Not the kiss—it was sexy as hell—but doing it in front of that many people, especially if it means my girl will never be safe again.

I'm also pretty sure Saylor hasn't forgiven me for it yet, although I don't see what the big deal is. I have no intention of letting her go once this tour is over, so who cares if the world knows she's my girlfriend? She'll need to get used to the spotlight at some point if she wants to be with me.

But maybe that's the problem. Maybe she doesn't want to be with me. I fumble over the chord progression and fight back a wince. *Head in the fucking game.*

Of course she wants to be with me. I've seen the way she looks at me, the way her breath catches in her throat when I touch her. The way she lights up when I wink at her. The way she absolutely saturates herself within seconds of being in my arms.

I miss the next few notes and mutter a mental curse. This is worse than after I dragged Saylor onstage last night. I didn't think I'd be able to play after that, but god, at least I wasn't missing actual notes in a song I fucking wrote.

Turning my attention to the fans singing along, I push all thoughts of Saylor from my mind. She's more distraction than muse these days.

Some of the groupies in the pit are wearing tees that say "I'll be your sailor tonight" and "Kiss me, Rhett!" A few of them raise their shirts and flash me when they catch me looking. I grin and shake my head. Nice racks, all of them. Uninterested, all of me.

We play the rest of the set, and at the end of two hours, I'm drenched in sweat. They weren't joking about this Texas heat. Thank god it's late autumn and not the middle of the fucking summer. I wave my goodbyes, knowing I'll be back in just a second for an encore, but playing my role perfectly regardless.

Before I can head backstage, the chanting starts. I sense the rest of the band tensing up behind me, unsure what we're supposed to do. I toss a glance at Jamal, because fuck if I know. The roar from the crowd only increases. If they were demanding another song, fine. We'd give it to them. The audience gets what the audience wants.

But that's not what they're demanding. They want Saylor.

"Saylor, Saylor, Saylor." I already know I'm going to hear that chant in my head over and over tonight as I try to fall asleep. What the fuck have I pulled her into?

I look at Jamal once more, but he just shrugs both his shoulders and his brows. He would probably throw her to the wolves if she was his, the fucking bastard.

I walk back to the mic and wrap my hands around it. Press my smile against it, search for the right words. "I don't think Saylor feels up to appearing tonight."

There's a chorus of boos, but I'm not about to make the same mistake again. Anything that puts Saylor in danger isn't worth it, no matter how much my fans may want it.

"Instead of Saylor, we'll play an extra two songs for you guys," I say, hoping this compromise doesn't send the label execs into a fucking tizzy. My girlfriend is off the table, and if they want to fight me on that, they can go fuck themselves.

We play the extra songs. I can tell it's a lackluster trade for the crowd, but screw them. Saylor is more important than their need for a show.

I wave good night for the last time and make my way backstage. My phone rings before I've even reached the last step. *Eddie.* He must have been watching the show live, even though it's three in the fucking morning back home.

"We have a problem," he says when I answer, because the guy doesn't believe in preambles.

My gut tightens instinctively. He wouldn't be calling me right now if it wasn't really bad. I brace myself for whatever is coming next. They're pissed I didn't bring Saylor on, there's been more bad press, they're dropping my contract. At this point, I'm even ready for the news that they're stealing all of my money, too.

"Have you been online?" Eddie says, his voice clipped.

I grab the towel Noah tosses my way and use it to dry the sweat on my neck. "Gee, Eddie. I forgot to pull my phone out between songs and check my socials." I throw the towel back to Noah with more force than necessary, and he gives me a look. "No, I've been playing a fucking show for the past two and a half hours."

I don't see Saylor or Leo backstage. After what happened, I hope he took her to the hotel. We had barely five minutes together before I had to get onstage. I would've blown off the entire show, but Leo assured me he'd take care of her this time and Saylor insisted I not skip it.

"You're going to want to take a look," Eddie says. "I'll wait."

I roll my eyes but don't ask what the hell I'm supposed to look for. Instead, I slide down against the wall, letting my muscles relax for the first time since discovering Saylor was missing. My hands are still shaking as I lower my phone, both from fear and the adrenaline from the show.

I type my own name into the search bar. Before I even spell it out entirely, "Saylor Seegmiller" pops up alongside it as a suggested query. The knife in my gut twists even further at the reminder that she was once his, that stupid fucking wanker who doesn't deserve her. I want to chop off her last name and any other reminders of him that she has.

She'll be pissed they've already figured out her last name, but those TikTok sleuths mean business. You can't hide that kind of information for long. It'll be fine. She'll see. She can legally change her name back to Jones and put this whole thing behind her.

The first article promises to uncover the identity of Rhett Cole's "secret" girlfriend. Is this what has Eddie's panties shoved up his ass? That my girlfriend is getting press? I skim the page, but they're just announcing Saylor's real name to the world, as if that part wasn't already obvious, given the suggestion in the search bar. The time stamp catches my eye as I'm hitting the back button. It was published this morning, so why the hell is Eddie calling me about this now?

I scan the rest of the search results, and a video grabs my attention. The headline says, "The truth about Rhett and Saylor." I click on it and watch as some girl with a high ponytail and too much makeup promises to uncover the truth about America's favorite pop star and his girlfriend.

The video already has thousands of comments and even more likes. I skip past her endless barrage of lead-up—I have better things to do with my time than listen to her nasally voice—and finally arrive at what she's been driving at this whole time.

"Not only is Saylor Seegmiller still married to her husband, Nathan Seegmiller, but she hasn't filed for divorce or even separated from him," the girl says.

I scoff and roll my eyes. Eddie got worked up over nothing.

"On top of that, her husband is *active military*. He's currently deployed, although his location is not disclosed—obviously. So while he's been out serving his country, his wife has been traveling the United States with a *rock star*."

Even though she can't see me, I flip the girl off through the screen anyway. With her stupid ponytail and her over enunciation of the words "military" and "rock star," I want to tell her what she can do with her bogus information. It doesn't even matter that it's not true. Thousands of people have already watched it, and they will all believe it. That Saylor's cheating on her soldier husband with me.

The whole thing is a crock of shit. I tell Eddie so.

He doesn't say anything.

"You still there?" I ask, thinking maybe the call disconnected while I was watching the video.

"I'm here."

"She's not married anymore, okay?" I get to my feet again. Noah's looking antsy, probably because I should've been at the meet and greet ten minutes ago. "She just hasn't changed her name back to Jones yet."

Eddie clears his throat. "As much as I wish that were the case, buddy, unfortunately it's not."

"What are you talking about?" The hair on the back of my neck stood up the second he called me "buddy," and it's not lying down any time soon.

"The label's been looking into it," he says. "Took us most of the day, but we finally confirmed it."

"Confirmed what?" I wish he would just get right to the point and spit it out. Better yet, I wish he'd get off the phone so I can get to my girl and make sure she's okay. God forbid she went online and saw any of this.

"There were no divorce papers filed, Rhett."

My heart stops in my chest. Where there should have been two beats, three even, there's just silence. "What?"

"There's also an interview with the husband already circulating."

I sink back to the floor without even realizing what I'm doing. "Tell me you're shitting me." It comes out as a strained whisper.

"I wish I was, trust me. You can watch the interview yourself if you want. But I'm warning you, it's not pretty."

I shove my hand into my hair and stare at the concrete floor. A million thoughts are swirling through my head right now, and not a single one of them makes any sense.

"Your contract was explicit about no scandals of any sort," he continues.

"What are you saying?"

"I'm saying this constitutes a scandal."

I drop my hand from my face. "You've got to be fucking with me."

"It's all spelled out in the contract. Have your agent send you a copy if you don't believe me."

"So you're canceling me?"

"We haven't made a final decision yet. But the possibility is something you should prepare for. In the meantime, we need to stay out in front of this, so we'll be arranging several interviews where you'll have a chance to give your side of the story." He clears his throat again. "Your responses will be prewritten by our team here, of course."

Of course. Because Rhett Cole is too much of a bumbling idiot to be able to speak for himself. He's too much of an idiot to realize that the woman he thought was his girlfriend is actually someone's *wife*. Someone who had no idea she was traveling with and fucking a famous pop star. No wonder she didn't want her name or photos leaked.

I end the call with Eddie and tell Noah to cancel the meet and greet. Screw the record label, screw my contract. I don't care if I never play another show again. There's no way I'm going anywhere until I get to the bottom of this. After pulling up the search engine once more, I type "Nathan Seegmiller" into the bar.

The same video pops up multiple times, shared by various commentators putting their own spin on this "crazy turn of events."

If there was any doubt in my mind before, it's obliterated the second I click on the first video. I would recognize that boring-ass crewcut anywhere.

29

"Drown" - Bring Me The Horizon

Saylor

The hotel room is aggressively air-conditioned, even though it's the middle of November. I'm buried beneath the thick duvet, because that seemed easier than adjusting the thermostat.

Images of the man in the alley have been playing through my head like an ad that shows up on every video you watch. I can still smell his sour breath and body odor even though I sprayed Rhett's cologne on my pillow and keep inhaling as deeply as I can.

I have no idea if Rhett expects me at the after-party. I didn't have it in me to attend the show. I was way too shaky, and Leo agreed to bring me back here so I could take a hot shower and go to bed. But attending the concerts isn't part of Rhett's and my agreement. Going with him to the parties is.

My hair has to be a huge mess by now, crushed by the pillow and tangled with the number of times my hands have been in it. The makeup I put on this morning is long gone, washed away by the millions of tears I've cried since this afternoon.

I don't know if I'll ever get over how close of an encounter that was. If Rhett hadn't come outside when he did, I probably would have been

217

raped. Sexually assaulted, at the very least. I was planning to punch him, but there's no way I could have actually overpowered that guy. I've already mentally set aside a fraction of the payment from Rhett for self-defense classes when I get home.

Until then, I'll be fine. No more wandering around alone. Leo hasn't left my side since it happened. He's been stationed outside the door ever since retrieving my phone from that creep and escorting me back here. Rhett threatened to fire him, so he's stuck to me like peanut butter on bread.

I took a nap earlier, but a nightmare woke me up. I've been too scared to try falling back asleep since then. Having Rhett's arms around me tonight will hopefully keep the demons at bay.

I'm scrolling social media when I see it. I initially swiped past, but then my subconscious kicked in, the way it does when you think you see someone you recognize.

There's no way in hell it could be him, but I scroll back anyway to double-check. A kind of paralyzing chill washes over me when I realize I was right. It *is* him. Nate. My ex-husband.

"—married to Saylor Seegmiller?"

I turn up the audio. It's a recorded FaceTime call with a white woman who looks younger than me. Who the hell is she, and why is she asking Nate about me?

Nate nods. "Yes, Saylor's my wife. What's this about?" He's still wearing his combat uniform, and I recognize the circles that form around his eyes when he's tired. I want to snort at his use of the word "wife." We hardly functioned as civil roommates the last time he was home. "Wife" is way too generous a term for what I was to him even before the divorce.

The girl looks disturbingly ecstatic at this information. I'm still trying to figure out what the point of all of it is when she says, "So you two never got divorced?"

Nate laughs. "Of course not."

I scramble to sit up in bed as the video continues. What is he talking about?

"Are you in the process of getting a divorce?"

Nate's brow furrows, and he shifts forward in his chair. "Why are you asking me these questions again?"

The girl adjusts the clear-rimmed glasses on her nose. "I'm doing a story on Saylor Seegmiller, your wife."

"Why would you assume that we're getting divorced?" he says.

Because we are . . .? The real question is, why hasn't he been served papers yet?

She ignores his question and says, "Are you aware that your wife is traveling in the US right now?"

Nate blinks in genuine surprise. I can see the wheels turning in his mind, wondering whether it's better to admit that he had no idea of his wife's whereabouts or pretend to have known so he doesn't look like a fool.

I'm still trying to figure out why he doesn't know anything about this yet.

Before he can answer her, the girl follows up with a second question. "Are you aware that your wife is currently touring the States with Rhett Cole? As his *girlfriend*?"

My heart careens across the room, and the phone drops from my hand onto the comforter. This cannot be happening. This cannot fucking be happening.

I bring my hands up to my face, willing the past twenty-four hours away. God, if only this were a nightmare I could wake up from. I would give anything to go back to last night's concert and never walk onto that stage. Any hope of slipping back into my quiet, normal life has just been obliterated.

The bedroom door opens. Not with a burst, like I half expect, but slowly and cautiously, the way you might check in on a sleeping person. Maybe Rhett doesn't know yet, and I'll have a chance to explain, although I have no idea what I'll say because I don't know what happened.

I filed the papers. I distinctly remember dropping the packet in the mailbox on my way to the airport. That was weeks ago, which means there was plenty of time for them to be processed and papers to be served to Nate, even on his military base.

I paste on a smile I don't feel as Rhett steps into the room, but it drops the second I register his face.

He looks haggard. He's still wearing his leather pants and red shirt from the show, but they're a crumpled mess. Did the groupies get their hands on him at the meet and greet? Or was he serious about the guy in the alley needing to die and decided to handle it himself?

His eyes roam over me, but it's like he doesn't see me. They're glassy and lifeless.

I push the blankets aside and swing my legs over the side of the bed. Before I can get to my feet, he speaks.

"Is it true?"

I'm still clinging to the hope that he hasn't seen Nate's interview. "Is what true?" But as soon as the words are out of my mouth, I can tell that they are the wrong ones.

His face turns stoic as he continues to watch me. "Are we really going to play this game?"

"Rhett," I say, moving toward him.

"Don't insult me." He narrows his eyes, and I stop in my tracks. "Is. It. True."

The way his voice clips the end of each word leaves no trace of doubt in my mind. He knows everything. I guess I should just be glad he came back here himself and didn't just have Leo throw me out.

"Rhett, please let me explain."

The hard lines on his face melt into incredulity. "Explain what, Saylor? That you lied to me about being married? That I just watched your *husband* laugh at the thought of the two of you getting a divorce? Which part are you going to explain?"

"I'm just as confused as you are." I take another step toward him and hold out my hand. "But I'll get to the bottom of it, I swear."

He shakes his head and paces to the other side of the room. "It won't change anything. According to the courts, you're married." Placing both hands on the windowsill, he stares out at the dark night sky.

"I swear to you I filed those papers. I don't know what happened," I say to his back.

He gives a derisive snort. "Yeah, but all we have to go on is your word."

His words hit like a slap to the face, a switchblade sinking into my heart. Tears burn in the corners of my eyes. "What do you want me to say?"

He whips around so quickly, I jump. "The label is threatening to drop me because of this."

I bite my lip as the tears finally spill over. I knew this would happen, didn't I? I knew that if I fell in love with him, it would destroy me. But silly me thought it would be at the end of the tour when he grew tired of me. Not because he thinks I betrayed him.

"I'm sorry," I say again in a watery voice. "I don't know what else you want me to say."

"You said there was no other guy."

A rush of air heaves from my chest. "Technically, you asked if I had a boyfriend, and Nate is the furthest thing from a boyfri—"

"Yeah, he's your *husband*," Rhett growls, eyes narrowed like an animal on the prowl.

I take a step backward, and his face relaxes slightly. "I don't love him," I whisper.

"You're still legally his wife." He spits the words out as though they taste bad. I guess if I found out he'd been married to someone this whole time, I'd probably spit those words out too.

"There had to be some kind of mistake," I say. "I'll call the courthouse and find out what happened." I wait for him to say he believes me and that we can go back to being what we were, whatever that was.

Shaking his head, he places both hands on his narrow hips. "You told me I shouldn't hide the fact that I was in rehab. But this whole time—" He plants a fist against his mouth. Is he fighting back tears? After a few seconds, he says, "At least I never *lied*."

The look in his eyes brings a sob to my own throat, and I clamp my hand over my mouth to keep it inside. There's nothing I can do to stop the tears, though. They rise up and spill over like a leaking dam. He still thinks I'm lying.

I scrape my brain for something, anything, that will convince him I'm telling the truth. "I love you." The words burst out of me, my last-ditch effort at salvation. They weren't premeditated, but they're no less true for it. "I wasn't expecting to feel this way, but I've fallen completely in love with you."

If he has any idea how much it takes for me to say those words out loud, he gives no indication. The pain on his face only deepens, as if by speaking the truth, I've only made what he has to do that much harder.

"I should never have pestered you to come on this tour," he finally says, his voice a soft rumble. "You were right to say no."

Another splinter of my heart breaks off and falls to the floor. The regret is so strong I can taste it, metallic and sickly.

"I gave you my heart, and you didn't have the decency to tell me yours already belonged to someone else?" he continues.

"It doesn't belong to him," I choke out between sobs.

"You're married, Saylor. To some bloke in the military who looked pretty torn up when he found out what we've been up to."

I want to snort at the thought that Nate gives a damn about our marital status. "He wasn't, trust me. There's no love lost between me and Nate. He's been hooking up with other people for years."

Rhett looks sick enough to vomit. "How do you expect me to believe anything you say after this?"

It's as though he's buried a knife in my chest. I'm afraid if I look down, I'll see blood pooling on the rug beneath my feet.

"This will ruin me." His voice is quiet, deathly quiet.

"We can talk to the label," I say, swallowing back the tears clogging my throat. "Tell them there was some kind of mistake. Maybe we can use it to your advantage. The publicity could be great." My voice rises at the end like a plea.

The expression on his face doesn't change. It's full of so much pain, it's brimming over. "I wasn't referring to my career."

30

"Breathe" - Taylor Swift + Colbie Caillat

Saylor

My chest is so tight it's hard to breathe. Rhett's words have punched two massive holes in my lungs, and I have to fight to get enough oxygen. He moves toward the door, presumably to attend the after-party.

I glance in the mirror over the dresser. My face is mottled from my tears, what's left of my mascara now running in twin black streaks down my cheeks. The T-shirt I've been wearing all day is wrinkled. "Do you want me to come with you?" I say. It will only take me two minutes to freshen up.

He stops with his hand on the doorknob but doesn't turn around. "I don't know why you would."

There's a soft thud as his words hit my heart, and I bow slightly from the impact. "Because that's why I'm here?"

He slowly turns toward me, his dark eyes dull and lifeless. "You're here because I wanted you here. Right now, that's not the case."

The door closes behind him, and I slump onto the bed. My heart crashes to the floor, shattering in spite of the plush carpet. This is it. The whole thing is over. Whatever we had, whatever we were, is in the grave.

I don't know how long I lie there crying. Thirty minutes maybe? When my inner well runs dry, I sit up and glance around the hotel room. Rhett's and my things are strewn around together like a normal couple's. His jeans over the back of a chair, my bra on top. Our phone chargers tangled together because there was only one outlet next to the bed. The shower holds both of our shampoos—mine a generic drugstore brand, his an expensive French one I can't even pronounce. I used it once, then walked around all day sniffing my hair because it smelled like him.

The memory releases a small reservoir of tears I didn't know existed. On impulse, I grab my stuff from the shower and shove it in my bag. I clear the vanity of my makeup and skin care, dumping all of it into my suitcase, not even caring if it spills.

I have to get out of here. If Rhett doesn't want me around, if I no longer serve the purpose of fake girlfriend, the only thing my presence will do is make things worse for him. I've ruined enough of his life. The best thing I can do is leave so he can pick up the pieces without me shattering any more of them beyond repair.

Most of my clothes are in the closet on the bus, but I retrieve the items discarded around the room and shove them in my suitcase. I change into a pair of leggings and an oversized sweatshirt from uni. My breakup clothes get pushed to the bottom of the bag. I'll probably never wear them again.

I should've filed for divorce sooner, made sure everything was squared away before leaving the country. I thought I had time, because I was never planning to go with Rhett in the first place, and I really needed that housing stipend.

And what do I have to show for my stupidity? A broken heart for me and a ruined career for him. I have no doubt any brokenheartedness he's currently experiencing will be soothed by the first girl he takes home after the party tonight. A week from now, he won't even remember Saylor Jones.

I stick my head out the door. Fortunately, Leo is still stationed outside. Part of me was afraid Rhett had dismissed him the way he dismissed me. "Can you help me carry my bags?" I ask the PPO.

A faint look of surprise crosses his face. "Are you sleeping on the bus tonight?"

"I need to stop there for the rest of my things, but I was wondering if you could take me to the airport? I have a family emergency."

Concern replaces the confusion, and he nods. "Of course."

Once I've retrieved my stuff from the bus, I rejoin Leo, who is standing by with a car. It's started to rain, which only feels appropriate, and we drive to the airport in dreary silence. What is there to say? Leo has never been much of a talker, and words have become foreign entities for me.

True to my nature, I ruined the person I cared most about. The only thing left to do is hope this publicity helps his record sales. I may not be able to undo the damage, but at least I can save him from me.

Once we're at the airport, it occurs to me that there may not be any available flights until tomorrow, but sleeping on the hard plastic chairs is still preferable to facing Rhett's anger and disappointment in the hotel room.

Leo helps me get my bags to the ticket counter, where he deposits them at my feet. "I hope things are okay with your family," he says.

I feel bad for lying to him, but I can't bear to tell him the truth and see the disappointment in his eyes. "Thank you," I murmur. "For everything."

He shifts uncomfortably. "It's been my pleasure."

After he walks away, I heft my bags into my arms and make my way to the smiling receptionist. I explain the situation to her, and she says she'll see what she can do. Several minutes later, she announces that she was able to transfer my ticket to a red-eye flight leaving in two hours.

Gratitude washes over me when the realization hits that I'm heading home. I'm finally going back to Wesbourne, where I'll be able to duct-tape my heart back together. It won't be pretty to look at, but at least it won't be strewn about my chest as though someone hacked it to pieces with a machete.

31

"Doomed" - Bring Me The Horizon

Rhett

The after-party sucks. To be fair, the glamour of them wore off after the first few weeks. I consider myself a party animal, but there's only so much schmoozing a guy can do before becoming exhausted. I miss my friends. If they were here, it would liven things up for sure.

I nurse my drink as I listen to a guy whose name I've already forgotten drone on about his plans to become a rock star. I want to tell him that he needs to hit the gym if he wants to make it on the big stage, but letting him talk frees up my mind so it can drift to better things.

Things like Saylor's huge fucking secret. I still can't believe it. All this time, she let me think she was into me. If she had just told me she was still married, I would've walked away. At least I think I would have. Maybe, if I'm being completely honest, even that wouldn't have deterred me. She got under my skin, and now it's going to take fucking surgery to remove her.

I set my empty glass down on a nearby table and wish the guy in the black-and-white-checkered shirt who is telling me about his millionth song, which I don't give a flying fuck about, would shut the hell up.

On instinct, I glance around the room for Saylor, hoping I can get her to distract me.

But then I remember that she's not here and why that is. Fuck me.

I pick my glass up and slam it back down, hard enough for the guy to startle and stop midsentence, giving me the perfect opportunity to escape. I wave two fingers at him and head for the door, Bear right behind me.

I'm dreading the confrontation with Saylor. It got ugly before, and I have no desire to relive that, but part of me is still eager to see her. Mostly the part below my belt.

Maybe I overreacted before, but she fucking lied to me. About being *married*, for god's sake. What else has she lied about?

I'm not delusional enough to think this won't affect my reputation. The label will likely drop me, unless they can find a way to spin it to their advantage. They'll throw me under the tour bus if it means more album sales.

My name's already been dragged through the mud, and it's only going to get worse from here. At best, I'll look like a bloody fool, at worst, a cheating bastard. All because she couldn't just tell me the truth. Maybe there was some mix-up with the paperwork, but she could've at least warned me, couldn't she?

The hotel suite is quiet when I step inside, and I assume Saylor's already gone to sleep. Good thing there are two bedrooms, because I'm going to need some space to process everything. There's only a week left on the tour. We can figure shit out after that.

As I'm grabbing my stuff from the room we shared last night, I realize the bed is empty. Maybe she's in the other one? Curiosity won't let me hop in the shower without finding out, so I walk across the hall and quietly open the door to the second bedroom.

It's empty as well. *Well, fuck.* Is she in the bathroom? I check, but the lights are off. Then I notice the vanilla-scented lotion she's always using is missing from the nightstand. She doesn't go anywhere without that stuff, which can only mean one thing.

She's not here.

I sink onto the bed and bury my face in my hands. Where the fuck did she go? I replay our last conversation in my head, when I told her I didn't want her here anymore. It wasn't exactly the truth, because now that she's not, there's an ache in my chest that's making it hard to breathe.

She must have moved to the bus for the night, which is probably for the best. We both need a little space to figure things out and calm down. We'll talk tomorrow and work something out.

* * *

In the morning, I grab a coffee from the hotel restaurant and walk with Bear to the bus. The roadies loaded the equipment last night, so the only thing we still need is the band's luggage.

I'm wearing Ray-Bans, partly to hide my identity from the other hotel guests and partly to cover the fact that I only got a couple of hours of sleep last night. Apparently, I've become dependent on holding someone who smells like vanilla in my arms in order to fall asleep. Stupid fucking wanker.

I hang out beside the bus, not exactly eager to face Saylor yet. The rest of the band staggers out of the hotel, appearing to have gotten no more sleep than I did, but for entirely different reasons. Jentry and Diego were going strong at the party last night, and Jamal had no less than three girls in his lap when I left.

Finally, everyone else has boarded, and I have no choice but to climb on as well. I've got shit to put in the bedroom, so I reluctantly make my way to the back of the bus. I hesitate with my hand on the knob, then remind myself that Saylor and I are both adults and can work through this.

I enter, expecting to find her still in bed, but it's empty. Not only that, but it doesn't even look slept in. My brow furrows as I step inside. The bathroom door is open, so I know she's not in there. A trickle of unease flits down my spine. I reach for the nearest closet, the one Saylor uses, and open it. It's empty.

I drop the bag in my hand, and it hits the floor with a dull thud. If she's not on the bus—

I run back to the front, not caring if I look like an idiot. The driver is already pulling out of the car park. "Wait," I say, breathless. "Saylor's not on yet." Before he can respond, I unlock the door and hop off.

The hotel receptionist looks up in surprise when I come to a halt in front of the desk. I give her my most dazzling grin. If Saylor didn't sleep on the bus, she must have gotten another room.

"Good morning, Brittany," I say after a quick glance at her name tag. "I'm wondering if my girlfriend got a room here last night. Saylor Jones?"

She gives me an apologetic smile. "I'm afraid we can't give out that information."

Something occurs to me. "It might be under Saylor Seegmiller. If you could just check?"

Brittany shakes her head, small smile still on her lips. I'm amusing her. "I can't do that. I'm sorry."

I place both hands on the counter and lean forward. "Brittany." I insert as much charm into my voice as I can. "Please. I'm begging you. I just need to know if she stayed here last night."

A flicker of hesitation crosses her face, but then it vanishes as she offers me another weak smile. "I'm really sorry. There's—"

"Do you know who I am?" I ask.

She blushes. "Yes."

"Listen, I'll give you free tickets to my next show if you'll just—"

"Rhett."

I turn to see Leo crossing the lobby toward me. My brows knit together as he comes closer. Why isn't he with Saylor? The nausea that's been churning in my stomach all morning rises until I can taste bile in the back of my throat.

"Where is she?" It comes out with more venom than I intended.

Leo doesn't even flinch. "I took her to the airport last night. You didn't know?"

"No, I didn't fucking know. Why the hell did she leave?" I say, even as the truth of it hits me between the eyes. *Because you're a grade-A asshole.*

"She said there was a family emergency. I thought you knew."

I stand there, like the idiot that I am, as the reality of my situation sinks in. There is no family emergency. Her parents aren't even at home, and she doesn't have any siblings. I drove her away with my anger and disbelief. God, I thought she just needed space. I didn't realize she'd *left*.

Leo looks at me, concern in his eyes, but I ignore him and head for the door. If he took her to the airport last night, it's too late to stop her. She's probably already back in Wesbourne by now, my heart tucked into her carry-on.

* * *

We spend a grueling day on the bus. The guys seem to know better than to bother me, but eventually I can't handle their chatter and retreat to the bedroom. I pull out my phone and stare at Saylor's picture. She's so goddamn beautiful it hurts to look at her. Before I can change my mind, I send her a text.

Why did you leave without saying goodbye?

After five minutes, there's no response, but I don't really expect anything else. I'm the one who fucked up. Falling back onto the bed, I gaze up at the ceiling and run last night's argument through my head again. No matter how you spin it, I was a shithead to her.

She still hasn't replied to my message, so I send another one.

I'm sorry for the way I acted. Forgive me?

What I really mean is *Come back?* but I know better than to expect that. We're nearly to the end of the tour now. The best I can hope for is that she agrees to let me make it up to her when I get home.

When we get to New Orleans, the concert bombs. It's the worst show we've ever played. I forget my own lyrics—the ones I spent weeks perfecting. I miss no less than three intros to my own goddamn songs. When I screw up the timing during "What We Never Said," there are several boos from the crowd.

I'm on a fucking roll.

And like the twat I've become, I take it out on the band. "What the hell was that?" I ask them as we all dry off backstage.

Jamal drapes a towel around his shoulders and looks me dead in the eye. "You mean you screwing up every single song? We were wondering the same thing, mate."

I clench my hands into fists to keep from pounding him. "It was a complete shitshow. Every single one of you is to blame."

"Mate, maybe you need to calm down," Jentry says.

"Don't you fucking tell me to calm down." I don't give a shit if he's right. Tonight sucked, and it was not all my fault.

Chase tosses me a water bottle. "Hey, so the show bombed. It happens."

"Not less than a week from closing." I unscrew the cap, then guzzle the water without stopping. When it's empty, I throw it at the nearest rubbish bin and miss. "We're practicing all day tomorrow."

A disbelieving laugh comes from one of the guys, but I don't bother seeing who. I pick up the water bottle and crush it in my hands before throwing it away.

"Dude, that's insane," Jamal says.

I whirl around on him. "Is it? Good thing you're not calling the shots, then."

"What's going on?" Noah approaches, goody-two-shoes face on and ready for action.

"Mind your own business," I snap.

He doesn't even flinch. "I am."

"I think Rhett needs to get laid," Jamal says, causing someone behind me to snicker.

"The girlfriend suddenly makes sense," Diego says.

My jaw is clenched so tight, something pops. "What did you say?" I ask, turning to him.

Diego laughs nervously and holds up his hands. "Nothing, mate. Just understand why you brought her, is all."

"Where is Saylor, anyway?" Chase asks. He normally doesn't say much, and I wish he'd keep it that way. I don't like the sound of her name on his lips.

"Yeah, man. I haven't seen her all day," Jentry says.

"Fuck off," I tell him. "That's none of your business."

"Rhett, you need to chill," Noah says.

I flip him off.

"Seriously." His face doesn't show an ounce of humor or fear. "Go outside and clear your head. You can't do the meet and greet until you've calmed down."

My nostrils flare as I glare at him, but he doesn't back down. As I head toward the back door, one of the guys mutters, "God, I sure hope Saylor comes back."

32

"Love in the Dark" - Adele

Saylor

Paula overwatered my plants. It's the first thing I notice after stepping inside. Well, that and the musty smell of a room that's been closed up for way too long. Before I left, I turned the thermostat as low as I could without freezing my pipes, and the plants haven't loved that either. Some of them look like they're barely holding on.

I drop the bag from my shoulder, and it hits the floor with a thud. The sound vibrates through my feet, making me feel something for the first time since I left the tour. Straddling one of the bar stools, I sigh and place my face against the cool countertop. I'm happy to be home—ecstatic, even. So then why don't I feel better?

Probably because the stack of mail Paula left on the counter is nothing but bills. I sift through it, and my attention snags on a large manila envelope on the bottom. After pulling it out, I recognize my own handwriting. This is the divorce paperwork, "Insufficient Postage" stamped front and center.

You've got to be fucking kidding me. I put five stamps on this thing, and that still wasn't enough? I blew up Rhett's career and my own heart over a lack of postage? This is taking the miscommunication trope to a whole new level. At least it revealed Rhett's true colors before I could fall any harder, if that's even possible.

I was right about the rest of the mail being bills. My rent is due, and I open my banking app to send the payment. When my balance appears on the screen, my heart freezes over. Forty-seven dollars and a few odd cents. Forty-seven measly dollars to my name. That's not even enough to cover my electric bill, which is also due, let alone my rent.

Thinking it might just be a glitch, I refresh the page. It reloads, but my balance remains the same. Did Nate somehow get ahold of this account, too? I scroll through the activity, but there's been none since I left five weeks ago. That can only mean one thing.

Rhett never paid me.

As I close the app, I notice that I have several unread text messages. They must have come in during the flight, all of them from Rhett. Just seeing his name on my screen brings a fresh flood of tears to my eyes. It feels like someone has carved my heart out with a sword, leaving nothing but a gaping hole behind. I shouldn't, but I read all of them.

Why did you leave without saying goodbye?
I'm sorry for the way I acted. Forgive me?
Saylor
Please
I miss you
I know I fucked up and I'm sorry. Can you please call me?
Baby

The last one hits me like a sucker punch to the gut. I don't need to be next to him to hear the tone of his voice—the low, sultry notes of it as he brushes my hair away from my face.

Pressing my thumb and forefinger into my eye sockets until the tears disappear, I take several steadying breaths. I cannot worry about Rhett right now. Obviously, I'm not going to call him or even reply.

What happened was inevitable. Sooner or later, we were both going to have to face the fact that whatever was going on between us could only ever be short-lived.

I drop my phone, and it clatters onto the counter. It's time to think about survival. I don't have anything in the flat that's edible, and forty-seven dollars will barely stock the fridge. I'll be lucky to still have a roof over my head and electricity by the end of the week.

Rhett must have forgotten to send my money, and after everything that's happened, I can't imagine he still plans to. It's not like I held up my side of the bargain. Nor am I about to call him up and ask where it is. I'd rather sleep in a cardboard box.

As much as I'd prefer to fall into bed for the next ten hours, I need to earn some money, and fast. I change out of my leggings and into jeans. Thanks to the flight, my hair looks like the aftermath of a tropical storm, but I don't have time to mess with it. I cram my bowler hat on my head and walk to the thrift shop.

Justine is sympathetic to my plight, but the schedule's already full. "I thought you weren't coming home until next week, girl. I don't have any open shifts."

I grab onto my heart before it can sink down to my toes. "That's okay. I'll figure something out." I smile to let her know I'm not upset, but my tears are ready to brim over. Again. Fortunately, they wait to do so until I'm outside the store.

It starts drizzling as I'm walking home, and for once, I'm relieved. At least now my tears aren't recognizable—they just look like rain. Water drips onto the floor of my flat when I step inside, and I wish for the millionth time that I had a dog to welcome me home. Someone who would be genuinely excited to see me, regardless of how badly I'd messed up in the past. But that would hardly be fair to him or her. I can't even take care of myself—how could I possibly provide for another being?

I sink onto the mat inside the door so I don't track in more water. Then I put my head into my hands and let the tears fall.

How did I end up here? Five years ago, I was doing better than ever. Uni was great, I had Timie, I was volunteering at Restore Hope in the evenings and on the weekends. I may not have known what I was going to do with my life, but anything felt possible.

Little did I know I'd fall in love twice, get divorced, have my heart smashed to smithereens, and face homelessness within a few short years.

My sweatshirt sleeves are growing soaked, but I don't care. I cry for myself, I cry for Rhett, I cry for what we could have been. I even cry for Nate, for all the places we went wrong. Isn't it funny how beautiful things can break just as easily fracture by fracture as they can from a huge crash to the floor?

I miss the tour. The thought surprises me. I thought I would be glad to be home—and I am—but I didn't expect it to feel so lonely. I miss the guys. I miss Leo and trying to make him smile. I miss having someone looking out for me. I miss not having to worry about how much things cost. I miss the fun and the energy that always coursed through the bus and backstage.

But mostly, I just miss Rhett.

The thought sends another rush of tears down my cheeks. God, I miss him. He feels like a phantom limb. You know it's missing, but you still feel it attached to you. Will this feeling ever go away, or am I doomed to live like this for the rest of my life?

I force myself to get up and move to my suitcase, which is still dumped on the floor. I heft it onto the bed, then make myself go through the motions of unpacking. Sleeping sounds much more appealing, but it's time to be mature and handle my shit.

Turning on the Bluetooth speaker on my nightstand, I start Spotify. I just need to focus on something else for a while. Eventually, I'll forget about Rhett and the past five weeks.

There's an email from Nate in my inbox asking what the fuck is going on. I ignore it and toss my phone aside. That shit can wait. I don't have the mental capacity to handle his drama or interrogation right now. His act for the camera was nothing more than that—an act. What I told Rhett is true. There's no love lost between me and Nate. Not anymore.

I tug a flannel shirt from the bag and hold it to my nose. It still carries a faint hint of Rhett's cologne, because the last time I wore it, he wrapped his arms around me and held me close for what seemed like hours. I could survive on this scent alone for the rest of my life.

Realizing what I'm doing, I toss the shirt into the laundry hamper. It gets caught on the side and hangs there, taunting me, reminding me that everything I touch ends up looking like crap. I can't even get a bloody shirt in the basket.

Then it happens.

At first I don't register it, but as soon as his voice starts crooning at me through my speaker, my heart starts oozing blood all over the place, my body aware before my brain of what I'm hearing. I can't stop it, the pain. It's a living entity much stronger than I am, taking over until I can't breathe anymore.

I sink to my knees on the floor, clutching my middle as Rhett sings. Fumbling for my phone on the bed, I try to keep the tears at bay, but they don't listen. Will I ever stop crying over this man?

When my fingers finally close around my device, I can't bring myself to end the song. I know the lyrics by heart, but I don't sing along, just let his voice wash over me as he belts out "One More Night." What I wouldn't give for one more night with him the way we were before. One more day before everything went to shit and I had to walk away from the only man I think I've ever truly loved.

What we had was different from what Nate and I had. I thought

I loved Nate, but it never felt like this. I never lived to see him walk through the door, never felt safe with him the way I did with Rhett.

Rhett unlocked something deep inside me that Nate never stood a chance of reaching. Everything was surface level with Nate. We were physically attracted to each other, sure, but it never went deeper than that. We didn't talk about our dreams or all the ways we'd been hurt in the past. He never had a desire to know me in a way that others couldn't. And whenever I showed him a part of myself that I'd hidden from others, he didn't like what he saw.

The song ends, and I wipe my face. This is the last time I will allow myself to cry over Rhett Cole. It's time to move on and create some kind of normal life again. I have no idea what this scandal is going to do to my chances of getting a job, but I'll just have to keep looking until I find a place that is willing to overlook the fact that my face is plastered on every magazine in the checkout line at the grocery store.

I make a mental note to myself: *Don't apply at grocery stores.*

My phone rings as I'm unpacking my toiletries in the bathroom. I brace myself for the sight of Nate's name on the screen—or, God forbid, Rhett's—but it's only Timie. I can guess why she's calling. I answer anyway.

"Hey!" she says cheerily. "How are you?"

"I'm good." I refrain from commenting on the fact that this is the second time she's called me in the space of a month. "How are you?"

"Great!" Her voice sounds fresh and brisk as always, but we've been friends long enough that I can pick out the notes of tension in it. "Are you working today?"

"Nope, not today." I set my shampoo back in the shower caddy.

There's a pause, and I know she's trying to think of the right way to bring up the real reason she's calling. I let her flounder.

"Sooo . . ." She trails off. "I saw something crazy today."

"Oh, yeah?" I have to force curiosity into my voice. I wish she would just cut to the chase and ask me.

"Yeah," she says. "I was grabbing some things at the supermarket since the farmer's market isn't open today."

I roll my eyes. Timie will never not mention anything about her quaint little idyllic village when given the opportunity.

"And I saw you on one of the tabloids there." She punctuates this with a tiny hysterical laugh.

I bite back the urge to ask why that would be so surprising. Clearly, she doesn't think my life could possibly be interesting.

When I don't respond, she continues. "Is it true?"

"Is what true?" I have a cruel desire to make her say it out loud, delicate sensibilities be damned.

"That you're dating . . . Rhett Cole?"

I sigh and toss my empty cosmetics bag into the cupboard under the sink. "Not anymore, I'm not."

There's a slight pause, and then she says, "But you were?"

"Yep." Placing a hand on my hip, I judge my appearance in the mirror. No wonder Justine didn't give me a shift. I look like a trainwreck.

"Oh." Her voice is quiet enough that I have to strain to hear it. "I didn't even know you were out of the country."

"Yeah, I kind of kept that one under wraps." The official story I gave Paula and Justine was that my parents invited me to join them on their trip for a few weeks.

"What about Nate?" Timie says.

"What about Nate?" I toss an armload of laundry into the hamper, and this time it all whooshes to the bottom.

"I thought you loved him."

I give a sarcastic chuckle. "Nate and I haven't loved each other for a long time."

Several beats pass. "I didn't know."

If you would stop gushing about your fairy-tale life long enough to ask, maybe I could have told you. "Well, you've been busy," I say, unable to keep the patronizing tone completely out of my voice.

"What's that supposed to mean?" For the first time in this entire conversation, she seems to have picked up on my lack of enthusiasm for her call.

"Nothing, Timie. Nothing."

"It didn't sound like nothing."

"You're right. It's something." I slam the lid of my suitcase closed. "It's the fact that you waltzed out of my life and expected me to be happy about it."

I picture her mouth falling open as she takes this in. "Is that what you think?"

"Yep." I give the zipper a yank.

"I see." She clears her throat. "It wasn't quite like that."

"Yeah, I'm sure there were a few times you missed me, but the picturesque view out your window soon reminded you of what you gained from ditching me."

"God, Saylor," she says quietly. "Glad you're finally saying what you think."

"It's true, isn't it?"

"No, it's not true. The view out my window? It's a fucking alley, and our neighbors always have too much rubbish for one bin, but they refuse to get a second one, so there's always way more than what fits piled up beside the building." There's a short pause as she takes a deep breath. "And as for missing you, I cried myself to sleep for almost a year after we moved. I missed you so much, and I had so many regrets. I wished we'd never left."

I'm stunned speechless by both of these admissions.

She continues, "I begged Javiar to move back to the city, and he reminded me of why we chose this in the first place. It wasn't because I thought I'd be happier away from you. God, I can't believe you'd think that. We didn't want to raise our children in the city. We both grew up there and wanted better for our kids."

I think about my own parents' struggle to make ends meet working inner-city jobs. Combine that with the tiny flats, the high cost of living, and the pollution, and it's easy to see why the countryside might be a preferable place to raise a family.

"There hasn't been a day that's gone by that I haven't missed you." Timie sniffs, her voice watery with tears. "I would've told you all of this sooner, but you stopped calling."

I breathe around the catch in my chest. She's right. I did stop calling. "I thought you were better off without me."

She lets out a strained laugh. "I've been miserable for the past two years."

"What about all the playground mums? Sounds like you lot are pretty chummy."

An unladylike snort comes through the phone. "They're all ridiculous. Obsessed with their hair and their morning yoga sessions. It's completely obnoxious."

I can't help but laugh. "Sounds awful."

"You have no idea," she says, a smile evident in her tone. "I'm sorry for hurting you."

"Back at you," I whisper.

"Now," she says in that voice that means business, "I want to know everything there is to know about you and *Rhett Cole.*"

33

"Had to Leave" - Babytakeoff + SouthSideAce

Rhett

God, I hate social media. Before the tour, I loved connecting with my fans, but since the comments started getting nastier, I've stopped monitoring them as much. Of course, that's because someone else was doing it for me, but I refuse to think about her.

She hasn't replied to any of my messages, not that I can blame her. What hurts the most, though, is seeing that she's read them and still chose not to respond. Before, I could convince myself that her phone was turned off. Now there's no denying that she's ignoring me. We're officially over.

The number of comments on my posts has only increased in the past few days, thanks to those stupid videos that went viral, talking about the scandal that was mine and Saylor's relationship. It seems everyone and their grandma has an opinion about it that they think we should hear.

They're calling me an asshole rock star who took advantage of a married woman. (That one might be half-true.) They're saying I hate the military, and that I set out to hurt a soldier who was protecting me.

(Definitely not true.) The worst ones, though, are the ones directed at Saylor.

They accuse her of everything under the sun, including seducing me for the fame, swindling me out of millions of dollars, and using me as some kind of ladder to further her career goals. All of that is absolutely preposterous, and anyone who knows Saylor will know how far it is from the truth.

But that doesn't stop the blood from rising to my face every time I read another comment. I nearly respond to some of them, telling them to fuck off with their stupidity, but Saylor's words come back to haunt me, reminding me it never does any good. It will only add fuel to the fire if they see me interacting with them.

I pressured her into this situation. She told me no so many times I lost count, but I couldn't stand the fact that she turned me down. I could have had any girl I wanted, so when she didn't fall at my feet in gratitude at my invitation, it frustrated me. I was determined to add her to my fan club.

I ended up doing a whole lot more than that. I should have seen it coming, I guess. From the beginning, she fascinated me. Even at summer camp, she stood out among the hundreds of other kids there. And it wasn't just her looks either, although those are fucking incredible. It was the way she carried herself, like she didn't need anyone else's approval.

I fell hard back then, and I fell hard again this time. Who knows— maybe I never really got over her in the first place. It's fucked up in so many ways, but I would literally give anything right now to be able to hold her one more time.

We're on the bus, driving to some city in the southern United States, but honestly, I've stopped keeping track at this point. After the disaster in New Orleans, the end of this tour can't come fast enough.

The record label hasn't made a final decision yet. I can't blame them if they cut me, although all of this buzz does seem to be increasing my downloads. Either way, I don't give a shit what they end up doing. None of it's worth it if she's not beside me.

Damn it, I wasn't going to think about her, and now I can't stop. Last night, I ended up sprawled across the other side of the bed and on her pillow. When I woke up, I caught a faint hint of her scent on the fabric. It made me angry that I hadn't realized it was there before, that I'd gone nights without inhaling it, that it was nearly faded and I hadn't clung to it while I could.

What is she doing right now? Did she patch things up with that bastard who doesn't deserve her? Or are they actually over, like she said? I clench my fists until I can feel my nails pressing into my palms at the thought of him having her, touching her body, his hands in her hair, on her hips. Their mouths pressing together, her moaning when he tips her back—

I toss my phone across the bus, and it hits a kitchen cupboard before falling to the floor. The guys look up from their card game.

"What the fuck, mate?" Jamal asks.

I ignore him and go to retrieve it. Not because I particularly want it, but because if Eddie tries calling, I'm contractually obligated to be available to him. And if Saylor decides to call—

What a fucking idiot. She's not going to call. That much became evident the second I realized she wasn't going to text me back. Why the fuck am I always chasing her? I finally went too far and chased her away from me for good.

I'm dreading the show tonight. I apologized to the band for the way I handled New Orleans, but it's only a matter of time before I screw things up again. Who knew a feisty girl with black curls, brown skin, and a smart mouth would be the key to me performing well?

There was just something about knowing she was close by that allowed me to relax and play my fucking heart out. The night I saw her in the pit, I thought I was going to explode. She looked so fucking beautiful, and seeing her was so unexpected, I forgot what the hell I was doing for half a second. I think that was the night I officially fell.

I pull up her contact card in my phone and stare at the photo of us she snapped one day when we were goofing around on the bus. I have my arm slung around her neck, pulling her in close. Her brown eyes are wide and sparkling with laughter, that beautiful mouth pulled into a dazzling smile.

God, I miss her so much it physically hurts. There's this ache in my chest that won't go away. Is that why they call it heartbreak? Because it literally feels like your heart is breaking into a thousand tiny pieces?

I never thought I'd say this, but I'm actually looking forward to going home. I miss my friends, I miss not being stuck on a bus for hours at a time, I miss being able to hop into my car and drive anywhere I want without a bodyguard hovering beside me.

Will I get the chance to see her when I get home? It's a question that's been playing on a loop in my head. With the end of the tour in sight, it's only a matter of time until we're both back in the same city.

The question is, does she want to see me? Judging by her silence, I'm guessing the answer is no. After the way I reacted, the way I fucking doubted her, it would take a miracle for her to ever trust me again. I don't deserve her trust, and I definitely don't deserve her. More than the douchebag she married, maybe, but not by much.

Still, I ran into her once. What's to stop it from happening again? Would pulling a dick move like that just push her further away? Or does she miss me just enough that she wouldn't run?

I rub a hand over my face and lean back against the sofa. It's all stupid anyway. It doesn't matter if I see her again or not. Things are fucked up between us, and there's no going back. She's married, and I'm not the kind of guy she wants anyway. I have enough fucked-up problems of my own that she doesn't need in her life.

I'd be doing her a favor by staying away.

So then why the fuck do I keep imagining bumping into her somewhere, watching the look of surprise widen her eyes, her mouth pulling into a small O, a faint blush creeping into her cheeks? I need to scrub her from my memory, but it looks like that won't be happening anytime soon.

I grab my guitar from where it's propped against the seat beside me. There's a melody that's been haunting me for days, and so far I haven't managed to capture it properly, which pisses me off. What kind of musician am I if I can't compose the song in my own head?

Opening the notes app on my phone, I strum the chords I typed out: G-flat, B-flat minor, E-flat minor, D-flat. I run through the progression several times, switching up the order.

Chase looks up from the table. "Something new?"

I glance at him and nod. "Can't quite capture it."

He tosses his cards onto the table and moves to sit opposite me. "Try adding an A-flat to the end of each stanza."

I do as he suggests, and he's right. It sounds much better. "Thanks, mate," I say, giving him a look that I hope appears appreciative. I am—I'm just having a hard time smiling these days.

"What do you have for lyrics?" he asks.

I clench my jaw and strum a few more times, suddenly wishing he would fuck off and leave me alone. He can even have his A-flat back. It's not that I don't have lyrics, but I'll jump off a building before I share them with anyone besides the person they were written about. "It's just a melody at this point," I say.

He nods, because he really is a cool guy. "I could help you put something together if you want."

I bite back the less-than-friendly retort on my tongue. "I appreciate it. I'll let you know if I have trouble."

"Sure thing." He slaps his hands on his thighs and stands, then moves into the kitchenette to grab something from the fridge.

I slump back after he walks away. The words are composed, but I haven't had the courage to write them down yet, maybe because doing so would only make it real. If I keep them in my head, I can pretend that this whole thing was a fluke, a dream, a fucking nightmare that I'll wake up from. I'll wake up, and she'll be beside me, that sleep-drunk grin on her face as she watches me watching her.

There won't be another guy out there with a claim on her. It will just be the two of us, in love and on the brink of a future I never knew could look so bright. The label can have their contract—I don't give a damn. Because without Saylor beside me in those beat-up combat boots, nothing matters.

34

"Fight Song" - Rachel Platten

Saylor

"Beggars can't be choosers" is one of my mum's favorite sayings. Now, I'm a nickel away from being an actual beggar, which is why I find myself staring at the red-and-white-striped polo shirt and cherry-red baseball cap the manager hands me with what feels like a boulder sinking to my toes.

I take them with a forced smile and walk to the bathroom he points out. Inside, I tug off my jeans and T-shirt and replace them with the restaurant's standard-issue uniform, complete with red polyester pants that must have been modeled on a gorilla, because they certainly don't appear to have been created for humans. The hat doesn't want to fit over my hair, but I shove my curls in until it's precariously perched on top of my head. Once I'm dressed, I glance in the mirror and immediately wish I hadn't.

I look like a fucking clown.

But at least said clown will be getting a paycheck, and right now, that is the only thing standing between me and homelessness. So I'll be a damn clown if I need to be.

My new manager, Larry, leads me around the restaurant, explaining the different stations and their responsibilities. I will be starting on the lowest rung of the ladder: as a cashier. I don't tell him that I much prefer the interaction with customers to that of flipping greasy burgers.

Fortunately, it only takes me a few minutes to figure out the cash register, which looks satisfyingly similar to one I had as a kid. (I don't tell him this.) Once he's assured himself that I'm not going to screw up everyone's order or run off with all of the money in the till, Larry walks away and leaves me alone.

It's midmorning, so there aren't many customers, which is both a blessing and a curse. A blessing because it allows me to take my time with the people who do come in. A curse because it gives me too much time to think.

I took the position at Donnie P's because there was not a single job posting that sounded appealing, and this one promised the quickest pay. The plan is to pick up as many shifts as I can and search for something else during every spare minute I have. As soon as I'm able to, I plan to leave the stench of grease and cooking animal flesh behind.

Without Nate's salary and the housing allotment, it's up to me to cover all the rent. The day after I got home and mailed the divorce paperwork—with an additional ten stamps, just in case—I was served with papers of my own from Nate.

The bastard just had to have the last word.

"You can't be that surprised," he told me when I called him that night.

"I'm not," I said. "Just not sure why you're so smug about it." According to his interviews online, he was devastated and heartbroken. I'd seen through his charade, but I was a little surprised he wasn't bothering to keep it up for me.

"I just think it's funny that your actions are finally coming back to kick you in the ass."

I lifted a brow. "And what actions are those?"

He sniffed out a laugh. "You know damn well what they were. You fucking cheated on me for everyone to see."

"Not exactly," I said, but he wasn't listening. That's the thing with Nate. He's only interested in what he has to say. Everyone else can fuck off.

"Whatever. I say good riddance to the whole thing. Our marriage was a fuckup from the beginning, so you won't catch me crying over it," he said.

"Really? I thought that was exactly what you were doing in all those videos."

A vein in his neck twitched, and his mouth grew tighter. "I was caught up in the moment."

I laughed out loud. "Bye, Nate." The laptop shut with a satisfying click.

I'm finally free of him, but part of me can't help but wonder if I'm any better off. Sure, my husband isn't draining all our money before I can buy necessities with it, but I'm currently punching buttons on a machine covered in a grimy film while my insides feel like they've been through a blender. So how much better off am I really?

Several hours later, Larry announces that I can take twenty minutes for lunch. I'm the last one to be given a break, but at least I'm alone. I take my food outside, needing fresh air after hours in the greasy haze, even if it is cold enough out here to see my breath.

I check my phone while munching my veggie burger. There's a text from my mum asking me to get in touch with her. I calculate the time difference and give her a call after verifying it's not too late.

"Hey, Mum," I say when she answers, bracing myself for her lecture on my life choices. I've been lucky they're away and that neither of them goes on social media much, but it's only a matter of time before one of them reads a headline. Apparently, that day has arrived.

"Hi, honey." Her voice lacks its usual upbeat charm. She pauses for a few moments before speaking again. "How are you?"

I glance around at the rubbish blown up against the dirty wall of Donnie P's, then at my clownish uniform and dirty sneakers. "I'm good. How are you?"

She doesn't take the bait. "You can probably guess why I'm calling."

"To tell me how amazing the Great Wall of China is?"

"Funny." She does not match the humor in my tone. "What happened, Saylor?"

"What did you see?"

"It doesn't matter. I want to hear the truth from you."

I sigh and crumple up my burger wrapper. "It's a long story, Mum. I can tell you when you get home."

"You'll tell me now." I can picture her at this exact moment—her arms crossed, biting on a nail, those familiar worry lines etched across her face.

With all the time I've had to think, you'd assume I would have mapped out the best way to explain the situation to my parents. Turns out, when actually faced with that scenario, even my best laid plans go to shit.

"It wasn't meant to go the way it did," I finally say. "Things just . . . happened."

"But you're always so careful, honey. How could you do that to Nate?"

My parents have always loved Nate. He was the son they never had, and I knew this news would hurt them more than it would hurt him. He always knew exactly how to charm them, and I never had the heart to tell them the truth after the two of us started having problems. I realize the error of that decision now.

"Mum, Nate and I haven't been working out for a long time. I filed for divorce before I ever left, but there was an issue with the paperwork."

She's stunned into silence for a few seconds. "Why didn't you tell us?"

"Because I knew how much you liked him. Besides, you would've just worried about me."

She can't deny that, so she just says, "I'm worried about you now."

"I'm fine, I promise." If wearing a ridiculous outfit for ridiculous pay is considered fine, then I'm thriving.

"And . . . Rhett?" The hesitation in her voice breaks my heart. Or maybe it's hearing his name on someone else's lips. Or being forced to think about him. "Are the two of you together?"

I swallow against the sudden lump in my throat, sending moisture to my eyes. "No, we're not." It's nothing more than a whisper. I don't trust my voice right now.

I never told my parents what happened at summer camp, and after Rhett dumped me without a proper goodbye, I was grateful there were no witnesses to my shame. Any knowledge of Rhett that my mother has was gained from the internet.

"Why not?" she asks.

I choke out a laugh. "Because he didn't want anything to do with me after he thought I lied to him." The knife buried in my heart jiggles a little, sending a sharp pain through my chest.

"And how do you feel about him?"

I lean back against the block wall of the restaurant and tilt my face up to the dark clouds gathering overhead. "I love him, Mum."

"Oh, honey." Her voice is soft and gentle, and it nearly breaks me.

"I chased him away." I swipe at the tears gathering at the corners of my eyes. Good thing I didn't put on mascara this morning. I doubt Larry would be thrilled about me working the till with raccoon eyes. "But that was to be expected, I guess."

"Why do you say that?"

I shrug, even though she can't see me. "Everyone always leaves me eventually."

"Oh, Saylor." Her voice adopts that disappointed mum tone. "Love doesn't push people away—it invites them to stay. If someone can't handle your love, they're not meant to hold it."

Keeping my face turned skyward, I let her words sink in. "Maybe my love is too messy to be handled."

She sniffs into the phone, unimpressed with my reasoning. "Coming from someone who has been a recipient of your love for your entire lifetime, I say lift your chin and go show the world what they're missing out on. It is their loss, not yours."

"Thanks, Mum," I say, and mean it. Whether she's right or not, it has lifted my spirits to hear her voice. "And thank you for not telling me you're disappointed in me."

"Baby, there isn't much you could do that would make me disappointed in you."

"Robbing a bank?"

She lets out a muffled snort. "I'd be disappointed you didn't invite me."

* * *

The next hour is busy with a late lunch crowd, and I don't have much time to think about our conversation. A mother with several small children comes in. They take a long time choosing what they want, and my heart goes out to her. She looks frazzled trying to corral them while simultaneously placing her order.

As she's counting out her money, I fill the cups with soft drinks and place them on the counter. She hands one to the oldest child, who can't be more than five or six. It is filled to the brim, and I wince as he takes it from her. He's only walked a few steps toward their table when he loses his grip on the cup. Red liquid splashes all over the floor.

He starts crying, and his mum looks like she wants to join him. One of my coworkers grabs a mop while I fill another cup. As the drink dispenses, my mum's words come back to tickle my brain cells into thinking that maybe she's right.

If someone can't handle your love, they're not meant to hold it.

35

"Zombie" - Yungblud

Rhett

It's the last day of the tour. We'll play our final show tonight, then fly home tomorrow. I don't even know how I feel about it, because my chest is numb. When Saylor left, she stuck a needle full of oxycodone into my veins and pushed the plunger.

I do everything as if in a haze. I just can't find it in me to give a shit. I'm sure that will change eventually—once I get home and forget about how she smells like a summer day, forget the way she felt in my arms, like a fucking daydream with legs. I might be able to lessen the sting of her leaving, might be able to get feeling back into my body, but I'll never be the same again. Like a riverbank that's been forever changed by the stream, I'll never be the man I used to be, thanks to her.

The guys are ready to get home. You can feel it on the bus. They're calling their significant others, and the excitement in their voices is nauseating. Because while most of them have someone to go home to, my condo might as well be an abandoned house for all the life it holds.

I've managed to get drunk the last few nights and send more

unsolicited texts to Saylor, begging her to forgive me, to call me, to please let me know she's okay. Naturally, there's been no response.

I grab a soda from the fridge and retreat to the bedroom for some solitude. I can only handle the guys' enthusiasm for so long. No wonder people fighting depression stay home. It's fucking misery to be out there.

I set my drink on the nightstand and throw myself onto the bed. The ceiling is a boring beige color, but I stare at it so long, I'm starting to think it's the most interesting thing I've seen all day.

If Saylor were here, she'd make me laugh and forget about feeling like a wolf has eaten my heart straight from my chest. Of course, if Saylor were here, I wouldn't feel this way. She *is* the wolf. Even if I get my heart back some day, it won't be the same. It'll be a mangled mess of flesh and blood. It won't resemble the organ it used to be.

Why the fuck am I still thinking about her? And how the fuck do I stop?

In rehab, they made us face our addictions head-on, admit to them, own them, then make the choice to put them behind us, to rise above them. I thought the whole thing was a crock of shit at the time, but looking back, I think it might actually have been effective.

Maybe I should try it again. Only this time, it feels like my drug of choice might actually kill me, regardless of whether I give it up or not.

I pull out my phone, a sudden idea in my mind. Something Saylor said weeks ago about telling everyone about my addiction rattles around in my head, and I'm hitting the record button before I even think about what I'm doing.

The only thing more powerful than your music is the story behind it.

I can still hear her voice, see her bright eyes in that hotel room as she said it. She always had faith that I would do the right thing, that no matter what, I would always have fans, even if they knew the truth.

It's time to see if she was right.

I'm recording the video live, because I am a glutton for punishment. I've only done a few of these in the past, but the numbness in my chest makes it feel like a walk in the park. Who cares if my career implodes after this? I've already hit rock bottom. At least there's not much further I can fall.

The red light flashes at me from my phone screen, reminding me I've already been recording for thirty seconds. Comments are rolling in, people ecstatic to see me, even if I'm lying on my bed, looking like shit with my bloodshot eyes and sallow skin. Turns out I need Saylor beside me in order to sleep the whole night. Apparently, I also need her in my life in order to have an appetite appropriate for my size. Now that she's gone, I'm surviving on fumes.

"Hey, everyone," I finally manage to say after tamping down the Saylor memories long enough to find words. "How's it going?"

A flurry of comments descends after that, but I don't bother reading them. I have a mission, and if I don't carry it out soon, I'm afraid I never will.

"I need to tell you something, something that will probably change the way you think about me. May even make you hate me." I take a deep breath. "I'm a drug addict. I was in rehab for three months. I've been clean for nearly a year."

The commenters are going berserk, but I don't pause to read what they're saying.

"Only a few people know about it. I did my best to keep it a secret, because I was embarrassed. I didn't want to be a disappointment, and I was afraid of what you would think if you knew the truth."

I picture Eddie watching this video later and try to imagine the kind of fallout I'll be facing when I get home. It won't be pretty, that's for sure.

"Someone told me once," I continue, "that the only thing more powerful than my music is the story behind it. I don't know if they were right; I'll let you be the judge of that. The truth is, most of my debut album was written in rehab."

I swipe at my nose and pray I can make it through this without choking up. God, crying on camera would be even more mortifying than this confession. "You guys love 'Take a Chance on Me,' but I bet you never guessed I wrote it after sitting in rehab for a month. It's a universal theme—we all want people to take a chance on us—but the truth is, I wrote it about my addiction specifically. I didn't want it to define the rest of my life. I didn't want it to change the way people saw me. Just like I hope this confession doesn't change the way you see me, even though I know it will."

I mentally scroll through the rest of my songs, then sniff out a laugh. "You'll love this one. 'Burning Through the Darkness'? Literally about being high, but from the perspective of someone who's no longer high. Listen to it again, and you'll see what I mean."

I share the details behind the lyrics of several more songs, including "Electric Heartbeat," "Fighting My Reflection," and "Stronger than Yesterday." I've ignored the comments up until now, but I'm curious to see how big the blaze is on this fire I've set.

My brother is in rehab right now. I can't wait to tell him to listen to your album.

This is so encouraging. I've struggled with addiction for years and always felt alone.

I want to know more! Did you write "Perfectly Imperfect" in rehab too?

My mouth falls open as I read. Those are just the tip of the iceberg. Saylor was right. People are eating this stuff up.

When I swallow, there's a lump in my throat that wasn't there before. I know I can't end this here. It was never just about the music, or even just about recovery. My story didn't end in rehab. In fact, rehab feels like the prologue to the real story.

I clear my throat and hide the comments for now. "There's actually more I need to tell you guys. I wrote the album in rehab, that much is true, but I hid that fact from my record label. They wanted someone without a past, and I knew they'd take one look at mine and decide I wasn't a good investment. So I hid it. Didn't tell them about the addiction or the recovery.

"When they sent me on tour, I knew there'd be drugs and shit. I wasn't sure I'd be strong enough to resist, so I asked someone to come with me. To help me abstain, and all that."

I rub a hand over my face at the memories that are flooding back as I relive this over a live video feed. "There was a girl. We knew each other like ten years ago. We had one of those cliché summer camp flings, but then I was a douchebag and never called her after we got home." I lift the corners of my mouth in a grim smile. "You'll find that's kind of a theme for me.

"When I ran into her again, I knew she'd be perfect for the job. She doesn't put up with my bullshit. She doesn't care about the fame. In fact, she pretended she didn't know who I was when we bumped into each other." I close my eyes and smile as I picture Saylor in that adorable hat, cheeks flushed with embarrassment as we picked up her stuff at the bottom of the stairs.

"But when I asked her to join me on tour, she said no. I should have respected that. But I'm a douchebag, remember? So I wouldn't leave her alone. I pestered her and pestered her until she finally agreed to come on tour with me and pretend to be my girlfriend. Technically, she was only supposed to keep me from slipping into using again, but since the label didn't know about my addiction, I needed to give them a reason for her being here. The fake girlfriend thing was exactly that—a lie to the record label, my band mates, and my fans to hide the fact that I'm an addict.

"It worked. Everyone bought it. They all thought Saylor and I were madly in love. We weren't, but then somehow, we were." My voice breaks, and I take a few seconds to compose myself before continuing.

"I didn't mean for it to happen. But have you seen her? It would have been impossible not to fall for her." I squeeze my eyes shut to prevent moisture from collecting there. I cannot cry on social media. God, I'd never live down the shame of that.

"She made it very clear that nothing was going to happen between us. Her boundaries were very firm, and she is a force to be reckoned with. But I hate it when people don't like me, so doing what I do best, I douchebagged my way past her boundaries. I'm not saying I did anything she wasn't okay with, but—" I stop, trying to find the right words for the next part.

"I screwed up. I see that now. If I could do it differently, I would, but only if it meant still keeping her. Because she's the best thing that's ever happened to me, and I would do anything to go back and change things so she wouldn't get hurt the way she did. I know I don't deserve her. I'm a fucked-up drug addict who manipulates people to get what he wants. At least now you know the truth."

I heave out a sigh, my chest lighter somehow. "I guess that's all I have to say. I'm going to do better. I'm going to be better. If there's anything Saylor taught me, it's that we all have the potential for greatness inside us."

I end the video and let the phone drop beside me on the bed. Shoving my hand into my hair, I play it all back in my mind, already thinking of a million things I should've said differently, but it's too late now. That video will determine the rest of my career, and I couldn't care less.

My text message chime goes off, and I glance at the screen. My dad. What the fuck is he texting me about?

Dad: *Hey, son. Just watched your video. Very commendable. I was thinking, I could fly to NYC to see you before you head home.*

My first instinct is to say yes, to tell him that'd be great. But then I remember how it was having him at my show in Nashville, and the interview he gave afterward, calling me "decent" for a newbie. Now, I want nothing more than to tell him to fuck off.

My thumb hovers over the keypad, itching to type out the words, to tell him what a jackass he is. But then the desire vanishes. Instead, I switch off the power on my phone. I won't reply to him. He's not worthy of one anyway. He'll just find a way to twist my words and come out on top.

I sit up and grab my guitar, which is still leaning against the bed from last night. I never even bothered to put it away. Not anymore. Starting now, I'm going to be a different man. A better man. Not so I can deserve Saylor—that'll never happen in a million years—but because if she ever loved me, she deserves to know it wasn't completely in vain. That what she saw in me was there, even if I didn't realize it until it was too late.

Because if I only accomplish one thing, I want it to be proving to her that she was right about me all along.

I settle the guitar across my legs and start to strum. This time, I'm writing the lyrics down. This song also deserves its time in the spotlight, even if the label drops me. Because Saylor *was* right—the story behind the song is even more powerful than the music.

36

"Colors" - Halsey

Saylor

"Do you think we'll ever get used to the smell?" I ask as I clean up the very runny present left by one of the shelter's newest residents—a small terrier mix with an upset stomach.

Selene looks up from the clipboard in her hands. "I've been here for six years and still want to hurl, so I don't think so." She blows a bubble with her gum and returns to the form.

I take a deep breath through my mouth and try to not think about what I'm doing as I wipe up the mess. The shelter is full, which only increases the animals' anxiety. An adoption event is scheduled for this afternoon, so hopefully many of them will find homes.

I wash my hands, then make my rounds greeting everyone. My schedule only allows me to volunteer once a month, so I rarely see the same faces twice. A good sign, even if it's hard not to get attached.

Stopping at one of the kennels, I squat down until I'm at eye level with a new addition, a solid gray cat whose fur looks as soft as cashmere. A quick glance at the name plaque tells me he's a male.

"Hi, big boy," I coo at him.

He walks to the front of the cage and sniffs my hand. That's when I realize he only has three legs. His gait is lopsided, but he seems to be managing just fine.

I glance over my shoulder at Selene, who is clicking away at the computer keys. "What happened to this guy?" I say.

She looks up long enough to see who I'm talking about before returning to her data entry. "Don't know. Someone found him beside the road and brought him here."

My heart shatters into tiny little pieces. Whoever his previous owners were, they didn't even have the decency to bring him in, just left him outside on his own to die. I bat away the tears that are forming at the corners of my eyes.

Giving the cat an extra scratch behind his ears, I whisper, "Someone wonderful will adopt you today, I just know it." While disabled animals aren't for everyone, there are plenty of beautiful souls in the world who have an abundance of love for these special cases. I'm convinced they're earthbound angels.

I finish greeting the rest of the animals, then it's all hands on deck to prepare for the adoption event. Kennels need to be scrubbed, dogs need to be walked, medications need to be given. My favorite part, though, is socialization time. It is crucial for the mental health of the animals, and downright essential for the well-being of Saylor Jones.

I sit on the floor and call the gray cat to me. He hobbles over on his three legs quite well before snuggling into my lap. My heart melts into a little puddle on the floor beneath us. The other animals come and go—some eager for pets and others more interested in the toys—but the gray cat stays curled up on my legs for the entire hour.

When it's time to put everyone back into their kennels, a pang enters my chest at the thought of parting from my little buddy. It's necessary, of course, and I know the rules about getting attached to shelter animals. It's not in their best interest—it only makes their transition to a new home that much harder.

But my heart isn't very good at listening to instructions. The way it plummeted over a cliff for a certain musician is proof of that.

The gray kitty doesn't look any more excited to be leaving me than I am him, but I reassure him that someone will be coming for him later. I don't know who could resist that incredibly soft fur or those soulful eyes, but whoever they are, they can't be human.

There's a good turnout for Gotcha Day, the shelter's official name for the adoption event. Over twenty animals find families and leave for better homes than the ones they came from. Unfortunately, the three-legged cat isn't one of them.

"I can't believe no one took him," I tell Selene as we clean up the back room. "He's a sweetheart."

She shrugs and pushes the broom across the floor. "I think a lot of people assume a disabled animal will require a lot of extra care."

I glance over at the cat, who is watching me with those heartbreaking eyes. "Do they? Need extra care?"

Selene stops sweeping to look at the cat. "Not really. He seems to have adapted especially well."

The kitty's face seems to say, *You promised someone would take me.*

I shouldn't have told him that, but I was so sure he'd be one of the first to be adopted. If I trusted myself to take another animal home, he would be leaving with me tonight. I crouch down in front of his cage. "I'd take you with me if I could."

He gives a tiny meow, then retreats to the back of the crate. It feels like a rejection, but maybe that's because he feels rejected. Tears well in the corners of my eyes again, and I quickly wipe them away before Selene can notice and accuse me of forming attachments.

Leaving the shelter that night is harder than it's ever been before. The gray cat looks at me with those huge eyes, and I hate myself a little at that moment. Why can't I be the kind of person who can successfully adopt an animal?

Those two weeks with Charlie were some of the best of my life. I looked forward to our daily walks. He slept in my bed—a habit I knew we'd have to break once Nate came home on leave—but I loved having his warm body snuggled up next to mine.

It happened so suddenly. The vet thought he must have caught something at the dog park, because one minute he was fine, and the next he was fighting for his life on the operating table at the animal hospital. They assured me there was nothing I could have done, but I knew the truth.

Saylor Jones's love is toxic and erodes the lives of the ones she cares about. Better to live half a life than to steal what's left of someone else's.

The flat feels especially empty and lonely tonight. At least I still have a roof over my head, thanks to my job at Donnie P's—literally the only good thing to come from that place. The plan is still to quit as soon as possible, but I haven't found anything better that allows me to make as much. The pay is shit, but I've been able to pick up enough shifts to cover my rent and keep the fridge stocked.

I heat up a bowl of ramen and do my best to ignore the last image of the cat in my mind. He watched me up until the minute I walked out the door, probably wondering if anyone would ever love him. How the fuck am I supposed to recover from that? How will *he* recover?

Taking my noodles to the sofa, I curl up under the thrifted afghan. I'm keeping the thermostat turned down to save on electricity, so the flat is always cold. But it's easier to wear an extra pair of socks and a second sweater than it is to make an extra fifty bucks.

Too bad Rhett never paid me for the tour. I know I would technically be within my rights to ask for it, but I can't bring myself to. Contacting him feels like acknowledging that something happened, and right now, the only way for me to survive is to pretend it didn't. Pretend he didn't weasel his way into my heart despite my best intentions. Pretend I didn't fall hard for him the exact way I knew I would if given half a chance. Pretend I don't still fall asleep remembering how it felt to be in his arms or the way his voice sounded as he quietly sang me to sleep.

I know we would never have worked out, but that knowledge doesn't lessen the sting of knowing that it's my fault he walked away. Yet another example of Saylor's love on display.

I haven't been able to bring myself to check the news, and I studiously avoid looking at the tabloid headlines when I'm at the grocery store, so I don't know if my deception ruined his career or if he was able to comeback from it. I only hope that leaving when I did gave him some kind of redemption with his label. He doesn't deserve to have his dream crushed because of me.

Scraping the last bits of ramen from my bowl, I think back to what my mum said a few weeks ago about those who can't handle your love. Work got busy after that phone call, and I forgot about it until now.

Is she right? If she is, that means my love isn't toxic at all, but that the people who left weren't worthy of it.

What about Charlie, though? He obviously deserved all of my love and then some, and it still killed him. He would've been better off in the shelter—

I stop and think about that statement. Would he really? Is the little gray cat? Are any of the animals better off in those kennels than in a loving home?

Is it possible that Charlie could still have caught whatever virus he did if he lived with someone else? I chew my bottom lip as I consider this. It's . . . possible. But if so, that means that the disabled cat would also be better off with me than without me.

I gave the rest of the world a chance, but no one wanted to adopt him. I want him with all my heart. I know I could provide him with a good home, all the love he can possibly hold, and a great life. The only thing stopping me is the belief that by loving him, I'm somehow going to hurt him.

What if I'm . . . wrong? What if I actually hurt him more by leaving him in the shelter than by bringing him home with me?

* * *

The next morning, I'm at the door of the shelter five minutes before they open. Selene looks at me with a cocked brow through the glass as she flips the deadbolt.

"Told you not to get attached," she tells me as she lets me inside.

"Well, this time it's for his good," I say.

He's even cuter than I remember, tucked into a small ball at the back of his cage. I squat down to greet him, and he lifts his head to look at me. It takes a few seconds of coaxing before he finally hobbles over.

"You haven't forgiven me for leaving you, have you?" I say, scratching his neck. He purrs into my hand, and my heart turns into a pile of goo.

Selene gives me the paperwork to fill out, and thirty minutes later, I'm walking home with my new best friend in my arms. He doesn't squirm or try to get down even once, and the reassurance that I'm doing the right thing grows.

I have no idea how I'm going to afford him—cats need food, litter, and toys after all, and I just spent my last paycheck on rent and the few groceries in my fridge. But I'll sell my sofa if I need to in order to give this guy the best shot at life.

It takes a second to fish my key out of my bag, especially with my arms full of cat. Before I can get the door unlocked, Paula sticks her head out of her flat. She takes one look at the bundle of gray fur and steps into the hallway, her floral kimono belted at her waist.

"What a beautiful baby," she croons, stroking his head. "What's his name?"

I blink down at him. I haven't considered it until now. "Leo," I say without another thought, wondering how my former PPO would feel about having a cat named after him.

"Leo," Paula purrs. "How delightful."

My key turns in the lock, and I shift Leo so he doesn't fall from the sudden movement.

"I have a bunch of things left from my last foster," Paula says, jerking a thumb over her shoulder at her own door while keeping one hand on Leo. "Luca is allergic, so you're welcome to it if you want."

"Um, sure," I say, choosing not to comment on the fact that her reborn doll can't possibly have allergies.

She disappears back into her flat, and I take the opportunity to nuzzle Leo under the chin. His eyes blink closed, and that familiar rumbling starts in the back of his throat.

Paula reappears several minutes later, carrying a pink-striped bag with "Victoria's Secret" on the side. I would have been happy going the rest of my life without knowing she shops there, but here we are. She hands me the bag, and it's quite heavy. A quick glance inside reveals a box of canned cat food, a half-full bag of litter, a litter tray, and a bunch of toys.

"Paula, this is too much," I say, and move to hand it back.

She shakes her head. "Take it. I was going to donate it to a shelter anyway." Scratching Leo's head, she murmurs, "This boy deserves it."

I thank her and shuffle the bag and Leo into the flat. There's the question of how to afford him answered, at least for the first few weeks. After that, we'll take it one day at a time.

It might be too late for me and Rhett, but it's not too late for this boy.

37

"Move Along" - All American Rejects

Rhett

It doesn't come as a surprise when Sam and I are called into the executive offices at Lunar Records within days of my plane landing back in Wesbourne. Sam is doing his best to hide it, but I can tell he's as nervous as I am. His foot keeps twitching where it's propped across his knee.

I spit out a splinter of my toothpick. I just popped it in my mouth when we pulled up, and it's already shredded. Maybe I should've listened to a fucking guided meditation on the way over here like my therapist recommended.

They're making us sweat. We've been here fifteen minutes, having arrived promptly at our appointed time, for which I'd expect a little gratitude. But no one has come out to greet us yet, besides the blue-haired receptionist, who keeps looking at me with hungry eyes. I ignore her.

Sam and I haven't talked much, apart from his directive to let him handle things. I'm trying to reassure myself that if they were going to cut me, they wouldn't waste so much time doing it. I doubt they'd even have called us in.

271

The door opens to the same conference room we met in before, and Eddie steps out. It feels like fucking déjà vu, except this time he's not wearing a smile. Instead, his face has this pinched expression that makes him look a little constipated. I refrain from offering him a laxative. Something tells me he wouldn't find that funny.

A handful of other execs are already seated, wearing expressions similar to Eddie's. Sam and I settle at the table, and the air in the room crackles with tension. I badly want to make a joke that is in nothing but poor taste, but even that part of me seems to have shut down.

Eddie clears his throat, taking charge again. "I'm sure you're aware of why we've asked you to come in." His eyes don't leave the paper in his hands, as though I'm not even worthy of a glance, let alone his full attention.

"To tell me how well the tour went?" I say with a smile that's only half-forced.

"What he means is—" Sam interjects. Fuck. I forgot to let him do the talking. "—we're not sure why this meeting has been called, since it seems like the tour was a success."

Eddie drops the page in his hand and looks at my agent. "It was a fucking shitshow."

Sam blinks in surprise, and I frown across the table at the guy who's supposed to be my liaison with the record label, but who has revealed himself to be my biggest naysayer. "I wouldn't say it's been *that* bad," I say.

Eddie's gaze swings over to me. "Really?" He punctuates this by tossing several tabloids my way. "Look at these headlines."

I scan them, but it's nothing new, just more trash talk about me and Saylor. If I hadn't already seen those photos, the sight of them now would shove the knife in my chest right up into my heart. But these articles are old. "These are from weeks ago," I say.

Eddie pinches the bridge of his nose. "The point is, Rhett, that you broke your end of the contract. We specifically said no scandals. I'm not sure there's a person alive who wouldn't call this scandal material."

Sam opens his mouth to speak, but only a grunt comes out before Eddie interrupts him.

"You had an affair with a married woman. What the fuck were you thinking?" Red splotches dot his neck, and I briefly wonder if he should get on blood pressure medication. Clearly, he doesn't have a good handle on his emotions.

"My client has no comment at this time," Sam says.

Eddie shoots him an annoyed look. "This isn't a fucking press conference."

"In my defense, I didn't know she was still married," I say. As soon as the words are out of my mouth, I wish I could take them back. They may be true, but it only makes Saylor sound like the bad guy, when in reality, she's the only good thing in this whole situation.

"I asked her to join me on tour," I continue, "because I'm a drug addict." I wait for the surprise to cross Eddie's face, and when it doesn't, I glance around the table at the other suits. Stoic expressions, all of them.

"Yeah, we saw your little confession," Eddie grumbles, his attention already returned to the paper in front of him.

I shift in my seat. Is that why I'm here? They're canceling the contract because of my addiction? As this sinks in, I expect to feel disappointment, anger even, or sadness. But I feel nothing. My heart rate hasn't changed, and my hands aren't shaking. In fact, I feel calm. Collected. Better than usual.

It hits me how little I care about their decision. Just eight months ago, when I sat at this table, it felt like my life was on the line. I wanted nothing more than this contract. When they threw in the tour, I thought I had arrived at the pinnacle of my career.

Turns out, the higher you rise, the further you have to fall.

If they cancel me right now, tear up my contract and throw it out the window, I won't give a single fuck. I will walk out of here with my head held high. If I never play another show again, I'll be just fine. Screw them and their fucked-up ideals. Life is about more than fame. I don't need this to be happy.

Not that I've been happy in the past two weeks, but that has nothing to do with the label, the tour, or the bloody contract, and everything to do with a girl with bottomless eyes, kinky dark curls, and a tattered pair of combat boots.

"Is that it, then?" I ask, planting my palms on the table to stand. "You're canceling the contract?"

The pen in Eddie's hand stops moving, just hovering over the page as he looks at me. "No one said anything about canceling the contract."

I'm already halfway out of my chair, so I pause there. A small laugh slips out. "Uh, yeah you did. You said I violated it—"

"—and that gives us the *right* to terminate," he says. "Whether we choose to act on that right is up to us." He glances at the rest of the executive team, who have yet to say anything this entire meeting. Maybe they're too scared to speak to the volatile artists they sign.

I sit back down.

Eddie raps the papers in front of him on the table. "We've been in discussion about this for a long time."

Is that supposed to make me feel better?

"We're not happy with how things turned out," he continues. "Instead of abiding by our no-scandal stipulation, you seem to have intentionally sought it out." I open my mouth to object, but he holds up his hand. "You're lucky it played out like it did. Fortunately, your fans seem to have sided with you instead of the girl."

White-hot rage grows inside me until there's a fucking inferno in my chest. How dare he refer to her as "the girl"? How dare he even talk about her at all? I clench my hands into fists at my sides so I don't leap across the table and punch him in the face. "Then they're fucking idiots," I grumble.

"Excuse me?" Eddie says.

"You heard me." I cross my arms over my chest and jut my chin at him. "I screwed up, okay? I'm the one who got hooked on shit in the first place. I'm the one who pestered her to come on tour with me until she finally agreed. I'm the one who didn't try harder to be a good person. Just leave Saylor out of this, okay?"

Eddie blinks at me, then turns back to the sheet in his hands. "Anyway," he says, as though I haven't spoken. "The label has decided to keep you on a probationary basis. If your record sales continue to climb and there's no more bad publicity, we will consider another album. A second tour is not a likely possibility at this point."

The urge to laugh bubbles up. Fuck them and their contract. "I suppose now is when I'm supposed to jump up and cheer? Maybe come kiss your shoes for saving my ass?" I say.

Beside me, Sam's foot jiggles even faster as he pops an antacid into his mouth. He's apparently given up on trying to do the negotiating, preferring to sit back and watch me burn instead.

Eddie's face pinches even tighter, and I feel sorry for his kids. "What I expect is a little respect."

I let one side of my mouth quirk into a smile, then let it linger there as I stare him down. Finally, I once again slap my hands onto the table. The woman at the end jumps slightly. I stand up, and it brings me immense satisfaction to be able to tower over Eddie where he's still sitting. "Fuck your contract," I say, and head for the door.

Behind me, I can hear Sam scrambling. I'm a shit for leaving him with this mess, but the guy wasn't doing his job anyway. At least now my money will actually be paying for something.

I give the receptionist a blinding grin on my way out, and she melts into a puddle on her desk chair. Unfortunately for her, it isn't what she thinks. I won't be taking her to bed later, or even calling her. That smile was because I never have to see that office or those fucking execs ever again.

The sun is smiling back at me when I walk outside, just spilling its happy rays all over the car park of the record label. I saunter over to my Maserati, feeling lighter than I have in ages. Who knew giving your dreams the finger could feel so freeing?

As I drive home, the final lyrics for my new song click into place. I belt it out in the car, and god it hurts, but it also feels so damn good to get it out there. With a clarity I've never felt before, I jog into my flat and grab my guitar.

Several practice rounds later, I'm ready. I set up my phone and hit the record button. It's time to let a new muse write my songs.

38

"Clean" - Taylor Swift

Saylor

Food service jobs should come with a warning label. I don't think I've ever been this tired in my life. The sofa calls my name as I stumble into my flat after a ten-hour shift at Donnie P's, but—much as I'd like nothing better than to rot on it right now—I have actual adult responsibilities calling my name. Or meowing my name, if you will.

Leo jumps down from his spot on the windowsill, knocking one of my spider plants to the floor as he does. I groan and set my bag down as he scampers over with that three-legged gait I adore. I'm happy for the company, but having a cat does mean I have less money to spend on frivolous things like food and less time to spend doing frivolous things like sleeping.

"Hey, buddy," I say, bending down to scratch his ears.

He purrs and presses his head into my hand, eager for my attention after being alone all day. In addition to cleaning up the plant he knocked over, I also need to scoop his litter box and get him dinner. I won't be getting to bed for at least an hour.

Sixty-nine minutes later (I checked), I finally fall into bed. Leo decides he got enough rest during the day and walks across me, begging me to get up and play with him. "Not tonight, buddy," I say.

I settle into the pillows, but sleep won't come. I'm so exhausted my body thinks it would be better to see how far we can push that, I guess.

With a groan, I roll over and grab my phone from the nightstand. I open social media, hoping a bit of mindless scrolling will convince my brain to give up the fight. Instead, Rhett's face fills my screen. On instinct, I swipe up before more than a second or two can play.

I can't even process what the next video is about. Finally, I lock my phone and lay it on my chest, panting. My heart is running circles around my chest for no explainable reason.

Why does he still have this effect on me? It's been weeks since the tour, weeks since I've seen him, weeks since I've allowed myself to remember the touch of his hands on me, the scent of his cologne, the electricity that surged along my spine every time he whispered in my ear.

It has not, unfortunately, been weeks since I've heard his voice. He wasn't whispering in my ear, but it had nearly the same effect. I'm no longer following him on socials, but that doesn't prevent his videos from occasionally popping up in my feed. The last one I watched sent me into a spiral for days.

He finally did it. He finally told the truth about his addiction. And considering how often I have to skip his songs on Spotify, it hasn't done a thing to hurt his reputation. If anything, he's only become more popular.

I'm proud of him, in spite of the fact that I have no reason to be. I have no claim on him. He did the right thing, and the most I can do is mentally applaud him for finding the courage to speak up. The rest of that video, though . . .

It was dangerous to watch, and I cut myself off after the fifth time.

It took me days to be able to go an hour without thinking about him. Now, he's back, filling my feed again with his beautiful face and his raspy voice and the magnetism neither I nor the rest of the world can resist.

I unlock my phone and swipe down, dragging the video back onto my screen. My heart bursts wide open at the sight of him, as though it doesn't realize he's not actually right here in front of me.

He's sitting on a chair in what is probably his flat, given the lack of personality and the excess of sharp corners. An acoustic guitar is on his lap, one he never plays onstage, but which he told me once is his favorite. A gift from his dad when he was young. Most of his guitars are, but that one is special.

It's hard to tell in the video, but he looks like he's been managing just fine since our breakup. No dark circles under his eyes, no weight loss that I can see. I tell myself I'm glad. He deserves to move on, to be happy. I want him to be happy, even if that means him being with someone else.

Is he with someone else? I haven't seen any photos of him with other women, but then again, I've been studiously avoiding the tabloids at the supermarket. Pain courses through my veins at the thought, but I remind myself it's for the best. We're never going to be together anyway. The best thing is for us both to move on. If he's able to do that years before I am, that's a me problem, not a him problem.

He finally stopped texting me, probably because I never replied. I considered blocking him, but I couldn't bring myself to do it. After several days went by without a new message, I realized he must have given up. That thought hurt more than all the others. Our coffin has finally been nailed shut.

On screen, his eyes flick up to the camera. He's lightly strumming the guitar, and the melody is haunting. "I have a new song to play for you," he says, and my heart careens over the side of a mountain. His voice has that hushed quality I love, like it's just the two of us here.

He's in a goddamn video, I tell my stupid, racing heart.

"I wrote it about a girl." That slow, lazy smile takes over his face, the same one that used to make my pulse pick up speed, the one that could turn me to jelly in the blink of an eye. "She changed me, so this one's for her."

He strums a few chords, and my brain is whirling. He never wrote a song for me. Is he already so deeply in love with someone else that he's writing her songs? Tears sting my eyes, but he starts singing before I can click out of the app.

"She's tough as nails / in her black combat boots / She never fails / to hide what's inside / Her battle wounds / a tidepool of pain."

Rhett's voice is a masterpiece. His fame has been well earned. He's an expert guitar player, to say nothing of the way he can captivate a crowd onstage or on video. His songs have brought me to the brink of every emotion known to mankind.

But this one? This one undoes me completely.

I'm sobbing so hard, I don't even hear all the lyrics. I have to rewatch it, but it keeps wrecking me every time. I cry for what we had, for the way he made me feel, for the hope he gave me for the future. I cry for what we could have been, for what we should have been. I cry for the mistakes we made that can't be undone, the things we said that can't be erased.

But mostly I cry because my heart is still firmly in the grasp of the man singing a song about me, and the worst part is knowing I'll never get it back, because how could I when he looks like that and he sounds like that and he writes songs about girls in combat boots who could only ever be me, yet I'll never be his and he'll never be mine. How am I ever supposed to recover from that?

I lose track of how many times I watch the video. It's enough that I have the song memorized by the next morning, when my alarm blares and I wake to find it still playing. Fresh tears spring to my eyes as I rewatch it one final time.

"Barbed wire wrapped tightly around a heart riddled with holes / But underneath and deep inside and hiding out / a wildfire heart burning bright / a flame untamed / She cloaks it well / smoke and mirrors / a gilt facade / But when she chooses to love you, look out / You're a brand-new man."

The song ends, and something catches my eye. I missed it last night, but right before he gets up to turn off the camera, Rhett tilts his chin down to his chest, then back up again. Our signal on tour for when he needed me.

I didn't know it was possible for my heart to shatter any more thoroughly, but that manages to do it. I close the app and toss my phone aside, not able to take another second of staring at the face that still appears in every single dream I have. I can't afford to think about him. I need to get to work, and if Larry catches me daydreaming again, I might not have a job at the end of my shift.

* * *

By the time noon rolls around, I'm beginning to wish I *didn't* have a job. Is being homeless really that bad? It can't be worse than scrubbing vomit off the bathroom floor or dunking so many fry baskets into hot oil that your hair permanently absorbs the scent, right?

Larry assigns me to the front counter right before the lunch crowd comes in, and I'm not sure if it's meant to be a reward or a punishment. I can never tell with him. I do know that if he ever brushes those disgusting hairy-knuckled hands against me, I will gleefully be reporting him to the authorities.

Despite the fact that I smell like grease and my hair is frizzing around my face, I am glad to escape the kitchen, even if it means I'll be standing behind the counter without a break for the next hour. The line curves around the store as more and more people come in for Donnie P's cheap-ass burgers and disgusting fries.

I don't know how long I've been standing here ringing up orders, but it's been long enough that faces are starting to blur together. I no longer even lift my head when someone steps forward, just keep my eyes on the keypad of the register, ready to enter their order and take their money. Larry prioritizes efficiency over friendliness, and for once, I'm happy to oblige.

The next person approaches the counter, and I wait, my fingers hovering over the keys. It's a man with his hands tucked into the front pocket of his gray hoodie. He doesn't say anything right away, so I look up to see if he has a question about the menu. He's tall, and it takes my eyes an eternity to reach his face.

When they finally do, I'm not sure how I'll ever tear them away.

Now that he's right in front of me, I can see all the things I couldn't on video. His cheeks are more gaunt than before, and there are shadows under his eyes the camera didn't catch. The biggest difference, though, is the dullness in his eyes, the lack of that spark that is so much a part of Rhett Cole that I hardly recognize him without it.

He looks . . . anguished.

Our gazes collide, and my heart gets caught in my throat. How dare he still look at me like that? The corners of his eyes are pulled down, making him look like a puppy that got left outside in a storm. I try to read what's hiding there, what message he's trying to relay, but I can't make it out. It's been too long, even though my heart still marches to the beat of his.

The man standing behind Rhett rudely clears his throat, and it shocks both of us out of our stupor.

I glance over my shoulder, sure I'll find Larry glaring at me, but he's not there. I turn back to Rhett, and in my cheeriest voice, say, "Welcome to Donnie P's. What can I get you?"

He looks at the menu board above my head and says in that voice I love, "Can I get the biggest order of forgiveness you have? And a little bit of your time?"

My heart stops beating.

He drops his gaze back to me, the question lingering there. I open my mouth, but no words come out. All I can think about is the fact that the first time he's seeing me again, I'm wearing the world's ugliest uniform.

The guy behind him says something, but I can't hear anything except for the crazy thumping of my heart in my ears. It's like I'm underwater, and Rhett's the ray of sunshine I'm swimming toward.

"I can't," I whisper.

"Why not?" he whispers back, and it feels like summer camp all over again.

I couldn't tear my eyes from him if I wanted to. His gaze is like sticky pavement on a hot day, and I could bake here forever. "Because I'm working."

"Fuck work," he says.

I'm aware that the tension level in the restaurant is rising, but it isn't until Larry barks at me over my shoulder that I snap out of the trance Rhett has me in. I jump and look at my boss.

His face is turning the color of the ketchup bottle in his hand. "What is going on, Taylor?" he says. He's never called me by my actual name, despite the fact that it's on my name tag.

I shake my head, and it's then that I notice the attention Rhett is attracting. Several people have their phones out and are snapping photos of him. Whispers are floating around the restaurant.

"That's Rhett Cole!"

"OMG, Rhett Cole is here!"

Rhett is completely oblivious, his attention still focused on me.

Larry, on the other hand, sees it all and is fuming. "We have a reputation," he snaps. "And you are holding up the line."

"Actually, Larry," I say with a hand on my stomach. "I'm not feeling so well. Do you mind if I take my break early?" It's not exactly a lie. My insides have been knotted since watching Rhett's video last night. Seeing him walk into the restaurant has scrambled my brain as well.

Larry looks at me like I just asked for a million dollars. "Absolutely not. Have you seen that line?" Using the ketchup bottle, he motions toward the people winding their way between the tables and chairs.

I don't even spare them a glance. "I know, but I really don't feel good. Can someone take my place?"

He shakes his head. "You can take your break in thirty minutes."

I turn back to Rhett to ask if he'll wait, but he isn't looking at me. His eyes are fixed on Larry. "That's okay. She quits," he says.

I suck in a sharp breath. He's going to get me fired. "Rhett, I need this job," I hiss.

The spark returns to his eyes as he looks at me. "Not anymore, baby." He tugs my apron over my head and tosses it at Larry, who looks satisfyingly dumbfounded, then leads me out the door.

39

"love song" - Yungblud

Saylor

Rhett pulls me past his gaping fans and out into the bright wintery day. My feet halt on the asphalt, causing him to stop as well. I'm still trying to process what just happened.

"What are you doing?" I say breathlessly. My heart is pounding so hard it hurts.

Rhett frowns as though he doesn't understand the question. "Getting you out of there."

"But—" My protest dies on my lips as I take in his expression. It's stormy, the lines around his eyes tight. "My things are still inside."

"I'll get them. But first—" He pushes me up against the exterior wall of the restaurant with his body, his hands coming up to cradle my face. At his touch, everything inside me turns the consistency of chocolate left in a warm car.

He hovers over my mouth, and I don't know if he's considering whether to kiss me or not, but I desperately hope he decides to, because I have never wanted anything in this world more than I want Rhett Cole to kiss me right now.

His lips linger over mine, tantalizing me, making me crave him, driving me to the edge of desperation. "Saylor," he says in a husky voice that tells me he's on the brink as much as I am.

Then he crashes into me with a vengeance, as though he has something to prove to the world. Maybe he has something to prove to me. He explores my mouth with the precision of an archaeologist, ensuring he leaves nothing untouched.

His mouth is like velvet, soft and luxurious, and I could live here for the rest of my life, I think. If being kissed by Rhett Cole outside a greasy fast food restaurant in forty-degree weather is the pinnacle of my existence, I think I'm okay with that.

Rhett's hands move over my face with the same greed with which his mouth moves over mine. His fingers splay over my cheekbones as though he's trying to contain all of me in his hands and can't quite manage it. He tilts me up toward him, his fingertips pressing into my skin until there isn't an inch of me that's cold.

When he finally pulls away, his lips tugging at mine, I whimper at the loss of him. I'm instantly freezing. His eyes drop to my bare arms, my red Donnie P's polo doing little to protect me from the winter air.

"Shit," he says, and grabs my hand. I follow him to his car, which fortunately is in a nearby parking spot. After helping me inside, he leans down. "I'll be right back."

I snuggle into the warm leather of the seat and refuse to think about what is happening right now. Rhett came back for me, he kissed me like his life depended on it, but none of that really changes anything.

The fact remains that he destroyed me by not believing me. Not only that, but we don't belong together. We never have, and we never will. I can't even sit in his car without being afraid of ruining his leather with the godawful smell of grease on my uniform.

The driver's door opens, and Rhett slips inside, handing me my purse and coat. I slip into my parka, even though the car has been keeping me warm. An extra layer of protection between us feels like a good idea.

"The divorce paperwork didn't have enough postage," I say, breaking the heavy silence between us.

He shoots me a glance before pulling out of the car park. "You don't have to explain."

"Don't I?"

Neither of us says anything else. When he stops in front of my apartment building, I grab my bag and turn to him.

"Thanks," I say quietly. "For the ride and—" Do I thank him for standing up for me, even though it cost me my job? Larry may be a dick, but I needed that money. Now I'll have to go back to job hunting.

"Saylor, wait," he says, his hand on the sleeve of my coat.

"What?" I say, resignation in my voice. I need to keep distance between us, even if it's just to keep me from falling again.

"I'm so fucking sorry for not believing you before." His throat bobs as he swallows. "About the divorce."

"You had no reason to," I say with a shrug.

"Yes, I did." He tilts my chin up with his finger. "You've never lied to me. It was shit of me to think you would." His eyes suck me in, threatening to drown me if I'm not careful.

"You can't just show up here and kiss me, as if nothing happened," I say.

As his eyes soften even further, he strokes my chin with his thumb. "Why not?"

"Because you hurt me, Rhett."

"I know. And I'm going to spend the rest of my life trying to make it up to you."

The determination in his voice scares me. What if he means it? "Rhett . . ."

"Can I come inside?"

My brows pinch as I consider him. There's no smirk on his face, no hint of anything other than pure, unbridled desperation for me to say yes. He's a man with his heart on the line. "Okay," I whisper.

Relief floods his face, and he clambers out of the car.

I know it's a bad idea, but I can't say no to those puppy-dog eyes, especially not when he has my heart tucked into the palm of his hand. Inviting him inside will only make his leaving that much harder, but I'm like an addict, only able to think about my next hit.

When we reach the door of my flat, I glance at him as I fish the key from my bag. "How'd you know where to find me anyway?"

He sticks his hands in his hoodie pockets. "Your neighbor told me after I pounded on your door for five minutes."

"Ahh," I say, turning the key. Looks like I'll need to have a chat with Paula about giving my location out to strange men.

"She demanded an autograph first."

At least the traitor didn't give it up for free.

We go inside, and Leo scampers over to meet us. "Hey, boy," I say, bending over to pick him up. He purrs into my neck.

"Who's this?" Rhett says, reaching around to pet him.

"This is Leo," I tell him.

His hand stays buried in the cat's fur, but his eyes flick to me. "You named him after your PPO?"

"What's wrong with that?"

"I didn't realize the two of you were that close."

I frown at him over Leo's head. "We weren't. I guess you think I should have named him 'Rhett'?"

The corners of his mouth tug upward, his boyish charm back on full display. "Yeah, why not?"

I set Leo back down and kick off my shoes. He runs toward his favorite spot on the windowsill. "Why would I want a constant reminder of you?" It isn't until I see the hurt on his face that I think about how that sounded. "I didn't mean—"

He pushes a hand through his hair, deflated. "Yeah, I know. I'm proud of you for taking a chance on another animal. I'm sure it wasn't easy."

"Thank you," I say. "It wasn't."

I move to the kitchen and put the tea kettle on the stove to give my hands something to do. I fight the urge to look over my shoulder to see what Rhett's up to. I can hear him moving around the flat, but the fewer images of him in my home that are burned into my memory, the better. It will be hard enough to recover from this encounter as it is.

When the tea is ready, I carry the two cups to the sofa and set them on the coffee table. As I grab the afghan and settle into the plush orange fabric, it hits me how similar this is to the first time Rhett was here. The *only* other time. I was nervous that day too, but it was nothing compared to the way my heart is threatening to bust its way right out of my chest now.

Rhett moves to join me on the couch, but he takes the seat in the middle instead of at the other end, putting him mere inches from my toes. I curl them into the cushion, suddenly even more nervous than I was seconds ago.

"How was the rest of the tour?" I say to distract myself from the fact that the man I am still very much in love with is sitting close enough for me to kiss. We can talk about his music without me falling apart, right?

"It was good, yeah." He nods, staring into his tea, then shakes his head. "Actually, it went to shit after you left."

My lips part in surprise.

He looks at me, and I see it now—the pain he's been in since that night. His eyes are wide and dark with it, threatening to suck me down into their miry depths. "Why'd you leave?" he says. Agony coats each syllable.

I swallow, but the lump in my throat is the size of a boulder and refuses to budge. "I thought you wanted me to."

He sets his cup down on the coffee table. "You thought I—" He stands up abruptly, jarring the sofa. "Fuck, Saylor. Why would you think I wanted you to leave?" His hands dive into his soft curls.

I clutch the blanket tighter around my shoulders. "You said you didn't want me there anymore."

He shakes his head and slumps back into his seat. I set my own tea down so I don't spill it with all of his shifting.

"I needed time to think, but I never meant I didn't want you," he says quietly.

"It's fine. We both knew it was bound to happen sooner or later."

"What's that supposed to mean?"

"Come on, Rhett." I pick at a stray thread on my uniform. "Let's not pretend this would have worked in the real world."

"Why not?" One glance reveals an annoyed look on his face. "Is this about summer camp?" he asks, a hard edge in his voice.

I sigh, letting my hands flop into my lap. "It's about camp and your past and my present and—"

"I'm not that guy anymore."

My eyes feel sad, heavy, and skeptical. "You expect me to believe that a month on the road is enough to change you?"

"No. But a month with you is enough to change anyone. Especially me."

Closing my eyes, I let out a shaky breath. "Why are you here, Rhett?" I reach for my tea again. My hands desperately need something to do, or they will end up tangled in his hair, buried in the folds of his hoodie, caressing the sharp edges of his jawline.

"I needed to give you this." He reaches into the back pocket of his jeans and pulls out a crumpled piece of paper. After he hands it to me, I realize it's a check for the amount we agreed on. "I left the name blank because I wasn't sure which surname you're using."

The implication stings, but I choose to ignore it, even though I can feel my cheeks heating. "It's Jones again." My voice is hushed. It was the first thing I did after the divorce was finalized. "You could have just mailed it. You know my address."

"Saylor, you know why I'm really here." His voice is velvet against my skin, his eyes dark wishing wells of promises. He leans forward, elbows on his knees, heart in his hand.

"You nearly broke me that night." My words come out in a whisper. "I knew it would happen the second I bumped into you on the stairs. I held my breath, knowing that when I fell it would hurt like hell." The ball of tears in my throat refuses to dissolve. "It did. It hurt so much more than I thought it would."

"Fuck, Saylor." Rhett leans his head against the back of the sofa and closes his eyes.

I sniff and wipe my nose with the back of my hand. "But I'm learning how to be okay. I have Leo, I have a job—well, I did"—I shoot him a meaningful look, and he winces—"and I'm trying to move on after you. Can't you just let me do that?"

"I don't want you to move on." He grabs my hand and tucks it between his own. "I want you to give us a chance. A real chance. Being your first kiss isn't enough. I want to be your last kiss, too."

Tears cloud my vision as I shake my head. "We don't make sense together."

"Baby," he says, setting my tea down before tugging on my hand, "you're the best thing that's ever happened to me. I would be a fucking fool if I let you get away from me again."

"I'm scared," I whisper.

Entwining our fingers, he says, "I'd rather do it scared with you than confident with anyone else."

My jaw trembles as I stare at him. Can I bet it all on him? He makes me feel safer than I ever have before, but he also scares me more than anyone else because he holds the power to tear it all away.

"You took a chance on Leo," Rhett says, as the cat begins licking his paws on the windowsill. "Can't you take a chance on me? I'll even sing you the song if you want." He waggles his eyebrows in that ridiculous way that always has me fighting laughter.

I bite back a smile. "I guess you did write me a song."

He leans forward until I can smell the peppermint from the toothpick he chewed in the car. "You listened to that?"

"I'd have to be living in a cave to not have heard it."

A cocky grin spreads over his lips. "I'll write you a hundred more if you say yes."

"And what am I saying yes to?" I ask.

"Be my girlfriend." His lips brush against mine, cool and tantalizing. "A real one this time."

40

"Make You Mine" - PUBLIC

Rhett

The look on Saylor's face scares me more than anything else. She looks unsure about me, and I panic for the first time since she left. How could I have been so naive? I thought she'd take me back if I apologized in person.

"Babe, I'm sorry," I say. "I'm sorry for walking out on you. I'm sorry for not listening to what you had to say, for not believing you the first time." I entwine our fingers. "But mostly, I'm sorry for hurting you."

I'm not sure what I expected—gratitude perhaps, or at the very least forgiveness—but Saylor still looks frozen.

My heart is pounding like I've just snorted two lines of coke. "Can you forgive me?" I ask.

"I—" Her words get trapped in that luscious mouth of hers.

"I know I don't deserve you. But I'm pretty sure I'll die if you don't say yes. You like to do charity work, don't you?"

This is enough to snap her out of her trance. Her eyes dance with that fire that hits me harder than any drug. "A charity case, huh?" she says.

I shrug and give her a small smile. "Whatever it takes."

She drops her gaze down to the colorful blanket in her lap, which looks like something my grandma would have had in her house in the seventies. "I'm sorry too. For everything."

It's quiet enough that I barely hear it, but the second it registers, I have to ball my hands into fists to keep from dragging her onto my lap. I know how easily she scares, and I'm willing to go as slowly as I need to in order to win her back.

I lift her chin with my finger, causing her eyes to find mine again. "Don't apologize. It was an honest mistake."

She starts to shake her head, but I can't resist any longer. I lean forward and take her mouth with mine. It's as soft as pillows and tastes like chamomile tea. She surrenders beneath me, and my heart soars all the way to the fucking clouds.

I gently release her and ease back just enough to read her eyes. It's become my favorite hobby. I allow a slow smile to lift the corners of my mouth. "I know what that expression means," I murmur.

She looks skeptical. "What?"

"It means 'take me to bed and fuck me until I scream.'"

A tiny gasp leaves her mouth, which is all the confirmation I need that I've hit the nail on the head, and now it's time for me to hit something else. I yank her toward me, depositing her into my lap.

She gasps again. "That felt like a move."

I bury my nose in her neck. "It was."

"A *practiced* move," she emphasizes.

I pull back to look at her. "And by practice, you mean . . ."

She rolls her eyes in faux irritation, which turns to bliss when I gently bite her collarbone. "I mean, you've done this before. Quite often, by the feel of it."

I continue nibbling my way across her chest, sweating at the thought of having her breasts in my mouth very soon. "Are you referring to sex or pulling girls into my lap?"

She tries to sound annoyed, but she can't hide how much she's enjoying this. It starts as a groan but ends as a whimper. "Everyone knows how much sex you've had, so obviously I was referring to the other."

"Mmm," I say into her skin. "This would be the first time." My hands are fastened to her waist, and I feel her stiffen.

"Please don't lie to me, Rhett," she says softly.

I draw back immediately. "Swear to god, baby."

"Then why did it feel so natural?" There's a caution in her eyes that tells me I still have a long way to go before fully earning her trust.

"Maybe because I've been dreaming about doing it since the first time we sat on this sofa?"

She blinks those dark eyes as she takes this in. "I *knew* you were up to no good that day."

I grin, guilty as fuck. "I've had a lot of fantasies about this particular piece of furniture."

"How many of them involve the world's sexiest polo shirt?" She glances down at her red work uniform.

"It's a different spin, but I'm here for it." I reach for the bottom hem and yank it hard, tearing it right up the middle. "There's a lot you can do with clothes, even if they're ugly as fuck."

She gasps out a laugh as she looks down at her ruined shirt. "Now what am I going to do?"

"I say we burn it." I pull it off her and throw it across the room.

She's straddling me, wearing nothing but a lacy black bra and a pair of polyester pants. It takes every ounce of self-control I possess—which I'll admit isn't a lot—not to tear both of them off her as well.

I take her breasts in my hands, flicking my thumbs across her nipples through the lace. Her breathing goes raspy. I press my mouth against her clavicle, savoring the flavor of her and wanting nothing more than to taste her further south. My dick pulses inside my jeans, eager to get to work.

"God, you're delicious," I murmur.

I reach into her bra and tug her free, letting the softness of her boobs fill my hands. She pushes her chest forward, so I take them into my mouth one at a time. A soft moan slips past her lips, and she shudders when I trail a finger down to her waistband.

"Let's get rid of these," I tell her, tugging gently on her pants.

She lifts her ass high enough for me to pull them off and discard them with the shirt, revealing a lacy black thong that matches the bra. I freeze.

"Who'd you wear these for?" There's no way she anticipated this happening today. The shock on her face when I showed up at the counter told me that much. My eyes are still on her thong, which— goddamnit—might be the hottest thing I've ever seen.

Her eyes blink open, and she glances down at her matching set of underwear. Then she shrugs, fucking *shrugs*, like it's of no consequence. "Myself."

I'm relieved, but also frustrated. "Don't wear this stuff around me unless you want to get thoroughly and properly fucked," I grind out.

She sucks in a breath. "I'll keep that in mind. *Sir.*"

My cock strains at my fly. "Careful, or I'll fuck that smart mouth."

"Is that a threat?" She quirks her lips into a teasing smile. "Or a promise?"

I give her a nonplussed look and flick her bra strap. "Take this off."

She does, and it hits a nearby potted plant. She doesn't even glance over, her eyes glued to mine.

"Good girl," I say, before taking her freed breast into my mouth again.

She moans and pushes into me even further. I reward her eagerness with an extra hard suck, and her back bows for me.

"Lie down," I say once I'm able to release her. She tastes so damn good, it's one of the hardest things I've ever done.

She complies, leaning back until she's resting against the orange fabric of this crazy sofa, which has starred in a few too many of my fantasies. I run my hand down the length of her, stopping when I reach her underwear. My eyes narrow as I take her in.

"What's wrong?" she asks.

"Nothing," I murmur. "Just considering how I want to play with you this time."

Her breathing turns more ragged the longer I stare at her, making me question how wet she's becoming for me. I drag a finger under her thong and through her seam.

"You're fucking soaked," I say with wonder.

A tiny hysterical laugh floats out of her mouth. "I could have told you that."

I grind my knuckle into her and relish the way she arches for more. "God, you're slick. I can't wait to eat you out."

Her face turns panicked. "Rhett, I'm going to come if you do."

I breathe out a chuckle. "Good." Then I drop down between her legs, take my time dragging her thong off, and bury my face in the lips of the only pussy I want for the rest of my life.

She gasps as I suck her clit. "Rhett, oh god." Her hands reach down and tangle in my hair, pulling me even closer in that way she does, until I'm pretty sure nothing exists in this world except me and her, right here in this moment.

Saylor is not quiet when I make love to her, and I hope the whole world hears how much she enjoys this. She screams my name as the walls of her pussy squeeze around my tongue. I continue thrusting it in, deeper and deeper, until she finishes.

When I rise up to look at her, she doesn't look satisfied, only more ravenous than before. "What do you need?" I ask her.

"I need you," she whimpers.

"I want to hear you say it."

She swallows. "I need you inside me."

I groan at the thought of finally pushing my dick into her again, of being buried so deep that my balls slap against her. "I'll be inside of you, all right. So hard and so deep you won't know what hit you."

She gives an answering moan. "How soon? Because I need you, like, right now."

"I'm coming, baby." I don't even bother taking off my pants, just roll on a condom. I reach for her legs and push them up so her knees are bent. She hugs them against herself, opening herself up for me like a flower in bloom.

Her pussy is red and raw from my mouth, and I can't resist one more taste. She bucks against me, but I hold her in place as I ravish her once more with my tongue. Finally, when my cock is screaming for his turn, I press a kiss to her folds and rise.

I slide my tip just inside her, making sure I'm positioned correctly. She shifts beneath me, ready for me to claim her, but I fully intend to savor every second of this. When I'm confident I won't last much longer, I thrust in as far as I can go.

God, she feels good. Like a fucking fantasy come to life. She arches her back off the sofa and tilts her hips in a way that allows me to drive deeper than I've ever gone before. I look down to watch the joining of our bodies, the place where our flesh is slapping together, making wet noises thanks to how drenched she is.

She opens her eyes, and together we watch as I fuck her on her orange sofa. Somewhere, her cat is probably watching, too.

I reach down between us. When I find her clit, I pinch it, making her cry out. She tightens around me, and when her release comes, my cock doesn't have a choice but to pulse into her as well. I hold her tightly as we both climax.

When it's over, I stay on top of her and inside her, not ready for this to be over yet. "I love you, Saylor Jones," I say.

41

"Wonderland" - Taylor Swift

Several Months Later

Saylor

"Tell us about your latest hit, 'Combat Boots,'" Sandra Clark says, directing her attention toward Rhett. She's fortyish, with that TV bob haircut in a blond that is definitely not natural, but which looks good nonetheless.

Rhett grins and looks at me where I'm sitting beside him on the sofa. These seats aren't as comfortable as they look on-screen. "I wrote it about Saylor, of course." Our hands are already twined together, which Sandra aww'ed over when we first sat down, but Rhett tightens his grip even more, his eyes telling me all the things he plans to do to me later.

"Of course," Sandra says. "And how does it feel to be thrust into the spotlight, Saylor?"

I feel the heat rising to my face, although it won't be noticeable to anyone else, thanks to the thick layers of TV makeup I'm wearing. "It took some getting used to," I say, glancing at Rhett. "But it's worth it."

"And have you thought about selling the boots?" Humor lines

Sandra's voice. "I'm sure they'd fetch a pretty penny on eBay."

We all look down at my beat-up Doc Martens, and the camera crew zooms in for a close-up. I laugh. "Nah, they're too special for that."

The live audience titters at this, and Rhett squeezes my hand again. I've said the right thing, even though it's not really true. Sure, I like them, but mostly because I got them for a hell of a deal when they were donated to Justine's Attic years ago, not because they were the inspiration for Rhett Cole's latest hit.

"Combat Boots" has taken the world by storm since he posted that video, easily outperforming all of his other songs to date. He's had more offers than he can keep track of since leaving Lunar Records.

"What are your plans, Rhett?" Sandra asks. "You left your label after a conflict of interest." *And had to pay a hefty sum for breaking your contract*, she doesn't add. "Are you planning to sign with a new label in the future?"

Rhett shifts on the sofa, but keeps a firm grasp on my hand. "At the moment, I'm happy dipping my toes in the indie waters. But I don't know what the future holds." He turns his eyes to me again, and I feel his smile down to my toes.

I moved into his condo last month. He would have happily moved into my flat with me, but I was tired of bumping into the fridge every time I turned on the stove. All that space was hard to turn down, especially given the way Leo likes exploring. I did make Rhett promise to let me decorate it, and he was only too happy to comply.

"What about for the two of you?" Sandra says, settling back in her seat across from us. "What are your plans for the future?"

I feel rather than see Rhett grinning beside me, but I keep my eyes on Sandra. The truth is, we've talked about the future, but only in vague terms. Am I willing to risk getting married again? Surprisingly, yes. What I share with Rhett feels like a universe apart from anything Nate and I ever had.

Does Rhett feel the same way? It's hard to tell. Every time the subject comes up, he evades it or makes a comment that could be taken either way. My verdict is that he won't be ready for a long time. Getting Rhett Cole to settle down would be the accomplishment of a lifetime, and I have no desire to rush anything.

"Every plan for my future involves Saylor," Rhett says, releasing my hand and putting his arm around my shoulders. "We'll have to see how they play out." It's a typical response from him, so I smile at Sandra to show her and everyone watching that I'm happy with our situation. And I am. Truly. Even if we never make it official, if I get to grow old with him, that's enough for me.

* * *

Tonight's concert is at a local music venue. It's a sold-out four-hour show, and Rhett is the headliner. All of the guys except Jamal stayed with him when he left Lunar Records. It wasn't hard to find a new rhythm guitarist, and Blake is great.

Rhett and the band do a few of these shows a month and are working on producing their first indie album. It keeps him just busy enough to not get bored, while still giving him plenty of time for other things, like spoiling Leo with too many cat treats and buying me things he shouldn't.

Tonight's crowd is smaller than the ones during the US tour. I assumed that since I'm local, no one would care about our relationship, but they eat it up almost as much as the Americans. Which means the pit is out of the question for me, according to Rhett.

"I look just like a groupie," I say, gesturing to my outfit—a Rhett Cole T-shirt, ripped jeans (from some high-end designer brand, thanks to Rhett's Amex), a flannel tied around my waist, and my trusty Docs.

His eyelids drop even lower over his eyes, a clear sign he's annoyed.

"Baby, that gorgeous face has been blowing up on TV and social media. Everyone would recognize you."

"I hate watching from the side stage." The view sucks, and tonight I want to feel the energy in the pit.

"I'll go with her," someone behind me says.

I turn to find Leo standing in the doorway of the backstage area, face devoid of expression as usual. "Leo!" I haven't seen him since the tour, and the memories he brings with him makes my eyes water. I walk toward him and throw my arms around his burly chest.

"Hey, mate," Rhett says, joining us. He reaches out a hand to shake Leo's, effectively positioning himself between me and my former PPO. "I didn't know you were in town."

Leo shrugs. "Thought I'd see if you needed additional security tonight."

I turn my best set of puppy dog eyes on Rhett.

He huffs out an annoyed sigh. "Fine. But you are not to leave her side."

"Yes, sir." Leo nods. "You have my word."

He escorts me toward the crowd after Rhett gives me a scorching goodbye kiss. I'm more elated at having gotten my way than I am about being in the pit for the show. The energy buzzing around in here makes me lightheaded.

When Rhett finally takes the stage, it feels like my heart will jump right out of my chest and into his arms. He is hands-down the hottest man I've ever laid eyes on, and he's all mine. Letting myself fall in love with him has been the most exhilarating experience of my life. No holding back, no fear of getting caught, just unbridled love.

Tonight he's wearing black straight-leg jeans, a paisley-print shirt over a white tank top, and several metal chains around his neck. His hands each have at least four rings on them as well. He pulls off the rockstar look well, but my favorite is when we're at home and he's wearing nothing but a pair of sweatpants. Or nothing at all. Rather partial to that one, if I'm being honest.

His eyes immediately seek me out, although I know he's trying not to make it apparent to avoid drawing unnecessary attention to me.

After several of his top hits, I know he's about to transition into "Combat Boots." Chase switches to a minor tone on the keys, and while the crowd may not recognize what's coming, I do.

Rhett told me his plan, and I agreed to it. Now that we are officially together, the spotlight has become part of our life. I'm still getting used to it, but Rhett makes it easier. His eyes catch mine once more, then land on Leo, who is dutifully standing behind me. They exchange a meaningful look, then Leo nudges me forward with a hand on my back.

From the stage, Rhett's voice rings out. "As many of you know, I went on tour last fall."

The crowd cheers at this.

"During that tour, I fell in love with the most amazing girl," he continues. More cheering. "She's actually here tonight. Would you all like to meet her?"

Fans across the venue go wild. Leo and I are at the front of the pit now, and Rhett meets us at the edge of the stage. Leo boosts me up, and Rhett grabs me. Then I'm onstage with him again, but this time it's under very different circumstances—namely, that I agreed to it.

The lights are blinding. I remember that from last time, but I still don't know how Rhett handles it all the time. The cheering is deafening, and a chant breaks out. "Kiss her, kiss her, kiss her."

Rhett grins and leans toward me, capturing my mouth with his, much to the delight of his fans. He swings his guitar behind his back and grabs my face with both hands. Catcalls ring out, but neither of us is paying any attention. Even in front of thousands of people, he has the ability to make my knees go weak with desire.

He finally pulls back, but only to nuzzle my nose with his own. "Stay for the song?" he asks. I nod in agreement, and he approaches the microphone, his arm slung around my shoulders. "As you may know, Saylor inspired my biggest hit to date." Rhett lets go of me to grab his guitar and play the first few chords.

If I thought the roaring was loud before, it's reached insanity levels now. The band plays the song, Rhett sneaking kisses between verses, and I don't know if I've ever been so happy before. Watching him do what he loves on his own terms—it's incredible. Our life is far from perfect, but it's also so far from where I was just a few months ago that it's impossible not to feel like I'm tripping out on bliss.

The song always ends with a big flourish, usually Rhett shredding his guitar in a dramatic way, but tonight, he just slips the strap over his head and hands it to one of the guys. I don't even see who, because I'm too focused on the way he's focusing on me.

I assumed I would leave the stage after the song, but from the way Rhett is walking toward me, I realize he has something else planned that we did not discuss. My heart is jackhammering in my chest. I trust him, but sometimes what he thinks is a good idea is still a far cry from my own.

When he's right in front of me, he leans in close and whispers, "Trust me?" as if reading my thoughts.

I nod silently, then gasp when he drops to one knee before me. Surprisingly, the crowd goes silent, as though we're all collectively holding our breaths.

Rhett reaches into the pocket of his jeans, and I know what he's pulling out before I see it. We all do.

The box is covered in black velvet, and with one glance, I can already tell this ring cost a fortune. He pops the lid open, revealing not the custom designer stone I expected but an oval-shaped sapphire surrounded by diamonds on a thin gold band that is clearly antique.

Tears are flooding my eyes before I've even processed any of this. "Rhett," I whisper, but he just smiles up at me.

"Saylor Elizabeth Jones," he says, and I'm glad there's no microphone. Everyone can see us, but no one can hear anything we say. "I love you. God, I'd move heaven and earth if you asked me to." He swipes at the moisture in his own eyes. "Will you marry me? I swear to love you forever and treat you like a fucking princess every day of your life."

I gulp out a laugh. "Will you let me have the biggest piece of cheesecake?"

"Always," he says solemnly, and I know he means it.

I wipe my eyes again, not sure which desire is stronger: the one to laugh or cry. "Of course I'll marry you," I say through the tears.

He gets up so fast it startles me, but he catches me before I can stumble backward. Holding me by the waist, he twirls me around in circles, and the crowd goes wild once more.

42

"The End of the Game" - Weezer

Rhett

"If I'd known you look this good in a tuxedo, I might have demanded you wear one sooner." Saylor gives me an impish smile as she straightens my lapels.

"Enjoy it while you can," I say. "It'll be the only time this year, if I can help it." While I may have grown up in suits and bow ties, that doesn't mean I enjoy wearing them.

Saylor smooths down the shoulders of my maroon Armani jacket, then stands on tiptoes to press a kiss to my lips. My hands fit around her waist the way they were meant to, and I tug her closer, not at all opposed to stripping off both of our outfits and hopping back into bed.

She pulls back. "You'll wrinkle my clothes."

"Nah," I say, glancing down at her tailored black pantsuit. "Too expensive for that." I've enjoyed nothing more than stocking her closet with as many clothes as it will hold, not that she ever wears them. Tonight is the exception.

Brushing her hands over the black jacket, she sighs. "Men."

I snort out a laugh and grab her waist again. Under the blazer, she's wearing a sheer lace top with a bralette underneath. She's tied the whole look together with a leather belt, simple silver hoop earrings, and pointed-toe stiletto heels. My girl looks hot.

"We're going to be late," she warns me, but there's no frustration in her voice. She wants this just as much as I do.

"Fuck the whole thing. Let's just stay home." I nuzzle her neck and nibble her earlobe. She's wearing a new perfume, and it makes me want to haul her to the bedroom right now.

"What about Maeve?" she asks around a smile. "She'll kill us."

"I'd forgotten about her for two blissful minutes," I say, pressing a gentle bite to the slender column of Saylor's brown neck.

She giggles and tries to squirm away from me. "Such a brave man."

I growl in irritation, but she's right. Maeve Wilson is not the kind of person you want to mess with. "Fine," I say, "but we're leaving early."

"Okay by me," Saylor purrs, dropping one more kiss on my lips before scurrying across the room to grab her handbag.

I've hired a car for tonight so I can feel up my fiancée in the backseat on the way to the charity auction. It's still hard to believe that this incredible girl has agreed to be my wife. As we drive to the Museum of Art, I hold Saylor's hand in mine and stare at her ring. "No regrets yet?" I ask her.

She rolls her eyes and tugs her hand away, but only so she can wrap it around my neck. She pulls my head down to hers. "None."

The car pulls up to the museum's entrance way too soon for my liking. Saylor and I separate, and I climb out of the car first, then reach out a hand to her. It's her first big society event, but she doesn't even look nervous.

We find everyone else once we step inside, or rather, they find us.

Maeve approaches, hands on her hips. "There you are. I thought you lovebirds had decided not to show." She says this with a smile, but it's covering thin ice. The ice queen is on the verge of cracking.

"Sorry we're late," I say, and press a kiss to her cheek. "Traffic."

She purses her red lips even tighter, because she knows traffic had nothing to do with it. She's wearing a floor-length black satin gown with sharp, structured shoulders and a deep V-neck, a diamond choker, and matching stud earrings.

Watch out, world. Maeve Wilson is out to kill tonight.

I move to greet everyone else, keeping Saylor tucked under my arm. She's attended a few poker games and even helped us with several revenge plots, but everyone is still a little on edge with someone new in the group. We'd all just gotten used to Slate being around when I announced that Saylor and I were serious.

Pierce, Heath, and Slate are all in tuxedos as well, although both Heath and Slate look as uncomfortable as I feel. Why do we do this to ourselves? One glance at the woman at my side reminds me exactly why. I'd have worn my fucking birthday suit to this thing if Saylor asked me to, and now I kind of wish she had.

"So, what's the plan?" I ask, rubbing my hands together. This thing will be boring as fuck if we're not bringing someone down at the same time.

"Deirdre Cox," Maeve says, eyes sparking with fire. "We run up her bidding, then back out at the last minute. Meanwhile, Lux will drain her accounts so she's left with a bounced check."

Lux nods her agreement, and I wonder where she's keeping her laptop. It's definitely not under that fitted white satin gown.

Pierce adjusts his black bow tie. "The shell bidder is already seated, but I gave him instructions earlier."

Maeve whirls on him. "What shell bidder?"

Pierce stares down at her for a few seconds before saying quietly, "The one we agreed upon."

If he were anyone else, I'd be scared for his safety right now. Maeve may be just over five feet tall, but she packs a lot of venom in those sixty-one inches. Her heels give her a slight advantage, but Pierce still towers over her.

"I'm doing the bidding," Maeve says. "Remember?"

"No, I don't remember," he says.

"We talked about this. In great detail."

Saylor sends me an amused look that asks *Are they always like this?*

They've always butted heads, but it's been especially bad since their companies had a mutual deal that went south, thanks to Deirdre Cox. Hence the reason we're all here tonight.

"The only thing I remember is agreeing we'd hire a shell bidder so Deirdre doesn't get wind of the plan," Pierce says, stepping closer until he's toe to toe with Maeve.

She fumes at him, refusing to back up even an inch. "No, we agreed that I would do the bidding to make her angry and keep her trying to outbid me."

Heath cocks a brow at me, and I grin back, shaking my head. "Maybe we could just fuck the whole plan and go play poker," I suggest.

Neither Pierce nor Maeve appears to hear me. Either that, or they're very good at pretending not to. Their staring contest is making Walker uncomfortable, and she fiddles with the new diamond on her hand. Heath beat me to it in the proposal game, but I couldn't be happier for the two of them.

"Maybe you were too busy fucking your boy toy to remember what we discussed," Pierce says. "Where is he, anyway? I thought maybe you'd bring him tonight."

Maeve's spine goes ramrod straight. "Fuck off."

"Oh, that's right." Pierce snaps his fingers as if he actually just remembered, the fucker. "He's probably here with his *wife*."

"So, anyway," I say, butting in and clapping my hands before Maeve can snap my best friend's neck. "What are we bidding on again?"

"A stupid hot-air balloon," Maeve says at the same time as Pierce says, "A vintage, fully restored hot-air balloon."

Saylor lets out a chuckle beside me. "You're kidding, right?" She was volunteering on the crisis hotline the night we planned this takedown, and she has yet to be party to any of the really ridiculous things that go down in this world.

Heath snorts. "Afraid not."

Apparently, Deirdre Cox has been talking about this hot-air balloon with everyone she meets, already planning parties around it and everything. A bit over the top, if you ask me, but hey, why have money if you can't spend it on ridiculous shit?

"Guys, it looks like the auction is about to start," Walker says, gesturing to the room where the bidding will take place. She's right. The foyer of the museum has mostly cleared out, and we are standing here like fucking idiots.

Maeve holds up her paddle and doesn't take her eyes off Pierce. "I'll be in the front row, bidding on a hot-air balloon like we agreed." Then she stalks off, leaving the rest of us in her hypothetical dust.

"Oi, mate." Heath slaps a hand on Pierce's chest. "You sure you want to take that on?"

Pierce is still watching Maeve walk away, but he shrugs. "It's nothing I can't handle, trust me."

* * *

The auction is boring as hell, but I could have guessed as much. Saylor and I sit in the back. She's watching the bidding, but I'm mostly trying to figure out how to get a hand into her top without anyone seeing. Why the fuck didn't she wear a dress?

When the hot-air balloon comes up for bids, though, I straighten in my seat. There are a handful of interested buyers, but they drop out one by one once the price climbs into the six digits.

311

"All this for an old balloon that probably doesn't work anymore?" Saylor asks.

Eventually, there are only three bidders left—Deirdre Cox, who looks like she hasn't been laid in a decade; Pierce's shell bidder; and Maeve, who also looks like she hasn't been laid in ages.

The number keeps climbing, and I feel Saylor tense up beside me. She's really getting into this. I grin and tuck her hand into mine.

"Two hundred sixty-eight thousand," the auctioneer says.

All three paddles go up.

"Two hundred seventy thousand."

Once more, three paddles in the air.

The auctioneer sighs. "Three hundred thousand."

The paddles continue going up with each number he calls. I yawn and settle back in my seat, throwing my arm around Saylor's chair. We might be here a while. Both Deirdre and Maeve look ready to murder someone—each other—and the shell bidder looks as bored as I feel. Something tells me this isn't going to end well.

Fifteen minutes later, the bid is at two and a half million. Maeve's face is as red as her lipstick, and Deirdre's has lost what remaining bits of color it had. Then—I'm not even sure how it happens—Pierce's bidder gets distracted at the same moment Deirdre gives up the fight. This leaves Maeve with the winning bid for an old hot-air balloon she'd rather smother herself with than take home with her.

I grab Saylor's hand and pull her from the room, needing a drink before this whole thing comes to blows. I can already smell the smoke coming from Maeve's ears.

We're sipping our glasses of champagne—Saylor's first, my third—when everyone else joins us in the foyer. Pierce walks up first, but Maeve is right behind him. He accepts a drink from one of the waiters with a grateful nod, then throws the whole thing back in one go.

Maeve smacks his arm, but he doesn't even flinch. "What the hell was that?"

"That," Pierce says, exchanging his glass for a full one, "was your stupid plan gone to shit. Happy?" He drains his champagne again without looking at her.

"I'm livid," she hisses, apparently no longer caring who can see or hear, because we are attracting quite a lot of attention.

"Hey, guys, we might want to take this elsewhere," I say, scanning the room for cameras. There aren't any yet, but it's only a matter of time.

They both ignore me and continue glaring at each other.

"You're going to pay for the stupid thing," Maeve says.

Pierce huffs out an amused sound. "Like hell I am."

"Your shell bidder is the reason we're in this mess."

He hands off his empty glass and crosses his arms over his chest, then bends down until their noses are nearly touching. "Actually, it was your constant need for drama and control that won you that fucking balloon."

Maeve gasps, and a chuckle slips past my own lips, which I quickly cover with a cough. "Go to hell," she says, glaring at Pierce so hard I half expect his tux to start smoking.

He smirks. "You're the one with the handbasket."

Her tiny hands are clenched into fists at her sides. She turns to the rest of us, and I swear I see Heath take a step back. "You guys were there. You heard us agree that I would do the bidding, right?"

No one says anything. Slate just stands there, arms crossed, like he'd rather be anywhere else in the world. Lux is suddenly absorbed by her fingernails. Heath is staring at the carpet, and Walker is twisting her hands into knots. Beside me, Saylor is watching the whole thing go down like it's a soap opera that she doesn't give a shit about but finds entirely too fascinating to turn off.

"Of course they didn't, Maeve," Pierce says. "Because that's not what happened."

Maeve jerks back to him and shoves a finger in his face. "Yes, it is, you manipulative piece of shit. They're just scared of what you'll do if they tell the truth."

"Hey, not true," I say. "I could take Pierce any day."

He narrows his eyes at me before focusing on Maeve again. "I'm manipulative? I just heard you last week bragging to one of the investors about the merits of dinner downtown, but everyone knows it's because you didn't want to be stuck with an hour-long commute."

"Oh, is that why you drone on and on about how 'inspiring' it is to mentor junior employees, right before dumping half your workload onto your assistant?" Maeve says, arms folded over her chest, armor on.

Walker steps forward, ever the peacemaker in our group. Her dark red gown rustles as she enters the battleground. "Guys, I'm sure we can work this out. What if—"

"No," Maeve snaps. "The only way this thing ends is if Pierce admits he blew the whole thing up." The two of them are still locking eyes, and if I'm being honest, it's getting downright awkward. They've never had a fight on this scale before.

Saylor touches my arm and leans in close. "Should I be worried?"

I give her my best smile. "Nah, they'll sort it out." Although we might all be ancient relics before it happens.

"I'm not admitting anything," Pierce says, "except that you're a pain in my ass."

Maeve's jaw grows rigid enough to snap. "Funny. I'm surprised you can feel anything at all with that stick shoved up there."

Pierce bites back a smile. He does a pretty good job of hiding it too, but I catch it just in time. This whole thing is fucking amusing him. Well, good for him, but I'm getting tired of it.

I sling an arm around Saylor's neck, tugging her in close to get a whiff of her scent. God, she smells good. "Why don't you two go fight it out in bed while the rest of us go home?" I say.

A red flush climbs Maeve's neck. She's always had a propensity for blushing at the slightest things—one of the main reasons I love to taunt her—but I'm not sure I've ever seen her quite this rosy. Pierce doesn't exactly look like a cool cucumber anymore, either. Holy shit, are they—

"I have an idea," Walker says, bravely approaching our two psychopaths again. "What if we held some kind of competition?"

Maeve and Pierce slowly break eye contact to look at her. Leave it to the word "competition" to get their attention. "What did you have in mind?" Maeve asks.

Walker gets a sort of deer-in-the-headlights look. She obviously has nothing up her sleeve.

I step forward, reluctantly leaving Saylor behind. "We'll work out the details. A challenge of sorts."

Pierce narrows his eyes, considering.

Maeve frowns but nods. "Winner gets the friend group," she says.

There's silence as everyone takes this in.

"Maeve, you can't be serious," Lux chimes in, finally interested in what's going on.

"I'm dead serious," Maeve says. "Unless you all agree that I was right?" No one meets her eye, and she takes a triumphant step backward. "Then it's settled. We'll fight for the right to poker nights and revenge plots."

I'm relieved to see that Pierce doesn't look any more gleeful about this arrangement than the rest of us. It seems Maeve has officially gone off the deep end. She actually plans to kick Pierce out of our group if she wins? And what the hell would we do without Maeve plotting the best takedowns and keeping everyone's sensitivity at bay with her cutting remarks?

Everyone else seems to mirror my thoughts, but no one says anything. There's no reasoning with her when she gets like this anyway.

When no one protests, Maeve gives a half-assed smile and tosses her hand up in a wave. "Call me when you have the challenge planned. Better make it a good one, too. I wouldn't want Pierce to say I cheated." She throws one more glare at him before turning her back to us.

"Hey, Maeve," Pierce calls as she walks away. "Don't forget your hot-air balloon."

She sticks a finger in the air and keeps walking.

Fuck. What the hell did we just agree to?

* * *

To read a bonus chapter of our diabolical friends plotting something besides revenge ;) → visit jessicajude.com/king-of-obsession-bonus.

Keep reading for an exclusive chapter of the next book in the Hand of Revenge series!

Exclusive Chapter

Maeve

There are few things in life worse than waiting, but I'll tell you one of them. *Waiting with Pierce St. James.* The man is absolutely maddening.

Take right now, for instance. I'm pacing, but he's on the couch in his living room, the one facing the large window with the panoramic view. The lights of the city are nearly hidden by the storm clouds rolling in. You might see him and think there's nothing particularly obnoxious about the way he's sitting there, but you'd be missing all the little details.

He has an ankle propped on his knee and an arm draped across the back of the sleek modern sofa, settled in as though he's relaxed, when I think it's safe to say "relaxed" is not an appropriate adjective to describe either of us right now. Which makes his posture a lie.

Then there's his face. It's not exactly a bad face, not what you'd call ugly. Sharp cheekbones and jawline, pouty mouth, symmetrical. It's passable, okay?

Fine, it's definitely in the top 1 percent of attractive faces in the country. Or it would be if not for those eyes. Dark brown, nearly black, and spaced the proper distance from his nose, it's not the eyes themselves that are the problem. It's what he does with them.

I spin on my heel in front of the window, and sure enough, he's watching me. Those stupid eyes travel the length of me—and listen, I know I look good tonight, but the way they linger over every inch of my body makes my muscles tighten.

Smoothing my hands over my long-sleeve dark floral-print minidress, I continue stalking the living room, ignoring him. A tiny huff comes from the sofa, like he's scoffing at me, and it takes every single ounce of willpower I have not to march over and smack that smirk right off his face.

The man is a menace, a godforsaken outright smudge on humanity. The only thing more shocking than the fact that I am stuck in the same room with him—*alone*—is the fact that we were friends up until this past year.

I *know*. You're wondering how I could've possibly been friends with a guy like him. Trust me, it has been the cause of countless sleepless nights. It bothers me that I didn't notice it before, not because I have regrets from the past twelve years, but because I'm afraid it means my skill at reading people is slipping.

If Pierce and I could have been friends for nearly half my life and I didn't recognize the signs, what other things am I missing? The thought is terrifying.

Movement from the other side of the room snags in the corner of my eye, and I turn on instinct. Pierce has gotten up and is removing his jacket. The man practically lives in custom suits—not something I typically have a problem with, but lately, everything about him makes my blood boil. Doesn't he own a pair of slacks?

Muscles ripple under his shirt as he tosses the jacket over the back of the couch. My mouth goes dry before I realize what I'm doing. I jerk my eyes back where they belong—the far end of the room—and resume my pacing.

I don't need to look to feel that infuriating smirk being cast in my direction.

When I reach the end of the room and turn around, I glance at the clock above the mantel. Pierce and I have been out here for nearly forty minutes. If the rest of them don't invite us into the game room soon, I'm going to snap. Why the hell is it taking this long to put together a stupid challenge?

"If they are in there playing poker," I mutter under my breath, "so help me god."

Pierce lifts his chin, and I realize I've spoken out loud. Fuck. I had no intention of being the first to cut through the silence filling this room like smoke. As if the man needs another reason to gloat.

"What will you do if they are?" he says, now that I've broken the silent treatment and nonverbally declared him the winner in our little standoff. He's perched on the arm of the sofa, just begging to be knocked over.

I briefly consider ignoring him, but do you know how hard it is to go forty minutes without speaking? God, I've been getting lightheaded with the backlog. "None of your goddamn business," I snap.

His eyebrows do this subtle upward flick, as though I've amused him, and you know what? He can go fuck himself.

"Actually," he says, standing and immediately shifting the energy in the room, "since this is my flat, I have a vested interest in knowing whether you plan to torch it to the ground to spite our friends."

I roll my eyes to let him know he doesn't ruffle me, even though my palms have become as clammy as a dead body's. "Don't be an imbecile."

This time his brows move up an entire inch. He shoves his hands into his pockets. "Me? The imbecile?" He takes a step toward me, and I instinctively take a matching one backward. "I'm not the one with a vintage hot-air balloon in my basement."

Tension radiates from my jaw to my head. I force a single deep breath in through my nose, out through my mouth, the way my yoga teacher is always blathering on about. It doesn't help, which confirms my suspicions that she doesn't know what she's talking about. "I wouldn't have that stupid balloon if you hadn't brought in that bloody shell bidder."

Once again, the corner of Pierce's mouth lifts into that ridiculous smirk that I swear will get him killed one of these days. My hands twitch with desire to do the honors.

"And yet, we agreed on the shell bidder," he says.

"For the thousandth time, we did not!" I say, my voice rising several decibels higher than I intended. I bring it back down to a normal range. "The plan all along was for me to drive up the bidding."

He shakes his head as though I'm a clueless child and he's humoring me. "Have you considered that you might be dealing with early onset dementia?"

My nostrils flare as I intensify the glare I have leveled at him. "I do *not* have dementia."

Forehead creasing with mock concern, he tsks and shakes his head. "And yet you own a hot-air balloon." Leaning in closer, he lowers his voice, and I catch a whiff of his cologne—sharp, smooth, a little spicy. "One you paid an obscene amount of money for."

"Because your bidder wouldn't back down!" I say.

Several months ago, we attended a charity auction with the express purpose of exacting revenge on Deirdre Cox. The bitch scammed both of our companies and dragged the name of our joint project, HavenNet, through the mud while pocketing hefty consulting and licensing fees from the people we were trying to help. She is scum of the earth, and I'd like nothing more than to etch my name on her back with the heel of my favorite pair of Louboutins.

You could argue that she's brilliant to have been able to pull off something like that, but I would like to point out that she didn't immediately flee the country after her little scheme. If she were truly smart, she would have taken her millions of stolen money and retreated to a tiny desert island somewhere, where the rest of the world never has to look at her mousy face again.

Instead, she decided to stick around to try to win some old, moldy hot-air balloon. The same one I ended up with, thanks to the bastard standing in front of me.

"Have you taken your maiden voyage yet?" Pierce asks, snapping me out of my fantasy of hunting Deirdre down and forcing bits of torn fabric from her precious balloon down her throat.

"Actually," I say, through a smile that feels more like a grimace, "I thought I'd save those honors for you."

His eyes narrow. "How thoughtful. But I'd prefer not to plummet to my death."

"How *would* you prefer to die?" I inject extra sugar into my voice. "I'm sure I could arrange something."

A flicker of amusement crosses his face before vanishing without a trace. "You couldn't kill me."

I let out a sharp laugh. "Is that a challenge?"

"Sure." He shrugs, hands still in his pockets. Those gray dress pants hang from his hips in a way I'm sure some people would describe as sexy, a subset of society of which I am not a member. "Hit me with your best shot."

"Gross," I say. "You did not just quote Britney Spears at me." Running my hands along the spearpoint collar of my dress, I double-check that it's still lying exactly as it should. I drag the black string tie through my fingers, then tighten the bow ever so slightly. It never hurts to look perfect.

Pierce is still studying me with an unflinching gaze, his eyes resting just below my chin. A tiny quirk of his lips has me reaching back to my collar, even though I just checked it.

"What would you prefer?" His voice has lowered and now sounds almost . . . sultry.

I repress a shudder. "I'd prefer you keep your mouth shut. Things were better before you spoke."

"Ah," he says, then looks down at the floor in a show of faux humility.

I brace myself for the next words from his mouth.

"So then you'd prefer I not tell you that we've made some tweaks to the budget?"

My head rears back a fraction of an inch. "You did what?"

He shrugs, nonchalant, then pulls his hands from his pockets and begins rolling up the sleeves of his white shirt, still in pristine condition despite being worn all day. Or maybe he comes home from work every evening and changes into a new suit. How would I know?

"You said you prefer my silence."

I grind my molars together and force my eyes to stay on his face, not on the way his fingers are dexterously folding his sleeves into perfect photoshoot-ready rolls. "Tell me what you did."

He tugs his mouth to the side and sucks air between his teeth like he's wincing, the bastard. "I wish I could, but—"

I close the distance between us, my heels clicking on the hardwood floor, the sound like gunshots. "This is a joint project."

"And yet you seem to have forgotten the meaning of *teamwork*." He finishes with his shirt and leans down until our noses are only inches apart.

I steel myself to keep from backing away. I cannot lose face now, no matter how badly I want to put distance between us. "We do not have the funding to go any higher—"

"Who said anything about going higher?"

"The only thing you've managed to do so far is increase our costs."

His brows arch upward. "Is that right? What about providing the tech? The team? The entire project is Luminara's—"

"But you don't have the contacts to get it into the countries that need it," I cut in. "Hence, the Wilson Foundation owns you."

A muscle in his jaw twitches, and I mentally pat myself on the back for causing him to break, even if it was just for a millisecond. "No one owns me."

I bite back a smile and cross my arms over my chest. Our verbal firing is finally shifting in my favor. "Really? Wasn't that Cinderella you were on the phone with earlier?"

"Her name is Amara."

"I don't care what her name is. She's nothing but a carbon copy of the last twenty-five women you've dated."

He rolls his eyes and takes a step backward. "What does this have to do with anything?"

"Nothing," I say. "Just that I've never seen you take a phone call from your girlfriend with other people around."

"It was an emergency." His eyes flash a warning, which I proceed to ignore.

I inspect my fresh and immaculate manicure—tiny red roses hand-painted on a bed of onyx. "I'm just saying it appears both the Foundation and Amanda have your balls in their pockets."

He moves so quickly I nearly miss it. One second he's standing a foot away, glaring at me. The next he's so close there's nothing but a hairsbreadth between our bodies, close enough that I can feel the heat of him through my clothes. His face is bent so near to mine that were I to raise my chin a fraction of an inch, my lips would brush against his. Disgusting.

"You're mistaken if you think for one second I will be owned by anyone or anything," he says in a whisper that feels as loaded as a gun to the temple.

I swallow, and his eyes flick down to my throat. He doesn't even bother to correct me about his girlfriend's name.

"Are we clear?" he asks.

A loud clap of thunder punctuates his words and reverberates through the entire flat. I jump, the involuntary movement forcing our bodies to brush against each other, and time stands still.

I've touched Pierce before. Obviously I have. We've been in the same friend group since we were fourteen. We even kissed during one particularly lame birthday party, but that was so many centuries ago, I'm not even sure he remembers it. I've certainly done my best to scrub it from my memory.

This, though. This is different. Accidental, for one thing. Not a hug and peck on the cheek goodbye. Not fingers brushing as he hands me a drink. Not sitting on his lap when there isn't enough room in the car for everyone to have a seat.

I am not a believer in sparks. I'm a grown woman with a career and the ability to make stupid creatures shrink back when they see me coming, for god's sake. So I'm not saying there are sparks as my chest makes contact with his, but I'm also not saying there isn't *something*. Because there is definitely something. It's enough of a something that I find my eyes focused on his mouth as I move away. It's the slowest motion in the world, as though I'm waist-deep in a vat of peanut butter.

He has a nice mouth, I'll say that much. Don't care much for what comes out of it most times, but the shape of it is just right. Big pillowy lips, not thin like some guys'. There's a dip in the center of the upper one, a neat little cupid's bow. His chin is shaded by a light amount of stubble that only seems to accentuate the lines of his face.

I bet he's a good kisser.

I blink in surprise. My mouth falls open of its own accord, because where the hell did that thought come from? His eyes track the motion, and now we're both staring at each other's lips.

Neither of us moves; neither of us says anything. We're stuck in this trance that I don't know how we got into in the first place. There is so much electricity coursing in this little space that I'm suddenly scared to touch a metal surface.

"Maeve—" he says in a raspy voice that sounds as though he's been screaming all night, but before he can finish his thought, the door of the game room opens.

"We're ready," Lux calls.

* * *

Every game must end . . . eventually.
Book 4 coming in 2026!

If you're in a reading slump after that or just want more of the same, you might want to try the Queen of Wesbourne trilogy, starting with Thrones We Steal, or the first book in this series, Ace of Betrayal, if you haven't read Heath and Walker's story yet!

Join Jessica Jude's email list to be notified when new books launch and to receive more exclusive bonus content. Visit jessicajude.com/newsletter to sign up.

Signed copies and book swag are available at jessicajude.com/shop

Lyrics to "Combat Boots"

Written & produced by Rhett Cole

Verse 1
She's tough as nails
In her black combat boots
She never fails
To hide what's inside
Her battle wounds
A tidepool of pain
Barbed wire
Wrapped tightly
Around a heart riddled with holes

Chorus
But underneath
And deep inside
And hiding out
A wildfire heart
Burning bright
A flame untamed
She cloaks it well
Smoke and mirrors
A gilt facade
Cause when she chooses to love you

Look out
You're a brand new man
Cause when she chooses to love you
Look out
You're a brand new man

Verse 2
I dreamed last night
Of those black combat boots
Our last fight
I was a fool
To let her go
She'll never look back
Barbed wire
Wrapped tightly
Around a heart riddled with holes

Chorus
Cause underneath
And deep inside
And hiding out
A wildfire heart
Burning bright
A flame untamed
She cloaks it well
Smoke and mirrors
A gilt facade
Cause when she chooses to love you
Look out
You're a brand new man
Cause when she chooses to love you

Look out
You're a brand new man

Bridge
I'd rather have
Her combat boots
Her combat heart
Her fighting love
Than anything

Acknowledgments

To Jesus, who never leaves me out and holds my heart more tenderly than I deserve.

To Curtis, who never lets me give up on my dreams.

To my family, who somehow manages to love me and cheer me on in spite of my shenanigans.

To my lovely sister / personal assistant / best friend, who by some miracle isn't sick of me yet.

To Jenny de Pierre, who always finds a kind way to say "this sucks, change it." You're a unicorn among editors.

To Haya in Designs for making a cover so stunning, it deserves to be framed.

To Rumaisa for helping to bring Rhett and Saylor to the world with your incredible artwork.

To my incredible Facebook group moderators: Madeline Hovey, Alexis Flick, Macy Holt, Althea Gutierrez, Heidi Lauper, and Kimberley Knott. I have the best crew!

To my VIP gang who helped create the perfect playlist for Rhett's book: Christiana Camacho, Kayla Bautista, Julie Pesik, Sophie Masannek, Angela Green-Carter, Morgan Fail, TWISTED BOOKWORM, Casey Ratliff, Cristina, Charlotte Søgaard, Katie Bessire, Robin Frum, Ashiki Welch, Brandy Frank, Kenzie Payne, Macy Fleetwood, Paige Miller, Bella Street, Emily Hall, Natty M, Hannah Rocha, DalekFrex, Jen Siena, Isabella Romine, Elisa Estrada, Danyele Henson, Ashley Coons, Selena Burke, Iris Wallace, Kat Kuruts, Trinity Rose, Maxi,

Leslie McBride, Samantha Reeves, and Heather Brooks.

To the early readers who helped catch pesky typos and small plot holes—you're the best!

To my entire ARC team, who believe in my books, my characters, and in *me*—thank you for loving Rhett and Saylor and for sharing them with the rest of the world with so much enthusiasm. I would be lost without you all.

And to you, dear reader, for picking up this book and giving it a chance. Authors get all the hype, but you're the real hero. Thank you for reading!

Also by Jessica Jude

Hand of Revenge series
Ace of Betrayal
Queen of Vengeance

They're rich. They're reckless. They're out for revenge.
A group of wealthy Gen Zers plays poker to determine the victims of
their weekly revenge plots. What they don't bargain on?
Falling in love with the people who could destroy them.

Queen of Wesbourne Trilogy
Thrones We Steal
Castles We Storm
Crowns We Save

Magnolia Parks meets The Princess Diaries in this angsty, slow burn
trilogy that will take you on an emotional roller coaster and leave
you completely wrecked.

*They want me to marry him. I know he's gorgeous and charming and his
voice makes your body sing. I know he's the bloody crown prince. I know
you think I'm crazy for hesitating. But you don't know him like I do. You
don't know what he did.*

About the Author

Jessica Jude loves nothing better than sending her characters on an emotional roller coaster of love, angst, and drama, but in reality her life is very ordinary, drama-free, and probably boring to anyone watching. (Which would be weird. And creepy.)

She married her high school sweetheart at nineteen. Being an author is a dream she's had since she was six years old and wrote her first book, which was ten pages long, about a girl named Mary getting lost in the woods. (It was never published, but good news: Mary was eventually rescued.) When she's not writing, she's reading, reading about writing, or eating ice cream. In another life, she would live in England in a sprawling manor house with hidden passages and secret stairways, but for now, she's content with her old brick farmhouse in the Midwestern United States.

Still a fan? Here are some ways you can ~~stalk~~ stay connected!

jessicajude.com/newsletter

Instagram @JessicaJudeBooks

Threads @JessicaJudeBooks

TikTok @JessicaJudeBooks

Discussion Questions

1. Why do you think Saylor was so reluctant to open up about her past?
2. Do you think Rhett was justified in his response to finding out Saylor's divorce hadn't been finalized yet? Why or why not?
3. If you could give past Saylor some advice, how would you recommend she handle her toxic marriage?
4. What do you think drove Rhett to addiction in the first place?
5. Describe your thoughts around Saylor and Timie's relationship. Have you ever experienced being left behind by a friend?
6. Do you think Rhett's decision to leave the record label and strike out on his own was a good one? Why or why not?
7. What scene in King of Obsession made the biggest emotional impact on you and why?
8. What quote or moment haunts you?